Praise for *Naked Girl*

"Wallack cleverly walks a tightrope in her writing, balancing the horrors with a child's unwavering imagination and naïve sense of wonder...a distinctive and emotionally rich voice delivering succinct observations...An endearing and fascinating perspective on a uniquely volatile and dangerous childhood. Verdict: Get it!"
-Kirkus Reviews

"Wallack's writing is evocative and lyrical, with a keen eye for detail and a deep empathy for her characters...For readers seeking a powerful and thought-provoking novel that combines rich character development with a gripping and emotional storyline, *Naked Girl* is an excellent choice. It is a remarkable debut that stays with the reader long after the final page and promises more great works from Wallack in the future. It is an unreservedly recommended Golden Quill read."
-Book Viral

"A lyrical and unflinching dive into a radical childhood, *Naked Girl* by Janna Brooke Wallack is an emotive novel about the meaning of home...Wallack's prose is alive with the open-eyed curiosity of youth...this revelatory novel is a poignant exploration of the stress and liberation of growing older in a world that never seems to grow up."
-Self Publishing Review

"The rugged elegance of Wallack's writing is everywhere, in which first-person accounts are both caustic and laden with style. I am reminded of Nell Zink's Nicotine in the chaotic nature of those who transit through the lives of Sienna and Siddhi, but with a panache that is singularly Wallack's. Very highly recommended."
-Asher Syed *for Reader's Favorite*

"Forced to adapt and grow in novel ways, Sienna and Siddi choose paths in response to their revised lives that are as unexpected as their father's choices...Janna Brooke Wallack cultivates an attractive, zany road trip through counterculture life...A heartwarming, fun experience lies in wait...Powerful descriptions create a masterpiece of insight and possibility..."
-Diane Donovan, *Midwest Book Review*

"Wallack's writing is sharp and professional. The pluck, or tenacity, these siblings have in the face of the world's indifference makes the reader want to see them overcome all their obstacles and find, in want of a better word, normalcy. This is an easy book to recommend and will make a great summer read."
-Mark Heisey, *The US Review of Books*

"Many readers will relate with how emotionally raw this book goes, and I think it will garner empathy for ourselves as people and for the people in the world of the book too. The book feels like a quick read...The blending of thought and action was well done. Book clubs will enjoy this, and readers who have felt out of place with themselves in the world will really appreciate."
-Writer's Digest

"*Naked Girl* by Janna Wallack is a tremendously funny book that I found myself crying into...a lose-track-of-time fictional memoir, it is a sociological examination of the institution of family... Sienna (the protagonist) is written so purely you have to remind yourself you don't know her in real life...This is a treasure of a book that speaks to everyone...Must read."
-John Burton, *Host of Home from Here*

"We're calling it. THIS is the book of the summer. A chaotic coming-of-age story with characters you won't be able to stop thinking about. A novel to sink your teeth into. Brava!"
-Jennifer Santiago and Jenny Leifer Fox, *Valley Girls/Literary Hudson Valley NY*

"*NAKED GIRL* grabbed me from the novel's stunning opening paragraph and held me in its grasp to the very end. The riveting, unflinching coming of age story of Sienna Shiva Karma Jones is told with devastating honesty and poignancy. You will not soon forget her."
-Elyse Title, Author of *Romeo*

"*Naked Girl* is a compelling, suspenseful, and moving story of the bond between a brother and sister who endure the hardships of neglect yet manage to hold on to the desire for familial love."
-Tova Mirvis, Author of *The Book of Separation*

"Janna Wallack is an extremely talented writer with a unique voice. *Naked Girl* is original and emotional—pulling the reader in immediately. I found the characters real and relatable...The perfect coming of age story. Looking forward to reading more of her work."
-Rochelle Weinstein, Author of *We are Made of Stars*

"Wallack is masterful at weaving multiple narratives together to create a vivid picture of Sienna's harrowing and hopeful life. She clearly illustrates – through flawless prose and a unique poetic style – the inherent tragedy of growing up."
-Jacqueline Dooley, Author of *Doorways to Arkomo*

"*Naked Girl* is a big, juicy read! Janna Cohen is a master at creating complex, likable characters. The details are painstaking and so illuminating. This novel will keep readers captivated with the hope of redemption, accountability, and survival. It's a complex unfolding that offers surprising details, humor, and a fitting ending. This book is impossible to put down!"
-Susie Warren, Author of *The Bolles Dynasty*

Naked Girl

A Novel

JANNA BROOKE WALLACK

CAMP KOCO BOOKS

For my giant, loud and crazy,
wonderful family.

Never forget that the universe is a single living organism possessed of one substance and one soul, holding all things suspended in a single consciousness and creating all things with a single purpose that they might work together spinning and weaving and knotting whatever comes to pass.
—MARCUS AURELIUS, MEDITATIONS

Nobody leaves this place without singin' the blues.
—ADVENTURES IN BABYSITTING

Prologue: Five Pictures, 1989

I only have five pictures of my mother, and she's naked in three of them. I keep the photos in the bottom of my Bee Gees backpack, in a jewelry box I took without permission. And if you look closely at the five pictures in order, you get almost the whole story.

Picture 1: A boudoir shot Jackson snapped. I recognize his chest trailing out of the frame and his penis in my mother's hand.

I found it in the downstairs bathroom, under the sink, on top of a stack of Jackson's Hustlers. The exposure has that stale fade of the 1970s. I threw it out once but fished it from the trash later that day, because I only have five pictures of her, and in this one, her hand looks just like mine.

The rest of my mother was stunningly beautiful. A Minnesotan snow princess, she clashed with Jackson's hairy, olive handsomeness but found her way to my father, no doubt as high on his sensitive guitar licks as they were on their bottomless bag of grass.

My parents, each mired in their own rebellions and reciprocally "cool" with free love, begat two babies in two years. My little brother, Siddhi, was their masterpiece, a doe-eyed demigod as brilliant as he was blonde. And fourteen months before him, they had me. I have frizzy, charcoal-sketched hair, and I'm broad-backed, heavy-breasted, and strong. I'm the sort of girl that men let carry her own bags, like I did today, boarding the plane.

Picture 2: "Sabrina, 1972" is scrawled on the back. My mother sits up against a carved headboard, one knee bent like a sunbather, the other extended across the paisley bed sheets. Head tilted down, eyebrows raised, with a joint the size of a cigar in her teeth.

1972 was the year she got pregnant with me when her parents (technically, my grandparents) disowned us.

Picture 3: A duplicate print of the Groucho Marx-smoking-a-wonder joint photo. I keep it because five pictures are better than four, even if one's a double.

Picture 4: My mother holds baby me and stares out at the ocean wearing a men's undershirt with cutoff jean shorts, knee-high tube socks striped green, then gold, then green, and dirty sneakers. The swollen round of her belly is baby Siddhartha growing inside.

Jackson told me that she wore these clothes to jog for miles and miles. I was too young to remember, but when I look at the picture, I do. When she got home and undressed, Jackson spanked her bare ass, and she whooped. I laughed because they laughed; that's what babies do. "Somewhere over the rainbow, 1973" is written on the back, and you can see she is fully stoned because that lightness is there on her face. The tops of her cheekbones push at the corners of her eyes as she tips her chin up into the breeze. I often stare at this photo until my eyes lose focus, and everything real blurs into a dream.

Picture 5: My mother holds baby Siddhartha like he's contagious. I'm down at her leg, a chubby crying toddler, forehead pressed against her thigh in a kitchen I don't recognize. She is still beautiful, but her eyes look dull, like a Mustang that's been broken and bridled. Her babies need and need, and she tries hard—I want to believe—until December 17, 1975, when, on her twenty-second birthday, she snorts far too much heroin, overdoses, and dies two weeks before I turn three.

The rest of my memory of her flashes in visceral snapshots of feelings too young for words. She is warm beads of sweat on sun-baked skin. She is bright blue slivers of sky, backlighting blond strands glowing gold. She is the scent of orange peels, applause on the Carson show, the chop-chop-chop of a knife on a cutting board, and the hissing sound of lit rolling papers. She is rageful, crying.

I keep the little I know of her filed under the five pictures in a jewelry box that, just like my mother, was never actually mine.

With my seat reclined, I close my eyes and spin an alternate past where she survives, gets sober, puts on some normal "mom clothes," and heads out to the grocery store. Then I bask in my invented memories of pancakes with bacon, school lunches packed in brown paper sacks, and my mother beaming in the front row as I advance a round in a spelling bee or perform the lead in a school play . . . but when I open my eyes, my mother is still dead. My family is still lost, and I am still sitting alone on this plane, flying home.

PART I

Xanadu

CHAPTER 1:

Ch-Ch-Ch-Ch-Changes, 1979

Jackson approached us on a wave of incense smoke undercut by a bittersweet gush of marijuana. He plopped down between us where we sat watching "Captain Kangaroo" on the wicker sectional left by some hopeful woman who wasn't our mother, but who might have intended to stay.

"Hey, you two munchies," he said, his smile as dilated as his pupils. "Who's in the mood for an adventure?" And, like magic, the whole room brimmed with mischief.

Siddhi raced to shut the TV, for if we hesitated, if we whimpered or hedged, it might be weeks before he asked again. I was six, Siddhartha five years old, and we loved our father intensely, the youngest kind of love, unflappable and fortified by need. We were lemmings, game to march blindly over the cliffs of his whim.

"What's the 'venture?" Siddhi wondered, blinking. Siddhi was dreamy and lithe, but with the perfect amount of baby pudge, too cute to gaze upon without that painful yearning you get with puppies in pet store windows.

"Can we please go to Africa?" I asked. Africa, the continent, had become my recent obsession. I planned to rule over a small-ish kingdom curated from the bounds of my extremely limited frame of reference: the dusty box of National Geographics that came with our rental, a half-day visit to the Renaissance Faire at Vizcaya, Rikki Tikki Tavi, and Babar the elephant. My version of Africa was a mini utopia where animals wore fancy clothing, and I was their queen.

"Pack up and meet me in the kitchen. It's adventure time!" Jackson said and thrust his long, tan arms into the air in triumph. "Remember the rule: if it doesn't fit in your backpack, then it's—"

"Bullship!" Siddhi shouted.

"Bullshit-t-t, Siddhi." I corrected him on our way upstairs.

"Right!" He grinned. "BullSHIT!"

We packed toys and necklaces, Siddhi's Teddy bear, Murphy the Great, and two pairs of socks (in case of skating or bowling). Jackson wore purple velour shorts and a rainbow spiral tie-dye, and he stood at the counter eating peanut butter out of the jar. His black curly hair met his beard to form a mane around his face. He took one look at us all strapped up with our backpacks and sandals and laughed so earnestly that he had to lean over and spit peanut butter into the sink. Siddhi and I were both still naked.

Breakfast was a fresh box of Cheerios, purchased at the minimart, where Jackson sunk a few gallons into Mellow Yellow, his '64 Thunderbird. He sometimes told tales of his years traveling in Mellow Yellow, driving from gig to gig, meeting new friends, and staying in their fancy mansions. His stories always began with him befriending some rich person and ended with him living with that person for a little while. He only had great days and bad days, both sometimes stretching for weeks or months in either direction.

Today looked to be a great one.

By noon, we might be anywhere from Key Largo to Kalamazoo. It was a crisp September Tuesday, cloudy, minus the usual haze, and since we never went to school, it was the same as any other day. Jackson put the top down so Siddhi and I could sit up high in the back, crunching handfuls of Cheerios and waving like pageant queens, looking out for better views of the coming hours.

Jackson accelerated onto the highway, forcing us to drop down into the seats and reach our hands over our heads to push against the whooshing air. And he drove for what felt like hours, eventually pulling off the highway and turning east toward the ocean.

If he'd told us we were headed for the moon, we would have believed that Mellow Yellow could sputter into space.

He parked along a barren stretch of grassy park that ran parallel to the beach for as far as I could see. "Here we are," Jackson told Siddhi and me, who sat drizzled in itchy crumbs from funneling the remnant Cheerio-powder into our mouths. "And no business for me until later!"

I felt it in my stomach when Jackson mentioned his business. Different from the dads on TV, he never wore a suit, held a briefcase, or kissed a pretty mother on his way out the door. He came and went at all hours with any number of emotions. There was no way to predict or prepare for who he'd be or what would happen to us.

We peed behind the car, mounted our packs, and tried to catch up with Jackson as he crossed the grass toward the expanse of golden sand.

"So, what's the 'venture?" Siddhi asked.

"This is it! We are going to walk on this beach until we're so pooped that we just can't walk anymore, and then we'll cool out and find a place to camp for the night wherever we end up! How do yah like that?" As he strode ahead of us, the dark hair on his head, arms, and legs luffed in the wind.

Heavy gray-black clouds moved in over the sun, whose rays seared out here and there, begging to be seen. As we continued our march, the ocean grew feistier, the sky went fully to nimbus, and raindrops began to polka dot the sand.

"How much longer, Jackson?" Siddhi whined. I wanted to know as badly as he did, but I felt very aware that big girls don't complain.

"Who knows? That's the adventure."

"That's the 'venture," Siddhi repeated, aping Jackson's shrug.

We passed a line of mansions on the beach. I chose a window

in each that would be my mother's chamber and imagined her looking out at us. The wind picked up. Waves crashed. Cold rain pelted our faces and hair. I put myself in charge of doling out the sleeve of crackers I'd grabbed from our kitchen cupboard in case of no lunch.

"Hey, I got one," Siddhi said. "How come the sky gets all the other colors, 'cept green?"

"Ooh…That's true, Siddhi. You're so smart," I said in my most maternal voice and threw an arm around his neck, both to show my approval and to use him as a crutch.

Siddhi's teeth chattered. He had barometric lips, and since they weren't yet blue, I knew we were not too cold to have to go indoors. With new people, Siddhi could sit silently for hours, taking them in and memorizing their details, letting his questions accumulate for safer circumstances, but alone with us, he just asked them whenever he felt like it.

We had to trot to keep up with Jackson's stride, listening hard to follow his answer: "…and that may be, but really, it's all about energy, man. Energy powers it all, all life…and the God-like substance that makes it all possible…everything from a car engine to your soul…" He poked into Siddhi's belly to make him giggle. "Energy is indestructible. Can't be destroyed, only changed into heat, and then heat changed back into energy, back and forth, eternally. Energy is forever, and we run on energy; therefore, we are forever. The only sure thing is change, back and forth, eternal, immortal. Understand, munchies?" We didn't really, but we always nodded either way. "And, God is energy, eternal and immortal, and everything!" Jackson looked up and opened his mouth to the rain, but I could tell his speech was far from over. He went on for gallons past my fill line for new information. "Isn't this great?" he shouted over the pelting rain. "God is giving us a drink!" He stuck his tongue out to catch more, and we did likewise. The cold raindrops stung at first, but once we were fully drenched, it stopped hurting and got fun again.

I noticed Siddhi's lips bluing up at the edges, but they stayed pinkish in the center. "Are we almost there, Jackson?"

"Funny you should ask," Jackson said and pointed down the beach. Past his finger in the rainy distance lay an oasis of swaying palm trees surrounding a massive building. "That right there is where we're headed!"

The rain soaked my long hair down into sopping curtains, heavy on my shoulders, and I wasn't sure if the goose bumps rising over my arms and legs were the fault of the chilly wind or the prospect of our visit to the castle that stood before us.

Jackson veered left, down a side street off the beach, and pulled over under a flapping awning. The wind whistled, impressed, as he expertly lit the joint he'd fished out of his backpack, inhaled sharply, and then exhaled a twisting burl of smoke. Siddhi and I stood side-by-side, waiting.

"Well, I tell you what, I didn't know it was going to pour," Jackson said, holding in his second hit. He blew it out and coughed a few times, "but it just makes the adventure wilder. Right, Siddhartha?" He and Siddhi exchanged smiles. I put on a smile, too, but no one was looking at me.

Siddhi's white-blond hair pasted itself all over his face and neck, and his lips pushed toward indigo and parted to expose the empty lower gum where, one week before, I removed his first loose tooth by tying it to a string attached to our bedroom doorknob and slamming the door. I got the idea from The Little Rascals. It was bloody, but it sure did the job.

We chased Jackson as he strode along the street, eventually veering to his right and coming around the corner to reveal the grand castle façade.

"The Breakers," Jackson announced with a revelatory hand gesture.

The Breakers must have been twenty windows across with towering turrets at either side, flags raised and flapping at their peaks, and a long driveway lined all the way with palm trees. Inside the entry doors, the lobby was loaded with massive Persian rugs strewn beneath a dozen extra-fancy sofas and chairs rimmed with golden fringes. Old paintings and gilded mirrors covered the walls leading up to a ceiling muraled with animals, clouds, urns of fruit, and flying baby angels.

I took a moment to pretend I was the Queen of Africa, casually coming home after a day out just queening around.

When Jackson addressed the man behind the glossy wooden counter, he said, "Hey, man. My associate left a key for me. The name's Gordon Lightfoot..." I elbowed Siddhi about the made-up name, but he was looking at the ceiling and didn't appear to notice the elbow or the lie.

"Certainly, Mr. Lightfoot," the man answered, and he handed Jackson an envelope and keys. Four men traversed the lobby carrying deck chairs and beach umbrellas from outside. Everyone looked steadfast, rushed, even worried.

David. That was the word. They said many things to one another but always mentioned David. The only famous David I knew of was David Bowie, one of Jackson's—and hence mine and Siddhi's—favorite rockers. "Think David Bowie's here tonight?" I asked Siddhi.

And Siddhi threw it to Jackson. "Are we here for a concert of David Bowie?" Jackson didn't hear. He took each of our hands and walked so quickly that we wound up next to each other behind him. "*Ch-ch-ch-ch-changes,*" Siddhi sang. "Hey, that's a good song for when you're shivering," he said.

I giggled and joined in, "*Ch-ch-ch-ch-changes...*"

Jackson walked down a wide hallway to a shop with tennis racquets and golf clubs in the windows. "Ha, there we go," he said. He dropped our hands and told us, "Go pick out some dry clothes."

It took no time for me to choose a pretty tennis dress. They only had one that was pink, and it was the biggest one. The arm holes went down below my ribs, but the skirt looked like an up-side-down coffee filter and flared out all the way when I twirled. Siddhi liked the flaring too and picked the same dress in blue. "For boys," he qualified. Jackson grabbed a shirt and a pair of pants, and without paying much attention, he added the dresses I handed him, tossing them all up on the counter without even checking. I remembered he shopped this way and got angry with myself for missing my chance to add in a pair of socks with pom-pom balls on the back and a couple of new T-shirts with no holes or stains.

"My word, ya'll went and got yerselves caught in Hurricane David!" said the lady behind the counter. She handed Jackson the shopping bag and his change. And she winked at him, smashed her fingers into the side of her hair to scoop it over her shoulder toward him. I copied the move in the store mirror, but my wet hair flopped back down.

"You're kidding me," Jackson purred, leaning in with his hand on the counter. The lady looked older than Jackson's thirty-two years of age and much, much older than the ladies Jackson took with us to Wolfie's Restaurant for breakfast sometimes.

She had red hair, red lipstick, and red fingernails. I could see that she really liked Jackson, because she licked her lips and then smiled before answering, "Oh, yes! The eye's meant to pass over tonight."

Jackson puffed his chest and propped his fists on his hips in a Peter Pan adventure stance. "A hurricane? Huh! What do you think of that?"

I wanted so much to tell him that I thought it was exciting but also dangerous, and to ask him if we were safe in this hotel, and if they would have some food and water for us, because Siddhi got very cranky when he got too hungry, and was there a nice place for Siddhi to maybe have a nap? And whose "eye" was passing over? An eye into heaven where maybe our mother could get a peek at us? But he wasn't really asking. He grabbed the shopping bags and headed for the shimmery elevators.

The hotel room was a palace chamber in miniature, every bit of it dressed in opulent fabric, wallpaper, golden tassels and trim. The bed practically filled the space, leaving only a little U-shape of fancy carpet for walking around.

Siddhi wasted no time flipping on the TV. He dialed through a few channels of fuzzy snow, stopped for a few seconds on the rainbow-beep emergency tester, then he flipped to what I thought was "General Hospital," but was actually just a Sanka

commercial starring a lady who looked like Monica Quarter-
maine. He flipped almost to the end of the dial before we got
lucky with some opening credits. "Godzilla! Right on. This is a
good one," Jackson assured us, and we sat hip to hip on the edge
of the bed, watching.

Jackson showered and changed into his new clothes: a pair
of beige slacks and a white shirt with a collar, three buttons, and
two embroidered palm trees on the breast pocket, that I'd laid
out neatly for him over the arms of our elegant chair. He peeked
out the curtains.

"Whoa, the storm's really mounting…" Jackson picked up the
phone and dialed once around the rotary. "I'd like to make a
room-to-room call, three oh two to ten twenty-two…" He sat on
the edge of the bed. "Heeeey, brother," he said into the receiver,
"…here, in the room…yep, and a couple new strains to check
out…fuck, yeah, frost resistant…no, no, beautiful…right on!"

Siddhi watched the movie, and I watched Jackson dig through
and readjust the contents of his backpack, which were mostly
wrapped packages filled with what he told us was expensive tobacco. He pulled the drawstring, closed the flap, buckled it in
place, and thrust it back over his shoulder. The storm brought the
kind of early darkness that made every noise a creak and every
shadow a ghost. The wind howled.

"Time for business!"

"No, Jackson," Siddhi whined, tensing up. His lips were almost back to pink. He hated it worse than I did when Jackson did
his business and left us alone, and I worried what would happen if
he had one of his famous tantrums in the hotel. "Stay and watch
with us, please!" I put an arm around Siddhi, administering the
strong squeeze that told him to calm down, and he got the hint
and relaxed a little into my hold.

"No can do, muncharoo. But do you like the room? Nice,
right?" We nodded. "Me too. So, cross your fingers because if tonight works out, we are getting a palace of our own!" I didn't know
what he meant. Would we be living in The Breakers forever more?
Were we moving to Africa? I had a day's worth of questions, but I

knew from the wild shine in Jackson's eyes that it was a bad time for curiosity. He jiggled the room key and shoved it in his pocket. "Hungry?" We answered with more vigorous nods. "Cool. Here," he handed me some cash, "order room service." On his way out the door, he leaned back and added, "Oh hey, get me a medium-rare filet mignon and whatever you munchies want, okay?"

We fought over the room service menu. I won by pushing Siddhi down, and he cried for a minute but then resumed watching the movie. The menu had no pictures, so I dialed the rotary once all the way around like I'd seen Jackson do, and a lady answered.

"Hi, my name is Sienna Shiva Karma Jones, and I'm six and a half, and I live in room 302."

I heard her giggle and then, "Yes, Miss, how can we be of service?" I pictured the lady from the gift shop as if a Stepford army of middle-aged redheads ran the whole hotel… I tried to sound like a queen.

"Yeah, so, me and my brother want to, please, order three medium-rare filet min-*yons*, please."

"Three medium-rare filets."

"Min-*yons*, yes, sure. And, yes, please, we also need plates and forks, please."

Siddhi bounced on the end of the bed and shouted, "And a Sprite with seven cherries!"

"Please," I corrected. "Oh, and one more thing, please, um, what is filet min-*yon*?"

Rain beat sideways into the window glass, and I pushed on it to make sure it would hold. Outside, the palm trees blew wildly, like punch dummies all the way down to the ground and back up and over the other way. Giant lips of white foam swallowed and then spit back out the whole length of the beach. I shut the curtains to block out the fright, and as I did, the golden rope tieback slipped down to the carpet. My tummy twisted with worry about what happened to Jackson. I wondered how we could pay the bill if they told us to leave the hotel before he returned. I decided I would be less worried if I had that length of golden rope. Maybe I could find a place to sell it if I needed money, and if it didn't come to that, then it would always be a memory of how brave I was ordering the room service, cutting our min-*yons* (which were nothing more than fancy steak) with such a sharp knife, and not crying about the ghost wailing outside our window. Even though it made me a bad girl, and I knew it, I grabbed the tieback and stuffed it into the bottom of my backpack. I had no other choice, really. There was too much already in my life that I didn't remember.

"Where's Daddy, CeeCee?" Siddhi asked, rubbing Murphy the Great's paw, like he did, over his worried eyebrow.

"He's doing business," I told Siddhi, "Like always." I didn't have the words to explain what I knew about our family. We lived a vagrant, furtive sort of life, always potentially grand but shaded by outsiders who disapproved of things too ethereal for them to imagine. I believed Jackson's theory that if they all just unpacked their bullshit, they would have space, like we did, for magic, and I saw myself as some sort of child enchantress in their margins.

Siddhi sucked on Murphy the Great's nose, and I worked my fingers through the tangles in his long hair and listened to his breathing until he was sleeping, and then I fell asleep.

I woke to a whisper. "You up, munch?" Jackson shook my shoulder a little and then leaned over me to the other side of the bed and did the same to Siddhi.

"Is the 'eye' opening?" I asked.

"Put your clothes back on," he said. "I had a big night!"

The bed was warm from sleep, our room thick with quiet, but when Jackson said get dressed and come, we little moons had no recourse but to orbit. Delighted that Jackson had returned, Siddhi scurried over to the chair and slipped his tennis dress over his head. Jackson laughed. "Where did you get that dress, man?" Siddhi opened his mouth to answer, but Jackson had already moved on. "Check this out," he said, and he opened his backpack to reveal more stacked bundles of cash than they kept in suitcases in the movies. He often returned from business smiling into new-found money, but never a whole duffel bag full.

Jackson laughed, hummed, and gaped. He appeared to love

the money in his bag, which made me wish I could open the window and dump it all out into the storm, sending it to flutter and flap away like the migrating Monarch butterflies in our magazines. Instead, I waited until Jackson and Siddhi both went to the bathroom, went for the bag, and took as many stacks of cash as I could fit in the remaining space in my backpack, to save, for the bad times, when Jackson wasn't all wide smiles and new clothes.

And after he checked three times to ensure that the room was locked, we rode down the elevator, Jackson in his palm tree shirt and Siddhi and I in our twirly tennis dresses, and walked a long hallway through a hefty set of brass doors. There we stood in a vast dining room full of tables covered in peach-colored linens strewn with flocks of white napkin swans. And in the very center of the room lay a real swimming pool.

Jackson handed a baggie of his special tobacco to a hotel employee who wore his same palm tree collar shirt.

"Thanks, brother," he said.

The employee eyed the baggie lustily, "No, thank *you*."

"Rock and roll!" Jackson whooped, removing his shirt and slacks and diving in. He splashed us, and I worried that he might wet the swans. I wondered where we would live after the piles of money ran out and the hurricane passed us by...

"Hey, munchies," Jackson called to us. "Get in here and have some fun!" If Jackson was swimming for fun, then everything had to be okay. Siddhi and I threw off our dresses and cannonballed into the pool. And while Siddhi and Jackson did handstands near the steps, I floated on my back, deciding how it would look to paint a mural of the hurricane, with my mother looking through its open eye, on the swimming and dining room ceiling of my castle in Africa.

CHAPTER 2:

Lend Me Your Comb, 1980

Jackson called it a Spanish Renaissance, but the house looked like a Dr. Seuss book that had come alive and let the trees grow through its windows, leaving shattered glass at the feet of its splintered sills. He referred to the previous owner as "Old Mother Havisham" because she had neglected the mansion and two acres on the water side of North Bay Road, letting nature and decades turn it inside out and upside down before she finally died in the green wingback chair on the sun porch at the age of a hundred and three.

Jackson bought the estate at a foreclosure auction "for a fuckin' song" and made us each sit in the green wingback chair to see if we could feel Old Mother's rebel soul energy.

"We're owners now, munchies!" I pictured Jackson handing over his beloved duffle of cash (minus what I stole) to the ectoplasmic shimmer of the oldest lady I could imagine, who in turn handed Jackson one of those square deed cards from Monopoly.

Dream come true or not, I feared this castle ruin. I worried the broken gates and missing door locks left us vulnerable to attack by bad guys and monsters. I worried that my own mother wouldn't have spectral access with Old Mother Havisham lurking all over the territory, and I felt uncertain about the rules and regulations with hauntings.

Also, I was sure our new neighbors would hate and shun us for our strangeness, like the time in our last neighborhood when a teen boy on a dirt bike chased us down. He caught hold of me, squeezed my arms until I had to cry, and whispered close in my ear, "If your dad smokes enough drugs, they send a lady in a suit to come take you to the orphanage."

Another time, we hid in Nana's car while she bickered with Jackson about booster shots, and when we returned to her condo with the puffy silver wallpaper, her neighbor Sylvia excused herself right away, telling Nana on her way out that we were, "ripe for a scrubbing."

But I shivered when I thought about the time when, three doors down from our last rental, we met a little girl named Saydi, who told us she'd stayed home from first grade that day with double pink eye. We played make-believe family and did a lot of hugging and kissing with Saydi, and when her mother came out and found us all swimming naked in their screened pool, she hollered that Saydi ought to be ashamed of herself, and shouted at Siddhi and I, "Why aren't you in school? Where is your mother? Get out of here you disgusting little pigs!" She was still spanking Saydi when I grabbed Siddhi's hand and ran us straight home without our clothes.

"We ought to name this place, right?" Jackson asked as he poured the shake, he blended with fruits picked from Old Mother's trees and we took sips and thought of possibilities.

"Ooh! What about The Dr. Seuss House?" I suggested, as an homage to the architect.

"No! Uh-uh," Siddhi protested. "Pleeaaassee, let it be Alderaan," he said, always with the Star Wars.

Jackson slurped the last of the shake straight from the blender and shook his head. "*In Xanadu did Kubla Khan a stately pleasure-dome decree,*" he recited. "*Where Alph, the sacred river, ran,*

Through caverns measureless to man, Down to a sacred sea…"
Our castle would take its name, he said, from Samuel Taylor
Coleridge. *"Gardens bright with sinuous rills, and many an in-
cense-bearing tree."*

Xanadu.

The name meant nothing to me until the movie by the same
name came out that August. "It's because of me that its time has
come again," Jackson said when he took us into the theater. "I put
it out there into the energy when we moved in."

Halfway through the ten o'clock showing, Siddhi fell asleep
with his head on my shoulder. Elated by the notion that Jackson
had the telekinetic ability to make roller skating movies happen,
I fantasized that Olivia Newton-John was my mother, alive and
lovely in her leg warmers and off-the-shoulder dress.

After Jackson named the house, I figured we'd stay a while,
and I needed to find a permanent hiding spot for my stolen treasure.

One afternoon, when Jackson and Siddhi fell asleep on the
sofa, I tiptoed to the kitchen and wrapped my thirteen stacks
of bills in a trash bag, like I'd seen Jackson do before, twisting
it and wrapping and then sealing it round and round with duct
tape until I held a squishy, silver brick. I then dug a hole between
the gnarled roots of the prettiest pine tree in the tall stand by the
seawall, placed my money brick down in the bottom, and covered
it over with sandy dirt and pine needles.

During the first several months, we'd spent whole days labor-
ing to help Jackson clean out Xanadu, but we tired long before
he did, and when we whined or hurt ourselves, he shouted and
cursed at us, often fleeing to his room to smoke a joint and rest.

By October, he caught a terrible sickness—the flu, he insisted,
though he neither coughed nor sneezed—and locked himself in
his room.

Siddhi and I continued to sweep, drag out the trash, and pull
weeds, but after several days of work, we barely made a dent,
and cavernous Xanadu still echoed with pollen-dusted ghostly
emptiness.

For Halloween, we wrapped each other in some Christmas decorations we found in a dusty box and trick-or-treated each other (for practice in the day) in the seven bedrooms of the second floor, naming them all, of course.

"This one's The Magic Carpet Room, where we'll bring the old rugs and beat them till they're fluffy...and this one's The Circus Room, like for juggling and flipping and—you think the ceiling's high enough for a trampoline? Oh, yeah, and this one's The Playing Room, where we'll put the thousand toys we're gonna buy..."

That night, we waited until dark and snuck out to trick or treat up and down the blocks until the old man with the four jack-o-lanterns on his stoop recognized us on our fifth trip and told us we were selfish and made us dig through our pillowcases to give him back three Smarties each. We still had enough candy for two days' food, but I felt embarrassed and made us go home.

We huddled together under a blanket on the couch and allowed ourselves seven candies apiece while trying to ignore the sounds of creatures skittering around upstairs and Old Mother Havisham inhaling the humid, salty air and wheezing her forlorn must into the darkness. We'd collected twenty mangoes to give out, plus we would have shared our candy. And we even lit a candle outside the front door, but not one single trick-or-treater came near Xanadu.

During his flu, Jackson only slept or drove off in the car for business. Sometimes, he returned with some food, most times not. Siddhi and I spent sunny days outside building a clubhouse in the roots of the massive banyan tree at the center of our circular driveway.

When it rained, we mined and looted the heaps of rubble in the house, scavenging for marathon sessions of make-believe. When that got boring, I used a broken piece of fence iron to pry open the "stuck door" closet, which turned out to be filled with sheets, blankets, and towels, and we spent the next few days building a colossal blanket fort over our couch and television. And once Siddhi had the idea to find an outlet and plug in the TV, we crouched underneath and tuned in for the comforting counsel of "The Brady Bunch," "Family Affair," "The Jeffersons," and "Leave it to Beaver".

We ate our way through all the food in the kitchen, including the stiff yellow sticks of uncooked spaghetti (the trick was to suck them long enough to soften them with saliva), and we gave ourselves diarrhea from eating bananas, kumquats, avocados, starfruits, and mangoes, ripe, unripe, and rotten. Here and there, we fought.

"I'm older and a girl," I said to my brother. "So, I'm in charge."

"So, what, CeeCee?" Siddhi crossed his little arms at his chest. "I have a penis, and you don't!"

We shouted back and forth until Siddhi lost his temper and punched me in the chest. Then we grappled in the dirt, each landing a few good blows until we'd had enough, and sat side by side, crying over our wounds. And when that was all done, we forgave each other because if not, it was too lonely.

The morning after the "Anne Murray Christmas Special," Nana pulled up in her Cadillac Eldorado. She didn't like to come to Xanadu, but we knew it was her because after she walked through the front door, all she said was, *"Oy gevalt!* This house is from hunger." She marched over to where we were watching the morning shows, lifted the protective wall of Fort Blanketania, and tossed in her usual command, "Come now! You'll eat something."

Nana wasn't the warm nest of motherliness for which I prayed. She'd grown up a poor Jew in the Lower East Side tenements of New York City during the Great Depression. Jackson said that as a kid, she had to cut the backs from her shoes when her feet grew, so her heels could flop over. You'd think someone so resourceful would be able to work miracles in the kitchen, but you'd be wrong. Even half starved, we knew to be wary of the paper grocery sack on her hip.

"On a scale of one to ten, how do you rate Nana's recipes?" Siddhi whispered.

"Maybe a one point three," I whispered back. "You'll understand that soon when I teach you *decibels*," I said, adding a pat on his cheek. "Let's be really good and do everything she says, okay? And maybe she'll let us move into her condo this time." He nodded and slapped me five, no jive.

We padded into the kitchen in time to see Nana, in her signature, Sergio Tacchini tracksuit, pour the brown and white Farina grains into the boiling water and stir them exactly once. Then she clanked the spoon down on the counter and sighed, "*Aiysh*! I'd like for this to just get done already."

In the EST trainings Jackson used to host in our rental living room, he told the crying people, "There is no saving time, only birth and death and rebirth, and the same old grooves on the same old record." But Nana lived to rush. When she took us somewhere, she dragged us. Her hugs and kisses were abrupt lightning strikes that grabbed and hurt, and after she released you, she checked her lobes for both clip-ons and her chest to turn her diamond encrusted Star of David right side up. And she never took the correct amount of time to cook her hideous hot cereal.

"Sid, come here. Sit down! Sienna, let's go already. What in the hell is taking so long? HERE! For god's sake, eat some hot cereal." She always called him "Sid" because, she said, *Who in the hell names a Jewish boy Siddhartha?*

Siddhi tried stalling. "Nana, knock, knock?"

"What is it, Sid?" Nana ladled the slop into the first bowl and set it in front of me.

"You have to say, 'Who's there?'"

"Who's there?" Another bowl found Siddhi.

"Boo."

"What?" She tore open the box of sugar packets and shoved it toward me. Without asking, she splashed far too much cold milk over each of our bowls. I stirred mine, horrified by the thinning effect and increase in volume. Brilliant Siddhi quickly picked up his bowl and slurped the offending milk off the top.

"You have to say, 'Boo, who?'"

"Boo hoo."

"Nana, why are you crying?"

"What? I am doing no such thing. What in the hell is the matter with you? Eat up before I give you a lickin'!'" Nana didn't bluff about lickin's, so under her one raised eyebrow, I began to choke down my cereal.

"Who can be in the clean plate club?" Nana asked as she left with a tray for Jackson. When she returned and spied me spooning lumps onto the floor, she turbo-stepped to my seat, lifted me off the chair by my free arm, whacked me three times on the tushie, and then refilled my bowl. After the cereal, she made us get dressed and tuck in our T-shirts. "Get in the car, *kinder*, we'll go run some errands and give your father a break."

Nana ushered us inside the little shop with the swirling candy cane pole out front and seated us on the waiting bench. I studied the dark, wood-paneled wall, covered in push-pinned Polaroids of satisfied customers, none of whom were females, let alone little girls. The lone barber wore an apron over his shirt and trousers. I admired its pressed, bleached-white cleanness. He had silver, side-parted hair, and friendly, watery eyes.

"What lovely granddaughters you have, Eleanor," he smiled.

"I'll tell you something, Ernie," said Nana, curling a feathery, spun-gold lock of Siddhi's hair behind his ear. "This one's a *boy*. For Christ's sake, let's make him look like one!" Nana plopped Siddhi onto the pile of phone books Ernie stacked on his chair. I waited on the bench, crossed my legs at the knee to show that I was the girl-child, and smiled at Siddhi in the mirror.

He knuckle-pinched Siddhi's cheek and then smoothed a shiny black cape by whipping it out into the air with a snap.

Siddhi flinched and then giggled as Ernie fastened the cape around his neck. "Such length. Have you ever been to the barber before?" Siddhi shrugged. If he had, he couldn't remember. One glimpse of Ernie's scissors and Siddhi began to wail. We loved our waist-long hair. We lifted each other up by it, made it into animal ears, wove it through with feathers and leaves for crowns, and avocado and Vaseline for horns and twists. When we played spy, it became walkie-talkies, and when Siddhi had nightmares, I stroked his hair to coax him back to sleep.

"Sid, sweetheart," Nana cooed. "Stop crying now, *bubbeleh*, before I give you something to cry about." Siddhi closed his mouth, working hard to sob soundlessly, but his body shook up and down.

I felt my own tears bubbling up. I didn't know this Ernie, and his friendship with the likes of Nana did little to help me trust him with Siddhi's precious locks.

"Nana," I hoped to help. "Siddhi feels a little sad 'cause he wants to keep his—"

"Hush, Sienna!" Nana barked, and fresh from the sting of her wooden spoon, I obeyed.

"No, Nana, please," Siddhi begged, his body melting down the phone book stack. "I like how it is." He had a snot caterpillar trailing out of each nostril.

"Don't be ridiculous. You look like a *faygelah*. Ernie here thought you were a girl. Now, I've had enough. Stay put before I give you a lickin'. Maybe I'll get you a frankfurter and a malted at the lunch counter if you're a good boy?" Nana always had a little smile for Siddhi. I went over to the chair and wiped the snot from Siddhi's nose with the edge of my shirt. Off went the smile.

"Lovely," said Nana. "Now you're filthy." The whole business must have rattled Ernie, too, because he switched his comb and scissors for clippers, and, in under a minute, he buzzed beautiful lion Siddhi into G.I. Joe.

Siddhi looked down at the blond hairy floor, then teary-eyed, he looked at me, but he kept quiet, as I planned to do. Restaurant food was on the way, and maybe Nana might agree to let us live in her condo where, in 7F, her friend Esther Cohn had a dish of Nip's candies, and her husband, Abe Cohn, had a slot machine that paid in real dimes.

"My, oh my, Sid," said Nana. "You look like a movie star." Ernie released him from the cape, and Siddhi climbed down from the chair, kicking the pile of his hair as he came back to the waiting bench.

"Your turn, Sienna." Nana beckoned me with her painted pointer finger. "Go short on her, too," she told Ernie. "God knows when they'll be back. My hippity-dippity son doesn't believe in haircuts. Tell me, what is so wrong with a goddamned neat haircut?"

"You're preaching to the choir ovah here," said Ernie, his New York accent much like Nana's. He traded the clipper back for his scissors and plucked a black plastic comb from the canister of blue water. Until that second, I was sure I'd get shorn like Siddhi, who sat with both hands rubbing his head. I patted his shoulder.

"See, didn't hurt a bit," I said and got up to take my turn. Siddhi met my eyes in the mirror, so I crossed mine and did fish lips to make him laugh. Ernie raked a comb through my uncooperative hair.

"Rat's nest," said Nana. He tied an itchy ponytail at the bottom of my neck. "Short," said Nana, as Ernie let the scissors chew across every strand right above the rubber band. Then he waved the severed hair in the mirror.

"See. There. Now I can take you into a restaurant!" Nana approved. The wet ends of my chin-length hair curled up toward the ceiling. It made me warm and dizzy to see so much of my body hanging lifeless in Ernie's hand. I wished that I were daring enough to eject Nana's Neil Diamond "Jazz Singer" cassette from her car stereo and yank out all the tape into a big mess so she could never listen to it again. But this was not Neil Diamond's fault, and there was a hot dog at stake.

I stood up and whispered, "Thank you."

At the lunch counter, I loaded my hotdog with ketchup and sweet relish. Without his hair to weigh him down, Siddhi swiveled round and round on his stool.

"Nana?" I asked.

"Mm?" she said without turning from her lunch.

"Can we go home with you from now on?" I prayed that if my wish came true, Nana could arrange for the yellow school bus to pick us up each morning and take us to the elementary school where I could learn to read and meet boys and girls my age and with whom Siddhi and I could giggle and share Wonder Bread sandwiches. Then, I could give Jackson back the buried money, which would cure his flu of sadness.

"Please, Nana? From now on?" Nana took another bite of knish, chewed it, and swallowed while I waited. Then she turned just enough to see my plate and said, "You eat a frankfurter with sauerkraut and mustard. You'll ruin it with ketchup," but for the first time ever, I'd lost my appetite.

A little girl with neat, even pigtails walked past our stools, followed by her young, pretty mom.

"Bathroom?" she asked.

Nana gestured. "All the way in the back."

"Thanks," said the mother. "Nice looking boys you have there," the mother said.

Nana smiled wide. "Thank you," she said. She let the lady walk away mistaken and took another big mouthful of knish.

When Nana finished eating and excused herself to the bathroom, Siddhi told me, "Let's grow our hair back so long that it goes past the floor." We swore on it and slapped each other twenty, that's plenty.

The next morning, Jackson jauntily reincarnated from his smoky room. He took us to cash the check Nana gave us to give to him—a five with three zeros—and then out to Denny's for pancakes and to tell us of his latest vision. He'd beamed an invitation, he said, into the greater energetic frequencies to bring us "special ones," he said.

"Followers. No, not followers...They'll be my...BABIES!" I pictured him gathering stuffed animals on his bed for some sort of game. But instead, he took us to the St. Patrick's Christmas carnival. Siddhi and I shared a chemical blue Slush-Puppy someone left practically full on the church steps while Jackson wandered around the grounds, wearing his mirrored sunglasses and army pack, swapping envelopes and baggies for cash, and then while we waited in line for the Dragon Coaster, he began to talk with the guy operating the ride. His name was Warren, and he looked a lot like Jackson but skinnier, with freckled skin and lighter hair. Girls in line noticed Warren, and one said he was "So foxy."

Siddhi and I rode the Dragon Coaster eight times in a row while the men talked, and by the time Siddhi had to go pee, Jackson had convinced Warren to come live with us.

"I'm kind of an existential Zen-ist," he told Jackson on the ride home. He pronounced Vietnam like it rhymed with ham and told Jackson how being there really fucked him up for steady work.

Then they passed a joint and discussed how the Dragon Coaster was a metaphor for *wu-wei*. Jackson walked him through the house and talked him through how it was a natural place for free love and meditation. He told Warren all the theories he always taught us, and about the *Bhagavad Gita,* and how all the working stiffs didn't have clarity of choice or space to meditate on the truth. And he told him about easy earning with Kublai Kush—his best strain of grass.

I didn't understand a lot of what they discussed, but I squeezed Siddhi, happy that Jackson had a buddy to keep him company so he might not catch the flu again. Over the next few months, Jackson brought Warren to the Coconut Grove farmer's market, the vita course, the health food stores, Lummus Park, and the beaches where they worked together to recruit new *Babies*, men, and women, all under twenty-five, the foxier the better, and all with our same style: free-flowing and frayed at the edges. Jackson quoted from Walt Whitman to Bob Dylan to the Upanishads, and Warren, by his side, closed his eyes and nodded assent.

The new Babies agreed and brought their stuff and their smells and their sounds back to our house, where Jackson promised abundant meditation, love, truth, meaning, and a place to crash. The Kublai Kush was plentiful, and when they took a rest from smoking it, the Babies were charged with measuring, packaging, and selling it. They did it all gratefully and well, returning all monies to Jackson. He praised them constantly as they repaired and regrouted the fallen Spanish tiles, filled the cracks in the terrazzo floors, sifted shards of glass from the soil outside the windows, scraped, patched, and painted the walls, unclogged the fireplaces, and trained the bougainvillea vines to grab at the rusting wrought iron spikes atop the outer walls, further shrouding the grounds in privacy. They even rebuilt the pool.

Though I'd lost out on my dream of training African elephants to run things, I delighted in Jackson's more achievable way. He maintained that we were one big family, which, at least in the beginning, seemed a wonderful antidote to my loneliness.

*

The night we planned to perform at the six-month anniversary dinner, we assembled a decent array of Babies for an audience (dinner wasn't always a thing at Xanadu, so this was a bit of good luck for us). Jackson sat in the wicker peacock throne at the head of the long, splintery table. To his right sat Warren, who'd become obsessed with transcendental meditation after reading a booklet Jackson gave him by Maharishi Mahesh Yogi. When he read it, he sat in the lotus position under the biggest mango tree and stayed there for two weeks, trying to levitate and affect world peace. Siddhi and I watched the bees buzz around his face, sometimes for hours, but we never saw him alight.

To me, he seemed cartoonish, even ridiculous, but Jackson vouched for his power, and so, if anything, I was skeptical of my own doubts. Next to Warren was Steve, a self-proclaimed love-shaman, and over his shoulders, he held his congenial com-panion, a ten-foot-long boa constrictor named Rat Daddy, who roamed freely through the house supposedly doing away with all vermin, but mostly Siddhi and I found him coiled in a pile and sleeping in the warm spots under the low-silled, sun porch windows.

Then there was Stacey with the black hair and giant boobs. After her dad kicked her out and before meeting Jackson, she worked as a mime in Key West's Mallory Square. I watched her as she rehearsed her act, willing her enormous boobs to stay clear of her gesturing arms. She once told me she dreamt of living in

France because, she said, they get it there. She sat with Warren, who played his mandolin on breaks from sitting with the bees. They liked each other so much that Jackson encouraged Stacey to move into Warren's room so they could make love together on her first night at Xanadu.

Jackson and the Babies made a lot of love, which often occurred in one or another of the bedrooms. On occasion, an orgy would erupt in the living room, a space, Jackson boasted once to Steve, where "twenty to twenty-five people could make love with each other comfortably."

The living room also served as a place for his daily teachings, winding speeches, so apparently wise that the Babies laughed and cheered and yelled and cried. It was after the laughing and the cheering and the yelling and the crying that Jackson would call for Warren to pour the Brugmansia tea and pass the chalice. Jackson claimed that drinking the tea and smoking the trumpet flower leaves had ancient, hallucinogenic properties that allowed him to hear God's voice.

Siddhi and I tried to wait up long enough to watch the love-making, but they took so much time with the tea ceremony and the smoking and wandering around and kissing and touching each other before they got to it, that often, we had to give up and go to sleep. But the Babies were encouraged to make love whenever and wherever they felt compelled to share of themselves, and so, even though it was still fascinating to observe an orgy from our perches at the upstairs banister, the sight of the Babies having sex was neither novel nor uncommon.

At the far end of the table sat Tomatoes. He'd lost his right leg from knee to foot after a car accident, and he'd subsequently dropped out of Skidmore. "Now that you've found the truth, maybe you'll skid less," Jackson had said to him, and Tomatoes, quite shy, flushed. Tomatoes refused to put a bite of food into his mouth that wasn't one hundred percent tomatoes, explaining that they contained all the nutrients he needed and that society's obsession with choices clouded clear thinking. Over his months with us, his handsome face grew gaunt and tinged orange, his body became lethargic, and it became harder for him to walk on his prosthetic, his stump got infected, and one of his teeth had cracked and broken. Still, he only ate tomatoes.

He only ate tomatoes, and he only read Kierkegaard. Jackson let the Babies explore their passions. Nobody but me questioned his motives.

"Why don't you eat other foods?" I asked him.

"I'm testing my faith," he said, his malnourished voice had a smoker's rasp.

"Like faith in God?" I asked.

"Uh-huh. See, a leap of faith proves the existence of your doubt. That's why it's a leap. To exhibit true faith, you must build a bridge over your doubt in the existence of the entity your faith rests upon."

"And you rest on tomatoes?" I tried to follow.

"They're more a means than an end."

"Siddhi said you still feel your leg?" I asked, though I already knew he could, because I saw him scratch hard on the plastic, and then I saw him realize what he'd done and start to cry. "How can you feel it if it isn't even there?"

"I suppose I want it back that badly," he said.

Next to Tomatoes sat Sariah. Jackson found her at the Renaissance Faire. Sariah initiated and administered all the "cleansing" wheatgrass juice enemas. She had everyone lay on our sides, and she'd come down the line to insert the bags and fill us all up. Then, she had us hang upside down, like bats, from gravity boots or tree limbs for better toxin absorption before finally letting us race to the bathrooms to poop neon green.

"Why do we need to do this?" Siddhi once asked, next to me on our branch, blood rushing his face and reaching to touch the grass with his fingertips as we held.

I thought of orphans in movies, always with sketchy guardians forcing them into odd routines and sipping spoonfuls of castor oil. *Because we don't have a mom,* I thought.

And finally, there was bone-thin Ximena, who never ate much, but since she was only seventeen, Jackson promised to heal her with meditation and high colonics. Ximena liked Steve best, so she slept in his room.

At dinner, Steve told Tomatoes how he and Warren fixed the pool. And the pool meant Siddhi and I filled our days with a slew of new games. We enacted under-the-sea voyages, dramatic drowns and rescues and Kraken releases followed by re-enactments of Perseus turning said Kraken to stone using a rotten coconut as the head of Medusa. We usually ended off with a session of repetitive back-diving to bleary-eyed exhaustion.

"Our pool is the best pool," Siddhi told the Babies at dinnertime.

"Way better than Nana's!" I agreed. When Nana decreed that the weather was "delicious," all the old ladies went to the condo pool, sitting on the lounge chairs in their skirted suits and Esther Williams caps with plastic daisies on the sides. The dedicated athletes swam slow laps and hollered at us for splashing while the others milled about, chatting in the shallow end. And we had to be quiet and kick with our feet under the water to keep their speckled, rotisserie chicken shoulders high and dry.

Nana paraded us before her friends as they took turns asking, "Do you remembah me?" And when we nodded politely, they followed up with, "What's my name?" Sometimes, one would bore deeper, "The boy looks just like the crazy mother. Such a shame...so young." They never said that I looked like my mother. "That Sienna is your little clone, Ellie. *Kinehora, Kinehora!* Poo, poo, poo!"

Dinner concluded when Warren passed the chalice and a joint around the table. Jackson had already hit both and pulled Sariah in for a kiss, and I elbowed Siddhi, knowing we had to act fast lest the lovemaking beat out our big chance. Siddhi dimmed the chandelier, and I pressed play on the tape recorder, and Billy Joel sang "Rosalinda's Eyes." We skipped and twirled. We hustled and bumped. We hokey-pokeied and turned ourselves around, did the twist, bus stop, and for the grand finale, I hoisted him up under his armpits and spun him around as he straddled his legs and pointed his toes.

As we bowed, the Babies met our feats with a standing ovation, and Jackson quit messing around with Sariah—*My children!*—herded us into his arms and carried us, both giggling uncontrollably, up the stairs; me slung over his right shoulder, and Siddhi hanging sideways under his left arm. I bounced high off the ground, sweating from laughter, bobbing upward and down, and watching the staircase curve and lengthen below me. He tossed us onto our bed and dove down in between us, letting us each throw an arm and a leg over his middle, rest our sleepy heads in his musky armpits, and wait for the magic. He kissed Siddhi on his downy forehead, and then he kissed mine.

"Close eyes, munchies," he murmured and recited the Eugene Field poem from memory: "*Wynken, Blynken, and Nod, one night, sailed off in a wooden shoe—Sailed on a river of crystal light, Into a sea of dew...*" I fell off into the twilight, sailing the sky with my nets of silver and gold, trolling for herring fish stars, ecstatic to have Jackson there next to me, murmuring into the darkness, "*So cried the stars to the fisherman three: Wynken, Blynken, and Nod.*"

CHAPTER 3

A Pain in My Ass, 1981

When Aunt Paula stopped by our house to pick up the important package Jackson left for her, and we told her he was in the Bahamas, she called up Nana and convinced her to let us stay—two nights—at her condo with Pop Pop's double-decker organ and the carousel of black-and-white photos from the olden days.

At least once a month, Jackson hopped over to the Islands for a bit and mostly left us home with the Babies, not in the way a real mom or dad would do it, with a list of special foods, emergency numbers, schedules, or bedtimes, but rather, we'd see that the new, thirty-foot Whaler and maybe one or two of the women would be gone, and then we'd know not to look for him for a few days.

I had a hard time sleeping when Jackson was away. I lay in bed thinking about how I would be able to take care of Siddhi and what I would have to do if too many days passed without Jackson coming back. Eating was also tough. Even fruit hurt my stomach.

Siddhi never lost his temper when Jackson was gone, but he cried every day for his return. He managed to smile when I yanked some Spanish moss from an oak tree and hooked it over my ears like a beard. And I made him extra snacks and stroked what was left of his hair to get him to sleep.

Some things were better when Jackson left; everyone slept in and did their lovemaking in their rooms, and without Jackson to kiss up to, there were no meetings, less enemas, and a lot less enthusiasm.

Because of her third divorce, Aunt Paula had a temporary set-up in Nana's convertible den. Like Ximena, she ran away from home at sixteen, then came back after her first divorce, then went to India for some other boyfriend. In India, she got a guru and grew out her underarm hairs in what she referred to as her "ZaSu Pitts," and then she came back and tried to go to work with Jackson, but they fought worse than I ever did with Siddhi.

No one could make Jackson lose his cool like Aunt Paula. She moved around too much for us to live with her, but she wore soft, gauzy clothes with tiny golden threads woven through them, and she smelled like orange blossoms. Spending time with her was magical because she really seemed to love us and want us around. She was an encyclopedia of our family. She prepared hot food that made us busting full, and she gave us presents—though, admittedly, they skewed older and were never toys. I had a vague sense it was not the right thing to feel, but I got incredibly happy whenever Aunt Paula got divorced.

"My God, you've got a full house," Ella Greenblatt from 14H said when she came to walk Nana to the condo's function room for mah-jongg.

"You're not kidding," Nana told her. And when Ella asked how Aunt Paula was handling things, Nana said, "She goes around barefoot like a *meshuggah*-no-brazier-peasant is how she's doing. Changes husbands like she's changing her socks. She's a pain in my ass..."

After they left, Aunt Paula made us brush our teeth and whipped out the presents. "Go ahead, you guys. Open 'em." They were, unfortunately, book shaped.

Aunt Paula urged us on. These moments meant something to her. I could tell by her giddy gusto versus most other times when she seemed so whipped. She told us she had a metabolic condition, but I wondered maybe if she just needed more things to feel happy about. Siddhi tore at the paper wrapping with great fervor.

"Ooh, be careful," she warned, "don't rip it." He held up the used notebook and screwed up his face, flummoxed. "It's my math work from the sixth grade. It's all filled out correctly—I was sensational at math, straight A's, not that anyone cared. Now you can teach yourself how to do all the exercises. See?" She flipped the pages.

"Siddhi, say thank you," I elbowed him. He had on a weird smile, the one where he was still waiting for a better present.

"Thanks, Auntie," he said, and she gave him a big hug. "I have to make," he said and ran off to the bathroom.

Aunt Paula turned her attention to me. She pushed her glasses up on her nose, tied her frizzy hair back in a bun, and swished her hands out into the air, jingling her piles of bangle bracelets to encourage me to open mine. "You are going to die when you open this…" She did a drum roll. Drama was Aunt Paula's milieu. She made everything too precious, in her desperate bid to transform nicked-up, mundane reality into delicate perfection with only the power of her need. Hers was a precarious method of living a life, with every person, every moment, every suggestion or outcome always falling short of a more peaceful and gorgeous one. She was the fragile sum of all of her disappointments, but you had to hand it to her because she kept on trying.

"C'mon Cees!"

"Sorry," I said as I sped up. My way was to make opening the present last as long as possible. I used the nubs of my bitten nails to peel back the tape and unfold the rest of the wrapping until I was left with a little stack of old paperbacks. I managed a big smile, formed mainly out of my appreciation of how Aunt Paula apparently loved me. Then her smile changed to a look of Obi-Wan Kenobi graveness.

"Sienna," she said and then paused, expanding the moment by tilting her chin toward her chest and looking down at me. Through her thick eyeglass lenses, her eyes appeared bigger and browner and much more tired, "These are my first edition paperbacks of all of my Salinger, and I am entrusting them to you." The name Salinger meant nothing to eight-year-old me, and yet, Aunt Paula's paperbacks felt so powerfully relevant to her, I feared the responsibility. I would have liked a nice Malibu Barbie, but instead, I held in my hands my Aunt Paula's beating heart.

"Wow, thanks, Auntie Paula!" She kissed me with a little hum and then lifted the top book, opened it, and sniffed the yellowed pages, closing her eyes from the good of it. "Franny and Zooey," she sighed.

"This is going to teach you that your inner world, the world of your heart and mind, is as real and important in life as what happens out here. You can choose to be with perfect beings always in your mind and let the world matter less if you need it to. There is a part of you, Sienna, an ageless, wordless, weightless piece of you that no one can ever hurt, and that part of you is always safe."

"You kinda don't seem like you really wanna give these away," I said. The books didn't even have pictures on the covers, just titles.

"Oh my gosh, no, honey, that's not it. I am just so envious that these stories I love most will all be new for you, and, well, I miss being the me who read these for the first time." I heard the toilet flush. She pushed her glasses back up her nose, "So you'll read them?"

"Okay, Auntie Paula." My promise had the power to bring a perennially let-down person a nugget of pure joy. "I'll definitely read all of them," I said, "as soon as I learn how to read."

*

For lunch, Aunt Paula cooked enchiladas with black olives sliced like Lego tires. "Is Nana mad all the time because Pop Pop Murray died?" I asked over a mouthful of cold cheese I grated myself.

My grandfather died before I was born, but I knew how some-one's death could squeeze you on the inside so that you looked the same but were not the same and never would be again.

"Nope. Ma was a bitch long before that," Aunt Paula said as she let Siddhi lick the sour cream spoon.

"Nana's a bitch," Siddhi repeated, dripping white from the corners of his lips. Aunt Paula didn't correct him. I gave him an elbow.

"And besides," she kept on, "it wasn't Pop dying that screwed us up. When he met Ma, Pop was already depressed because of his brother Schmuly. They went into the army together, Pop and his big brother, but Pop got shot and sent home early."

"Pop Pop got shot for real?" I got set to hear another one of Aunt Paula's tales of our family. She was the quietest one in the family. Like Siddhi, she didn't need to talk as much as Jackson, Nana, and me, but if you got her going on about the family, she could spin her bitterness into beautiful webs of family history.

"Yep. Right here," she said and poked herself in the tushie. "Another soldier in his own squadron shot him by accident. That's what happens when you draft a bunch of teenage boys and send them out with guns." She cracked the oven and peeked. "A few more minutes. Anyway, they shipped him back to the Lower East Side after only three months in Salerno."

"What about Uncle Schmuly?" I asked, delighted by the new relative on the scene.

"Schmuly got killed in the war. A nineteen-year-old kid gets slaughtered storming a beach, and this makes him a national hero? There were medals they awarded him, and a town parade. Pop was very jealous…But also devastated. He idolized Schmuly." Aunt Paula seemed to forget she was talking to us because she looked away and stopped swishing her hands in the usual way that made her silver bangles jingle and her soft belly shake. Siddhi took the opportunity to plunge his fingers into the sour cream.

"He always compared them," she continued, "Jackson and Schmuly. He tried so hard to get Jackson to live out and become whatever Schmuly might have been…Like, ugh, when he forced

Jackson to go out for football." She stared at the white door of Nana's dish cabinet. "And Jackson didn't even like sports, but he'd have to be out there with Pop throwing the ball." She spat the word Pop like the jolt you feel when a balloon bursts before you're ready.

"Staggering around, soused on his damned whisky, and throwing the ball in the bugs and heat, back and forth, back and forth, back and forth, and with all the advice and screaming and yelling. *My father didn't tumble off the boat from Russia, so my boy could throw like a broad!* He'd yell at Jack. As if Pop were ever a quarterback, like Pop even knew how to play! And then, when poor Jack didn't make the team, he went on about how Jack lacked discipline, how he needed to toughen up, and he took off his belt, and—" Siddhi dropped the spoon on the floor with a clang that distracted Aunt Paula, and I got mad at him for halting the history lesson before she reached the end.

She rinsed off the spoon and handed it back to Siddhi. "Jackson may be, well, whatever he is, but at least he doesn't beat you guys," she said, stroking her finger down my cheek. "I give him a lot of credit for that." She sniffed and flipped her frizzy, Roseanne Roseannadanna hair in a way that said she was all done with that subject, so I went with a new question.

"How does Nana get money without going to a job?"

"Oh, well, between Pop's life insurance, army pension, and selling the house, he left her pretty comfortable." I pictured Nana snuggled into a cozy nest of fluffy dollar bills.

"How much do me and Sienna have in life assurance and army?" Siddhi interrupted, and Aunt Paula laughed again.

"So, was Pop Pop a rich businessman, too, like Jackson?" I asked.

"What?" She laughed. "No, baby. Jackson? What?" More laughing. "No, Pop was not rich. He went into the army from high school. He didn't want to work in Nana's father's grocery store. Said it was low class, so he taught himself to be a bookkeeper. He was always ashamed of the fact that he never went to school. He used to holler, "*Without an education, a man is nothing!* If Schmuly were here, he'd have been a doc-tah!"

Aunt Paula took Siddhi down from the counter and used one arm to sweep us both to the side so she could pull down the oven door and take out the enchiladas. The cheese and sauce bubbled and sizzled, and the savory aroma made us jump up and down and cheer for good food. But she said we had to wait for them to cool.

"Did Nana and Pop Pop Murray love each other?"

"Good question, Siddhi," I said, and he smiled. I'd collected Nana's story of Pop Pop Murray a sentence at a time. When the plumber asked Nana if her husband was at home, she said, "*Ai-ysh*! That man is better off in the ground!"

"You want to know a little something about Murray," she told the friend we ran into at the Green Stamp store. "Here's something: He was a Goddamned pain in my ass." And when I asked how they met, she said, "Your grandfather was a soldier in the service. Very handsome in his uniform, so you'd never know he was a nincompoop." And to Aunt Paula, she said, "All you kids get dahvorst nowadays. You didn't get a dahvorse in my day. You went to your parents for a week, and then they sent you back to your philandering schmuck-of-a-husband."

"Did they? Did they love each other a lot?" I asked.

"Love was different back then, CeeCee. Ma married Pop to escape her own parents, the same reason I married Gary. They were tickets out," she said. "And sometimes those are the only tickets available."

I didn't know what any of that meant, but with the answers getting steadily sadder, I decided to stop with the questions.

CHAPTER 4

Be True to Your School, 1982

It was Sunday, May ninth, a day when every girl should have a mother. Siddhi woke me before dawn, as was our custom. We tried to wake Ximena to help us fill the early hours with a game of pretend school. She was our friend and, at seventeen, the youngest of Jackson's "Babies." But she'd spent the night with the rest of them, smoking pot and drinking the Brugmansia tea, splitting off in groups and pairs for love-making rituals, until everyone wound up passed out and draped throughout the house like they were under a spell from Sleeping Beauty.

I tucked my hair behind my ears and smoothed out my teacher costume (the pink tennis dress which was getting closer to fitting me covered by a pillowcase-cum-tunic I'd cut head and armholes in and belted with my golden curtain tieback from The Breakers).

Siddhi, my student, sat on a flipped milk crate, crooked smile peeking out from under a straw hat someone left lying around, his pencil threaded through his closed fist. The day before, he'd thrown one of his finest temper tantrums, for which Jackson locked him in our bedroom "to cool out." I didn't dare let him out, as Babies had been kicked out of Xanadu for lesser infractions, but I did spend the day soothing him from the other side of the door and sneaking him food and water, as I believed a good mother would do.

When Jackson got home around sunset and freed him, Siddhi was drained and long past screaming and crying, but I could see a part of his fury remained, a red ring in the hazel of his eyes.

"Good morning, class," I announced. "Today, we're gonna learn all about the planets. Who can name them?"

Siddhi shook his head. I didn't know them all either, but I hoped Siddhi and I could put our heads together.

"I can name them all," a voice rang out from the yard as a tall, new Baby joined us on the sun porch. "Let's see," she said, "there's Mercury, Venus, Earth, and Mars," she had wavy brown hair and a pink hibiscus stuck in above her ear. "Jupiter, Saturn, Uranus, Neptune, and the littlest, farthest one is called Pluto."

"Wow," Siddhi sighed. She took care with her bare feet to step over all the party mess as she sat down and then swung her pretty legs over the knobby sea grape branch growing right into the porch where there used to be French doors. Through the opening, light spread across the sky, and green parrots flocked from tree to tree, trying to make up their minds about where to call home.

"I get up early, too," she said. She seemed different from the others. She had an aura of sweetness. "You must be his kids," she said. "I'm Libby."

I aimed to impress. "I'm Sienna Shiva Karma Jones."

"Whoa, now that's a name," Libby said. She had sparkly teeth, a reminder that Siddhi and I were days past due for a brushing. My name origins were a source of great pride for me.

"Sienna is Jackson's favorite color," I told her. "And Shiva is the God of Destruction, like how you can destroy all of the bad things you do and then make everything more beautiful in your next lifetime." Siddhi nodded along. He was a little shy with new people, but more than that, he had no need, like I did, to fill the space between strangers with his words. "And Karma is when you do good stuff and then good stuff happens to you back, and you can do that in other lives also. All of it counts. Everything is the same. One big thing."

"Very smart," she said. She wore a shimmery seed-pearl brace-let. "And too true." My cheeks flushed with her praise.

"Anyways, they couldn't decide, but when my mother asked why they even had to pick one, they didn't pick just one, and I got both names, which I think was certainly the right decision."

"Certainly," Pretty Libby agreed. She had a beauty mark next to one of her eyebrows.

"Jones is the name my father changed to from Litzkin, which is my Nana's original last name that she got from my Pop Pop Murray, who was a pain in her ass and also dead like my mother, and I'm glad Jackson switched it because Sienna Shiva Karma Litzkin sounds very, extremely weird."

"Very, extremely," Siddhi echoed. Libby smiled at him.

"Well, it is very, extremely nice to meet you, Sienna. And you must be," she knelt beside my brother, a motherly move. "Let me guess. Siddhartha?" I revved up to give the speech I had about Siddhartha Kahlil Gibran Jones, but Siddhi had his own notions.

"Call me Bliggins," he said. I slapped my hand to my forehead, like Nana always did before hollering that she was fed up with our baloney. Libby put her thin wrist to her lips to stifle a giggle.

"Well, Bliggins," she said, tipping back his hat and touching his soft chin, "can I play, too?"

Wearing her shimmery, turquoise panties and Jackson's pen-guin T-shirt from the Fleetwood Mac concert, Libby cooked us scrambled eggs with rice cakes and peanut butter, and she played school until Jackson called out for her. Then she gave us each our own hug and trotted back down the hall.

"What about Libby for a new mom?" I asked Siddhi.

"Where's the old one again?" he wondered. Siddhi memorized science facts, whole songs, and lengthy poems with ease, but he had no good place inside to keep our mother.

"Remember, Siddhi," I said, needlessly cautious, "Mommy

died when you were a tiny, one-and-three-quarters-year-old."

"Oh yeah!" he said, suddenly delighted like the answer had been stuck on the tip of his tongue.

"So, what about Libby?" I asked again.

"How come her? What happened to Shella?" Shella was the Baby who slept over with Jackson before Libby. He often paid special attention to the newest woman, like she was the only one he wanted to make love with for a while. Shella had banana-shaped boobs and hair down to her thighs that she wore in a ten-pound braid. Shella didn't give hugs, but she made good granola and macraméd a few plant holders for the dining room.

And then, one morning, we woke to find that Shella had decamped. "Jackson, is Shella coming back?" Siddhi asked.

"Nah, I think she caught a ride out with some cats headed to Myrtle Beach."

"Why'd she leave us?" I asked.

"I don't know, munch. Huh...I'll have to meditate on that one."

"Shella's not as good as Libby," I told Siddhi. "And not as pretty, and anyways, gone. And Libby knows the song of the fifty states..."

"Hmm, yeah," he said, pondering. "And she has the fancy underpants...Yeah. She could be our new mom. Okay."

"And maybe after they get married, with me as the flower girl, Jackson could plant a seed in her butt so we can have a sister."

"And a brother," Siddhi added.

Thrilled with our consensus, we ran down the hall and burst into Jackson's room to find him and Libby naked, her crouched on top of him, facing backward, and hopping like a frog. She caught sight of us, screamed, and, sticking with the whole frog thing, hopped off into the sheets and pulled them up to her neck. Jackson rolled over on his side, rested his head on his bent arm, and looked at us with his morning eyes, glassy and reddish from smoking.

"Hey, munchies," he grinned. "What's shakin'?" His penis was still pointing out straight.

"Are you and her gonna get married?" Siddhi asked, pointing

at Libby.

Jackson laughed. "Never, you silly munch! Libby is one of my Babies. We were just doing some lovemaking." Libby exhaled, laid her head down on the pillow, and looked at the ceiling, blinking. "Right, baby?" Jackson reached back and squeezed her upper thigh through the sheet.

Libby grimaced as if he'd pinched her. "Mm hmm," she agreed.

My heart squeezed hard and then plopped into my guts when Libby and I found out at the exact same time that Jackson didn't love her especially at all. When she went into the shower, I snuck into the bathroom and took her seed-pearl bracelet from the side of the sink so I could keep it to look at and remember lovely, unbroken Libby.

Two days later, Jackson invited Ann without an "e" and Anne with an "e" into his room to make love with him and Libby all together, and halfway through, Libby stormed out crying and carrying her backpack and purse.

"Bye, kids," she said before leaving. "I'm sorry for you." We never asked Anne With and Ann Without to play school. They were nothing special like Libby might have been, and I really didn't want them teaching me anything.

There was a month left before the regular kids got out of school for summer break, and since my courage surged in the morning, that's when I chose to tiptoe once more into Jackson's room. The Libby business inspired me to try and get Siddhi and I into elementary school, a building filled to the brim with pretty teachers, a parking lot packed with moms honking from their station wagons, and a cafeteria stocked with chocolate milk and French fries, just like on TV.

I found Jackson sitting on the floor, cross-legged in meditation. Sariah, Ximena, and Ann Without were all asleep in his bed. I waited quietly until his eyes slit open.

"Hey, munchie-sweet," he opened, bolstering my resolve.

"Hey, Jackson. Can me and Siddhi please go to school today? Real school?" I threw in a batting of eyelashes and pressed my palms together in begging prayer.

"Siddhi and me," Jackson whispered, languidly stretching his neck to one shoulder and then to the other.

"Siddhi and me. We want to be enrolled in school from now on. Pretty please?" I made sure to sound exceedingly studious. Jackson smiled at me, tipped his chin down, and stroked his beard. He turned his face toward the window to the sunrise and asked, "Why would you want to go to another school when I have you enrolled in the finest school on the planet?"

"You do?" I believed that Jackson had regular tête-à-têtes with God, so it would follow, naturally, that he possessed the power, as he did with the Babies, to sense my needs and summon the appropriate miracles.

"Really? Which one?" I asked, "North Beach?" North Beach Elementary was the nearest elementary school I knew of, and its proximity to Xanadu lent it a certain tops-on-the-planet potential.

"Nope."

"The orange one on the way to the farmer's market in Coconut Grove?"

He shook his head.

"Hmm...The green one with the metal slide near Nana's condo?"

Jackson gazed out his window with sullen dreaminess, like he was waiting for someone who wasn't me, and somehow, I knew I'd blown it. I would have been better off doing something praiseworthy to get back in his graces: make up a song, do a headstand, or cartwheel through the room, but I didn't waiver.

"The one in the church on the way to Bay Harbor?"

"No, Sienna," he sighed, sounding bored. "I have you enrolled in my own school." This was big news to receive without warning, and my stomach sizzled inside me, like a shook-up soda can. He sighed, stood up, and said, "See, that school down the street is a nice-looking building with the flower bushes and the nice American flag waving from the nice flagpole on the lawn. And all the nice little children lined up in rows at their nice little desks and the nice teachers at their blackboards teaching all the nice things."

"Uh huh," I nodded along calmly, though it all sounded so nice, it was hard not to squeal. TV taught me that school lunches came in little molded trays with walled squares for the different foods, so they didn't even touch each other, and there was a space on each tray for a miniature carton of milk.

"And all that nice stuff that the nice teachers go to work every day and program into the nice children is nothing more than one, giant, Machiavellian mind fuck."

"Too early..." Sariah groaned. "Come back to bed."

"Keep it warm for me, baby," Jackson answered and bent to kiss her on her tushie before taking my hand and leading me down the hall to the living room.

"Sienna, you and your brother are gifted in your intelligence, which gives you the unique ability to derive all you need to learn energetically from the sky, earth, and water and from me. And I learn from God. Look around, and you'll find teachers every-where." He waved across the space before us, and following his gesture, I saw Siddhi on the couch napping with Rat Daddy. A topless woman I didn't recognize sat on the floor across the coffee table, giving Steve a tarot card reading. Stacey and Warren snug-gled in the purple papasan chair, watching "One Day at a Time."

"Guardian angels lurk in the elements and in your mind. You gotta get into serious meditation to draw them up through your chakras, and that'll be all the school you need," Jackson said.

Education by way of divine osmosis sounded easy enough, but not fun, not my style, not for me and Siddhi, who had questions to ask and games to play and friends to make and lockers to fill with textbooks and fresh school supplies from the drug store.

I was halfway through gathering up the nerve to tell him so, when he moved to the front of the room and announced, "I AM MADE OF GOD!" He paused after he said it, a signal to the Babies that it was time to listen up. "You are of ME," he said, and the Babies turned to pay attention, "So you," and here he meant everyone in the room, all those who followed and worshiped and descended from Jackson in body or thought, "are of God!"

I stole another glance at my brother, fast asleep with his head resting on the fat middle of a snake large enough to unhinge its jaw and suck him down like a Milk Dud.

"Is Siddhi God, too?"

Jackson lit a joint, pulled the smoke deep into his lungs, and held it, nodding. "Yep," he said through exhaling smoke. "And I'm not sending my two little bodhisattvas to get all of the organic godliness torn from your skulls and instead get brainwashed with a load of standardized fear-bullshit in that sugar-coated, government-machine, mind-fuck-atorium." Tomatoes and Steve thought what Jackson said was very funny. He took another deep toke, exhaled, and laughed with them. "You and Siddhi'll grow up to be *their* teachers," he said. "You understand?"

I didn't. All I heard was blah blah, organic…blah blah…Siddhi is God, blah blah… fear bullshit…blah blah, mind-fuck-atorium, which I gathered to mean I was *not* enrolled at North Beach Elementary. I also knew if I cried or mentioned that I needed the bathroom, Jackson would become angry and unpredictable, so I tried to distract him with another question. "So, what's your school called?"

"What school?" Jackson took another hit.

"Yours. The tops on the planet."

"Yes." He looked up and thought for a moment; even a kid could see he was making one up on the spot. Not that I believed he wasn't capable of such a feat of education, but I was positive that whatever he said wouldn't involve a class hamster or a science fair. "My school is called, uh…The School…of Love."

"Right on," said Steve. "The. School. Of. Love."

"And for your first lesson, I gotta tell you a story…"

"Ooh, can it be Sleeping Beauty?" I begged with prayer hands.

Jackson rolled his eyes and sat me down.

"Once upon a time, back when I lived in India," he said, "I encountered…a tiger." Jackson hadn't ever traveled to India, but he had a way of commandeering a parable and telling it in the first person. By the end, you'd realize it was just a lesson, but for the part where you thought it was real, you'd really connect with him, right there in his danger, and so when it all worked out in the end, you'd feel his relief.

I'd heard him tell this story before and seen how he drew people in with it. He was a fantastic storyteller, and this one, where he winds up hanging from a cliff face with hungry tigers above and below and two little mice chewing through the vine he holds to keep him from certain death, well, it was one of his greatest hits. Jackson used his whole body to deliver this speech, drawing it out with pauses, facial expressions, and wild hand gestures.

Siddhi woke up in the middle and interjected with a question, "But then, what did you d—"

"Shh!" Jackson said sharply and pointed down at his feet that Siddhi should come and sit with the others. As Jackson described the tigers, I looked around the room at Siddhi and the Babies and wondered how all of them, any of them, hanging on Jackson's every breath, could really be my teachers, let alone gods! The room was dead quiet, but for Jackson's voice and the sipping sound of whoever's turn it was to hit the joint.

"I'm shit-scared," he went on, "just packed with fear, y'know, like the worst paralysis. I am one who looks up for my lessons, not usual for me to be looking down, but in this case, my ass is on the line…"

Jackson went on as the Babies sat at his feet, brains agape for his wisdom, and I wondered if this would be the rest of my life, getting lessons about India-stuff I didn't understand on the dirty floor of our motherless house, never learning how or being allowed to read the real children's books I saw in store windows with big pictures printed in bright candy-wrapper colors. Jackson held one arm over his head like he was holding the vine for dear life, "… so that when I get out of this cliff-pickle, I'd go live my life more truthfully, right? And next thing I know, two mice crawl out…"

My stomach cramped and twisted as I listened to him riff, wanting to understand and, even more, to believe. But I couldn't help wondering if Jackson knew what he was talking about at all.

"...and if those mice chew all the way through the root, then I'm screwed, right?" The Babies filled the room with joyful anticipatory 'Nos' and supportive woo-hooing. "Oh yeah, man. I. Am. Tiger. Pastrami. And I'm frantically looking around for a way to save myself, and guess what? There isn't one. There is no way to save myself from my birth, my death, or all the bullshit in between..."

This was the part where he always hit it home, slipping in his philosophy just before the payoff, exchanging all the Babies' questions for all of God's answers. And finally, when everyone was high on the kush and Jackson's rhetoric, and even Siddhi and I were cheering along, he brought it in for a landing. "...over to my right, growing out of the rocks, I see this strawberry. One luscious, red, sensual little strawberry growing on the cliff face, ripe as can be."

The Babies went bananas, wolf-whistling and howling. "So...I reach over," he pantomimed reaching way over to the side, "and I say to myself, *'I'm gonna die here.'* That's inevitable, you know, that's cool, that's the same for everyone. Them's the breaks! But before I succumb to that energetic transition," and he plucked the circulating joint from Tomatoes' fingers, like picking the strawberry, and he licked his lips and took a record-breaking pull. The Babies went hooting wild while he held it for a second or two and then exhaled, the vibration of his voice texturizing the smoke, "I'm gonna eat. This. Perfect. Fuckin'. Strawberry!"

I didn't understand how the anecdote related to me and Siddhi, but I stomped my feet and cheered madly along with the rest of the Babies, which was so much fun to do, at least for that morning, I forgot all about wanting to learn to read.

Whenever it revved up like that, the Babies and Jackson liked to do some lovemaking, and when the telltale kissing began, I suggested we get some crayons and papers and play explorers and take field notes like the Babies were Jane Goodall's band of chimps in Africa, but Siddhi felt like taking a swim. Rock-paper-scissors-shoot! Paper-covered rock. We swam.

CHAPTER 5

Let My People Go, 1982

Nana sprinkled Jewishness over our existence like monosodium glutamate, and to me, it tasted delicious. She insisted that Siddhi and I were Jewish, and that along with the genetic genius of Spielberg, Einstein, Meir, and Dershowitz, we too shared responsibility to our fellow Jews, like Nana's friend Elsie, who had a tattoo of numbers on her arm, because she survived the Holocaust.

"They're always trying to wipe us out, you know," Nana said. I'd made the decision to consider Judaism for three reasons. First, I wanted Nana to love me, and whenever she said, "Next year in Jerusalem," she became affectionately happy. Second, if we were Jewish, she might take us with her when she played mah-jongg at Elsie's.

The one time she did bring us along, Elsie called us "dahlinks" and let us play with her grandchildren's toys and *matryoshka* dolls, and she encouraged us to eat the chocolate-dipped cocktail sticks and Nips candies in the crystal bowls on her coffee table. Third, and most key, I loved the idea that an entire people, without having met, tested, or even smelled me, were willing to include me in their group and want me unconditionally, that I was *chosen*, without having to change anything about myself.

On what Nana called the Ides of March, she took us with her on errands and stopped by Temple Beth Shalom, where a Hebrew-accented teacher read us a book about Passover.

For Siddhi and me, the Exodus from slavery was less exciting than the fact that Passover came with a special dinner with custom crackers. And while we took turns peeing in the big stall in the ladies' room, Siddhi and I agreed on a plan to invite Nana and Aunt Paula, who had, that year, FINALLY taught us to read, to come over to our house for Seder, and when Nana asked Jackson if we could do Passover, he said, "Sure, Ma. Sure."

Nana offered to bring the dinner and seder plate, but Jackson told her, "We got it covered Ma." She was so delighted about the idea of a Jones family Passover, she even offered to take us afterward for a weekend visit at the condo, a sure bet for more Aunt Paula food and even more reading lessons.

We packed our bags that night in March.

We counted the days, and Ximena lent me her wrap-around skirt with the sunset and clouds printed on it. "It used to be my sister's," she said, looking sad for a second before adding, "Keep it. It looks weird on me anyway." Ximena had become so skinny that everything but naked was too big on her. She wrapped the skirt around me right under my armpits and tied the bow on the side of my chest. "Like a strapless princess gown," she said.

I wanted to beg Ximena to eat and eat until I could "pinch an inch," but whenever Siddhi and I offered to share our rice cakes and cheese, she looked at the food like I thought about getting a new mother, with love and wanting, wracked with suspicious trepidation. Siddhi said she told him she was on a hunger strike for world peace. But I could see she didn't think she deserved the food.

On April 7, the El Dorado pulled up at four-thirty sharp. We ought to have predicted they'd come early—Nana's stomach alarm always went off at five-thirty, and she had to leave time for the seder—but Siddhi and I hadn't finished getting the Babies to help us with the meal and no one had reminded Jackson, so we were all surprised to spy the car, and before he trotted off to stall them in the driveway, he ordered the Babies to clean up, burn some incense, and get dressed.

Babies scurried to and froe to make it all happen while Jackson gave Nana and Aunt Paula a drawn-out tour of the updates on the outside of the house, pool, and gardens. When they came inside, Aunt Paula hugged each of our heads into her soft belly, and Jackson ferried Nana into the dining room, where I'd clothed the table in pale pink bed sheets and lit votive candles. Never one to arrive empty-handed, Nana set down a box of matzos, a Tupperware full of eggs, and her stack of Maxwell House *Haggadahs,* worn and stained from decades of exodus. Sariah skipped barefoot from the kitchen draped in a gauzy, white garment too sheer and ineffectual to count as a dress. She held a cloth-covered basket, and Jackson dimmed the old crystal chandelier, maybe to make Sariah's areolas less discernible.

Sariah held up the basket, peeled back the napkin, and announced, "Something special for Mrs. Jones…"

"Mrs. Litzkin, sweethawt," Nana corrected. "My son changed his name to Jones when he was a famous singer." Nana once told us Jackson's given name was Yonatan Shmuel Ben Moshe, Jewish for Jonathan Schmuly, son of Murray.

Sariah turned to Jackson, who smirked, cryptically amused. She started again, "I baked a fresh loaf of bread, still warm, for Mrs. *Litzkin,*" Sariah beamed as she presented the basket.

"Far out," said Stacey.

Nana's eyes bugged out. She looked away from the basket and snapped at Sariah, "Not a chance!" And then she crossed the room to put some distance between herself and the *shande.*

"What just happened?" Sariah asked the room.

"You don't eat bread on Passover," Siddhi told her. "You only eat matzo crackers," he said, adding in a creepy whisper, "or else you burn in hell forever." He winked at me. Siddhi and I were not big fans of how Sariah had been hogging Jackson.

"That was a real nice thought, baby," Jackson told Sariah as she slunk back toward the kitchen with her sinful loaf.

"Here you go, dahling," Nana said, quickly shoving her offerings into Jackson's hands. "I need to use the toilet."

Stacey showed Nana to the bathroom.

Aunt Paula pushed up her glasses and snickered, "She almost drove me nuts with bringing the eggs."

Aunt Paula once told us that when she and Jackson were kids, every morning Pop Pop sat at the breakfast table, read the paper, and ignored her while criticizing Jackson for playing guitar and having long hair, "like a queer." Meanwhile, she said, Nana boiled six eggs, three hard and three soft, that she set to cool on either side of a single plate. And when Nana walked it to the breakfast nook, the eggs rolled around, changing loyalties. "Preference be damned," she said, "if Jackson didn't eat the egg he took, Pop cuffed him on the back of his head for wasting food."

Jackson set the Tupperware on the table as Nana returned to the dining room. "You're not going to put them on a serving dish?" And then, "Where is the seder plate, dahling? Where is the *gefilte* fish? Where is the goddamned Manischewitz wine?"

"Ma, we're not into that stuff here. You know that. Come sit and have a beautiful, healthy meal."

Nana eyed the table.

"What in Christ is going on here?" she asked, clutching her box of matzos but half-smiling, preserving grace in case Allen Funt should leap out from behind the potted Ficus to tell her she was on "Candid Camera." Her short, salt and pepper hair was set in stiff, airy curls, and she had bits of Estee Lauder, free-with-purchase lipstick on her front teeth. Her diamond star glinted from the exposed triangle of her chest above the zipper of her burgundy velour tracksuit. Had Nana ever been invited to dine with her beloved President Reagan, she'd have shown up at the White House wearing a velour tracksuit.

Jackson took her by the hand and led her to the seat beside his wicker peacock throne at the head of the table. He never let me sit in that chair, and by the enviable care he took with Nana, it was plain to see that if he wanted to take care, he was able; in terms of doting and covering Nana's needs for a while, appearing concerned, he had the aptitude.

"Let's have dinner, Ma. Why don't you come and sit down?" Each time he handled Nana with care, I felt a wave of hot tingling in my cheeks and chest, and I squeezed Siddhi to go with it. I squeezed and pinched him so many times he must have thought I was messing with him, and he got impatient with me and shoved me hard under the table. Stacey and Warren consoled Sariah. Steve, Tomatoes, Ximena, and a couple of others sat silently, observing. Pink Floyd played on the living room record player some song about being able to tell the difference between blue skies and pain.

The hot mushroom and cabbage fumes from the casseroles on the tabletop rose and mingled with the musky incense cone smoldering in its usual saucer atop the buffet. Nana sat next to Aunt Paula, whose modus operandi in the presence of both her mother and Jackson was to assume childlike disinterest. She acted vague, awkward, and humorless. Siddhi and I were energetically back in sync, and I couldn't figure out the source of my tension. Something weird was afoot.

"Where is the Godforsaken food?" Nana asked as she dug around her pocketbook, found and mounted her reading glasses, and tilted her head to the side to scratch a fingernail into the depths of her hairdo.

"Ma, I think *this is* the food," Aunt Paula said, goading.

"*Aiysh*! Shut up Paula, will you please?" Nana preferred Jackson, and Aunt Paula seemed both to revel in and fume at that fact. I elbowed Siddhi under the table, a warning that we must brace ourselves for the inevitable.

"Ma, we are peaceful here," Jackson said without hiding his amusement, "Try to be nice."

"Well, she should shut her trap once in a while. It's *Pesach*, for Christ's sake!"

"Those slaves went free," mumbled Aunt Paula as she folded her arms across her chest in protest.

"Speak up," Nana huffed, waving her stack of *Haggadahs* in a manner to suggest that everyone in the dining room ought to pick one up and get Jewish quick before the seas folded in.

Aunt Paula, short to Jackson's tall, pale to Jackson's tan, chubby to his slim, sighed her resignation. "Nothing, Ma."

Gauzy Sariah swooped in. "Mrs. Litzkin, we are so honored to have you here with us tonight. Happy Passover," she cooed.

"Yes. Thank you, dear," Nana told her. "Dear" was for waitresses and bank tellers; you didn't matter to Nana until you hit "sweethawt" or "dahling."

"We have a beautiful, fresh meal here, let's just enjoy it together, yes?" Sariah looked to Aunt Paula, who unfolded her arms and tucked in her seat.

"That's the stuff," said Jackson, and he pulled into his wicker throne.

"Yes, yes...fine, fine, good," Nana put her napkin on her lap, "but I don't see what you're eating here. There's no brisket."

Warren—a militant vegetarian—let out his sick hippo groan, and Siddhi and I burst into fits of giggles. We'd made an extensive study of the emotional energy that Jackson and the Babies put toward discussing, debating, and proselytizing about the right food, eating cooked or raw, balances of prana, yin and yang, nutritional philosophy, macrobiotics, and frequency and quality of bowel movements. We were old enough to appreciate the irony that despite their food fascination, they rarely remembered to purchase, cook, or serve us any.

Sariah placed her hands on top of Jackson's shoulders, like he belonged to her, which pulled the start cord on my stomachache. "Some of what we've prepared here, Mrs. Litzkin"—she kept using Nana's proper name, as if Nana was sure to warm to her when Nana didn't really like anyone except for Jackson—"was grown right here on our land."

"Oh my. Well—" said Nana.

"We have a homegrown alfalfa and broccoli sprout salad with tahini," Sariah pointed to the first bowl. "And this is warm, fermented cabbage, split pea porridge, and a beautiful nut loaf with mushroom and lentil gravy, all completely raw."

I looked at Nana, who rewarded me by wincing.

"And here," Sariah did a game show hand flourish over the next dish. "We have a coconut, avocado, banana, and papaya salad, with fruits fresh from our tr—"

"Say, Jackson, what do you hear from your old friend Arnold Selznick?" Nana railroading Sariah gave me such a jolt of family pride I almost had to excuse myself to pee. Plus, I recognized that name. Arnold Selznick and Jeffery Schwartzman had been Jackson's two best friends when he was a kid, just after Nana and Pop Pop moved the family from New York City to Miami Beach.

Jackson said that his two friends tried to play the music for the songs he wrote, but they were terrible, and they mostly hung out in Flamingo Park to smoke cigarettes and talk about pretty girls. Arnie, the smart one, could eat a dozen donuts by himself and was the top student in their class, and one time in the park, when an older bully called them a bunch of big nosed kikes, Schwartzy, the tough one, ran up and knocked that bully's block off.

I coveted such stories and mulled them over in my head until I'd cast Arnie (David Cassidy) and Schwartzman (Donny Osmond) and "Young" Jackson (Robbie Benson) and imagined them chatting all together beneath swaying palms, making bad music, and trading good secrets. And because their friendship took place in the Sixties, I pictured it all in black and white. I wanted to be a part of their group, to know Jackson closer to my age, because I had a theory I would have liked him before he grew up and needed to be so much larger than a kid knows how to handle.

"I heard Selznick moved back to the city," said Jackson.

"So, you're in touch then?" Nana licked her fingertip and flipped a page in her *Haggadah* as if we were moving properly through the seder.

"Nah, Ma. I haven't spoken to those guys since I left home," he said. "So, what? Sixteen, seventeen years..." Jackson told us as soon as he got some money, he bought Mellow Yellow, packed two suitcases and his guitar, and ran away from home. He said he made like a banana and split.

"Word is he's running for Congress," Nana said, and when Jackson made no response, Nana elbowed Aunt Paula in the arm. "I told you we should have brought the chopped liver," she said, which elicited another mammalian death groan from Warren as he excused himself from the table, *to meditate on the beauty and sanctity of our animal brethren*, he said.

Siddhi and I dipped our heads under the table to laugh so hard there was no sound.

"Ma!" Jackson raised his voice a bit but then looked up, took a deep breath, and dialed it back. "We eat food for our souls here."

"Well, forgive me, but I don't see how anyone could get full up on all of this mango something-or-other and nut *schmutz*."

Sariah massaged Jackson's shoulders. "Well, Mrs. Litzkin, how about a little taste?"

Nana furrowed her brow, and I was pleased to witness her loathing Sariah, who currently dominated Jackson's bed, and Siddhi and I had real concerns.

I still believed I had a responsibility to keep the way clear for the right woman to come along and marry Jackson, love us the most, adopt us, and make me two French braids in my hair separated by a perfect white line part, and Sariah's puff of dark pubic hair showing through her sheer dress spoke poorly for her potential. Once she stopped rubbing Jackson and took her seat on his far side, we dug in. Nana ignored her plate, nibbling a board of matzo and determinedly continuing her own microservice, which she eventually concluded with a rousing, under-the-breath, "*Dayenu*." I used the matzos to make Siddhi and myself each a nut-loaf sandwich.

As he ate, Jackson launched into a lengthy sermon on the benefits of raw foods, and the Babies chimed in here and there with lots of quasi-scientific evidence to support his claims. "And a raw diet makes you look great, too!" he said.

"Amen," said Sariah.

"Who cares how you look?" spat Aunt Paula. "Why is everyone

so concerned with looks these days, when what really matters is how you feel." When Aunt Paula was eighteen, she ran off and married a bum. Then she married and divorced some more bums. I never met any of them more than once, but her current bum was probably still Uncle Hobie. "I'll bet the families of the Hama Massacre victims in Syria have huge concerns for the vitality of fresh squeezed juices," Aunt Paula said. "There are more important things in the world, Jackson. People are suffering. I've been crying for a mon—"

"How do *you* feel, Jackson dahling?" Nana spoke right over her.

Aunt Paula huffed, "Ma, I was talking about my feelings…"

"Who could forget? You and your feelings…You have too many goddamn feelings, you know!" Nana deadpanned. A few of the Babies giggled until Jackson held up an open palm, and they got serious right away for him.

"Ma—" Jackson began.

But Aunt Paula burst out, "Oh, that's your big attempt to defend me, Jackson: *Ma, Ma, Ma,*" she mimicked. The usual family problem was upon us, and Siddhi must have been worried, too, because he grabbed my hand. Our bags were all the way upstairs, and I began to lament that we hadn't hung them on the backs of our chairs. No one moved or spoke at the table. I felt like one of the Jews in Egypt, and I wished Moses would come and make a path for me to Nana's El Dorado.

"Paula, why don't you cut the shit and stop making this about you, okay?" Jackson remained mellow.

"Because it's always about me, right? Ma is always going on about me and my wonderfulness. Never a thing about Jackson and how handsome he is, and how talented he is, and how Jackson was in The Sandcastles and Jackson wrote 'Tiny Flowers,' and Jackson is so talented, and he looks so wonderful."

"Jackson wrote 'Tiny Flowers'?" Sariah asked Tomatoes, who shrugged.

"Paula, cool out with the sarcasm, okay? We are peacefu—"

"Shut up, Jack!" Aunt Paula snapped.

Siddhi squeezed my fingers, and I scooted my chair up to his, so

I could reach to pat his back. I would have played with his hair, but I didn't want to point out to Nana how much it had grown back.

"Like, the *song*, 'Tiny Flowers'?" Sariah was rambling. "*My pretty girl so fair, da, da, dee, da, da, da, and she had tiny flowers in her hair?*" she sang.

Nana nodded; her chest puffed up with the most resilient stuffing: pride. Her star glinted in the candlelight. "Yes, he did! This man came to the house and told my son he was really going places. Gave us a check for five thousand dollars. A fortune in those days—"

"A fortune now," added Tomatoes.

"—and changed his name to Jackson Jones because it sounded less ethnic or some such," said Nana. She grabbed an egg.

Sariah smiled and closed her eyes. "My dad used to sing that song to me as a lullaby. Before he got sick and…," she paused, opened her eyes, and one tear ran down her cheek. "I…really… love that song."

"Yes. Yes. Everyone loves the song, but no one remembers about my son!" Nana raised her voice, poking her finger upward, gesturing to her point. Aunt Paula rolled her eyes.

"How could you have written that song?" Sariah asked Jackson.

Siddhi leaned over to explain to Sariah what we'd been told about Jackson's younger days. "Jackson was the singer in The Sandcastles. They said he was the next Elvis."

Sariah's eyebrows shot up as I rounded out the rest of the story. "'Tiny Flowers' was a big, huge hit, but then the British invasioned America and messed everything up, and then that's when God told Jackson that everyone remembers '96 Tears,' but no one remembers the real name of Question Mark from Question Mark and the Mysterians."

"Oh, Christ! He got lucky for five seconds in nineteen-sixty-four!" Aunt Paula cut me off before I could tell Sariah that Jackson once wrote a song about Siddhi and me, but he hadn't played it in so long that I forgot all the words.

"He was a genius," Nana gushed.

Aunt Paula let her fork clang down on her plate, "Right!" she screamed, "Because Jackson is soooo talented, and Jackson is soooo handsome, and..."

"SHUT UP, PAULA!" This time, it was Jackson and Nana together, and sharp enough to make me jump.

"It's enough already. I can't even think," said Nana. "Sweethawt, what are you talking about planting and farming, I thought you're a businessman, dahling?" She looked at Jackson.

"That's the understatement of the year," Aunt Paula laughed, but Jackson shot her the look. She'd gone too far with her hinting; it was time to put a cork in it, and she did.

Jackson took a breath and addressed the Babies. "The lesson here is simply that I was one of you, and I need you to see what biological family versus chosen family can do to block God and damage the soul." They nodded and made knowing mumbles. Aunt Paula put her head in her hand. Nana dug around in the box for another matzoh and missed the whole thing. I got another twist in my stomach, knowing that I was just the biological kind of family and not the chosen kind.

"Ma," Jackson said, reclaiming Nana's attention. He sighed, ran his fingers through his hair, and continued, "Let's get back to talking about natural foods, and how I feel and look so much better since going raw." Even I was relieved to change the subject.

"He's lost around five pounds," Sariah chimed in as she wiped her hands on a cloth napkin.

"Well, I think you are looking very well and handsome, sweethawt," Nana said.

"Thank you, Ma," said Jackson, but his eyes were trained on Aunt Paula. He waggled his eyebrows at her and let his lip curl up in a taunting smirk.

"Well, I think you look like SHIT!" Aunt Paula shrieked, and stood up too quickly, causing her glasses to slip down her nose and her wooden chair to tip backward and hammer the floor.

"Oh yeah?" Jackson smiled, "Well, I'm makin' love to about four different women right now, and none of them think I look like shit." He and the Babies shared a laugh; Sariah excused herself to the bathroom.

"No one cares who you're making love to, Jackson!" Aunt Paula went to stomp out of the dining room, but then she turned back and looked at the remaining diners.

"You want to know why you never heard of him? Because he was a one-hit wonder. He never followed it up with anything worth a damn!"

"That's enough out of you, Paula," said Nana.

"He almost got on Ed Sullivan, and then he…" she started to laugh, a crazed, creepy laugh. "He got bumped for Topo Gigio. He got bumped for a puppet. Ha!"

"GET OUT!" Jackson screamed. Everyone went stiff.

Nana followed her daughter, not her favorite child, but nonetheless, her date for the evening, and from the living room, and in a markedly sweeter tone, I heard her say, "Paula, drive for me sweethawt, and stop at the delicatessen on the way, will you? I couldn't eat one goddamned thing on that table."

Siddhi and I raced up the staircase to fetch our backpacks and library books, but by the time we retrieved them, ran back down, and burst out the front door, they'd already driven away.

CHAPTER 6:

Christmas Special, 1982

My big reservation about being a Jew was letting go of the dream of my own Christmas special, like Anne Murray's or Charlie Brown's, surrendering my right to holler exhilarating commands like, *Siddhi, quick, call Santa! We need to save Christmas before the gang gets back from the Snowflake Ball!* I'd fantasized about featuring a guest appearance by Frosty the Snowman to sing exclusively Cat Stevens songs, because all of Cat Stevens' songs made me feel like crying in a good way.

Then, as if Christmas itself felt threatened by my potential abandonment, Sariah came out and ordered us to write letters to Santa Claus. She'd suddenly come down with a case of the Christmas spirit, and her holiday delight made her categorically nicer, thereby thrusting Christianity into the ring as a contender in the battle for my soul.

"Where should we put the tree?" she asked Jackson.

"What tree? Who's getting a tree?" he whispered from his lotus pose.

"We are. Here, near the television is probably best. We can

have a trimming party, and the kids can make paper chains, and then I can bake salt cookie ornaments like I used to when I was a kid, and we can make eggnog and…"

"Shh," he murmured. He opened his eyes to slits, "I love your rear end in those shorts."

Sariah smiled. "Thank you, but I am talking about Christmas. Let's bring a huge Christmas!"

"You bring that rear end over here," he told her. I didn't like it when Jackson spoke to Babies about sex stuff in front of us. No one did that on "Family Ties," and it always gave me a bad shiver in my stomach and thighs. How would he ever get married if he didn't even try to be romantic and open doors and bring flowers to one special woman…If Sariah had a chance to be that woman, then I had to do my best to help.

I dedicated to Sariah's cause by sampling her eggnog and helping with the house. And I did my favorite job of cleaning and reorganizing the downstairs rooms. I went around the house, taking a pillow from here and a chair and lamp from there, and I added a pot of rosemary on a little end table to create a warm, comfy little space for Jackson. I'd hoped to watch him snuggle into the little home I'd spun for him.

Siddhi was a paper chain master. As he worked, he dropped hints about which action figures he needed to pad out his meager Star Wars collection. The holidays improved Sariah's attitude enough to rekindle my long-lost hope that she and Jackson could get married, and as she grew nicer still, she might finagle Siddhi and me entry into the fourth and fifth grades, and maybe, after my tenth birthday in January, take me shopping for a training bra. Nana only wore brassieres, vast and frightening ecru-colored garments with straps like masking tape. What could she know about a dainty little training bra?

After we draped Siddhi's paper chains around the tree and pinned the rest across most of the living room windows, Sariah mixed salty dough that we baked together (almost like a real mommy and kids) into hard, tasteless cookies we then painted with Santa faces for ornaments. The kitchen smelled like I felt, warm and homey in that way that smells make you remember things about mothers. She warned Siddhi not to eat the ornaments when she took them out to cool (watching out for his safety, a value added), but his Siddhi-like impulses got the best of him, and he had to run and spit his hot, salty bite in the trash.

Sariah directed us for almost an hour—interspersed with her doing a lot of humming—as we adjusted tinsel and rewrapped colored lights until they shimmered and spiraled to her satisfaction. I preferred that she kiss and hug us and tell us we were smart and wonderful, but I had faith that her love would all follow in time.

Next, she let us watch her unwrap several ornaments from her big, burgundy suitcase and told us stories about each one. "This one we ordered through the mail. It's a moon rock. See how hard it is?" We sat before her on our knees, taking turns touching the otherworldly item. "And this seashell I found in the Keys. See? My father drilled a little hole in it, and we looped the string through..."

I pictured Sariah as a little girl in a ruffled bikini trotting after her kind father, turning cartwheels on the sand to pass the time as he drilled holes in her seashells. She took down Siddhi's paper chains and moved them to the mantle because they just didn't work for her on the tree. When I saw Siddhi deflate, I assured him she needed to make more space for presents, and although he understood I was just trying to cheer him up, he let it pass.

Christmas versus Chanukah. We had ourselves a race.

On the last night of Chanukah, December 17, as the Babies passed a joint and finished the remains of Sariah's Christmas dinner practice run (including scalloped potatoes, a novel slice of heaven), Jackson led Siddhi and me around the giant Banyan in our circular driveway and out the front gate for a surprise. Major reversal! Chanukah had made a break in the home stretch by sending Nana with two ten-speed bicycles tied into her open trunk, thus pulling Jewish up from behind and leaving Santa and Hashem neck and neck...

"Happy Chanukah! Use them in good health, *kinder*," said Nana, giving us each an aggressive kiss and hug before leaving.

Jackson lifted Siddhi's kickstand and helped him perch awkwardly on the seat while holding its underside, keeping the boy and bike upright. I thought of Sariah and all her efforts waiting for us inside.

"Now?" I asked.

"There is only now, Sienna. Every minute of your life is now," he said and turned his eyes back to Siddhi on the bike. "Okay. Riding a bike is a spiritual thing, man. You need to keep pedaling and keep up your speed. Stay balanced. You gotta feel around for that perfect spot where you just aaaahhhhhh…you just coast on a cloud, man, because if you lose your groove, you go down."

I was getting little pains in my guts, but Siddhi wore a huge grin. He fidgeted, raring to go.

"Keep up that aaaahhhhhh." Jackson ran, holding the seat as Siddhi veered side to side, pedaling hard. And when he let go after just a quarter of a block, Siddhi wobbled for a couple of seconds, then flailed his legs and nimbly dove to the grass. Jackson sent him a wolf whistle to commend the effort before turning to me, "Okay, munchie, you're up!"

"But doesn't Siddhi need another turn?" I was less athletic than Siddhi and spent his brief, wild ride picturing my own wretched fall, which was more dramatic and involved an ambulance ride.

"Get up there and worry about yourself."

"Maybe I'll wait for later."

Jackson didn't like apprehension, especially when he decided to involve himself in our activities. "We gonna do the fear bullshit thing now?"

"I'm not afraid," I lied, tummy twisting. "I just don't feel like it right now."

"Yeah, yeah. You're afraid, and you'll never get anything done that way. You remember that day at Six Flags Atlantis? You went right down that water slide you were afraid of and turned out to love water slides?" Of course, I remembered. Jackson had pushed me down the waterslide because I was holding up the line with my fear bullshit. I cried for the first half, but somewhere in the middle, my terror turned to exhilaration, and when it was over, I ran right back up to slide again.

"Exactly like that, munch. You started out scared, and then it was just…. aaaahhhhhh. That's why people say it's like riding a bike because riding a bike is so fuckin' easy. Now, straighten out your tushie. Good, here we go."

Jackson pushed the back of my seat, and I began to pedal, thinking to myself, that is not what that expression means. Jackson is not as smart as everyone thinks he is. I pedaled fast, meaning to impress him and to force him to run, maybe even cause him to trip and fall. He told everyone how they were so afraid, how their parents gave them so much fear, and how the world would never teach them the truth until they listened only to him, and I really wanted to know if there was someone else who could answer my questions and see if that person's answers were as different from Jackson's as I hypothesized a normal answer would be.

I pictured myself falling over rocks and bloodying myself, breaking bones, and Jackson having to know it was all his doing, me in the hospital bandaged head to toe with a leg up in the triangle thingy and remorseful Jackson crying by my bedside…Then I heard the whistle from what sounded like a mile behind me. I turned around and saw Siddhi and Jackson, back at the gates, tiny in the distance. I had my balance, and I kept riding. I crossed right over the street (thank goodness there were no cars coming because I didn't know how to stop) and then made a wide turn down around the block to Alton Road where there were smaller lots with loads of smaller houses.

I slowed down and then backpedaled into a fall on one of the softer-looking front lawns and sat for a minute, reveling, before I noticed that my knee was cut and throbbing.

"Oh my god! Are you okay?" Two girls ran toward me. The little one was younger than Siddhi, with brown pigtails as skinny as shoelaces, and on her T-shirt, Snoopy slept atop his red doghouse. The other girl was taller than me, with long auburn braids, a bow at the bottom of each, like Anne of Green Gables. She looked my age and so…normal. "We like totally saw you fall from our playroom window. Do you live around here? There's lots of kids in this neighborhood, but most of them are like total snobs. I can't be friends with snobs. So stuck up and spoiled. Whatever." She smiled.

I didn't think of saying anything until she was done because she was so lovely and friendly, and I wanted her to tell me everything about her and her Snoopy-shirted sister and why snobs were no good until the sun went down and she had to go to sleep.

Her name was Courtney, and her birthday was in March, ten months before mine. She was born, and then ten months later, in the same hospital, I was born, and we were just now meeting each other. She was halfway through fifth grade at North Beach, and her sister Dava was in second and had asthma and allergies. Courtney was only allergic to mango. The skin made her tongue itchy. I thought about all the times when we were younger, Jackson got depressed, and Siddhi and I lived on mango, and what I would have done if it turned out we were allergic.

Courtney liked math more than all the other girls in her class, and she already had to wear a bra when I was still, as Stacey taught me to call it, "on the wait for pubes and boobs." Last year, Courtney visited her great-aunt in Rome, and ever since that trip, she couldn't eat American spaghetti because she'd been ruined by Italian pasta. For Chanukah, her mother and father, a teacher and doctor, got her a pasta maker because good pasta was her new favorite food.

I wanted to listen to her talk forever, but when her mother called out to see if I needed help, and Courtney answered that I was unharmed, her mother gave me a wave and called the girls in for dinner. "Come over again, okay? Ask your parents if you're allowed to come in," she said before running up the walk to her waiting mother.

*

Christmas Day, Sariah rose at dawn, decking the halls with fresh pine boughs, wearing her red and pink striped leotard, humming nonsense songs as Siddhi and I picked up where we left off in the huge stack of vocabulary and writing workbooks we got from the "Freedom Box" at the library. We were diligent and proficient!

For gifts, Sariah got me a pair of pinstriped Jordache jeans straight from the commercial and a legitimate Cabbage Patch Kid. She bought Siddhi the Imperial Cruiser play set and an Adidas shorts outfit. Not bicycles, but a brilliant bounty in place of the usual Christmas gifts, which were none. Christmas dinner was served promptly at four-thirty, and it grew harder and harder not to embrace a religion that understood when children feel hungriest. And never in all the years before had our dining room table been so stacked to overflowing with such regular, American food.

With the help of Stacey and Anne With an E (Ann Without had left Xanadu without a word), Sariah had baked days' worth of biscuits and muffins, pumpkin and date breads, a tray of little quails, roasted shoulder to shoulder, like the Chinese Terracotta Warriors from the Childcraft Encyclopedia, candied yams, the "for real" scalloped potatoes, and a creamy miracle she called "green bean casserole," baked with crunchy onion rings on top.

Warren stayed upstairs. Tomatoes and Ximena also retreated to their rooms. Jackson treated the whole thing as a novelty, like we were all having a great time mocking convention by participating in it with such fervor. Siddhi and I were drooling Pavlov's dogs, parked in our seats at the table and poised to eat ourselves silly, when Sariah stood up in front of us and Jackson (and a few other Babies who were around that afternoon and cool with the presence of cooked meat) and clinked her spoon repeatedly on the side of her water jar.

"Thank you all for sharing this special Christmas with us," she said, and as she spoke, I noticed that even though Jackson's mouth was smiling, his eyes were doing the glazed-over, go elsewhere thing they did whenever I asked about food shopping or taking Siddhi to the doctor. "When I was a little girl," Sariah went on, "Christmas was a time for joy, for new beginnings, for family, and for big announcements. And this year is no different." She turned to Jackson, took his hand, pulled him to standing, and placed his palm down on her belly. "Jackson. My guru, and my love...I'm pregnant!" Sariah said and followed up with a jump and a happy little squeal. "I'm pregnant! We're having a baby!" She hugged Jackson, who hadn't hugged back or even moved. "Honey?" With each further word, she sounded more like a mother to me. "Are you surprised? Happy? Honey? So? What do you think?"

Siddhi giggled with glee and kicked his legs under the table, and I shivered with a wave of love, instantaneously devoting myself, for better and for worse, to Sariah and our new baby.

"Jackson?" she asked. Her smile flattened with a worry I knew to feel without even looking at Jackson.

Jackson shivered awake and took a sharp breath. "Well, how do yah like that?" he said, punctuating with a round of forced laughter.

*

In the weeks between Christmas and my birthday, Sariah henna dyed her hair back from bombshell blond to her natural honey brown. She quit smoking pot and nude sunbathing, and she went to bed early, before Jackson's sermons and the group lovemaking. She took Siddhi and me to a clinic where we each got an exam and five shots, each covered with a circular Band-Aid. "When the baby comes," she cooed, her hands making circular motions round her belly button, "you guys will need to be healthy, so you don't make him sick."

"Right," said Siddhi, happy to oblige.

Never had two children taken such delight in vaccination. I even showed her where to tuck the copies of our immunization records with our birth certificates and passports in the top drawer in Jackson's dresser.

And it was mother-like how she loved to bake bread. Bread, bread, bread. Sariah was serious about her bread. She left the dough on the counter for a whole day before mixing it again and leaving it again to rise the rest of the way. She never let us help measure or knead, but she let us watch as she made the most delectable loaves, brown and crispy on the outside and warm and chewy on the inside.

The free-spirited sex goddess veneer that Sariah had cultivated for almost two years ebbed away and left her looking healthier and more beautiful than I had ever seen her. I began to hum along with her as we spent over an hour in my room getting rid of everything unsavory and unsafe for babies and left the place looking spit-spot, dragging a black, contractor bag full of I-still-don't-know-what out to the trash. And when he was away on the boat doing business in the Islands, she did the same in Jackson's room.

The new and improved Sariah pruned all her rough edges, which turned out to be a big mistake because she hadn't left any wild vines for Jackson to hang on to. She left him in free fall.

Then, the fight. In Jackson's room. A whopper. Sariah wailing, pleading. Jackson shouting. I tried to focus on our movie, but Han Solo being frozen in carbonite only stressed me out more. I tiptoed halfway down the hall and made out enough of what they were saying to get the idea.

Him: …pretty fucking stupid suggestion.

Her: Maybe you ought to…how you do things…

Him: …father already, and…don't know what kind of shit you're getting…or maybe it's not even mine.

Her: …freedom is not…love you, and I…the baby, Jackson?

Him: …get an abortion.

I knew the word. Abortion. For unwanted babies. I learned about it from a rerun of "Maude." But Siddhi and I really wanted Sariah's baby, and she did, too. With so many wanters wanting so much, I got really mad at Jackson for saying no. He could bring new grownups home whenever he liked and give them bedrooms and food and kisses and sex and jobs and money, leaving little left over for his biological family. Siddhi and I discussed how if he asked us what we thought, we would tell him all the things we could do to help make it easy. No trouble at all. He wouldn't have to do anything. We were willing to work for this baby. I knew better, though, and just before bed, I hedged my own grief by lifting one of Sariah's precious ornaments from its bough and tucking it away with my other stolen memories.

Jackson came out the next morning outrageously high, with red-watery eyes, and walking in slow motion. Sariah dragged out behind him, keeping her own puffy eyes trained on the floor. She'd skipped putting on her usual makeup and looked younger to me and oddly smaller. Her mouth fell at the corners, and her cheeks hung slack, all of yesterday's bliss painted over by its tragedy. They left together, and when they returned four hours later, Sariah looked smaller still, and she staggered into the bedroom without a word and went to sleep for the rest of the day and night. I tried to tidy up for her while she rested. I picked a bouquet of scarlet ginger flowers and placed them in a ball jar of water next to her baking things. And when she emerged the next afternoon, she looked frail and tiny, the way old people get as they find more and more of their lives behind them.

A few days later, while Jackson was out doing business, Sariah stood before us with her suitcase in hand. "Have you guys seen my moon rock?" she asked, tearing up and trying not to let us see. "It was right there on the tree..." We looked over at the tree, bare without the rest of Sariah's ornaments. We both shook our heads. "Yeah. Okay." She let her tears fall freely after that, and my throat tightened up, and then we were all crying. "I won't be seeing you guys again, so take care of yourselves, okay?" With her free arm, she half-hugged us, each in turn.

"But, why?" Siddhi pleaded, "Don't go. We want you to stay." We had secretly made baby dolls out of Nana's control-top pantyhose, pillow stuffing, and a hotel sewing kit. We'd written lists of our favorite baby names. But Sariah had this look on her face. I knew it, the broken look, the one my mother wore in the last and saddest picture. If Sariah stayed, she'd end up dead.

"It's right that you go, Sariah," I said. "It's better that way. You can find someone nice to marry and have a better baby." I meant it to be kind, but Sariah burst into fast, terrible tears and went quickly out the door and away.

Siddhi and I agreed to give Jackson the silent treatment upon his return. And after he said "hi" a couple of times and sensed the snubbing, he came over to the couch and stood in front of the TV.

"Sariah needed something different than we have for her here. We can't give her what she needs."

"What do you mean we?" I screamed. I couldn't help it. There would have been a baby that would have connected Sariah to Jackson, and therefore to us, by blood, forever, that would have made her a mother to our brother or sister and therefore, a mother to us, and he'd ruined it like he ruined everything. Siddhi put his arm around my shoulders and stomped his foot in solidarity. I fingered the moon rock in my pocket. Jackson sent us to our room without dinner, as if he'd planned to cook one anyhow.

CHAPTER 7:

Diff'rent Strokes, 1983

When we got tired of riding bikes together in a pack, Courtney Laytner invited Siddhi and me into her super normal-looking house, gave us each a handful of jellybeans, and added that President Reagan ate a pound per day and that his favorite flavor was coconut. She also knew that the actor who played Long Duck Dong in "Sixteen Candles" was twenty-nine years old in real life. We took a turn blowing her mind by informing her that it was possible to hold your breath for five minutes without dying and that, "Yeah-huh, swear to God, Paul McCartney was *definitely* in a band before Wings."

The Laytner house was clean, cozy, and carpeted, and the kitchen had a clock of a cat, that moved its eyes and tail, hanging on the wall up above a Rotary Club calendar where May 18th was marked "Courtney's recital" in cursive. A pair of floral chintz sofas squared off in the "fancy" living room, where Courtney warned us, "You can't play in here," and a carved marble chess set lay over the lemony-fresh coffee table.

"Let's go to my playroom," she suggested, passing us each our own foil two-pack of Pop-Tarts. "Don't mess this up," she said, pointing at the pillow-covered daybed with her elbow as she used her hands to tighten the ribbon tied around her auburn ponytail. Her little sister Dava followed, but Courtney stopped her in the doorway.

"You're not coming in, Dava. You have the cooties." Courtney looked back at us with a fiendish grin. "Right, guys?"

I had no idea what was going down. I looked at Siddhi, who shrugged. "Right!" he said, but he appeared to be guessing. I didn't want Siddhi to contract any illness; it was too hard to find the right medicines. I felt relieved, at least, that we were now immunized.

Dava stood her ground, eyes tearful. "But Mommy said—"

"Well, Mommy is in the garage, and anyway, if you tell on me, I won't let you play with my Easy-Bake *ever* again." Dava stayed put, crying now over her dilemma. "Okay, fine, Dava. You can come in, *IF*," Courtney looked back at us again for suggestions, I supposed, but I had no objections to Dava (besides her rampant cooties) and was flummoxed as to Courtney's issue with her own sister. "*If* you...go get the Crest." Dava ran off and returned seconds later with the tube of toothpaste in her hands.

"How many?" she asked.

"What do you think, guys?" asked Courtney. "Four squeezes?"

"Four?!" Dava sobbed.

"Ugh...fine. Three squeezes, and you must swallow it! And then you still must stay in the baby corner."

Then, I understood. This was hazing. Siddhi and I watched with mouths agape as Dava squeezed a lump of Crest the size of a chocolate kiss over her tongue and swallowed it whole. Then she downed a second, and then the third, a feat of derring-do, all to gain admission to the playroom. Like TV show kids, Courtney had the luxury of being mean to her sister for the fun of it. I sort of envied her, but the thought of making Siddhi earn his place beside me, of not wanting him around, of being mad at him for longer than an hour, or wanting him elsewhere was, to me, what Nana would call a *shande*.

Apart from the untouchable guest bed, the playroom was loaded with the history of Courtney's childhood. Siddhi and I entertained her as we held each toy up and performed the corresponding commercial jingle, and she laughed (as did Dava from the baby corner), sometimes joining in. The Fisher Price Houseboat! Sesame Street Puppet Theater! Roly Poly Pooh! Snoopy Sno-Cone Maker! Pink and Pretty Barbie and her Electronic Piano!

"This is so old," she kept saying. "Oh my God, I've had this one since I was five. I don't know why we keep these things!" But these things were all new to us.

In Courtney's playroom, I didn't want to be ten. I wanted to be seven like Dava. No, I wanted to be born all over again as Courtney Laytner's fortunate twin, daughter of Mrs. Laytner, who shuddered and corrected me when I casually called her Roz.

We rode to the Laytner's every afternoon, and when they were home, they invited us in. We got to know Courtney as we made closed-eye charcoal sketches of each other on her easel with the attached roll of blank newsprint. Courtney's bedtime was nine o'clock (right when the good TV started). She'd never read a Penthouse Forum letter, never smelled pot, and never seen anyone have sex. She'd never even seen Dr. Laytner's penis! She loved gymnastics and hated piano lessons, and she had to finish her broccoli at dinner in order to *earn* her dessert, and she and Dava abided by countless other exquisite, inexplicable rules involving but not limited to steering us clear of the "fancy" room, no swimming in their little pool without a grown-up watching, and no crossing the big roads, no more than two TV shows per day, and no using the stove, toaster, or blender without permission.

The granter of the many permissions, Mrs. Laytner, wore knee-length skirts or Bermuda shorts and poured ruby-red Hi-C into souvenir glasses from the Calgary Stampede, served grilled cheeses on white, and taught us to dip our pudding pops into warm water first so the icy coating wouldn't stick to our lips. Mrs. Laytner even played the fourth position as Courtney inducted us into the convivial voodoo of Hungry, Hungry Hippos.

Siddhi and I worked hard to acclimate. We took showers and combed the snarls out of each other's hair before going over. At the Laytner's, we said please and thank you and helped Courtney and Dava clean up the playroom before we left. Courtney suggested I should borrow her "roll on," which eliminated the weird new chicken soupy smell in my ZaSu Pitts. She even said I could keep the rest of the deodorant bottle and proved it to me by opening a whole new one she retrieved from the shelves in her garage, where Mrs. Laytner kept backups for each of their household needs from toiletries to toilet paper to towels.

The night we all sat down at the dining room table together, Mrs. Laytner served everyone Caesar salad from her generous wooden bowl. She'd made the dressing right at the table, shaking her hips back and forth and humming the melody to "New York, New York" as she tossed her homemade concoction into the lettuce with a level of showmanship I could only describe as adorable. Then, she placed the bowl on the table and scratched her wedding ring finger into her frosted perm. "The secret," she said with a wink, "is that I substitute Pecorino Romano for Parmesan and add an extra clove of garlic for a kick." To which, she lifted her foot and managed a little sideways kick that cracked Dava up so hard she did a spit-take with her milk and had to be excused to change her shirt.

Dr. Laytner, a big man with a square head and a side part in his receding hair, led off with a whopping story about a patient who had one hundred percent blockage of his left anterior descending artery for almost twenty-four hours, and after Dr. Laytner did the surgery, the man lived! I wasn't sure about the man's odds of dying, but Dava and Court oohed and aahed and Mrs. Laytner leaned over to grab his cheeks and plant a kiss on his lips. I had to deduce that Mr. Laytner had accomplished something even more impressive than regular heart surgery.

"Did you get to see inside his heart?" Siddhi asked.

Dr. Laytner tipped his head like a dog hearing a weird noise, and then, he smiled, widened his eyes, and leaned toward Siddhi. "I sure did!" he said, and I saw Siddhi overflow with the fascination of it.

"So, usually, they die a lot?" I asked. I wondered if my mother had had a complete blockage of her heart, and died on a surgeon's table, rather than from snorting too much heroin, would things be different for me? Would I be more like Courtney, in a home more like this one?

"Well, my dear, the unfortunate answer is, yes," Dr. Laytner sighed. "With that sort of blockage, it is very risky." Mrs. Laytner cut and served fat squares of lasagna along with a story about one of her students winning the National Merit Scholarship, and as we ate, Dr. and Mrs. Laytner went on to discuss the male chauvinist pig, whom Mrs. Laytner bumped into in the Pantry Pride parking lot, the grandparents' impending visit, the Libyans, their daughters' days at school, and Halley's Comet.

Court and I helped clear and load the dishwasher, and then we passed out clean plates for dessert. Courtney told her story about a boy in her class who almost died from being allergic to peanut butter. Then Siddhi raised his hand, and when Dr. Laytner called on him, out of nowhere, he asked the table, "If you had to choose, would you rather wear a hat that screams you awake every time you fall asleep or a pair of pants that sometimes bites you?" Siddhi asked me questions like that all the time, but somehow, in the context of the Laytner dining room table, his question sounded random and out of place. A brief, awkward pause followed, but then they laughed and took turns answering what Mrs. Laytner called, *a very creative query*.

Nervous that Dr. and Mrs. Laytner would think Siddhi and I were weirdos, I decided to try and be more like them and take a turn to tell a regular story. Because Courtney brought it up, the peanut butter story was the one I thought of first.

In March, Jackson and his new favorite Baby, Belinda, brought us with them on a short trip to Jamaica. At the airport, on our way there (we took a strange boat home, which later got picked up from our house by a man with an eyepatch), Jackson and Belinda met another couple of travelers and brought both them, and some jerk goat meat, beer, and magic mushrooms, back to the house we had rented, where they all got high and had sex together while Siddhi and I swam in the ocean.

I wasn't an idiot. I left everything but the goat meat and beer out of the version I told the Laytners, because I knew full well that normal people like the Laytners stared and whispered about people like Jackson and about children like Siddhi and me, walking down the street with people like Jackson. Nana called the Babies "seedy," which I thought meant that they had green thumbs, but when she said it to the children's librarian, her tone was wrong for a compliment. I asked the librarian to look it up. It meant sordid and unwell. Sordid? She turned a few more pages of the dictionary to Sordid: Ignoble. Unsavory. Squalid. Contemptible. I asked her to look them all up.

"The jerk sauce was way too spicy," I told the Laytners. After a while, Siddhi and I got so hungry that we decided to take some money out of Jackson's pants pocket and take a walk to search for food. "There was a restaurant right across the street, but we wanted to get, like, groceries, not just one meal, so we asked around, and the bartender told us there was a store far down the road. We were hungry, so we went anyway, and it was getting dark when we finally found the place." We hadn't understood about the exchange rate, so the fifty Jay we brought with us ended up being worth about seven dollars. "But the guy at the store was super nice, and he helped us pick out a jar of peanut butter and a loaf of cocoa bread and even gave us each a free soda."

"Well, that was lovely of him," Mrs. Laytner said, clearly thinking I was done with the story, and if only I'd sensed her apprehension with where I was headed, I might have just said that yes, it was, and the food was yummy, the end, but everyone had told an interesting food story, and mine wasn't finished yet.

"So, we walked the whole way back in the dark, and it took longer to get there because we stopped for a while to pet this stray dog, but then we realized it was covered in ticks, like a hundred ticks, head-to-toe. So then, Siddhi insisted on picking all the ticks off before we left." The Laytner's idea of edgy living was allowing Courtney to roller skate without elbow pads. I should have stopped there, the end. Dessert! But I kept on.

"Oh, and I forgot to tell you, we didn't have any shoes on, because there were these poor children begging on the way from the airport, and Jackson gave them our shoes and most of our clothes so they would have some for themselves. We got some flip-flops and T-shirts later in the trip, but on that first night, we were just barefoot." I told them that when we got back to the house, they had no idea we'd been gone, but I left out that they'd eaten the magic mushrooms they bought along with the goat meat and were all still naked and wandering around the house touching things and each other, staring and breaking into fits of laughter.

"So, we snuck into our room with the food, but neither of us could open the peanut butter!" Our hands were too small. Both of us heaved and hoed and tried until my hand got too sweaty right when Siddhi attempted to release the seal by hitting hard on the bottom, and the jar slipped and smashed into the metal doorknob and broke in half! "And this is the crazy part of the story," I said. "We were so hungry, we didn't even care anymore and picked out the broken glass pieces and tore off hunks of bread and used our fingers to eat the clean part."

"Yeah!" chimed Siddhi, "and there was even a crunch in my first bite, and it was a piece of glass I had to spit out."

I nodded confirmation.

Dava and Court gave little laughs, mostly in response to Siddhi and me cracking up. Dr. Laytner took Mrs. Laytner's hand and squeezed. I had no idea what that meant, and they changed back to their regular faces before I could get a good enough read to figure it out.

"Well...what's for dessert, honey?" Dr. Laytner asked in a TV dad voice, as if Courtney lived in a sitcom. "We don't want to let Sienna here get too hungry!" Then everyone laughed. By the time Mrs. Laytner passed out her version of strawberry shortcake—a slice of Sara Lee pound cake with a handful of berries dumped on top and a big blob of Cool Whip—Courtney and Dava were sent off to do their homework.

"Hey guys, uh, what are you up to now?" Mrs. Laytner asked

us when Siddhi and I went to their den couch and turned on the TV. Siddhi shrugged and looked at me to answer.

"Dukes of Hazzard is on till nine, just till they finish their homework. Want to watch with us?" It was dark out and Dr. Laytner insisted on driving us home even though it was only four blocks away. We thought he was crazy, and we opened the window of the den to see Dr. and Mrs. Laytner loading our bikes into his car in their driveway.

"I know, honey," Dr. Laytner said to Mrs. Laytner, after Siddhi's bike disappeared into his trunk. "But we can't get involved with that man and his crazy cult."

Mrs. Laytner wiped a tear from her cheek, which I sort of realized was about us. "They're so intelligent, Paul. That boy is gifted. And she is so warm and tries so damned hard. They need to be in a good, safe family like ours…" Dr. Laytner had to tie the trunk closed with some twine because he didn't have room to fit our bikes inside.

Before we left for the one-minute drive back home, I ignored the pain in my stomach and asked Mrs. Laytner if she wanted us to maybe just pack some things and then come back and stay at their house for a while. "We can sleep on the floor, so we don't mess up the pillows on the guest bed," I promised. But her eyes only welled up with that pity again.

"No, honey…No, we can't do that… I know! Maybe, on a weekend sometime, you and the girls can have a little sleepover."

CHAPTER 8:

River Crazy, 1984

Mellow Yellow took three hours to get us from Miami Beach to Aunt Paula's near Arcadia.

"Can we swim when we get there?" Siddhi asked, fanning out the Florida tourism brochures he'd collected at the Miccosukee rest stop on Alligator Alley. His mouth dripped orange drool from the gumball he found on the floor outside the men's room.

"Ooh! You can see Siddhi's amazing dives!" I said. Tomatoes taught him how to dive the week before, dangling his one leg over the side of our pool while coaching Siddhi on his form. "I still have to hold my nose when I dive."

"We'll see," said Belinda, who had the passenger seat reclined almost into my lap, her hand claiming Jackson's arm, her eyes resting. That was the one mothering thing Belinda mastered after four months in Jackson's bedroom: "We'll see." The only mother skill she possessed was the most infuriating one. Jackson popped Dr. Hook into the cassette player, and we sang along. Belinda hadn't spent enough time riding around with us to learn the words to "Freakin' at the Freaker's Ball," so she lit a joint and filled the car with bittersweet smoke, sending ribbons out the cracked windows.

Another hour and we made the final turn, past the field where Aunt Paula's last husband, Uncle Hobie, grew what Jackson called, "the finest shit around," to Aunt Paula's two-bedroom cottage nestled in vine-wrapped palms and moss-covered cypress swamp. Siddhi raced me through the doorway to the land of three meals a day of hot, Aunt Paula food, mostly topped with melted cheese and sour cream.

After a couple of Aunt Paula's good hugs, we dumped our backpacks on the living room hide-a-bed, grabbed Siddhi's trunks and my silver lamé bikini (another hand-me-down from Ximena, and my favorite, sexiest bathing suit out of the three I ever had), and made off to the damp bathroom to take turns peeing and changing.

By the time we got out, Aunt Paula and her newest husband, Uncle Merle, had walked Jackson and Belinda half the distance to the sunset.

"Shit!" I said as I watched their shrinking silhouettes head for the horizon, "There goes our swim."

"Fuckin' shit!" Siddhi agreed. I was happy he wasn't too angry because if he revved up a tantrum, he might spend the whole weekend locked in the back bedroom like he did last time.

"Wanna go catch lizards?"

"Nah." I poured us two cups of honey-sweet Red Zinger. I left Siddhi half a glass and made mine huge because I was older and super thirsty.

"Rummy Q?"

"Yeah, okay," he shrugged. "Hey CeeCee, this'll make you pee yourself! Doesn't Uncle Merle look just like Sweetums the Muppet?" We often categorized new people by who they looked like on TV to help remember all the grownups, and he'd just nailed Uncle Merle. With his yellow, shaggy hair, rosacea-bulb of a nose, hanging lower lip, and overgrown limbs, I'd thought Uncle Merle was like Paul Bunyan cross-pollinated with Bruce Vilanch, but Uncle Merle was Sweetums, for sure.

I walked over and handed Siddhi the larger pour, because he'd rather play Rummy Q with me than lizard hunt without me. "I'll go get the game."

I explored the little items Aunt Paula displayed all over her bedroom, lifting each and making sure they still had their dust rings, making her roots be part mine, our treasures, and memories, year after year, right where we left them. I rattled her strands of beads—love, costume, and prayer—and cuffed my hand around her feather boa, pulling my loose fist down its length.

My favorite photo hung near the closet, a black and white of Aunt Paula in India, her true home, she said. She sat on the ground in her drapey clothes, gazing up at her guru, an old Indian man with white hair wisping off the sides of his ears like a bat. I imagined that guru was kind to her in a way Jackson and Pop Pop and her three bygone husbands weren't, but at least she kept trying. She looked short and round, same as now, in a stuffed bear kind of way—skinny arms and legs sewn onto a thick, mushy middle, pale skin like Siddhi's and dark frizzy curls, like mine and Jackson's that she parted in the center and looped behind her ears. On the table beneath the photo, there was a little vase of dried flowers in the spot where she used to keep the pink ballerina jewelry box she had since she was a little girl.

On that last trip, when Jackson locked Siddhi up for the day, Aunt Paula and Uncle Hobie stayed out of it. They went out to the river without helping Siddhi at all, so I stole that jewelry box and pushed it to the bottom of my Bee Gees pack. When I got it back to Xanadu, I found it to be the perfect addition. I could store my other treasures—the golden curtain rope, the pearl bracelet, the moon rock, and the pictures of my mother—within it.

✳

Belinda cut me off after four enchiladas. "Sienna, that's enough. You'll need bigger clothes, piggy." Siddhi stuck his tongue out at her back. And then, after dinner, we watched "Star Wars," again, on Betamax, and then crawled under the hide-a-bed covers, not twenty feet from the dining room where the grownups stayed up talking.

Siddhi fell into his light, puppy-growl snore, and I closed my eyes and allowed myself to float in the ether of the conversation and the stench of the pot smoke billowing overhead. When I smelled the smoke from farther than the backseat, enough to smell it but not enough to get the red eyes and stomachache, it smelled sweet green, like lawnmower incense, and it reminded me of a time when I knew less and laughed more and liked Jackson every day.

"The Lamb's Bread won't be fat enough by September," Jackson said through intermittent coughing.

"It's never enough for you," Aunt Paula said. Merle loosed a giggle. "I grew what you gave me."

"It's not how much you planted, Paul. You went in late..."

"It's only me here, Jackson."

"Well, it was supposed to be you and Hobie," Jackson said.

"Hey-there-just-a-minute, friend—"

"Relax, Merle," said Jackson. "This is business now, man."

"Jackson, don't be an asshole. Hobie's gone. I planted it all. I did what you said, and I *need* my money."

"Well, there's no money for any of us if there's not enough product for my people to fuckin' move, Paula."

"Pass that, Merle," said Belinda.

"Your people," Aunt Paula snarked. "Maybe inform Warren that half the clones were no good, and you know the cold front stalled germination."

"We gotta go back to Jamaica if we are going to recoup. Shit, Paula. I have to get more runners and borrow the cash and start all-the-fuck-over."

I found it all very confusing. Why couldn't we "recoup" here? And why did they have to sell pot? Why couldn't they all be doctors and teachers like the Laytners so they didn't have to sneak and whisper and talk in codes?

"If I had to transplant those acres myself, we'd have nothing, Jackson. Jesus! I asked you for fresh clones, but you had one of your flus and never delivered, remember?" Aunt Paula sounded so upset.

Jackson exhaled. "Calm down, alright?" It was quiet for a minute. "You'll need to call the Guys in Negril." I knew Jackson was telling Belinda. Jamaica was where he'd acquired her. She'd been living in Negril with some old man boyfriend who knew the ironically named, twin, drug dealers Happy and Smiley Guy. When Jackson had them over, which was almost never, I made Siddhi hide in our bedroom closet with me until they left.

Aunt Paula groaned. "Jackson, don't get involved with them again."

"Are you kidding me? They bank-rolled Xanadu!"

"They're too connected. We said we'd stay small time with this thing. No—"

"Bottom line, they have the cash."

I couldn't help worrying, even as I fought sleep, that this whole problem was my fault. That I could save Jackson if I took him to my pine tree and dug up the duct-taped treasure to fix the mess that my own wicked selfishness had set in motion. But then I wondered about what would happen if he found out I stole so much cash. Jackson kicked people out of Xanadu all the time for far less. Sometimes, when a Baby hadn't even done anything, Jackson ousted him just because he didn't think he could be trusted. I couldn't risk it. I had to stay and protect Siddhi.

"Their margins are bullshit," Aunt Paula pleaded, "and they're both fucked up on blow. Forget it. Bad karma."

"Pauli-girl, c'mon. You know I need you there," said Jackson. "When are we doing this?"

"Merle," said Aunt Paula, "can we still get a loan from your mother for a booth at the Giant Flea?"

"I'll go," sang Belinda. "It'll be fun. The Guys are harmless; different generation is all."

"Good. Send one of your followers. I'm out!"

"Shut up, Paula," said Jackson.

"Hey man, y'all are fixin' to kill my buzz."

"Shut up, Merle," Paula said in an exasperated whisper. Then, even with my knotted stomach, sleep won out.

*

The water's edge was polka-dotted with clumps of mangroves and pink knobs of young cypress. Several old palm trees stretched way out over the river, reaching for sunlight. Aunt Paula stepped onto the dock to watch as we swam when there was almost no current, and when we tired, she took us on a long canoe ride down the creek to a place she called The Boys' School.

I imagined that the school, her closest neighbor, was a fancy prep school like in movies, and as we came about, we passed the basketball courts where I spied a hunky, Leif Garrett clone with feathered hair and a great smile. He waved and blew a kiss. When I blew one back, Aunt Paula yanked my hand down and lectured me about strange boys, adding the actual name of the school: *Desoto County Juvenile Detention and Rehabilitation Camp for Boys.*

Jackson and Belinda emerged from the back bedroom around lunchtime, just as Uncle Merle pulled up in his mud-spattered pickup, his cap covered in greenish-white splotches of fake bird poop read, *Damned Florida Seagulls!*

"You want I should go get the motor, baby girl?" Merle inquired, without removing his cigarette from his mouth. Siddhi elbowed me, impressed, and he picked up a twig and hung it from his own lips.

"Nah, we'll take a paddle. Manatees, Merle." Uncle Merle shook his head and smiled. We sat in the boat, inside the bed of the truck, loving the windy drive until Uncle Merle pulled over on the side of the road near a path into the woods.

"Here's the drop."

"Go a little farther up, man," Jackson told him, winking at us. "We'll scout that hidden acreage from the water and time the trip back." So, Uncle Merle drove past the two-hour drop spot, where Jackson once floated with my mom before she died.

*

We drifted along Horse Creek with the current while Jackson pushed us off the Zodiac into the cold water, dragging us back in and howling with delight. He turned his straw hat sideways and spoke in a French accent, "I am Capteen Crunch, and zees eez my sheep!" On a river, with only family (mostly), he went into play mode and became so loveable. Belinda giggled and patted his back, but when Jackson paid her no mind, she tied her long, flowy hair up into a knot, took off her top, and pointed her naked nipples toward the sun.

I took a rest, holding the back of the boat.

"Merle said there are yellow ties on a few of the trees," Aunt Paula said. "Keep an eye out."

"What's the acreage?" Belinda asked.

"I think, for seven grand, they will give us about fifteen land-locked acres, no road. Much cheaper than Negril."

"True, true. But it's risky in the States and—"

"No more than Hobie's field and much less than smuggling in from the islands," Aunt Paula interrupted.

"Paula, listen, you know he's gonna deal with them either way. We need the product now."

"If he works with those cocaine cowboys, I am *OUT!*" I thought she made up that clever name. I didn't know what co-caine was yet, but as far as cowboys went, my guess was, like our family, the Guy brothers were *outlaws*.

"Yeah, well, it's not your call, Paula," Belinda yawned.

*

Siddhi took the finishing sip off the water jug, and the creek wound on ahead, shrinking in the distance like in a painting. Sid-dhi and I held onto the pontoons and let the boat drag us through the cool water. The forest shaded the sides of the creek, but we had to stay in the middle because Belinda needed her boobs to get full sun. Spanish moss made the trees look dressed for Halloween, and the air smelled of fresh mud pie. I watched my legs go brown to orange to beige as I lifted them up through the creek water. Siddhi's face and shoulders were lobster red. Thank goodness the sun started to slide further down the sky.

"You guys okay? Getting hungry?" Aunt Paula asked.

"You have food?" Siddhi brightened.

"No, baby, but the dock ought to be right around the next bend."

"I'm hungry," I said to the air around me.

"What else is new?" Belinda muttered. She was not like Libby or Sariah. No amount of rehabilitation could make Belinda into mother material. I was old enough now to understand Jackson's real type: skinny, sexy, and rotten with kids.

Siddhi kept a lookout for the dock. I looked for ties on the trees and thought of that yellow ribbon song. We compared fingertip prunes, thumb-warred, and sang, "A Hundred Bottles of Beer on the Wall," reaching sixty-seven before Belinda ordered us to shut up. We played geography until we got stuck in the never-ending A's.

When the Zodiac got stuck on a submerged, fallen tree trunk, we all got out and yanked it over, causing a tiny tear on one pontoon. As he hopped back in, Jackson rubbed Belinda's tushie through her bikini bottom, which she kept on, I supposed, for Aunt Paula's sake. At home, she and Jackson always walked around naked.

"We should have brought the cooler," said Aunt Paula.

"Calm down and enjoy the day."

"I will not calm down. Your children are hungry."

"The children are fine," Belinda interjected. "They ate more already today than most children in the world. And besides, it's all rainbows here...look around."

"Right...right, baby," Jackson agreed and then laughed for too long. "No one's starving," he added, poking Aunt Paula's belly. "Capteen Crunch veel not allow eet!"

"Nothing's marked here. We should have tried from the road. Stupid." Aunt Paula waded to the bank, patched over with nettles, stickers, and pebbles. Her feet were bare as ours, and so she was back in the water after a few prickly paces.

"Sienna, Siddhartha," Jackson addressed us, though his eyes were trained on the space above our heads. "This little adventure is taking longer than we thought, a special opportunity afforded to us by God. *Hey you!* God's saying, *why not stop and appreciate?* See, you're not gonna die from a little hunger, so focus on the beautiful energy around us. In temporal reality, we're only here for a split second..."

"And look! A million rainbows," said Belinda, "dancing in the everywhereness."

Aunt Paula called from the water, "Oh, Jesus. Shut up, will you?"

"No, you shut up," he yelled back, "You're ruining my trip!"

"Your trip?" Then she paused a beat before saying, "Wait a minute, are you tripping?" Aunt Paula thrashed through the shallows, dipped into the deep section, and swam to the boat. I thought we were all taking a trip on the creek, but the way Jackson and Belinda were doing it really pissed Aunt Paula off.

"Let me see your goddamned eyes!"

"Uh, last I checked, my eyes were not your business," Belinda said.

"You took Merle's tabs?" Aunt Paula put her forehead in her hand. "If you mean the ones you plan to get rich selling under the table at the Giant Flea, then...*Oui!*" said Jackson.

"Two customers! Are you rich yet?" Belinda laughed.

"I'm gonna kill Merle," Aunt Paula mumbled, and the subject faded along with the current.

*

At twilight, Aunt Paula swam Siddhi and me to the shallows for a drill. "How do you tell the difference between a coral snake and a king snake, guys, remember?"

"I know!" Siddhi answered. "Red on black, good for Jack; red on yellow, kill a fellow!" Aunt Paula nodded and hugged him. Siddhi beamed like he'd just advanced to the Showcase Showdown.

"How do you know poison ivy?"

"The leaves," I said. "One, two, three; beware of me!"

"Great job, you guys," she said, but she looked troubled. Maybe she realized, like I did, that if we stepped on a coral snake while tromping over the banks in the dark, her poems might not prove all that helpful. It felt nice when she tried, though.

Jackson mocked her, "It's a comin' soon, right 'round the bend!" After every turn, he said, "C'mon Paula, it's a comin'! Can you feel it?"

Only Belinda found him funny. Siddhi and I held a meeting in the water. "I'm hungry and thirsty and tired," I whispered. "And this is really boring now."

"Yeah, this sucks. It's getting dark, and I didn't even see one snake yet or alligator. Shit." His lips were still mostly pink.

"Fuck," I whispered, putting a finer point on it. I was going to say something about how the alligators come out after dark, but I didn't want to scare him. "You know that brochure you have for Disney World?" I asked.

"Course," he said. "The Magic Kingdom."

"When I'm old enough, I pinky-promise to take you someday, okay?"

*

The sun hid far behind the trees. Jackson and Belinda ran out of jokes and began to make out. "Get a room!" Aunt Paula whined and pulled Siddhi and me ahead, walking purposefully over a long sandbar. She said it looked familiar, but she wasn't fooling me. Other than the violet sky, everything else looked black. I listened to the *threep threep* of the crickets but mainly homed in on the throat-clearing grunts Uncle Hobie once taught us were the sound of alligators out to hunt.

We moved quickly and soon lost Jackson and Belinda and the raft somewhere behind us. We slapped mosquitos from each other. Siddhi guessed that every noise was a snake. I couldn't find the moon. I distracted myself for a bit, imagining Belinda, like

Captain Hook in the Disney brochure, standing with her feet holding open the jaws of a ticking crocodile. I told Siddhi, and even Aunt Paula laughed.

"Rule of threes," Siddhi mumbled to himself.

"What's that, hon?" Aunt Paula asked, sniffling.

"Three weeks no food, three days no water, three hours no shelter."

"Till what?" I asked.

"Till you die," Siddhi explained. "Ouch!" he yelped, a split second before I felt a hard crack on my left shin and echoed his cry. From then on, we had to walk, swishing our arms in the water in front of us to feel for fallen trees. The cool pockets got colder, the noises grew loud enough to scare me, and it was too dark to check Siddhi's lip color. I wondered if we'd already passed the dock, it being so little, but then I realized we'd never overlook the lighted buildings and the long grassy lawn of The Boys' School.

Aunt Paula had forbidden it, but to slake my thirst, I stealthily slurped some creek water, which tasted like pennies. Aunt Paula seemed to lose more heart with every step, mumbling phrases like "death march" and "son-of-a-bitch," until I heard her really crying.

"It's okay, Aunty Paul," I said, "Siddhi and I'll take care of you. Almost there." We rounded another bend where the bank sloped so steeply upward, we had no choice but to swim.

"Look for lights...anywhere, any lights," Aunt Paula commanded as we slowly breast-stroked in formation, close enough to bump feet. The woods were tall and dark.

First, Siddhi spotted the alligator. "Whoa! Look there!" The armored animal waddled down into the water not twenty feet away from us.

"SWIM! Goddammit!" Aunt Paula shrieked, yanking hard on my hair to turn my head toward the rising bank just down river from the encroaching animal.

And as we scrambled to the shore, yanked and scratched by Aunt Paula's desperate helping claws, Siddhi stood up and shouted again. "Tent! Tent! There's a tent!" There was no light. It was amazing he could see it. A squat, red dome sat on the rocky ledge.

"Let's go," I said, stepping slowly as the nettles took tiny bites of my feet. But, in a surprising move, Aunt Paula lunged after me, grabbed my arm, and pulled me backward.

"Let me go!" I squealed, twisting my wrist from her grasp.

"No! We don't know who might be in there. We'll stay here, wait, and see. Come and sit down for a second." She sat on a lower rock ledge above the water and below the tent and directed Siddhi and me to sit side by side between her legs. Then she wrapped her arms around us and leaned over our shivery bodies in a bizarre, human-shield maneuver. Bent over, with Aunt Paula's cold, wet bathing suit pressed at my back, I wished for some normal adult to appear and take control of the situation. If there'd been a phone, I could invoke our rule: *If Jackson ever doesn't come back, if you're ever lost, call Nana.*

Siddhi, who'd been quiet for a long while—exhaustion always hit his mute button—wiggled out from under our sobbing, ragdoll aunt, rushed up the bank, and with a yawping war cry, scrambled over rocks, roots, and thorns until he reached the tent.

"You get back here, young man," Aunt Paula shrieked. Siddhi ignored her and unzipped the entry flap.

"It's empty, CeeCee! Come on!"

"Coming," I whooped, and with new enthusiasm, I hopped up, grabbed Aunt Paula's wrist, and dragged her behind me up and into the tent, delighting in the grating sound of metal on metal as Siddhi, my hero, zipped us inside.

"One down," I said.

"One what?" asked Aunt Paula.

"Right!" Siddhi agreed.

"Shelter!" I spooned up to him for warmth, waited for his snore, and let my eyes close.

*

I woke to the sound of a motor…a darting beam of light…Siddhi roused and went for the zipper.

As the boat passed, Siddhi shoved his head and one arm out what little of the zipper he could get open. "Help us! Help! We're here!" He shouted to the boat, lurching forward, and dragging the tent down on our heads with his force.

"Paul? That you?" A slow drawl called from below, the voice of Uncle Merle, Muppet-rescuer. We crawled out and stumbled down the bank to his little fishing pram, and Aunt Paula collapsed into his arms. "Easy there, baby girl," he said, smoothing her hair and squeezing her to his chest. He wrapped a towel around my shoulders like they did with a fur cape when a girl in a movie learns she was a princess all along. Siddhi got a towel cape, too.

"Wrong way," Aunt Paula said as he turned upriver.

"Jackson and his lady ain't showed up either, Paul."

"No way," she spat. "We go home first." Merle came about again. Another ten minutes by motor, and there was the dock. Aunt Paula told Uncle Merle what happened and how Jackson and Belinda ate acid and didn't give a crap about the kids.

I wanted her to be wrong. "Jackson would never have played Captain Crunch with us if he didn't care," I whispered in Siddhi's ear. "Aunt Paula said those things because she went river crazy with night terrors and tent fever." Crazy or not, I knew she was right.

"What time is it?" Aunt Paula asked.

"Four in the morning," said Uncle Merle. "You had me a little scared there, darlin'."

Not scared enough to come looking for us at ten? Midnight? Two? We'd been on the river for almost fifteen hours. Once on the dock, Siddhi and I made Uncle Merle laugh so hard that his cigarette fell out of his mouth as we dropped to our knees and kissed the moldy Astroturf.

Uncle Merle motored out again and returned with the others a few minutes later.

"We made it!" Belinda said, unbothered.

I went hot and weak with relief when I saw Jackson back safe, but then, on his way past me walking toward the house, he cupped my chin in his hand and winked. "Adventure," he whispered, which made me want to punch his face a hundred times until blood poured from his nose. Belinda's and Aunt Paula's, and Uncle Merle's, too.

Inside, Siddhi and I guzzled Red Zinger, as Jackson and Belinda retired to the second bedroom, and Uncle Merle and Aunt Paula disappeared into hers. I refilled the iced teas, but when I got to Siddhi with them, he was already sleeping.

*

Jackson shook me awake. "Hey, I have a surprise for you, munchie." I stood, half asleep, while Jackson shook Siddhi awake and padded after him toward the table.

"Whaddaya have, Jackson?" Siddhi asked, getting to his feet.

"Shhh! If we wake the others, we'll have to share. I was saving this for the ride home, but I'm in the mood now."

This was the love Band-Aid. Jackson knew, somehow, when it got too terrible, and though it didn't make us any safer, he'd wake us for a midnight swim or cuddle and recite a little poetry; always when we were already exhausted because of his madness, he'd come up with a way to acknowledge he'd gone too far. He gestured toward the table where he'd laid out a huge metal mixing bowl and three boxes of Lucky Charms. Then, he poured the cereal out all over the surface of the table.

"Marshmallows only," he said. We fished out every pink heart, orange star, yellow moon, green clover, and blue diamond and threw them all into the mixing bowl, leaving on the table a hill of beige cereal, while the bowl between us contained a beautiful mound of pastel-colored, marshmallow sugar puffs. Jackson passed out spoons and waterfalled the milk from high above the bowl, until all the empty space was creamy white. Then he stirred for a minute to let the milk pink up, but not so long that the marshmallows lost their crunch.

"Dig in," he commanded, and we ate and ate, mouthfuls of cold milk saturated with crunchy sugar, here and there munching on fistfuls of dry cereal from the table. "To cleanse the palette," he said.

"Hey, do you like seafood?" I asked them both. And because I knew he hated it, I turned to Jackson and showed him my opened, full mouth. "See food!" I said, to which he frowned at me, stood up, petted Siddhi's head, and returned to Belinda in the bedroom. Siddhi shrugged and showed me his own rainbow tongue, and spoon-by-spoon, all bad things digested into bellies full of sweetness.

CHAPTER 9:

The Night the Lights Went Out, 1985

At harvest time, the Babies spent a week weighing and packaging mountains of nickel and dime bags, quarters, halves, and ounce bags, stuffing the measured drugs in corresponding-sized envelopes and wrapping them in multiple layers of cellophane until the whole first floor reeked of grass and skunk. We wanted to ride bikes, but we weren't allowed to go out. Jackson didn't want anyone drawing attention to the house.

Siddhi and I spent most of the morning in our beds, reading Ender's Game (him) and Peter Pan (me) before we tiptoed down the stairs for a snack, and Siddhi had the idea to go find Ximena as a third for Chinese jump rope. Jackson called Ximena a pure spirit, a Jain, a Sufi. To me, she was Tinkerbell, starving herself until she became light enough to fly, for Ximena looked too thin to be a human. Like the boy in the Keane painting in Nana's powder room, her overgrown eyes reached out at you. Her hungry chest had long ago consumed her breasts, and her arms and legs had withered down to pipe cleaners, bony and coated in an oddly thick, baby-soft fur that reflected light and made her appear to glow. Siddhi liked to pet her arms, "Here kitty, kitty," and she'd purr and nuzzle him with her head. She wasn't a big talker; she was shy… and she never gave inspired answers to our questions, but she was always game for a round of poker or Twister or Three-Way Checkers Supremo (Siddhi's invention).

With the Chinese jump rope stretched around our ankles, Siddhi and I stood three feet apart to form a generous rectangle. "Just a few minutes, okay, guys?" She said, seeming so tired.

She jumped from side to side a bunch, and then, using her toes to crisscross the ropes, hopped both feet up and out and then landed outside the ropes, facing me. Then she repeated the process, but before she cleared the crisscross, her knees buckled, and she came down on them and then fell onto her back, pulling on the elastic cord and bringing both of us down with her.

Siddhi landed on his tushie with his hands behind him, and I landed on my hands and knees over Ximena's body like we'd just finished a game of Twister. I thought she was messing with us and began to giggle until I saw the terror in her eyes. She grimaced and grabbed at her jaw, and as I tried to get the tightened cords from my ankles, she moaned and then flopped, fish-like into a weird, whole-body spasm. I dragged my top half over to see her face.

"Ximena, are you okay?"

"Whatsa the matter with her?" Siddhi cried out. Ximena sucked for breath and clawed at her neck.

"Get Jackson!" I shrieked to Siddhi, and he fumbled with the cord until he freed his legs and stumbled off.

"Tell him to call 9-1-1!"

"CeeCeeees…" Ximena wheezed, trying for air, smacking her palm to her naked chest. Her wet eyes bugged out, and she raked my face before making a sort of ruffled spitting noise, after which her big eyes rolled backward.

I screamed for help, holding her head in my lap as her body continued to rattle. Warren ran into the sun porch, snatched her up like a pick-up stick, and ran her to Jackson and the others. He laid her flat on the living room rug. Stacey rushed in with a wet towel and began to dab at her pale, sweaty forehead as if a cool rag could steal a fairy back from Death.

I watched as Warren placed two fingers on Ximena's neck and shook his head at Jackson, who backed up to the wall and banged his head one time into the plaster, hard enough to make the hanging mirror go crooked.

"Motherfuck," he said and then crouched down against the wall until his head pushed into his knees.

I wondered if it went down this way when my mother overdosed. Did Jackson do nothing but curse and pity himself? Did he even try to save her? Warren stacked his hands between Ximena's flat breasts and pressed her sternum up and down, causing a sickening little crack. I'd seen people do CPR in movies, but never did I hear the little noises, the brittle snapping of little ribs to allow for the compression, the squeaky hiss of stale breath, and foamy spit forced out of the loose mouth of the dying.

Warren's hands pumped, "One and two and three and four and..." Ximena's skin gave like pudding. At "fifteen and," Warren stopped, pinched her nose, and blew his breath into her mouth. I watched her rib cage rise and fall, rise and fall, her flat chest glaring at us. Warren sat back down on his ankles and resumed pumping and counting. I waited for Jackson to tell God to heal her, rally the Babies to scurry around with their flopping parts while he made a rousing speech, fired up a joint, and put life back to right, but he froze watching Warren, like everyone else.

"Do something!" someone shouted, and I realized that someone was me. "Before she dies!"

Warren breathed another long, slow exhale into her lungs, and I crawled quickly to the side of Ximena's ribs. "I'll do the pumps!" I hollered and placed my hands, as Warren had, on her chest.

A second later, Jackson ripped me out of the way and took over. "One and, two and, three and, four and, five and," he said as he pushed her sternum up and down over her heart. Siddhi was at her other end, rubbing her feet, which he did all the time because everyone loved his foot rubs. I had him on track to be a doctor of the highest caliber. Jackson stopped at fifteen, Warren did the breaths, and Jackson bent forward to start again.

"Wait! STOP!" Warren yelped. "She's breathing," and in that second, they sat back on their knees to give the girl space to come back to life. My throat lurched with hope, and my chest went hot with yearning. Warren, still on his knees, eased her upright until her head dropped forward like an unmanned puppet's, and then he leaned her back to rest on his shoulder.

"She needs a doctor, man," he said.

"I'll call 9-1-1!" Siddhi and I shouted in unison. We'd both been keen to dial it ever since learning of its existence.

"NO, YOU WON'T!" Jackson barked, so close to my face that his breath, which smelled like pot and sunflower seeds, moved my hair. He was drenched in sweat. "Get your asses upstairs!"

"But—" I didn't want to leave her.

"NOW!" he hollered. I took Siddhi's hand and ran us halfway up to crouch on the landing, where we could still hear Warren's defiantly peaceful breathing. Jackson said Warren had "tuned in, turned on, and dropped out" after being in the Marines and seeing some heavy shit go down in Mayaguez, which explained his emergency skills and his tattoo of a skull in a green hat.

We crawled over near the banister where we could get a better view of the scene.

"This could be real, real bad for us, man," Jackson said to Warren.

"I get your drift, brother," said Warren, "I do." He nodded at Jackson. "Okay, but this is serious shit. I'm pretty sure she's having a heart attack." He put two fingers on Ximena's neck. "She's still got a pulse...time's tickin'."

Jackson stood up and shooed the Babies out of the living room. He told Stacey to go start her Datsun, which was silver and always had the T-tops off so Siddhi and I could jump into the seats when we played Dukes of Hazzard. Stacey ran past us to her room and came out with car keys and clothes on.

"That's right!" Jackson said, resolute. I crept lower, down a few of the stairs, to see more. As for Jackson, it was clear now that the control-power had come back into his eyes. "She's a sick girl, poor thing. She's, uh...anorexic. She needs doctors!"

"Yeah, man, that's right. Right," nodded Warren. He lifted Ximena and supported her as Stacey slipped a sundress over Ximena's head and shimmied it down her body like she was dressing a Barbie. Then, Warren picked her up again and ran her to the car.

Jackson stood, fists on his hips, facing the windows and his reflection in the glass. When Stacey approached, he kissed her lips and drew her into his stare. "Take her to the emergency room." When Stacey nodded, he held up a finger, "Wait a sec." He ran off to his bedroom and returned seconds later with a little denim purse. "Here. And, go get the rest of her stuff, quick, quick, quick." And to Warren, "Get her to the car!" He waved a hand around at the waiting Babies who'd returned to the room. "This isn't part of things here. They'll help her at the hospital. They can make her eat. They can help her."

Stacey ran back past us on the stairs with Ximena's sun-flowered duffle bag, and Jackson met her at the threshold, grabbed her upper arm, and pulled her up close for a hug. "Drop her off at the ER," he whispered. "You found her like this. You don't know her. No paperwork. Don't leave a name. You don't know anything. No bullshit."

Stacey formed a creepy half-smile, obviously feeling important to the cause and in Jackson's grace, and dipped her chin once, a nod of yes. We watched out the window as Warren positioned Ximena into the reclined seat. After he shut the door, he gave her hair a little pat, which made me cry fiercely into Siddhi's shoulder.

*

When Stacey returned alone, Jackson was waiting. During her debriefing, she admitted to answering a few questions at the hospital— nothing in writing, she said. She gave them Ximena's bags and ID, no big deal. To me, Jackson looked freaked out, but Stacey didn't seem to notice.

Other Babies crept in until all fourteen were present, the whole "family." Every flat surface of the living and dining room was covered in precarious pyramids of packaged drugs. If Ximena's heart had not attacked, this would be the time when Jackson and Warren divvied up the product, distributing a full backpack to each of the Babies, and then sent them out in pairs, over the whole of Florida, from Key West on up to the Panhandle, the universities, festivals, concerts, bowl games, and tailgating parties.

And day after day of their absence, we would get their envelopes in the mail. Regular mail. Stacks of cash. And in return, Jackson mailed them shoebox packages of replacement products in fat cans of Folgers Crystals to hide the smell. The postal service never lost or confiscated a single package. The pairs of Babies would trickle in as they tapped out, and then life went back to normal—parties, enemas, meditation, lovemaking—until the next harvest.

But now they whispered and wept and looked to Jackson, as usual, for what to think. "I have to meditate and let God in on this one," Jackson said, to unanimously bobbing heads. Stacey wept softly. Warren kissed her temple, and then he kissed her lips and led her upstairs to their room. Jackson took Belinda down the hall to his room, and they brought Anne With and Tomatoes along too.

My brain throbbed, pulsing through the possibilities, shot through with random rushes of fury at both Jackson and God for sending Ximena off to die alone. And yet, as Jackson's daughter, God's sort-of granddaughter, I believed I was duly charged to create some kind of prayer, even with my faith battered by the vision of Ximena's boney, pudding chest, Jackson's fists on his hips, Warren's warnings, and the smell of fresh pot and burnt tire rubber.

I couldn't unsee Ximena's terrified eyes and foaming mouth as she tried to ask me to help her. Stupid though it seemed and useless, I sat facing Siddhi on his bed, our legs crossed, and we clapped for Ximena, hard as we could, and with our eyes squeezed shut, avowing a hundred times, "I do believe in fairies, I do believe in fairies, I do, I do…"

*

Jackson emerged after dark and gathered the Babies by candle-light. "The body," he began, and I knew it was sermon time, "is nothing more than a set of clothes that the soul sheds at death in order to prepare itself for reincarnation." And the Babies knew right away to listen as he moved around the room. "You do your time in this human suit." He touched Belinda on her back. "This body you incorrectly believe to be the real you, and you memorize this life." He massaged Steve's hunched shoulder to loosen. "You suffer your pains," he said, giving Warren half a hug, "gather your experiences and learn your lessons." He touched each Baby as he spoke. "And when your soul and God agree you've got something figured out," he investigated each set of eyes, filled them with his warm smile until they mirrored the little smile back to him, clearly believing in him, "you make the karmic adjustments. In some lifetimes, you need only a little tweak, others a tune-up, and some give you a big shove in a better direction."

A joint began to circulate, and the palpable tension fizzled into the usual mellow because Jackson used his power to make it so. He read a section of the Bhagavad Gita, a conversation between the ambivalent Prince Arjuna and the god Krishna, something about how choosing to do nothing is still a choice. Fear is a choice. Taking the next breath, a choice. No matter what, we are always choosing. "So, we must do so consciously and without fear." And by the time he was finished, all the Babies seemed calm and comforted and high.

Siddhi whispered to me from our perch on the upstairs landing (which gave us a great view of the whole scene), "Makes sense, kind of." And I had to agree. Jackson's talk made me feel a little bit better, too.

Stacey, Warren, and Anne With began kissing and touching one another, and Jackson obliged, letting himself be entwined into the human paisley blur. The lovemaking never ceased to equally pique and horrify me, and I made us retreat to our room before the rushing and slapping and suctioning sounds and the moans that wrung my stomach and heated my legs, throbbed down to my feet and left me wishing I had the guts to flip on the bright lights and shame them for their nastiness, send them all to bed without their supper, and run to the far end of the earth to get away.

*

By the next afternoon, the house was so cleaned out, on Jackson's order—*no papers, no roaches, not even one seed*—everything smelled bleachy fresh, and I couldn't help replacing little tables and fluffing sofa cushions because Xanadu had never looked so nice and normal.

That was until Jackson shocked everyone, "Let's go sell out as usual," he said, "and then we'll settle through the mail, and once this crop is cashed, we'll all go on to live our next karmic journeys. Xanadu has been a beautiful dream, but it is wake-up time. It is not safe here anymore."

Just like that, he chucked everyone. Even Belinda.

Smiles fell, eyes twitched, and darted. It seemed, few, if any, of the Babies had alternative plans. I wondered if Jackson's decree included us...Xanadu was our world. Where else was there?

"When it is safe again, I'll ask God to send you back to me, but until then, silence. Silence is healing. Silence is solidarity and love. We are all connected in silence. Silence is the only way to hear God." To avoid taking questions, he put his hands up, "Gandhi said that in silence the soul finds the path in a clearer light, and whatever is elusive and deceptive resolves itself into crystal clearness." Then he layered in some Thoreau, "Silence is the universal refuge, the sequel to all dull discourses and all foolish acts, a balm to our every chagrin." Then he got Zen, "Silence is the essential condition of happiness."

But the Babies continued to shift around, mumbling worried sounds and projecting uncertainty and indecision, which might have been what inspired Jackson to sharpen his point. "Listen up! If you give in to fear bullshit and get off the karmic path, if you choose to break the silence of our family, you will be implicating your own selves in any number of...legal problems. You don't need that, or me, anymore. You will live blessed lives with me in your hearts. It's time to grow up."

I still couldn't be sure if he was including Siddhi and me. Did we need to grow up and move on? Were we allowed to talk about Xanadu? If we got kicked out of Xanadu, how would I take care of us? Who might hire a twelve-year-old? I used the abundant silence to plan. If Jackson abandoned us, I would sneak back to Xanadu and dig up my buried treasure. That, plus the rule: Call Nana, was enough to keep me calm.

Once the last of the Babies left the house, Jackson drove us to Howard Johnson's hotel on Arthur Godfrey Road just a few miles from Xanadu, warning us that if anyone, police or otherwise, asked us any questions, we were to tell them we were renovating. The house had mold. Then he keyed into our HoJo's room, got into the bed closer to the window, rolled on his side, and promptly contracted the flu.

PART II

Take it on the Run, Babies!

CHAPTER 10

The Sundance Kids, 1985

Once a day, Jackson got up to stretch his legs and went out to check his post office box. Some Babies sent fat envelopes with cash wrapped in newspapers, and to them, he sent fresh bricks of plastic-wrapped marijuana in big cans of coffee. Many failed to mail in their money, and with the mounting cost of our HoJo's hideout, Jackson's flu intensified.

He ordered a pizza some nights, and we ate half and left the rest in the box for breakfast, saving all crusts for Jackson because Aunt Paula once told us that when he was a kid, pizza crust was his favorite food.

At noon, we took two dollars from his wallet, which bought us each a candy bar and two games of Pac-Man in the arcade near the laundry room, more if we found any quarters in the pay phones or vending machine change cups.

During Siddhi's turn at the video game, if no one was inside, I snuck a small amount of our clothes into whatever washing machine was in use. "Nobody looks when they switch to the dry-er," Siddhi had said when he gave me the idea. Then we waited for their dryer to buzz and sifted our clothes from the foreign ones. The one time we came in when a woman was folding, we performed the script we'd worked out:

"Excuse me," I said in my naïve kid voice. "We are missing some clothes from our wash, and we used that same dryer."

And as the lady began to sift her pile, Siddhi added, sounding all sweet and innocent, "Um, it's my Hulk shirt, and hers is Little Twin Stars—"

And I interrupted, feigning surprise, "Oh my God, those are our underwear, too. So embarrassing!"

The lady, of course, obliged us, thoroughly charmed by the two of us—children too charismatic and articulate to be so unkempt—there on what ought to have been our mother's errand.

Siddhi commented on the pleasant feel of his warm, fabric-softened undies, but the shame of it made my stomach twist. I wanted to be a regular girl with lip gloss, a nice haircut, and pretty ribbons adorning a set of neat braids. I wanted clothes that looked just bought, or at least without pizza grease stains on the front and holes in the ZaSus. I wanted to be someone who had a kitchen with groceries in the cupboards and a school to attend, instead of one who hunted for quarters to spend on food and video games. Sneaking my dirty clothes into a stranger's wash, watching her fold them, and fantasizing that she was my mother made me hate Jackson even more for being such a quitter and for making me steal from people in order to take care of Siddhi, and it made me hate myself for not being smart enough to think of a better idea.

The upside was that as outlaws on the lam, with no access to the rice cooker and Champion juicer, Siddhi and I got to live in pizza–Ring Ding–Cheez-Doodle heaven, and we coasted through three weeks playing gin rummy and watching cable TV, practically in the shadow of Xanadu. We might have been able to manage a few weeks more, but lying around all day in the dark, wood-paneled room made us tired and headachy, and there was Jackson, sleeping, cursing, and gassing the room up with his farts and pot smoke. Plus, he kept using up the quarters to make calls from the lobby phone booths.

"Forget about Nana," he told us. "She's on a cruise to China." Jackson always lifted one eyebrow when he was telling us a lie, and I already knew that Nana thought cruise ships were, *Feh,* Yiddish for *Yuck!*

We told Callie, the HoJo's restaurant waitress, that we were fraternal twins, and it was our birthday, and she administered two free, hot fudge sundaes, a harmless hustle considering we'd never be around to claim the reward on our rightful birthdays. Siddhi told Callie, who had one side of her head shaved like Cindy Lauper, that her ice cream was superior to Carvel, and for the compliment, Callie gave us a refill.

As we slurped the melty parts out of the bottom of our silver sundae bowls, she gave us the check for the order of fries we shared before the ice cream and asked me, "Wanna sign it to your room?" I did what any scraggly outlaw would do: I nodded, forged Jackson's signature on the bill, and pocketed the three dollars he gave us, along with my little silver sundae dish, to remember Callie's good heartedness.

The last Saturday in April, we pretended to go to the pool but walked to Courtney's house instead, where we were treated to leftover turkey sandwiches and an epic Monopoly game with the whole family. What began as a perfect visit (meaning we showed up in clean clothes with clean hair and brushed teeth and got through a meal and two-hour board game without even once offending their normal people's sensibilities) wound up a horror worse than ever before.

This time, it was Siddhi. Not wanting to abandon a great hiding spot during a simple game of hide and seek, Siddhi deposited a sizable number two in Mrs. Laytner's houseplant, and when she caught my "genius," eleven-year-old brother, pants to his ankles, wiping his tushie with a leaf from her overgrown peace lily, her high-pitched shrieking summoned the rest of us out of hiding to find that Siddhi had been unfound in his hiding spot because he'd forgotten and breached the all-important rule and hidden—and shat, for that matter—in the fancy room!

"I'm so, so, so, so sorry," Siddhi said, doing the thing where he looked down at his hands when he tried not to cry or tantrum, and Mrs. Laytner's eyes and mouth popped and agog like a Panic Pete squeeze toy, sank quickly into unbearable pity. That was until he rushed to clean up after himself by scooping his mess up with his bare hands, and, while running it to the bathroom, sprinkling poop-contaminated soil over the creamy white carpet. Mrs. Laytner shrieked once more as she ran after a boy, old enough to be in fifth grade, apologetically trotting a double handful of his own feces toward her kitchen garbage. The shame turned out to feel as familiar as the pity. Blood rushed up and filled my face, arms, and legs, heating the parts of me farthest from my heart, my extremities threatening to rocket into all directions just to escape being associated with me.

We were degenerate aliens. No matter what or where.

"I think," I said to Courtney when she walked us out to the front stoop (she'd made several offers to bring us the registration packets they kept on a table in her school office), "we definitely need the school forms."

Jackson's flu took on a new symptom: paranoia. As fewer and fewer envelopes arrived at the post office, and without the Babies' devotion or the walls of his castle, Jackson was left with crunchy, polyester bedspreads, stinky shag carpeting, pizza crusts, soap operas and us. He took to pacing the room, mumbling about time and money.

Siddhi and I held court with the rotating sets of families at the HoJo's pool. We cozied up to and joined those who schlepped the floats and coolers, the ones prepared to spend the day. We told them, "Our Daddy is on his interview for a big job," crossed our fingers and held them up. "Wish us luck!" We followed and babysat for their toddlers, taught them dances and cheers, directed little plays and led long relay races and games of Marco Polo Boffo Socko (another of Siddhi's punch-ups). Two out of three times, we were invited to order or share some lunch.

I knew something about this felt conniving, sneaky, and essentially wrong, but after a long morning spent with a new family, memorizing their names and ages and anecdotes, hugging their most precious children, I cared about them. I felt a part of their clan. And what good was an extra tuna on wheat if you couldn't share it with family? Siddhi and I invested time and genuine heart into our lunch hustles, and our sincere affection for the people made the wrapped subs, handfuls of chips, and baskets of fried clams more digestible.

Sometimes, when Callie was on her shift, she'd spot us and shout, "It's the twins! Isn't it your guys' birthdays today?" She'd wave us over and, with a sly wink, hand us our free ice cream sundaes. By our fifth "birthday" in as many weeks, she knew Siddhi was a mint chocolate chip with seven cherries, and I was peppermint stick with hot fudge and whipped cream. By week five, the ice cream got too sweet, and the days too long.

*

As Siddhi and I burst out onto the sunshine-flooded sidewalk, riding the bikes we'd broken into Xanadu to retrieve, I felt triumphant like we were starring in an awesome movie about us, and I sang the corresponding Cat Stevens song, "Can't Keep it In," to soundtrack our victory. Siddhi held two good pillows under his left arm, and I rode with the envelope marked "Munchies," the one I took from the bottom of Jackson's underwear drawer, tucked under my elbow. Siddhi rode ahead of me, wearing his own underwear drawer find: a T-shirt Jackson brought home from one of his Jamaica trips. It was bright yellow and said, *NO PROBLEM.*

Back at Hojo's in our usual booth by the window, I practiced Jackson's signature until I had it spot on. The School of Love kept no records and assigned no grades. I wrote, HOME SCHOOLED in the "Previous Schools" space. The identification and vaccination requirements would have been our Achilles' heel, but thanks to our trip to Jamaica, we had passports, and thanks to Sariah, we had all our shots, and thanks to Jackson, all the documents were together in the manilla "Munchies" envelope.

I poured over my work, obsessively scrutinizing every block-printed letter. I intentionally answered the questions in felt-tip pen and then forged Jackson's signature in ballpoint as a contingency—should my handwriting be child-like and suspect, I was prepared to claim that I filled out the forms, and then my Daddy signed them before leaving town on a cruise to China, for business, of course.

As I rechecked and collated the papers one last time, I caught a glimpse of Siddhi, ashen-faced and frozen to the vinyl banquette.

"You okay?" He stared down at his folded hands. "Siddhi, do you need St. Joseph's?" I'd taken a bottle of the chewable aspirins from the Laytner's backup stores, mostly to use for Siddhi but also to keep as a memory. "You have a fever?" I pressed my lips on Siddhi's head, checking for I-had-no-idea-what. "Cool as a cucumbah!" I said in Nana's accent, but Siddhi wouldn't smile.

He'd had a legendary temper tantrum that week after Jackson returned from the P.O. Box with less cash than he was expecting and a letter from Aunt Paula.

"She's getting married," Jackson told us.

"Again?" I asked.

"Indian guy," he said. "She's moving back to India with what's-his-name, uh, Prakesh."

Siddhi must have been missing her, maybe imagining, or hoping, like I always did, something about her rescuing us, because he lost it and exploded so hard and fast that Jackson smacked his face and shoved him into the bathroom for two hours until he stopped crying. He threatened to kick us both out on the street if I didn't shut up and quit trying to soothe him. So, I sat with my back against the door, tapping every so often to let Siddhi know I was right there.

"Siddhi? Are you sick?" I asked again. He kicked his legs against the booth seat and wrung his hands in his lap.

"I'm scared," he said.

No problem, I thought. I just had to talk Siddhi out of a little fear bullshit, something we did for each other. When at first I'd been afraid of Rat Daddy, Siddhi was the one who convinced me that pythons were gentle and nice. When on his ninth birthday, Siddhi had a deep, wet cough and a fever, and Jackson gave him shots of wheatgrass juice and handfuls of chewable vitamin C with rosehips, I took him to the upstairs bathroom, held him while he puked pink and green, read him Treasure Island as he squeezed Murphy, crying and sucking in steam from the hot shower, and promised him he'd be okay. When I woke in a pool of sweat after a nightmare about our mother, Siddhi gave me Murphy to sleep with, and when Murphy didn't work, Siddhi held Murphy, and I held Siddhi until I fell back to sleep. I knew I could be whatever he needed now.

"What are you afraid of?" I started vague, to not get ahead of myself and assume the problem was bigger than it was. Jackson taught us that in negotiations, "He who speaks first loses," and Nana maintained (to her friends at the bridge table) that ninety percent of all problems could be solved with a good *schtup* and a slice of cheesecake. I had no idea what that meant, but I knew that Hojo's had cheesecake on the menu in case it came to that.

"What if the school calls the police on him?"

Jackson had been arrested once, when we were very young, in the first years after our mother died, in the rental house with the broken swing set. Nana sent in an attorney, and there was a mild hullabaloo that ended in dropped charges. I remember the click of metal handcuffs and flashing blue and red lights, waiting for hours in a playroom full of dirty, broken toys with a bluish-haired lady named Hilda who gave me three Chessmen cookies but wouldn't let me sit on her lap.

"Siddhi, we got the forms we need and filled them out perfectly, right?" He nodded. "We went over them a million times, right?" He nodded again. "The signature looks perfect, right?"

"Yeah, but what if they call the house and ask Jackson if it's really okay?"

Convincing Siddhi turned out to be easier than I imagined. "Jackson isn't home, silly. None of us are."

"What about when we move back?"

"So what? What does he always say about the phone?"

"Don't ever answer it. If it is so important, they'll come over."

"Right! It's like so dumb that we even have a phone, right? And two: we'll ride bikes to school every day and get back by three. I mean, Jesus, has he ever asked us where we go on our bikes? Ever? Even once?"

Siddhi shook his head. "Uh-uh."

"Right. He doesn't even wake up till three o'clock sometimes. He didn't even notice that we snuck home. He doesn't even know who Courtney is, or Dava. He doesn't even care." I couldn't be sure how much time I'd spent, over the years, waiting for Jackson to ask me more questions, wishing he wanted to know us, wondering why sex and pot were so much more worth loving.

Siddhi sat up straighter, stopped his handwringing, and gave a sheepish grin. When I suggested we ride off for a good *schtup* and cheesecake, he opted for a vending machine Snickers, and a game of Pac-Man instead.

The following Monday, we donned our cleanest clothes, which I pressed with the HoJo's iron, and we rode down Arthur Godfrey Road, all the way to the school office and presented our bundle of paperwork to the secretary, whose lipstick was so red that it made her teeth look yellow. She put on the bifocals that hung from a strand of beads around her neck and looked at my opus.

"It's all there," I said. "My daddy's sick," I clarified. "He said we can start today, though," I added without her asking. She smiled at me with exactly half of her mouth.

"Ay, I'm es-sorry," she said, with a Spanish accent. "But you cannot enter es-school until your daddy gets better and comes to es-sign you up himself."

I'd been dashed! I'd failed so quickly after so much preparation, stunned like Wile E Coyote after running full speed into the *trompe l'oeil* tunnel he had painted himself.

Back again to Hojo's, with the truth that I would never, ever go to school, I sat on the resting chair in the ladies' bathroom and sobbed until my tear ducts felt drained and empty and took another few minutes to fill the sink with cold water and splash it over my eyes and face, to hide that I'd been crying.

"It's the twins!" Callie said when she saw us. "Happy Birthday, you guys!" We never failed to take her up on her kindness, and I ate to the bottom of my peppermint stick sundae, even though the look in her eyes when she served us, like the office lady's, made me stop liking the taste of ice cream.

*

The first week of May, Jackson sat up each night in our room calculating the value of his remaining product against the total cash he'd received. He counted and recounted, and by the worried look on his face, his wan solitude and fading tan, it was evident the math was not working out. I stood by the bed as he counted and recounted, knowing I had the power to save the day. A quick ride to Xanadu to shovel up my silver brick, wait for Jackson to go pee, and slip the cash into his next count. Problem was I'd sworn to save that money for a real emergency. I had no idea what a real emergency might look like, but even the most minor scenarios revolved around saving Siddhi. Hojo's wasn't so bad.

On Mother's Day, Jackson woke us at four a.m. to pack and load into the car. He told us to keep silent and kept looking, like he was checking to make sure no one saw us leave.

CHAPTER 11:

Good Guys?
1985

Jackson rented a twenty-five-foot Whaler and told us to go to sleep for the couple of hours it would take him to motor across the Gulf Stream to Bimini. Siddhi and I cuddled up on the damp and dirty V-shaped mattress vibrating from the motor and slamming up and down on the water as Jackson sped into the breaking waves.

Even though I fanned my hair out all around to block the dirt and gasoline stink from our faces, it was too disgusting and scary to sleep. We played funny movie line geography instead. When it was still dark, and it seemed I couldn't go another minute without getting sick, Jackson slowed to idling, and I came out to throw up over the side. Siddhi's pallor had a greenish-blue hue, but he was so tough and never as prolific a pooper or barfer as me.

"Okay, that's enough," Jackson said. "Don't go overboard," he added, laughing at his own pun, but not in a nice way. Not warmly. He didn't even look at us as he refueled the boat and took a slip in the marina. I wanted the morning to come. I needed the sun to come out and make it all less foreign, so I could figure out what to do just in case...but the sky had no light.

Jackson took us into a hotel, The Compleat Angler, and I got so excited to have walls around us, a clean bed to sleep in, but he never got a room. We followed him to the bathrooms and then to the bar. Without asking us, he ordered us two cheeseburgers and left us at the table to go over and chat with the impossibly muscular bouncer whose sleeveless T-shirt allowed for a vista of his upper arm acne. Jackson looked to already know him. He was bald on top with a ponytail in the back and he didn't seem to notice that his pants had bunched way up between his thighs, another bit of spot-on casting in the absurdist troupe of Jackson's acquaintances. They went to the bathroom for a little while. I prayed that the man was not too bad, and I watched the door, waiting for Jackson to come back out.

I could still taste the sick acid in my throat, like burning salami, but when the food came, I forced myself to eat it all, even the garnishes. Siddhi did the same; no way to predict when the next food might come.

Jackson was extra jumpy when he got back, and the anxiety must have affected his tummy the way it did mine because he didn't eat anything.

Back on the boat, he ordered us again into the horrible V-bed to sleep for a few hours. This time, we took off our T-shirts to block the smell, and I did sleep.

When he woke us, I still felt so sleepy, it hurt to peel myself out of the cabin. The never-ending night was still dark, but I could see a little light rising at the edge of the sky. We left the boat in its slip and followed him on foot through the crumbly little lanes and allies of Bimini.

He'd been nasty to us for almost a day and night without really doing anything about it other than taking us on a boat ride and acting like a paranoid jerk, so I calmed down enough to want some answers, though Siddhi beat me to it.

"So are we on vacation, or is this like for busine—"

"Keep your fucking trap shut and MOVE!" Jackson barked. It wasn't his usual way of talking, even when he was angry. He was different, pissed off, erratic, body snatched. Siddhi and I held hands and stayed quiet.

He turned down an overgrown lane, too small for a car. In the blur of dawn, green parrots squawked at the sunrise, and a pit bull pulled at the end of his chain barking hard at our intrusion until a sleepy man in boxer shorts came out cursing and dragged him back inside. It was a morning full of anger, and though I wanted more than anything to find a safe place to sleep, I braced myself for another journey into the unknown.

At the very end of the lane, Jackson knocked on the fence gate of a shanty house and drew out an elderly woman who had deep blackheads all over her face, smelled like coconut, and wore a scarf over her head. She told us to call her Mama B. Jackson handed Mama B a fifty-dollar bill, at which she smiled, baring a wildly incomplete set of teeth and handed him a key, which turned out to start another, smaller motorboat, the only boat tied to the random dock across the road from her shack.

When we paused after Jackson boarded, he said, "Get on!" When Siddhi gave a little shake of his head, and we both stood still on the shore, Jackson got off the boat, grabbed Siddhi under his armpits, roughly picked him up, and deposited him into the boat. I scurried to get in on my own when he returned to do the same to me, but when I was getting on, my flip-flop slipped on the side and my leg went down between the boat and the dock, and I lost my shoe in the water and banged my ribs on the side. I yelped from the pain and surprise, and before I could do it myself, Jackson scooped me up by my own *ZaSu* Pitts and muttered, "That's what you get when you don't listen."

I needed to, but I knew better than to cry.

Jackson took us out a ways offshore, and then cut the motor and let us rock and drift while he opened his bag again. He counted a pile of hundreds, one at a time, from hand to hand. He seemed to have a lot of money, I thought, and I was relieved about my decision to leave that emergency stash safely in the ground. I smiled at Siddhi, and he patted me on the place where I fell and mouthed, "Sorry, CeeCee."

About his money, Jackson appeared to reach the opposite con-clusion. After another count, I saw him grimace and then shiver a little. His upper lip beaded with sweat even against the ocean breeze. He dug around in his duffle bag a lot and tapped his feet up and down like he might jump out and swim away. He bounced his knees, and moved his lips, feverishly mumbling nonsense to himself.

I looked at the controls and tried to figure out how to drive the boat, trying to remember what side of us the sun rose on as we motored out to this spot, and then I thought about how long we'd been adrift and changed directions and my stomach began to twist. Siddhi stared down and began to wring his hands, and I sucked slow, deep breaths and thought of Cat Stevens songs, a little trick I developed to keep myself from crying or needing the bathroom. I didn't want to make Siddhi any more frightened. I dipped my head down to meet his eyes and mouthed through a fake smile, "Don't worry. We're fine."

For a fragile minute, I wondered how mad this new Jackson could really get... If we did the wrong thing or asked the wrong questions, would he get angry enough to whip us, like Pop Pop did to him, with a leather belt? Throw us overboard into the sea? Leave us in Bimini with Mr. Arm Pimples and Mama B? I scooted closer to Siddhi, determined to shield his body for the duration of any trouble.

The little boat bobbed in the chop. Another observational pass revealed no life preservers or floats, no first aid kit, no food or water or visible shoreline on any horizon. No place to hide, no plan we knew of, no time clock. I got furious with myself for being stupid and childish enough to let us get stranded again in the elements.

Jackson kept counting until, abruptly, he widened his eyes, threw his head back and screamed to the sky, "FUUUUCK!"

We had big problems, ones about pot and money, which, un-like family and sex, had yet to play out in our laps. My chest felt to me like a metal birdcage, one of the old-fashioned kinds from Sylvester and Tweedy, except with my heart balanced on the inner swing, whipping back and forth in the hollow of my chest, shuddering in my core.

"Thieving motherfuckers!" Jackson shouted, louder and worse than his loudest and worst. He sounded body-snatched, like a completely different man. I jumped, and Siddhi stiffened in my arms. And without even looking in our direction, Jackson turned his back to the breeze, and furiously, obsessively, counted the whole bag again. "FUUUCK!"

Siddhi and I clung to each other. His lips were a safe pink, so the shivering had to be fear.

"GOD-FUCKING-DAMNIT. I'M GONNA KILL THAT FUCKING WARREN!" He grabbed a little tiny bottle out of his duffle bag pocket, tapped some white powder on the top of his hand, and then sniffed it up into his nose, recapped it, and set about counting the whole bag again.

So, Warren was the thieving motherfucker, not me. I hugged Siddhi tight, let him put his head down on my lap, and told him to try to go to sleep.

*

Jackson motored us to a secluded, tiny island with a deep, private cove somewhere in the Abacos. We floated in the lake-sized circle of water with nothing on the land across from the cove mouth but a crescent of white beach with a small dock. Someone owned this island and was not at home. The beach was quite a distance from our anchorage, but not so far that I couldn't see two large cranes parked on the sand. No people though, just the birds.

He dropped the anchor and stood on the stern to pee into the water. Then he sniffed the white powder from the vial again and recounted his bag of money. I lowered my bottom half until the water came up to my waist and finally got to pee.

"I need to go, too," Siddhi said, splashing head-first into the water and swimming about a hundred feet from the boat to do his own kind of business. I was amazed by his ability to relax his sphincter while simultaneously treading in deep water, but if he could go in a houseplant in broad daylight, then pooping while floating was not such a stretch.

"So gross, Siddhi!" I said when he squeezed his face.

"When it comes out, I just swim away fast," he hollered from his spot.

Minutes later, another boat idled into the harbor, and from the cockpit, I saw the evil twins. Happy and Smiley Guy. They looked like cute little grandpas, smiling and waving from beneath the roof shading the tower of their bigger, snazzier yacht. Jackson threw them a line, and they tied our little dinghy up to a cleat on their stern, the vessel's name painted on a teak panel in black script: *Orgazmatron*.

"Ahoy, Jacksie!" Happy did most of the talking. Both men were short and strong looking, but in a lean, veiny way, muscles strapped to bones and shrink-wrapped in skin so intensely tanned that they appeared almost purple. Happy had a full head of thick silver hair styled and sprayed on top so that its only way to move was to flap up and down like petals. Smiley's hair was mostly combed back over his head and trapped under his Kangol. He kept an unlit cigar in the right side of his mouth.

Jackson and I climbed aboard the *Orgazmatron*. And with his poop safely scuttled, Siddhi opted to keep swimming.

"Hiya," Smiley grunted. His unbuttoned *guayabera* shirt struck high contrast with his deep suntan and the black metal gun holstered near his armpit. He patted me too roughly on the head and then embraced Jackson, who hugged him back with gusto.

"This place is beautiful," Jackson said. His voice was different than ever before, like a kid's, the way I sounded when I asked him a question I knew he'd say no to.

"Told yah so, didn't I? Beau-tee-ful. And the only fella lives here's out for the season, so it's poy-fect. Nice and private." Happy sounded like one of Nana's friends when he spoke, part New York, part Jewish, and the rest Popeye. "Drink?"

Jackson shook his head, his eyes flat, "Nah," he said. "But don't let me stop you."

"Already three sheets to da wind. Ha!" Happy said and used

his knuckle to jiggle out an itch in his ear. He wore three, chunky gold rings on each hand.

Jackson offered them his tiny bottle, and you'd think from their reaction that he'd pulled out a bucket of Reese's Peanut Butter Cups. Happy trotted into the cabin and returned with a mirror and a razor blade he used to chop and move the powder around, forming lines which they all took turns snorting. I meekly accepted the soda I was offered, chugged it, and then asked for an extra can for Siddhi.

"Okay, Jacksie. Very hospitable," said Happy. "Now, let's get this ball rolling!" He punctuated his friendliness by clamping his heavy hand on Jackson's shoulder.

Smiley looked at me, offered a crooked smile. "Hey, kid, go for a swim, heh?" he said. He was the quieter, scarier one.

Happy added, "Yeah, honey, grab a snaw-kull and take a good look down under the water. Big surprise down there." He turned me toward the back of the boat and gave me a little *potch* on my tushie to hasten my departure. With two masks and snorkels plus Siddhi's soda in my hands, I cannonballed off the boat.

When I surfaced, I heard Jackson. "...won't fuckin' believe this brother, but I got nabbed by the Coast Guard on the way to the Angler." Jackson was lying. No one ever stopped us. I held onto the side of our dingy, stilled myself for better listening.

"Hey, what gives with the brats?" Happy asked. "Don't ever bring yah kids to the drop again, y'unduhstand me? I could give you a real smack in the head."

"Yeah, you're right, you're right," said Jackson, again in that foreign voice, unrecognizably witless, pleading, and defeated.

"Kids ain't stupid, Jacksie. That little girl of yours ain't so little anymore. She's got some big eyeballs, and poy-fectly good hearin'."

"Hey," Siddhi called, swimming toward me. "CeeCee!" I tried to wave him back. "Watch out for brown floating sharks!" he giggled.

I waved my hand, shushing my finger to my lips for Siddhi to stay quiet, and his face changed instantly to solemn and knowing, because we were accustomed to that thing that happens in life where you're just skipping along, tra, la, la, having a great ole time, and suddenly you hear the click that tells you you're standing on a landmine.

"Fifty fuckin' *grand?*" Happy yelled. "You coulda bought those *shmucks* off with five! The fuck's wrong with you?"

I listened carefully for Jackson's answer. I needed to hear each of his lies, so that me and Siddhi could back him up if needed. Then I heard the punch, and Jackson crying out. Then I heard another and then a third and fourth. Jackson whimpered in pain, sounds eerily like those he made with all those women behind the door of his bedroom.

"I didn't know, Hap," Jackson managed out of breath. "I'm sorry. I didn't fuckin' know that, man. I'm sorry. Please. I'm sorry."

"This ain't Amway we're runnin' here. This is serious business. It takes forethought. You gotta expect this kinda shit's gonna happen here and there."

"Fifty grand, huh?" I heard a strange click, and I'd seen enough movies to think it might be Smiley's gun.

"Oh, Jesus. No. Please, God, please, no. I'm sorry." Jackson was crying now. I held the dinghy line with one arm, and Siddhi with the other. He looked at me, terrified, and I started thinking through how I could untie the dinghy and motor us to the island for help. Then I remembered that no one was home. From my stomach up through my neck, I felt both frozen and burning hot, sort of like the time we got into Nana's Bengay. "Please. Jesus Christ! Oh, God. No," Jackson begged.

"Oh, c'mon, Jacksie," Happy laughed. "He ain't gonna shoot yah." Now that I'd stopped breathing entirely, I could hear every word. "He's got the pistol to your head to make sure you're payin' attention. We're gonna let it slide this time, because it's our fault we didn't know you were so stupid, and we didn't prepare yah. Next time, though, you pay bribes out of your own cut, yah hear? You pay us in full or we take a pound of flesh. Y'unduhstand me?"

"Yes, yes. I-I understand," said Jackson.

"Smiley, cut it out before he shits his shorts," Happy laughed again. "We'll let you keep ten g's, make sure those cute little brats of yours don't go hungry, but if you evah, EVAH..."

"Never. Never again, I promise. I'm sorry. Thank you. Thank you," Jackson sniffled.

"One more thing," Smiley interrupted. "If you bring those fuckin' kids near a drop again, I'm gonna drown 'em!" he said coldly. "Ya hear me, you dumb shit? I'm gonna hold them under the fuckin' water till they're dead."

I gave Siddhi a mask and snorkel and motioned for him to swim away. Then I put mine over my face and dove down, under the water and swam hard and fast toward Siddhi's white legs thrashing beneath the surface. When I came up, out of breath and shaking, I peeked back at the boats, but Jackson and the twins had disappeared into the cabin.

"Are they really gonna drown us?" he whispered.

"No way, Siddhi." I tried to sound very sure. "They're just bullies, like in the movies." I helped him adjust his mask to make good suction and was glad he couldn't see the tears forming inside mine.

Happy was a criminal and a psychopath, but he wasn't a liar. When I put my mask into the water and focused on the bottom, what I found was indeed unbelievable. The entire floor of the little harbor, every inch of it, was covered over in green sea turtles, hundreds of them, lying still, their bodies and shells overlapping each other, stuck like us, leaving only peppered dots of sunlit sand where they had no corners to cover it.

CHAPTER 12:

Ashram,
1985

We conquered hours and hours of I-95, Georgia, the Carolinas, Virginia, Maryland, Delaware, Pennsylvania, and New Jersey, with thumb wrestling, reading, and sleep. "Gonna be great for us, munchies," Jackson muttered, when he woke us both up for "a look" as we drove right past the New York skyline.

I wondered if we would ever see home again, if we had enough money to live in the real world, and I whispered my worries to Siddhi, but he started to look down and wring his hands, like he always did when he got scared, so I cut it out.

I'd been to the ashram once before, as an infant, Jackson told me, and as the purplish shadows of the Catskill Mountains rose out of a never-ending bed of green forest, I wished I could remember my baby years. One thousand and eighty whole entire days living with my mother squashed into the forgotten corners of my cortex by too many newer, shittier events, like Courtney being so excited for sleep-away camp she didn't even seem sad to say goodbye, or Jackson driving the whole way from Miami Beach to New York at ninety miles per hour, with the constant insistence of his fuzz buster that he slow down, mumbling about his guru helping him *straighten out.*

Jackson took a long, gravelly road that led to a huge, grassy opening in the forest, then up a hill, past a pair of old brown barns where a bunch of goats stood around apprehensively, like they were waiting to take their driving test. Jackson pulled up to a circle of little buildings he called *bungalows*—creamy-yellow clapboard with lacy-railed porches—and parked at the sign that said, "MAIN OFFICE," just as a circle of naked women upended themselves into headstands. They looked like a rack of lamb.

*

Baba Goshananda made speeches from his velvet meditation pillow. He wore an orange fabric diaper wrapped around his hot cocoa body. The white hair on his arms and chest created the illusion of a T-shirt. Jackson said he was sixty-seven, which we thought ancient. He seemed kind, and everyone sort of revered him like he was Yoda, and it wasn't long before I, too, wanted him to notice and approve of me.

Baba greeted us with a deep appreciative bow. We all bowed back. "Inside this sanctuary is your home," he said. "I bring to you, share to you, my peace." Most of the people—who all looked more like Babies than Laytners—made happy humming, yum-yum sounds as if Baba had popped Hershey's Kisses into their mouths; some wept. "Outside these valls, you may mire yourselves in desire and fill up your mind vit your attachments. But here vit me, in me, in love, there is freedom, and in freedom vee sit, vee meditate, and vee release."

I loved the schedule: time to eat, time to clean, time to meditate before the distraction of breakfast. If I went to the rope swings where Siddhi preferred to stay for free play with the few other younger kids, I would never be held to any grown-up standard, and the Baba might miss me.

I was a horrible meditator. I counted to a thousand Mississippi before falling asleep, replayed whole episodes of "Family Ties" and "Facts of Life" behind my closed eyes, and peered around at other people and studied the lengths of their breaths and the shapes of their bodies, especially Sister April, not least because Jackson had started sleeping in her bungalow. She was beautiful as per usual for him, with large, freckly boobs, and she threaded chains of daffodils through her flaxen hair. She'd been a schoolteacher in Princeton, New Jersey, she told us over dinner, but she heard the call of her spirit guide and left her family so she could find herself. "You should meet Wren," April said. "Brother Bill and Sister Nancy's daughter. That one's full of beans."

Baba agreed with Jackson that clothing was a barrier to truth. So, everyone at the ashram was supposed to be a nudist, but each wore some combination of woolen socks, ponchos, scarves, beads, blankets, bandanas, barrettes, and flowers. I looked down at my own body. *Sienna is afraid of the truth*, I imagined Baba thinking. So, I took off my T-shirt and underpants, mortified by my poof of black pubic sprouts, and I fidgeted too much during the hours-long meditations, sighed, cleared my throat, styled my hair to cover my parts, and when I asked Jackson, "How much longer," he made me go outside to play with Siddhi.

*

Wren Raintree had been sick in the infirmary for my whole first week. Sister April said she had something called *hypochondria,* which I thought sounded serious, but when I asked Wren, she said, "Tell Sister April I had *fuck-you-itis.*"

She was fourteen, and to my delight, she treated me like I was fourteen, too, instead of twelve, and she was taller than me, skinnier, and with full boobs where I only had grapes. Her hair was longer, straighter, and darker than mine. She said it was because she was Black Irish. "But you look like a white person to me," I had to say.

"Shut up, stupid!" She laughed. Her parents used to be normal, she told me, but after they almost died in a plane crash the year before, they went crazy, moved to the ashram, and changed their last name to Raintree. When they lived in White Plains, she said, her name was Wren McGuire. I wanted to make some joke about how at least she had *two* crazy parents, but the thought only made me long for my mother.

Wren had a way with words. In the buffet line, spooning food onto her tray, she'd say, "Mm, I want to stick my dick into these mashed potatoes," and, "I'm gonna make sweet, sweet love to that split pea soup." Once, she fanned the air near her crotch toward my face. "Smells like hot broccoli, doesn't it?"

"Sort of," I agreed, marveling at how her fart smelled vaguely green.

Wren made funny faces out of her leftover scraps and polished my nails and toes black with pink dots. And she was a serious yogi, far more skilled and flexible than I. "Yoga helps you be awesome at sex," she told me from her downward dog pose. Her naked vagina looked like a scream. She looked backward through the V of her legs to where I sat behind her. "Wait, are you still a virgin?"

I attempted cleverness. "We're both virgins because we haven't seen 'The Rocky Horror Picture Show.'"

Wren shook her head. "Seen it three times. So, um, that makes you a double virgin," she said, giggling. Being a double virgin made me feel broken somehow, because Wren seemed so satisfied not to be any sort of virgin at all.

*

As the eldest kid, Wren ran the job wheel. She assigned herself to bunk clean up, and I got the "most important job," of scaring the seagulls off the compost heap by the barns. "Like this," she said, waving a red washcloth around like a matador and shouting, "Blah blah blaaah!"

I got a few of them to fly up and then land back down on the heap, fly up and land back down again, until a man approached, introduced himself as Brother Mojave, and asked me to stop frightening the birds.

"But it's my official job," I argued.

"Is it now?" he asked. He wasn't a teenager, but he was much younger than Jackson. "Wren Raintree told me to do it," I explained. He smiled, accentuating a Rob Lowe level of cheekbone gorgeousness.

"Okay, Little Sister," Brother Mojave chuckled. "Wren was pulling your leg. See, the seagulls eat from our compost and then poop all around here, and we mix it all up with the manure over there," he gestured somewhere past me near the barn, his voice like warm cookies. "The seagulls are a part of this community, and we love them, just like we love you." My face went hot when Brother Mojave said he loved me and made me hate being naked even more than usual, and I draped the hand towel as best I could across my chest.

"I'm Sienna." I didn't want to be his little sister.

"Do you smell that?" he asked. I smelled a lot of things, rot and pine needles, the barbeque smoke of the burn pile, cow turds on the breeze from the pasture, and when Mojave put his arm around my shoulder, I smelled his skin, musky like the woods. He leaned us over the compost heap and took a big sniff. "That, Little Sister, is the scent of transformation. Baba teaches that nothing ever dies, only transforms into something else. Everything is compost, even us." Jackson said stuff like that all the time, but he didn't hug you at the same time.

The next morning, I returned to meditation to watch Mojave. He sat still in the Lotus. His shaggy brown hair lopped over darker brown sideburns that faded out along his jawline. His pubic hair was lighter than Jackson's, which made his penis look bigger, and because he wore shorts and sneakers to run every morning, his tushie and feet were whiter than the sandy brown rest of him.

I kept my crush a secret from Wren. Mojave was a grown man.

✳

"What do you mean you haven't done a gathering walk?" Sister Liana accused me. Wren and I usually spent work time laughing at entries in the communal journals, adding prank passages of our own, rifling through people's stuff, holding scavenger hunts for the boys, and doing each other's hair and nails.

Wren stepped in front of me, hands on her hips mimicking Sister Liana's stance, and I had to bite my lip to keep from laughing. "Sister Sienna's been helping Brother Mojave mix the compost every day!" Mojave stopped chopping cabbage to listen, and half smiled, exposing a complicit dimple. "She *even* helped him mend the garden fence." He raised his eyebrows at that one.

Brother Mojave nodded and winked at me, which shivered in my thighs.

"Oh. Well," said Sister Liana, "Can you do without her for a spell? I really need the greens today."

"Of course," he said. "But she's the best, so just for today."

"Don't you need *my* help?" Wren asked him in a tone I'd never heard from her, like she'd finally reached the cupboard and found it bare.

Mojave looked back down at his cutting board. "Nope. You can help Sister Liana, too." I felt a shameful relief when he rejected her.

Wren and I chatted and gathered a bushel basket of dandelion greens and wild chives in less than half an hour, then got quiet for a while in the brutal sun, as we walked back to camp, each holding a basket handle, until Wren said, "I didn't lose my virginity to my boyfriend."

"Oh?" I asked.

"When my parents went away on their trip to California, the one where on the way back their plane crashed, they left me with my aunt and uncle." She stopped walking. "And on the second night they were gone, Uncle Sean came into my room in the middle of the night and put his hand over my mouth, and, you know…then."

I knew she meant sex, but I had so many questions. Wren picked up a stone and threw it hard at a tree trunk. I stood still and quiet. I didn't want to do anything to keep her from finishing the story.

"So, yeah, that's how I lost my virginity, and then the plane crashed, and it was all insane and they went crazy and took me to like ten therapists and everyone cried all the time and hugged me saying thank goodness I wasn't with them, that I was *safe*."

I didn't know how to respond. I wanted to hug her and say I was sad for her, but she didn't even sound that upset about it. We walked some more. Then she turned and grabbed my arms, dug her polka dot fingernails into my skin. "I never told anyone that. Ever."

"Wren, you can always tell me—"

"Shut the fuck up and listen!" She squeezed me tighter. "If you ever, *ever* even think about telling, I swear, I will *never* be your friend again." Then she released me with a little shove.

I crossed my heart and swore on my life I'd never tell, even if she wasn't my friend anymore, even if she hated me.

I wanted to ask her why they hadn't taken her to California, if Uncle Sean had come to her room more than one time, if we should report him to someone, but that all seemed wrong. "My mother died from drugs," I blurted.

At the edge of the clearing, Wren showed me how to harvest fiddleheads. "Liana will love these," she said. "Plus, she'll feel so guilty for bitching you out."

*

"You guys wanna come play tag?" Siddhi asked outside the morning meditation.

"Nah, I'll catch up with you at lunch," I said.

It wasn't that I didn't want to be with Siddhi. Really, I missed him tons, but Wren and I were naughty girls, and I didn't want to subject innocent Siddhi to Wren's and my wild ways. I still ate with him and read with him and checked on him often, and my bunk was right next to his, because I could be the real me with Siddhi when Wren went off by herself.

Wren got to us before Siddhi left, and I worried she'd say or do something I couldn't explain. He already asked me daily if I knew when we were headed home, but with what little we saw of Jackson, it was anybody's guess.

Siddhi scratched at his peeling forehead. He'd been so badly sunburned he'd taken to wearing some departed kid's long-sleeved pajama top.

Wren sang her usual greeting as she walked up, "How ya doin', homos?" She had an elaborate fishtail braid in her hair that she'd promised to teach me that afternoon.

I turned Siddhi by his waist and nudged him toward the other kids on the ball pitch. "Go, Siddhartha!" He looked wounded, but he obeyed. "I'll eat lunch with you, okay?" I called behind him, but he'd already broken into a run.

"Hey," Wren said, giving me a friendly yank on my not-as-good braid, "Want a piece of gum?"

"Yeah, sure," I said. We hadn't had real sugar in over two months.

"Kay," she said, and then bent her knees and stretched a piece of her vagina lips toward me. "Here you go! Already-been-chewed gum."

I stifled my shock and skipped straight to laughing.

Siddhi and the boys played tag for hours, while I hung out with Wren. I told her how I wished to go to school and how I buried thousands of dollars in my backyard and how Jackson sold drugs for money. She asked if I ever French kissed anyone, and when I shook my head, she took me to the empty Children's House to teach me. She gave me some peppermint rinse to make my breath fresh. She told me to gargle a lot and spit.

"Is your boyfriend here?" I asked as I poured the mouthwash.

"Duh!" she said. "How do you think I would be having sex all the time if he was in Westchester? I sneak out and meet him at night. That's why I'm too tired for chores."

"But I never hear you leave."

"Ye-ah. That's because I'm slick, and all you kids sleep like you're dead." I didn't appreciate being lumped with Siddhi and the handful of other little boys, but I let it pass.

"But, like, what if you get caught?"

"Don't be retarded, Sienna. No one *cares*." She was right. Whatever boy was meeting Wren in the woods at night could have had sex with her on the buffet table, because everyone at the ashram was so wrapped up in themselves, they'd never notice, just like they never questioned or cared about all the other bad things we did. But *I* cared about Wren and her happiness and her safety and who this secret boyfriend was and if he put his hand over her mouth. *I* cared if she was in deepest love or if she only had sex in the woods because of the loneliness we all felt with no parents at night. So, I gave Wren my undivided attention, the kind I paid when I walked the trunk of a fallen tree or spied the cops driving behind us when Jackson lit up in the car.

"But who is it? How old is he? Who?"

"I can't tell you."

"Why not?"

"Because it's a secret. Jesus! Do you want me to teach you how to French kiss or not?"

I imagined kissing Brother Mojave in the woods, him wanting me and loving me. I gargled the mouthwash and spat it in a glass. "Yeah."

"Kay. So, for *Frenching*, you use your tongue. Here, open your mouth." Wren put her parted lips over mine and pushed her tongue into my mouth, licking around and over my own tongue, and a hot weakness spread through me, good and shameful, as Wren put her arms around my body, and pulled me up to her warm skin.

"You're getting spit in my mouth," she said. "Swallow."

I did.

"That's better. Here, now," she said. "Try again and put your arms around me. Boys like that." I hugged her shoulders.

"No, here," she said, and she put one of my hands on her lower back and my other hand, she put on her boob, holding my wrist, and making my fingers press and circle around on her nipple, which was hard and pointy even though it wasn't cold outside. She rolled on top of me and kissed me harder.

I asked her to stop, but her mouth on mine muffled my words.

Her eyes were squeezed shut. She had a cluster of four small pimples on her forehead. I started to push her away with my arms, but she took one of my hands and put it between her legs. She let go of my hand and used hers to make a circular rubbing motion on my vagina that sort of hurt but also felt amazing. The longer she rubbed me, the more it built until I had to press into her hand to try to make the hurt feeling stop.

"Mm. Dirty girl," she whispered and kissed me again. There was her rhythmic pelvis pulling on my wrist, her fingers searching between my legs, the sweat on my neck, the remembering to swallow, and the hot hurt welling, the squeaking of rusty springs.

"Yeah, yeah, more," she moaned.

"Don't," I said. Wren ignored me, continuing to writhe above my balled fist. Her touches felt pleasurable, like scratching a mosquito bite, but also wrong because I wanted Wren to be my friend and for us to be girls, not like Jackson and the Babies and her Uncle Sean.

"Wren, I don't like it anymore, plea—" She did something with her finger that made a pain inside me.

"OW! STOP!" I shouted it right into her ear. And Wren stopped. She sat straight up, like it was nothing, stood, and walked to the window.

"Whatever, retardo. If you want to be shitty at sex, that's your problem."

*

All of the kids sat together at dinner. Wren was super talkative. "That new lady in Rama House looks like a monkey had sex with a pig, and they had a baby that got hit by a car," she said. The boys all cracked up, even Siddhi.

After Kirtan chants, she fanned the air in my direction, shouting, "Organic asparagus, baby!" But it sounded different to me now, like acting, and when I saw her on her own, braiding her hair on her cot, getting ready for him, her face looked younger to me. And she looked so tired like Jackson did when something went wrong with his business.

And something else: Wren's finger flipped a switch on inside me. Each day, I'd wait until the shower house was empty, and then I'd go inside, using my own fingers to rub and rub in the pursuit of trying to make the hurt feeling stop. One day, after I held my breath and went as fast as I could, stroking and swiping more and farther than I'd gone any day before, the ache exploded like a burst balloon, like a sudden fall over a straight-down water slide into a pool of warm chocolate.

*

"I never see Brother Mojave in the Houses," I said, working the knots out of my hair.

"So?" Wren said.

"So, like, how long has he been here?" I asked.

"Mojave lives here," Wren answered, re-braiding her own.

"Whadda you mean?" I asked.

Wren rolled her eyes. "What I mean, Sienna, is Mojave lives here. He doesn't have another home. Just here. God! You're so dumb sometimes."

"Okay, fine."

"Yeah, fine," she said, mocking my tone. Wren finished her braid. Something came over her, some different emotion, not the usual sarcasm or teasing; something darker lurked in her grin. "You love him, don't you?" Wren poked her finger hard into my chest. Then she fell back onto a cot, lifting her arms overhead to expose a little patch of dark hair in each armpit. "You love him, and you want to have hot, nasty sex with him!"

I felt myself flush, not with embarrassment, but with anger. I thought of Mojave when I played with myself in the shower every day. I thought of French-kissing him, but I was afraid that Wren would be jealous because I didn't want to kiss her anymore. Wren pointed her body at me like a gun. "You better tell me if you love him, Sienna, or I swear, you retar—"

"Cut it out, Wren! You don't know what you're even talking

about," I said, ashamed of myself for fearing her. And then she pushed me, and, cursing, she punched me in the arm, and it—being the last thing I expected in the world—hurt like hell. She half grinned before shoving me to the floor, pinning me under her greater height and strength, and drumming my body and face with both fists shouting, "Bitch... fucker... cocksucker... You better stay away from him, you hear me... you... virgin... retard... bitch... cocksucker..."

Beneath Wren's punching machine, a rich, rising thing gathered up its power within me, from a place before Wren's teasing, the beating, from before I even came to this place and before I hung posters of movie stars on my bedroom wall. I saw my mother, and my question was why she wouldn't take care of me, and my rage lifted me out from under Wren, who'd been, for three months, my world.

I saw my mother's face where Wren's ought to have been, and the redness filled my heart and shot out into my arms and then my hands. I threw Wren from my chest and onto the wooden planks. I scrambled up quickly, kicking her in her side with my flailing feet. Wren popped up fast but made no move at me. Her eyebrows creased her forehead.

"Ha!" she laughed, wiping the blood from her nose with her fishtail braid. "Now, you look even uglier than you already were."

My face bled and throbbed, my arm and shoulder ached, and my skin swelled from being slapped and scratched.

"You're *not* my friend anymore," I screamed, but I didn't mean it.

*

To avoid Wren, I promised the boys I would play tag by the swings, but first, I swung by the compost heap, thinking I could get some sympathy from Brother Mojave, and maybe, if he felt badly enough, I might get a kiss.

The usual cocktail party of seagulls perched and waddled atop their poop mountain, but no one worked in the noontime sun. I detoured through the barns for a little shade, and there I found him, lying flat on his back on a torn serape, napping in the shade of the storage barn, naked but for the cowboy hat over his face. Silently, I crouched down next to him, turning on my side to bend my elbow on the ground and rest my head in my hand. One of my knees crossed down over the other one which Wren had taught me was a sexpot pose. Beyond listening to him breathe, I lay in the pose, realizing that I was not ready to kiss a man, that I didn't even want to, and that I needed to give up the whole thing and get back to Siddhi and the kids.

Brother Mojave took a deeper-sounding breath and then spoke without moving his head or the hat. "What do you want?" I didn't know how to answer, though his silky voice made my skin burn from my neck all the way down to between my legs, and I squeezed the tops of my thighs together to either stop or maybe increase the feeling. "You want something from me, baby," he whispered. "I know what you want."

Then, he reached out and grabbed a big chunk of me. He touched me so hard, squeezing my knee. I stayed quiet, even though it hurt. He rolled his whole weight on top of me, and the hat fell away, but his eyes were closed as he smashed his lips into mine until my muffled squealing opened them. When he looked at me, his eyes widened, and then he smiled. He took both of my hands and pinned them next to my ears, grunted in a way I recognized from the Babies at Xanadu, and pushed his penis, which had tempered into a boner, hard between my legs. It swiped into my vagina a little bit at the tip and stabbed me, but the feel of it did something else to Mojave, something that glazed his eyes over in a way that made me think he didn't see me at all or care about me, or even remember who I was. He yanked both of my wrists over my head and held them together under one of his huge hands, so he could use his other hand to aim his penis.

I wanted to kick him hard in the nuts like movies taught me, but my legs were already spread far apart with his heavy body smashed between them. He issued angry grunting noises like a hunting gator, and I was caught, in his teeth, a stupid, little virgin drowning in his death roll at the bottom of the river. I didn't know if it would hurt to be raped or what he would do with me afterward to keep me from telling on him. I wondered if I was living the last moments of my life and was about to spend them with a drooling sex monster. I called over and over for help, but no one could hear me, and the more I wanted to freeze and vanish, the more I made myself squirm and kick, trying to wiggle free. But then he put his penis hand around my throat, pressed it down against my windpipe so that I truly couldn't breathe.

"Don't you move," he whispered, and his spit came out on my face. There was no caring at all in his voice. "You came for this, and you're gonna get it." Getting a breath was my only focus. I stilled myself, and he let go. He spat a big gross amount of saliva on his hand and then swiped it between my legs so hard I could feel the scratch from his calloused fingers, and after whatever he'd done, he was able to force the rest of his penis up into my body so hard and fast that my vagina felt torn and filled with fiery pain as if his penis had thorns.

In my head, I screamed furious words, words Wren would say if she wanted something to stop right away. "Get the fuuuuck off me you fucking motherfucking shithead cocksucker. I'll kill you, motherfucker. Help! Help me! Fuck you…" And finally, he hurt me so badly that a scream came out. And it felt so right to do something against what was happening to me that I kept screaming, as loud and as horribly, and for as long as I could make it last. And I think all the shrieking woke Brother Mojave out of whatever spell he was under because he pulled his penis out of my body and fell away with one hand blocking his groin, and before I could stand up, the other hand that released my wrists returned to grab my chin.

"You keep your mouth shut, little girl," he hissed. I'd never heard him sound like that, scary, drooling, and nasty, and that's when my crying really got going. "Hey, hey, hey," he softened, putting his arms in the air like it was a stick-up. "Hey, you wanted it, right? You came here for it, didn't you, baby?"

It was true. I was a terrible girl who had abandoned Siddhi in hopes of stealing a kiss from this man, so I gave the most honest answer.

"Uh-huh."

"Yeah. I'll take it slow, baby. Come lay back down." Brother Mojave got up on his knees, rubbing his still-hard penis with his free hand. And when he leaned around me to straighten out the serape, I threw a handful of gravel in his face, scrambled up, and ran.

As I sprinted, as fast as possible, back to the bungalows, I had one clear thought: I was no longer a virgin, and it was my own fault for sex-potting around, a naked girl with a grown man.

I ran first to the shower house to wash myself. There were several women in there already, but no one noticed the panic on my face or the scratches and the little smear of blood on my inner thigh. Safely behind the shower curtain, I did expert silent crying.

By the time I got out and finally arrived at the soccer field to meet Siddhi, all the kids— except for Wren—stood in a huddle with several grown-ups, including Jackson. Siddhi had been hurt. There was a lot of talking and yelling, but Siddhi's pain cries cut straight through, tying my stomach into a pretzel. Jackson took a seat on the grass, and each time he touched Siddhi's broken leg, Siddhi screamed, and we all flinched.

"What happened?" I asked as my crying took on great volume. One of the twins, I didn't have time to figure out which, said, "Wren dared him to jump from the swings at the highest up he could get to."

"YOU didn't have an eye on your brother, is what happened," Jackson snapped. And a few of the other adults nodded. Then he touched something else on Siddhi's leg and made him scream again.

"Don't worry, Siddhi," I said through tears and snot. "I'm calling 9-1-1." I lunged toward the infirmary when Jackson shouted at my back.

"Sit down! We have a doctor." A new guy, Brother Raymond, the one with a thicker mustache than Magnum P.I., carried Siddhi to his car.

"Raymond has hospital privileges," April said.

"Where's Wren anyway?" I asked.

"She checked herself back into the infirmary," April said with another of her eye rolls. "She just needs so much attention."

"You're wrong about the hypochondria," I said. "Wren doesn't have that. She just needs more love."

*

I waited on the main road for hours, watching for Brother Raymond's car, and when it appeared, I ran for it and found Siddhi smiling and licking rainbow sprinkles off a melting ice cream cone. His leg was up on the dashboard in a thick, white cast that stopped just below his knee. Brother Raymond let me hop into the car with them for the rest of the long road to the clearing, and I hugged Siddhi from around the seat.

"I'll never let anything happen to you again!" I promised.

In the side mirror, he smiled back at me, but his eyes told me otherwise. They were tired and swollen and to me, so sad, hovering above his sunburned and peeling cheeks. He shrugged and smiled. "Wanna lick?" he asked and offered me his cone.

*

The day after Siddhi got his cast, Jackson said, "Pack it up, munchies, and meet me at the office. I'm not feeling the energy here anymore." Hospital privileges were expensive, I supposed. And four months was a whole life. Time to go home.

"Where's Wren?" Siddhi asked after we hugged and said goodbye to the rest of the kids.

"She's contagious," I muttered. Siddhi and I settled into the backseat, relieved that the front seat did not contain Sister April. Jackson popped in the tape of Steely Dan. Siddhi brought along a book of Ray Bradbury stories for later. He used a pencil to scratch inside his cast while thinking of a "thing" for twenty questions as we drove past the barns and the foul, rotten, putrid scent of transformation.

It was six a.m. and Brother Mojave was probably still off at his camp in the woods, but I looked for him anyway. I felt so dumb for it, but I wished I could know if he'd miss me. The seagulls waddled around, taking brief flights and then landing back on the mound. I wondered if they'd really forgotten how it was to soar high up in the sky and hunt for fresh fish, or if they remembered it perfectly, wishing for the salty ocean every single time they dove into that heap of shit.

PART III:

Sienna and Siddhartha

CHAPTER 13

Weird Christmas, 1987 (Siddhartha)

Siddhartha opened his eyes to the music.

Oh, come all ye faithful, joyful and triumphant, Oh come ye, oh come ye, to Bethlehem…

For a moment, he believed that he'd woken elsewhere, in someone else's home or in another universe, but once he roused enough to confirm he was in Xanadu, the bass-baritone continued to zigzag the terrazzo, up the stairs, down the hallway, and into Siddhi's ears.

He looked over to see Sienna's bed tidily made, which she always did immediately upon waking, and so he had to skip the upstairs bathroom, finding the door locked and the familiar scent of her hair mousse and perfumes seeping from its seams. Sienna was such a foreigner to him lately.

Sing, choirs of angels, Sing in exultation, O sing, all ye citizens of Heav'n above…

Siddhi floated down the staircase on Bing Crosby's crooning, like Donald Duck, toward a cooling pie on a windowsill. He traversed the grand foyer with its cracked flooring and chipped paint and continued through the archway into the living room, expecting to find some unique, idyllic, other child's vision fit to accompany such a delightful symphony. So, when his eyes caught up with the actual scene—his dad slung over the couch with his latest, the ever-heinous Gloria, both stripped to their waists and strung out from the night's party—Siddhi felt instantly sorry he'd left his bed. No one who lived in the new, cocaine-fueled Xanadu, not even a bookish twelve-year-old boy, could escape the nitty-gritty primer on life with narcotics.

Jackson took a bong hit and rambled, "...like my own father, a real son-of-a-bitch, but he would have liked you, baby. He loooved redheads..."

Gloria wore an open bathrobe and a pair of fluorescent green, spiked heels. She was child-tiny, elfin, with strawberry tart tits that Siddhi couldn't help but memorize, pixie-cut red hair, moderately "Blade Runner," and she hung around Xanadu all hours without ever actually moving in. The constant coke made her twitchy and disruptive. Hair and breasts aside, Siddhi preferred Jackson's stoner-girls to the tweakers; they were more thoughtful, quieter, and left less of a wake. Gloria was less hot and more hot mess.

Plus, CeeCee mandated that he steer clear of Gloria after the hideous bathroom incident. She'd been brushing her teeth when Gloria had clamored into the bathroom with dried blood at the base of her nostrils and squatted in the tub to wash her face, armpits, and crotch. While scrubbing, Gloria doled out two pieces of unsolicited advice: "Yah gotta fuck your man every day if yah want to keep him happy," and then, "Yah gotta remember to wash your asshole, honey, so your *punanny* don't stink." Then she hopped out, winked, took the towel from CeeCee's hand, dried it between her legs, and dropped it on the floor before trotting out. Even for Jackson, Gloria was a new low.

When his dad started selling and snorting cocaine—and made enough money and peace with the Guy brothers to return to Xanadu—the house took on a whole new vibe. Gone was the band of tawny, long-haired stoners, granola chicks, veggie gardens, and raw cleansing. The new Xanadu was commercial, toxic, soulless, and dangerous, a seedy frontier inhabited by an all-male band of unseasonably leather-clad thugs with no other aspirations but to get high, screw hookers, and scrape together enough cash to exchange their rhinestone earrings for diamond studs. Xanadu had become the Wild West, all the drug-addled depravity of the old version with none of the ethereal curiosity or community spirit.

"Heeeeeey, man. Good. Morning. To. You." Jackson took another toke. Siddhi had come to appreciate the morning marijuana come down session, a brief return to mellow. A squat, white-plastic Christmas tree had been erected in the slot between the crooked old mantle and the new big-screen TV. It was a festive object, and each of its albino pipe-cleaner boughs curled to beckon Christmas cheer back to Xanadu.

Gloria was a junkie and dumb as a bag of hair, but Siddhi had to give her propers for sneaking in whatever outer-world, tinselly fun December might deliver, and Sienna must have taken a clandestine shopping trip because the floor beneath the little tree was littered with gifts wrapped in red paper, each labeled with a large Rudolph sticker reading, *To: Siddhartha Khalil Gibran Jones, From: Santy Claus,* in Sienna's chicken scratch. She relished the chance to spell out his ridiculous name in full, the same as he had when on the first night of Chanukah, he handed her the short story he'd written for her—"The Butcher, the Hippie and the Doomsday Robot," cheaper and more personal than a bought gift—with the card that said, "Happy Chanukah, Sienna Shiva Karma Jones!"

Siddhi listened to the music, sighing in relief when Gloria saw him and folded herself into her robe. "Hello, Gloria."

"Hiya, Sex Pot," she said, scraping her fingernails across his chest. His dad snoozed, as Siddhi quarantined himself in the kitchen to pass a little time making some breakfast. He opened the fridge and smiled, grateful no one had gotten in last night, and raided CeeCee's groceries. Another notable difference from the erstwhile reign of Mary Jane at Xanadu, the cokeheads left off the food.

He scrambled a dozen eggs, using a fork to rake them through the hot butter like CeeCee taught him, and he toasted a loaf of bread and slathered the slices with butter and jam while juicing a shitload of oranges into a pitcher large enough to share.

When he returned to the living room, Jackson moved his feet to allow Siddhi to clear away the foul ashtray and empty bottles off the coffee table. Siddhi didn't dare move the powdery mirror and rolled up dollar bill as he wiped the rest of the surface clean with a wet paper towel, left, and returned to set down his breakfast platter and juice. Siddhi felt sure his little feast, along with the tree and gifts, might be sufficient currency for a decent, quickie Christmas.

Jackson scratched his head, flipped channels, and downed half of the toast while Siddhi and Gloria spent a few minutes spreading the one bag of tinsel and twelve-pack of red ball ornaments over the tree.

"Whoa-ho-ho, boy!" When he happened upon the fake fireplace channel, Jackson put on his Foghorn Leghorn voice. "Now we got us a fire going. I say, I say, I say, boy, now we got ourselves a fire!"

Gloria sniffled, then coughed, and then repositioned herself on the couch and slung her skinny legs over his lap.

Once the tree was trimmed, Siddhi looked around for something else to distract him from his gifts until CeeCee concluded her bullshit preening rituals. Courtney had introduced her to eyeliner and mascara and this thing called a "diffuser" that, apparently, did magical things to her curls.

On the floor, beside the couch, Siddhi spied a Santa beard made of white fur, and holiday giddy, he swept the elastic over his head and hooked it behind his ears. The straps were broken or something, no mustache, but it worked well enough. To complete the get-up, he took one of the pillows from the sofa and shoved it up under his T-shirt.

"Ho, ho, ho," Siddhi bellowed in his best, jolly old voice, causing Gloria to burst forth her hoarse, machine gun laughter just as

Sienna found her way into the living room. "Merry Christmas, CeeCee!" Siddhi announced, holding the beard in place on his chin as he spoke. "Fresh O.J.?"

From across the foyer, he saw her smile, leading him to believe that his jovial spirit and beard-festooned chin had handily staunched any impeachment for violation of the Anti-Gloria pact. She looked from Siddhi to Gloria, and her face fell, but then the doorbell gave her a start, and she came about to answer the door.

"Good morning, Siennala!" Nana burst in carrying a brown paper bag of food and administering to Sienna the expected, aggressive kiss. Upon hearing his mother, Jackson untwisted his limbs from Gloria's, calmly stood, and pulled on his pants. Siddhi saw him seem to realize something and then scuttle the coke mirror to the end table on the far side of the couch. "All the old goyim have scattered," Nana announced. "I brought Chinese."

"Hi, Nana," Siddhi called across the foyer.

"Hello, Sid, sweethawt. I thought we could eat chow mein and catch a matinee. What in the good God damn are you wearing?"

"Hey, Nana," Sienna said. "C'mon, we'll put it right in the kitchen and get plates." CeeCee steered Nana quickly past the living room to avoid her noticing Jackson and Gloria entirely, giving Siddhi the perfect angle to see Nana's eyes bug out when she spied the glittering little tree in the corner. She stopped dead.

"What, we're Jews for Jesus now?"

Jackson kept his cool. His mouth stretched into a broad, marijuana-kindled smile, and said, "Yes, Ma. I have always loved Jesus. He was a great teacher who preached peace, and I honor all peaceful people. Why not celebrate that with a beautiful piece of nature that the children decorated with their perfect art?" Siddhi wondered if his dad was hallucinating a better tree.

"Oh pah-lease!" Nana did her signature hand swipe, "How about because you and your two crazy children are *Jewish*? I gave you a goddamned Bar Mitzvah in Temple Emanu-El in September of nineteen hundred and sixty! How about that's why?"

"Ma, you should study the teachings of Jesus," Jackson said, and Siddhi couldn't help grinning as Nana visibly flinched. "He was a great rabbi, a leader of the Jews. A guru, Ma, a great guru."

"*Aiysh*! You're *meshugganah*, the lot of you," she said, and then checked the star at her neck.

"That may be true, but my children and I are Jews and Christians and Buddhists and Hindus, Ma. The whole spectrum commingled into the white light of love and kindness. We are *total love*."

Catching Siddhi's glance, CeeCee stuck her finger down her throat to fake barf.

Nana didn't notice the joint or the stench it left hanging or the remaining line of cocaine on Gloria's poorly hidden mirror (or if she did, she didn't let on). She kept her focus on the little plastic tree. "Well, I have news for you, you get that *shanda* out onto the curbside, or I'm leaving."

"Ma, relax, will ya?"

"Oh, for God's sake, Jackson!" she shouted as she hurried toward the front door to leave, but not before Jackson called after her.

"No, Ma, for Christ's sake!" he said, which bent Siddhi over laughing. He tried to ignore the crappy feeling that crept in just after the laugh, the niggle that stayed, where he regretted his inaction, and that he hadn't followed Nana out after she announced, "If you *kinder* want to come with me, I'll wait in the car for five minutes, and then I'm leaving."

CeeCee nodded her head toward Nana's trail. "Open 'em fast, Siddhi," she said, and by her face, he knew they were going to Nana's. For CeeCee, a day away, anywhere else, was better than even a Christmas Day in Xanadu.

Jackson and Gloria resumed playing footsies in front of the fake fire. Siddhi wasted no time tearing the first box out of its red wrapping paper. A Lego Space set. He was twelve, probably too old for such a toy, but he'd had so few of these things when he was younger, and he loved that Sienna knew he really wanted this type of gift and the time to sit on the floor and make perfect sense out of its many pieces. He also got a model plane, a small but complicated erector set, and an old high school physics text that he recognized from the "Freedom Box" at the public library. The gifts were a solid haul, and so long as he put Gloria out of focus and shut out how he'd dissed Nana, he could look at his father and sister and listen to Bing Crosby by the shimmering tree tinsel and funnel it all into a feeling of happy holiday, family joy.

"Merry Christmas, Siddhi," CeeCee said, giving him a hug from behind and, with it, a whiff of her *Anais Anais*.

"Merry Christmas!" Siddhi said, holding his Santa beard in place.

"Merry Christmas!" Bing Crosby announced at the end of the record.

"Merry Christmas!" Gloria answered in earnest. "Wait a minute, who else is here?"

Jackson jumped to his feet in a panic, dropping Gloria like a ragdoll to the strip of terrazzo between the sofa and coffee table and looking wide-eyed toward the door. The paranoia was a drug reaction his father had succeeded in breeding out of his weed strains, but with his new affection for cocaine and quaaludes, there was no way around jumping out of his skin a few times a day.

"It was on the song," Siddhi assured him. "Glo answered the song!" Siddhi's furry beard slipped down around his neck, so he hooked the elastic band back over his ears to replace it. Jackson dropped into the couch cushions with an obvious grunt of relief and a residual chuckle.

Sienna sat on the floor next to Siddhi. "You like the Legos?"

Siddhi nodded, and the furry triangle shifted again.

"Leggo, my Eggo," Gloria said, as she got up and repositioned herself over Jackson.

CeeCee and Siddhi exchanged the usual eye roll, but then her eyes lingered and searched his face. "What?" he asked.

She tilted her head like a dog, hearing a siren. "What the hell is that on your face?"

Siddhi blushed, feeling dissected. "Duh! Santa beard."

"Wait," she said. "Oh my God! Ew! Ew! Siddhi, get it off now!"

"What? Why?" Teenaged Sienna was hard to pace with emotionally. He found it nearly impossible to read her these days. She constantly had her period, she came and went, and she was so fucking fantastically dramatic about everything.

"This is why we made the pact!" she yelled, "And you broke it. Ugh! Take those off right now!" She grabbed at the beard and practically tore it from his head.

"What's your problem?"

"He was just having himself a little goof, honey," giggled Gloria.

"I wasn't talking to *you*," CeeCee snapped back.

Siddhi had the sensation that though he and CeeCee had once been so connected, he was waving to her from another planet. How could he have been such a stupid little kid? She slingshot the beard across the room, shook her hands out, and twisted her face into an almost gag, like she used to do at Nana's hot cereal.

Gloria got up and took the item and, giggling, stepped one high heel through the elastic and then the other and pulled up what Siddhi now conceived was a pair of furry G-string panties back on and up under her robe. And with that act, a moment passed between Siddhi and his sister, a millisecond, a subatomic speck of time, during which CeeCee crossed the threshold of their togetherness into another realm and even with all his newfound understanding, Siddhi stayed on his side. He sat, cross-legged on the floor with his child's gifts, dunce-capped in a way that made him want CeeCee out, of their room, of the house, out and away, and he trembled with how he both chased and feared that fantasy. But worse, he wanted to choose to stay a boy, in a boy's life, one with Lego and chow mein and Bing Crosby's idyllic crooning, and even, if it had to be so, even with Gloria, the devil he knew.

CeeCee had left for Nana's car what felt like an hour ago (though it might have been five minutes). And like a child, he knew she wouldn't let Nana pull away without him. And like a child, he collected up his toys to bring along with him. And like a child, he followed to where his big sister waited for him rather than spend the day alone.

*

"It vas a dream I had," said Elsie. Siddhi continued building his Lego at Nana's condo, where a little game of mah-jongg had broken out when he and CeeCee and Nana's gaggle of girlfriends got back from seeing "Empire of the Sun" at the cineplex. CeeCee played the fourth seat to Nana, Elsie, and Ray, he thought as a ploy to avoid him more effectively.

Elsie put down a tile and went on, "'A dream once lost in sorrows and songs...'"

"Whaddaya talking?" Nana chided, exhaling her smoke, like one of the dragons on her mahjong tiles.

Siddhi knew the quote, "It's Rilke, Nana," he said.

"Dat one's headed to Harvard," said Elsie, whom Nana referred to as, *the last of the bigtime readers*. She waved her Auschwitz-tattooed arm toward Siddhi. "Smarty-pants, dat one," she said in her diehard Polish accent.

"We'll see," said Nana. "Three crack."

"He'll be such a catch," said Ray. "Siennala, your turn, cookie."

"Four bam."

"Ooh, look at dis one!" said Elsie. "Dis one's da beauty, no?" She shook CeeCee's shoulder. CeeCee had grown up a lot and become very pretty, though if you asked her, she'd just tell you she looked fat or some other self-effacing, girlie crap.

"What was your dream?" CeeCee asked.

"Well, I dreamt of my Oscar," Elsie said. "How he'd planned to marry a different girl until I turned on my charms, and he chose me instead."

"How'd you meet him?" CeeCee asked, "A dance?"

"No dahlink," she said. "He vas the soldier who liberated me."

Siddhi could see her about to cry.

"You've become a little lady," Ray chimed in. "Any boyfriends yet?" To which CeeCee shook her head.

"Well, don't you bring me one unless he's Jewish," Nana threatened. "You understand me, miss?"

Elsie ignored Nana and continued, "Well, if you vant to get

him good, you need to sit right up close and let him know you're interested."

Siddhi watched his sister get ordained into an old lady, circa World War II romance.

"Once you have him on da hook," Elsie went on, "Keep yourself handy, and be vitty, make him laugh."

Nana nodded along. And Siddhi wondered why Sienna was eating this garbage up. These ladies were training CeeCee to get boys to adore her rather than telling her what a great person she was, and how none of those boys would ever be good enough for her. And then Siddhi wondered, again, for the millionth time, how moving to Nana's might be just as bad for them in a different way. If turning themselves inside out to be acceptable to others was Nana's *yin* to Jackson's *yang*, then both extremes were equally fucked, and he could just excuse himself from trying for anything.

"Mah-jongg!" Elsie sang.

"Oh, for crying out loud," shouted Nana. "I'm going to the toilet." She got up from the table. "You're a ringer, Elsie. You and your goddamned Rilke," she said on her way to the hall. And then, her usual bomb, "You two get your shoes on. Your father will be worried if I don't get you home soon." To which Siddhi felt himself begin to boil.

CHAPTER 14

Total Eclipse of the Heart, 1987 (Sienna)

Mrs. Laytner pulled her Volvo wagon into the Miami Beach Convention Center's fire lane. "I'll pick you up at five. Right here, okay?" She had a long, narrow face, unsupported by her short stature, though the same freckly face looked regal and quite pretty on Court, who was lanky like her father.

"Sure," we agreed in unison, and then to each other, "Jinx! Buy me a Coke!" The day was rebounding from a rough start, with Siddhi stonewalling me, slamming doors, and tearing apart his side of our room while I got dressed and did my hair. He was always such a dick when I was on my way to sleep over at Court's house, huffed and brooding. He'd whittled, honed, and polished his sarcasm, and he never wanted to go anywhere, just stay home alternating reading with *kvetching*. Something about puberty—old news for me—was so angering for him, worrisome, and really, I hated leaving him. He accused me of being obsessed with the Laytner family.

The thing was, I was the kind of girl who no one asked, no one checked, and someone raped, and Court was the kind who had to meet expectations, be appropriate, and "make us proud." Court was accounted for, and I couldn't resist being a part of that, even though it meant leaving Siddhi unaccounted for sometimes.

"How much did you bring?" Courtney asked as we walked inside. The extra thick layers of blue eyeliner and shimmery frosted lip gloss she'd applied to the both of us looked worlds prettier on her fair, pinky coloring than on my swarthy, olive skin.

"A hundred," I said. My bangs were sprayed-stiff in the way Court taught me to blow them out with a curl brush and fan them into an airy poof.

"That's a lot. Did you steal it?" she joked. Stealing was the latest craze at Beach High; Court, a freshman like I would have been, said her friends described the buzz they got fresh off the take.

"Nah. It was luck. Jackson gave it to me on his way out to the boat," I lied. Of course, I'd stolen the money. Hundreds were like tissues to Jackson. He even snorted his coke through one. He'd always been a counter, but there was so much, and when I took money, he ought to have spent on us for clothes and stuff anyway, he never seemed to notice.

Court pushed out her bottom lip. It wasn't like her to wish I'd done something wrong, though it was precisely like her to hop on a trend. I wondered, now that it was cool in her high school, how pleased she might be if I told her how I'd stolen many thousands of dollars when I was six and buried them, Blackbeard-style, in my yard.

But I wanted to trade my badness for Court's goodness. I hoarded free samples of Court's nice and normal life, how her reddish-brown, spaghetti hair fit daintily into the small elastics that snapped in two when I tried to use them on my rat's nest, how she'd kept a diary since she was five but never wrote anything personal in it, and how her favorite mixtape contained songs by Barbara Streisand, Quiet Riot, Tchaikovsky, and The Sex Pistols, all of whom she obliged with equal worship. She got straight A's in geometry to earn ear piercing, and Dr. Laytner demanded she stitch up the slits in the men's boxers we wore as shorts. Court insisted she'd never notch up the social hierarchy with a lame, sewn-shut wiener slot. She wanted admission into the small clique of girls at the apex of the ninth-grade food chain, but for so many factors—not just Mrs. Laytner's outlawing of any "rhinestoned-Madonna-slut-crappola"—she'd hit a glass ceiling. I was glad to have her be a little lonely, so she'd always need me around, but I wasn't proud of that feeling.

She flicked my hundred-dollar bill. "Aw, that was cool of your dad," she said. She'd never met Jackson, but she always asked about him and pretended familiarity, maybe to downplay that her parents forbid her from entering Xanadu.

The annual flea market was the ninth wonder of the world, a vast expanse of consumer madness with hundreds of vendors lined up in rows, wares staged for perusal: leather goods, costume jewelry, knife, mop, and kitchen demonstrations, posters of baby animals, jingoistic sweatshirts, dream catchers, sundry beads... Patrons herded through the aisles, leisurely tightening the gaps between themselves and the items they never knew they always needed. Funnel cakes, cheese steaks, and soft pretzels wafted the air, alluring thousands of nostrils.

After a lunch of assorted fried foods coated in powdered sugar that all tasted the same, Court spotted two of the ninth-grade elite girls sharing an arepa at the food tables. She stiffened, asked me if her bangs were okay, told me to be cool, and then introduced us. They just looked like any other girls to me, but something about me really intrigued both Shana and Jennifer.

Court kept elbowing me to answer their questions. "So, like, you totally don't, like, go to *school*?" I sensed Court's delight and played along. "Are you like super Christian or something?"

"Uh-uh," I said. "Nothing religious." Unless she counted Jackson's personal relationship with the Big Man.

"Oh shit, do you like have cancer or M.S. or something?" asked Shana. "Sorry to sound like a bitch." She didn't sound sorry, but she *did* sound like a bitch.

"Nope. Not dying."

When the two girls (neither one as interesting or as cool as Court by any stretch) pulled over to test perfumes, Court filled me in. "Shana has a perfect body, right? And she wears like the most awesome clothes!"

Shana did look awesome in her painted-on jeans, slouchy socks, and new leather Keds. Her bang-fan was a wonder; she had the right hair for it. Jenny was also skinny, rich-looking, and stylish but an obvious second fiddle to Shana. Someone had to be. Court informed me that both girls were competitive figure skaters. But they were total jerks, and Court had somehow missed the memo.

The four of us shared a giant slushy, on me, and then Shana led us to the karaoke station, where we crammed ourselves into this foam-padded phone booth to create a low-quality recording of "Total Eclipse of the Heart." Courtney sang all the *Turn-Arounds*; Shana, Jenny, and I each took a verse, emulating Bonnie Tyler as much as possible, though we ended up sounding like tone-deaf Alvin and the Chipmunks.

We each got a copy of the tape, on me, and then we walked some more.

"Dare me?" Shana asked with a knowing look at Jenny.

"Totally!" Jenny nodded.

"'Kay. Stay here," she ordered, and Court squeezed my arm as we watched them walk up to a long display pallet of silver jewelry.

Shana got the attention of the man working the stand. "Can I try some on?" She led him away to the watches and placed her bags down atop the ring table between her and Jenny. Shana smiled and talked to the man for a minute, tried on the watch, and then gave it back, thanking him, and then she and Jenny returned to us, canary-eating grins intact.

Shana took us by the elbows and pulled us quickly to the next aisle, which, by the look in her eyes, gave Court the tingles, and when we turned the corner, Jenny held up her hand, exposing two silver rings. "Heh, five-finger discount," Shana added.

"Awesome, right?" Jenny gave Shana a ring and kept the other two on her finger. I saw Court deflate.

"Okay, you guys," Shana said. "We gotta go. It's been real."

"Oh, cool," I said, relieved. And then, for no reason, everyone hugged each other and kissed the air while touching cheeks saying, "Mwah," which Court explained was the Beach High method.

After they left, Courtney dug around in her purse and came up with her lip gloss. "CeeCee," she leaned toward me and whispered, "ever steal anything?"

Court was the pristine part of my life, my secret stash of pure goodness. Once, after errands with Nana, we ran into the Laytners at Wolfie's, and Court gave a dollar to the homeless man outside despite Nana's admonishment: *Feh*! He'll only use it for drugs! She volunteered at a soup kitchen with her family on Thanksgiving, and she sold candy bars for her service club fundraiser to benefit The March of Dimes. She told Dava she was proud of her when she ate the toothpaste. She only lied to protect people's feelings. ("Sorry you can't sleep over again. My mom doesn't feel well.")

Court was a good girl, and with her, I got to be a good girl, too. "I don't know," I answered, feigning deep interest in a heap of men's argyle socks.

"That means yes, doesn't it?" Court had no idea that I long ago stole the little pan from her Easy-Bake oven and shoved it in with the other "memories" in my backpack. Nor was she privy to the hundreds of times I'd taken money from Jackson to buy Siddhi and me pizza, deodorant, sneakers, and Robitussin DM. Stealing, for us, was like cocaine for Jackson: a necessity for everyday function, as coated in shame and badness as our funnel cake was in powdered sugar. I wanted no such shame for Courtney, but when she looked at me, eyes begging for my help in her adventures in growing up, I found no words that wouldn't betray the version of me I was with her. All I did was shrug like an idiot.

"I'm gonna do it," she said. "Tell me how."

"No, Court. It's stupid." Court had a mother and a father, and they made dinner and had so many expectations, and they laid out fair and easy rules, not stealing implied by almost every one of them. Court focused lustily on the silver displays. "Yeah,

I know, but I just want to try it one time, like to see what the big deal is, get the *rush*."

"Don't, Court. It's not worth it. Tell me which one you want. I'll totally buy it for you." I hoped she'd relent, but she fidgeted, devil-eyed with anticipation.

"Not the same! I want to see what's so great about it. I'm gonna try." I had to do something to stop her, to keep her good.

"No," I grabbed her hand and tried to walk her away. "Look, kettle corn!"

"Stop!" she said, planting her feet at the silver seller and yanking her hand from mine. She got like this sometimes. When the Laytners took us to the church carnival in the Saint Patrick's parking lot, she swore she would conquer her fear and ride the Zipper. And even when Dr. Laytner reminded her that it made her throw up, she planted her feet and yanked her hand away, and Dr. Laytner smiled and bought the tickets and whispered that he was proud of her while she puked in a trash can after getting off.

Telling Court no, was the wrong tack.

"What if I show you?" I asked her in an Artful Dodger-esque whisper. "Okay?" The notion of doing it myself, for the sake of Court's virtue, didn't even feel like wrongdoing.

"I don't know," she hedged, but she loosened her stance and lowered her eyebrows, and I knew I had her.

"I don't know means yes! C'mon."

"The best way," I told her, "is to *not* be like Shana and Jenny. Don't make a big deal about it. Here," I said, handing her the sterling silver watch I'd casually lifted during my explanation, hoping she'd see that without the audience, without the build-up, the dare, that stealing was nothing, less than nothing, boring.

But her eyes, mouth, and nostrils flared with amazement like I'd done one of those ninja backflips that starts with running up a wall. Then, a proud smile made its way across her frosted lips, and she slowly shook her head.

"Just now? But how'd—"

"Yeah. It's not hard. See, it's dumb. Just forget it."

"Not yet," she said.

"You're not doing it," I told her.

"Fine, but I need to actually see you do it, so I know how."

When I knew she was not going to insist on trying for herself, an indemnifying happiness warmed over me. I felt...cool. Who was I to deny Courtney my one talent? We walked and talked, and over the course of our last hour, I snatched a little bauble from each silver place we passed, a few rings, a couple of bracelets, a second watch, and a few pairs of earrings, silver hoops, chandeliers, rhinestone studs. I was slick, smooth, and blameless because I was keeping my friend pure.

"This lady I talked to here last year told me a lot of people steal, so they work some loss into the prices," I lied. It sounded wrong, and my fun feeling fell away.

Court already knew I'd never been to the flea market before. She furrowed her eyebrows, and her abetting smile gave a faulty twitch. Her subconscious let something slip, a little dismay, a fleck of regret breaking free and illuminating the part of her that knew this was wrong. It was short-lived, she stuffed it down and soon was piqued again. "Now it's my turn!"

"No, Court," I said. "Here, have all these." I hung the heavy bag of silver on her wrist. But it wasn't about the booty. I think Courtney just wanted to feel what it was like to be a villain. She tiptoed like Boris Badenov, subtle as a blinking neon arrow, as she pretended to browse, all under the gaze of the vendor who obviously "made" her immediately and followed her back and forth, rolling his eyes with his arms folded across his chest, waiting.

When she couldn't evade his gaze, I called her name out loud, and she gave up and slunk back over to me, wearing her regular, good smile. "I suck," she said.

"That's because you're good, Court. And now you don't have to wait in a holding room while they call your mom and the cops."

"Here," I said, and I put one of the watches on her left wrist, "I don't need two." We headed out the main doors to find Mrs. Laytner and Dava waiting in the idling Volvo. Same spot, like they'd never left.

"Jeez, Mommy, you're like clockwork," Courtney said. Every

time she called Mrs. Laytner "Mommy," my heart turned over and beat hard for a minute. I followed her into the backseat.

"Buckle up," Mrs. Laytner said, pulling out.

"We ran into Jenny Sachs and Shana Lesser. Listen to this!" Courtney leaned between the front seats and stuck her copy of our tape in the cassette player, and we heard a bunch of static, then the song began, chipmunks warbling, *"Total eclipse of the heaaaaarrrt…"*

We all laughed so hard that Dava had to blow her nose. Court reached for the ejected tape. "Hey, hon, where did you get that fancy watch?" Mrs. Laytner asked.

"Oh, uh, well, I, um I bought it at the flea market just now, to-day," she babbled, awkwardly, horribly, and then smiled a crook-ed, pained, liar smile. Lies were a power-of-protection Court never needed before. She was a piss poor liar.

Mrs. Laytner could have been a total stranger and known that Court was full of shit, a giant whitehead pimple of a liar, an em-barrassment to the criminal world, with the great irony being that she hadn't even done anything wrong.

"Oh, yeah? Really? How much was it?"

"Well, *I* chipped in for most of it," I cut in evenly, but a beat too late. It didn't matter anyway because I could have produced a receipt, and it still wouldn't mask Courtney's unraveling.

Mrs. Laytner looked furious. "I believe you did nothing of the sort, young lady," she said to me and pulled over on the shoulder of the road.

"Whattid Courtney do?" Dava asked, looking up from her *Sweet Valley High*.

But Mrs. Laytner shushed her and turned toward the back-seat, focusing completely on her older daughter. "Tell the truth *right now*. Did you shoplift that watch?" The heat spread up my neck and through my cheeks, as my degenerate influence hatched into full daylight.

"What? No! Uh…no. God, what do you mean?"

Mrs. Laytner's incredulous look turned fierce, explosive, as Court continued to stammer her denials. Mrs. Laytner turned back toward the steering wheel and exhaled. She shook her head slowly with disappointment. "Well, I thought I taught you better, but apparently, you need remediation." She brought a protective arm up in front of Dava in the front seat, made a hard U-turn, and drove back to the Convention Center without another word.

I wanted to fess up and tell Mrs. Laytner that Courtney was incapable of stealing a free sample and that *I* was the no-good thief. But I said none of it. I sat facing forward and boiling in shame. Courtney looked super scared. Dava blew her prolific nose.

"Go on!" Mrs. Laytner barked, and Court, who seemed to know something I didn't, got out of the car, sniffling back tears, and headed back into the building.

"Dava?" Mrs. Laytner asked. She opened the windows and shut off the ignition, and the heat quickly reclaimed the car. "Remember when you took that lollipop from LaGorce Market, and Courtney and Mommy told you what you'd done wrong, and you had to give it back to Mamoud and tell him you were very sorry for stealing?" Dava nodded and pulled her pigtail hair to make it tight. "Well, I never thought this would happen, but that is what your big sister is doing right now. Please, Honey, when you turn fourteen, and your ding-dong friends all think it's cool to shoplift, please remember that I will know and drag you back to do the right thing." Then she turned one eye to me, and I could tell she knew I was some kind of bad influence on her daughters. "And it ain't too cute when it's jewelry instead of a little piece of candy," she said, shaking her head again.

"Mrs. Laytner?"

"Yeesss?"

This was my chance to tell her to be proud of Courtney. I should have come clean to her about my terrible behavior, showed her all the rest of the silver, and had her teach me a lesson by making me go back in and apologize to everyone I ripped off. I *wanted* her to be disappointed in me, to expect better from me, like she did with her own daughters.

I was not, however, one of her own, and she had just resumed letting me sleep over. If I risked it and told her everything, the most likely scenario was that she would kick me out of the car, their home, and possibly their lives. No more Caesar salads. No more playing geography until someone fell asleep. No more of Dr. Laytner's lame, dad jokes. No more lining up chairs to listen to Dava's abysmal flute concertos, and above all else, no more Courtney.

"Nothing."

"Don't try to defend her, Sienna. Just go in there and check on her. See if she's finished, will you?"

"Um, sure," I said and got out of the car. I caught up with Court as she was coming out into the vestibule.

"Oh, my God! I am so, so, so sorry," I told her, adding a hug. "Are you okay? D'you give it back? Oh, God. I'll tell your mom the truth, so she'll know you didn't really do it. Okay, c'mon, as soon as we get back in the car, I'll tell her the whole story and that it was me and— "

"NO!" Court grabbed both my shoulders, "Don't tell her you did anything wrong! Just please stick with what she already thinks."

"But why? It's not fair. Plus, I can just—"

"Just shut up about it, CeeCee!" She sounded older when she said this. "I freaking returned it, and I said I was sorry. That's all she wants. She'll be mad for a day, and then she'll forget all about it."

"But you didn't do it!"

"Just *please*, don't tell her it was you." She squeezed my shoulders and shook me a little. "Promise me?"

"I promise." Then she hugged me, the real kind, not the Shana and Jenny kind.

Back in the car, she fastened her seatbelt, nodded at her mother, sat back, and looked out the window, new tears pooled at the corners of her eyes. I joined her in the backseat, trembling, reeking with guilt and staying quiet, but Mrs. Laytner had those magic mother senses.

"Sienna Jones," she said, staring out the windshield rather

than looking at me. "Do *you* have anything to return before we go?" Court mashed her foot hard against mine.

"No, Mrs. Laytner," I answered. I wanted to spend the rest of the day wandering the aisles of the convention hall and returning each item I stole with a mother-ordered apology. So, it surprised me how easy it was to lie.

"Courtney Hannah Laytner, do you swear on your *patooties* that you returned that watch?" Swearing on one's patooties was the Laytner's sacred family vow.

"I swear on my *patooties*. I even told the man I was sorry for taking it, and I *am* sorry, Mommy. Really sorry."

"You *should* be," Mrs. Laytner said, softening in a way that allowed us to move and breathe somewhat normally again. She and Dava rolled up the windows and put the air conditioning back on. Court stopped crying. Dava reached to put on the radio, but Mrs. Laytner laid a hand on her arm to stop her. "One more thing. I know this won't happen again because stealing is for self-ish, desperate people, and you are much too wonderful, smart, and kind to behave that way, Courtney, but you put Sienna in a position to have to lie for you, which is doubly disappointing. I believe you owe *her* an apology, as well."

"Oh no," I yelped. "She really doesn't ha—"

Courtney kicked me again and mouthed for me to shut up. As she sincerely apologized, I tried hard not to vomit.

✳

Having been briefed on the day's events, Dr. Laytner took his turn to lecture Court for a few minutes while she squeezed my hand under the table to remind me that I promised. We ate flank steak in awkward silence. I kept waiting for them to kick me out, but they didn't think to do it.

Later, I couldn't sleep. Court and Dava were both out cold, and the clock radio said it was 12:16 a.m. I got out of the trundle bed and left their room to sip some water from the bathroom sink. Dr. and Mrs. Laytner were up late. I heard the television and some talking in the den and was sure I heard my name. I crept down closer to listen from behind the stairway wall.

"...she has to go through, you know, but you should've seen her. She was so embarrassed!" She made a little garbled, amused sound, almost a giggle. I heard the ice cubes clinking in Dr. Laytner's glass.

"Well, she's always been a horrendous liar... I still can't believe it was *our* kid and not Sienna. She's more like the type, no?"

"Paul, c'mon," she said, but she didn't disagree.

"What? With the *schmuck* father in the crazy cult house? And no one expects a thing from those kids."

"Well, that's why we let her spend time here."

"Yes, I'm aware of that, Roz, but she's over here quite a bit, and I'm starting to worry about her influence on the girls." More clinking ice. "And if Courtney was shoplifting, I have no doubt Sienna had something to do with it, too," he added. "What about when they're sixteen, and it's beer and boys? Or sneaking over to that wreck of a house to do God-knows-what drugs with those degenerates? Sienna'll cover for her, you know."

"Anyway, they're still young, but I worry about that, too."

"I told you last year not to let 'em get so close," Dr. Laytner said.

A sigh. "She's a good kid, Paul. Smart. And Courtney loves her. This is a *mitzvah* we're doing for her."

That was enough for me. I crept back upstairs.

✳

After another hour of lying awake, feeling my own pulse pounding in my chest and wrists, I had to go. Mr. and Mrs. Laytner had turned in, and I left a note about being sick from all the fried junk food and rode back to Xanadu.

When I got to my room, I fell into my bed before noticing Siddhi's side of our room was empty. He'd cleaned it out. There was nothing left but detritus and dust bunnies.

"Wha–?" I heaved in a whisper. Had he run away? I scrambled

out into the hallway, pacing up and down the closed doors, not wanting to knock on any of them only to wake the dumbass junkies who, at four a.m., were probably in their first hour of sleeping it off and then, at the end of the hall, on the last door across from the laundry closet, "KEEP OUT!" was spelled in segments of black electrical tape.

I knocked gently but audibly. "Siddhi? You okay? What's going on?"

"I moved rooms," said his sleepy voice from inside his new one, the one he chose to live in to get away from me. "Read the sign."

CHAPTER 15

Action-Reaction, 1988 (Siddhartha)

Siddhi watched the videotape until he memorized every deep knee bend and swinging arm, every board grab, ollie, rock, slide, and fall. He began to worship Lance Mountain, a twenty-four-year-old, Powell Peralta-sponsored skater with lanky knees like Siddhi's own. Siddhi was nearing fourteen and had grown about a foot in under a year. Lance Mountain looked happy and free, skating the cracked asphalt of Los Angeles, while sexy girls with sun-kissed cheeks shouted, "Ride the big one, dude!"

Siddhi borrowed the video from this guy named Travis, who'd spent a couple of months living at Xanadu and dealing for Jackson. Travis was a skater dude, who'd grown up in Gainesville and claimed he learned how to skateboard in Rodney Mullen's garage. It all meant nothing to Siddhi until Travis lent him "The Bones Brigade Video." Siddhi found skateboarding intense, visceral, and poetic... Instantly, he was hooked.

Travis had shaggy black hair and was older and taller than Siddhi, with bony legs, pigeon toes, and a praying mantis slouch. His belongings consisted of his board, his spare board, an army duffle of clothes, and a dinged-up milk crate filled with back issues of *Thrasher* magazine, he was all too happy to lend. Siddhi read them top to bottom, savoring each as part of the primer on his new obsession, and—researcher's perk—they helped him learn the argot, to think and talk like a real skater.

As Xanadu rimmed the lower circles of Dante's Inferno, Siddhi kept to his room a lot. He wasn't sure whether it was him growing up or Jackson swimming down that changed how he saw the place, but everything seemed smaller, seedier, and everyone more vapid, aggravated, and lost.

In the past, Siddhi and Sienna had had the run of the place. They built forts in the trees and laid claim to the couch, satellite outposts from the central quarters of their shared, sunny, corner bedroom. They played games and biked around and spied on the old Jackson and his band of sun-tanned, sex-crazed, hippie-hooligans, who danced with or without music, screwed like someone threatened to discontinue screwing, and laughed easily with or without humor. The house was his dad's pleasure dome, but at least in the past, Jackson and his old litter of Babies had had some ideology they perceived as a positive goal: peace and love and health and enlightenment and all that garbage. In hindsight, it was a more well-intentioned fuckery.

Now that his dad had agreed to captain the *Orgazmatron* for the Guy brothers, he was often away, heading back and forth to whatever island, with whatever chick he was banging as first mate. An increase in the cocaine trade and recruitment of Jackson's trafficking and sales force caused further devolutions. The house was a shitpit. Gloria had been a gentle teaser. These days, Xanadu was lousy with junkies. When the hookers began to cruise through the migrating occupation, Siddhi and his pubescent loins were intrigued, but watching paid sex from the sidelines just about ruined sex. Quaalude-fueled, paid copulation was loveless, animalistic, clumsy, drooling nastiness that started with a jonesing addict begging for drugs and ended with two people headed in opposite directions from a little pool of moisture.

If not for his sister and Travis, Siddhi would have been happy to see Xanadu burn down, if only to scatter the filthy new crowd and kill their remaining germs. Yet, the more Siddhi wanted out, the deeper he felt himself wedging in. Like the rest of the new flock, Travis sold pot, coke, and pills for Jackson, and, for the job, he was out most of the night and asleep half the day, but he was young, only nineteen, and pretty friendly. He had a crucifix earring dangling from his left earlobe. He wore a black undershirt with baggy plaid pants and Vans, and he seemed cool.

Siddhi didn't ask about the drugs; he already knew more than he wanted to. Travis never snorted coke that Siddhi could tell, and didn't seem the type, plus he listened exclusively to punk rock. He didn't fit in with the other guys, and Siddhi knew Travis's days might be numbered because his dad was quick to jettison square pegs, and apart from the others who spent their afternoons sunning themselves in the back and side yards by the pool and greenhouse, Travis was out front every afternoon in the driveway, filling the air with the hardcore enmity of The Circle Jerks blaring from his boombox speakers as he skated up a sweat, free-styling on the asphalt.

"Dude that was righteous!" Siddhi had learned to say. "Can you teach me that one?"

"Course, bro'," Travis said, which filled Siddhi with a desperate joy—such was his loneliness, with CeeCee finding every pop-generic, mall-chick reason to disappear and dip in and out like a sun shower—and so he played it cool, not jumping too quickly for a turn.

He watched Travis do a few more tricks first, finishing his own turn, while Siddhi took the chance to ask his new friend a few more questions. "So, like, how long does it take to 'get it?'"

"Depends…" Travis bent his knees deeply, lowering his torso almost to the board and then jumping up, board following his feet, and landing on the driveway, running a few fast steps to get his balance while the board flew at Siddhi.

"On what?" Siddhi asked, handing back the board and feeling stupid about not knowing the "skater" way to handle the exchange. He marveled at the sure commitment of Travis's feet and ankles, his body's ability, like water, to find level, his easy rebounds from gnarly falls. Travis persisted, determined to master his board, to dominate the hard surface below its wheels. Siddhi manned the front steps and continued his education, watching as Travis balanced both feet on his board and rolled forward, and he tried to anticipate the exact second when Travis bent down and popped it all off the ground, using his foot to flip it over in the air before landing hard, both feet up on the board, all four wheels to the ground, everything upright, everything stable.

"Depends on how big your balls are, son," he said, and he dropped the board and jumped back on, kicked off hard, and flipped another trick. Then he circled around back to the stoop, kicked the tail of the board so hard it popped up, and he caught it in his hand and passed it over to Siddhi. "No better time to find out!"

*

Siddhi heard the idling motor and got to the window in time to see Jackson loop the *Orgazmatron*'s stern line from the dock piling and shove off into the waterway, gone without a word, and probably not to return for about a week of back-and-forths to the Bahamas, the Keys, Jamaica, sometimes even Cuba, but Siddhi was long past caring whether his dad remembered his birthday.

While he finished up the trigonometry worksheets he'd Xeroxed at the library, CeeCee burst into his bedroom singing in Spanish, *"Feliz cumpleaños a ti, feliz cumpleaños a ti..."* then segued into, *"Que pequeño mundo es."* Because, she said, "it just feels like they go together."

"You scared the shit out of me," he laughed.

She carried his birthday breakfast, a square pan of gooey brownies ablaze with candles that he knew without counting numbered seventeen—fourteen for his age, one to wish on, and two more to make the total number a prime. CeeCee mothered and nurtured, and Siddhi was a math guy.

"I baked them for you this morning." CeeCee's other life out in the world had a way of caulking up old cracks and somehow making new ones. She rode her bike all over the place and returned with rented videos, filling the "mini bar" in their room with snack cakes, chips, and the kinds of cereal that were meant to be eaten in dry, sugary handfuls. She also brought two apples for them to eat with the brownies "For our health."

At first, he loved the privacy when she found her way back into sleeping over at Courtney's house every Saturday night. He could read until three a.m. without having to listen to her whine about the lamp light or, worse, telling him he was staying up too late, that he needed his sleep to help him grow big and strong, or some such infantilizing shit. Plus, she cleaned the room like three times a day. Every time he got off his bed, she smoothed and tucked until he felt bad about lying back down on it and messing up the pillows. With CeeCee out of the room, he could grab a *Hustler* from Jackson's bathroom and whack it in bed instead of in the shower. It was different with the pictures, better lying down. Some mornings, like this one, after a good session, he was able to fall back asleep for a few hours.

He and CeeCee had an agreement, though, about sharing their room, their home within the house. Siddhi wasn't big on sports or the related, clichéd metaphors, but there was something vital, crucial even, about sliding into home plate. He knew it, and until then, CeeCee seemed to know it as well.

But then CeeCee discovered Mrs. Laytner's decorating magazines and began to renovate. She rearranged the furniture to be "cozy" and "homier," but what she meant was more normal, conventional. And all the shit she did to it really *did* make it better, more organized, and nicer to inhabit, but then there was the problem of contrast.

Their perfect room made the depraved remainder of Xanadu feel like more of an assault, a cross-section from a Hieronymus Bosch painting, where Siddhi, the newly crowned prince of the sullen and irritated, awoke from the long, odd dream of his childhood to find himself trapped in his sister's delusional family sitcom set, but knowing that if he dared open a door or peel back the Afghans and soft, cotton sheets, he'd find that they were draped over a river of crap, gurgling three underworlds beneath Courtney Laytner's home-baked, American dream. Once CeeCee resumed sleeping out every weekend, he found it even harder to bear the dichotomy. He had to move out, and though she insisted she understood, he could see in her face that he'd hurt her.

"You have eye-crispies," she said, and she flicked a bit of sleep from the corner of his eye.

"I must be tired from all the *growing*," he snarked. How old was old enough to handle his own shit?

"It's too hot today," she said. "Court and I want to take you with us to the movies." She and Courtney invited him most of the time when they went places. Sometimes he obliged, but then they chatted on and on about boring crap, clothing trends, their near-constant menstrual cycles, heinous pop music, and *Oh my God, that awesome guy was like one hundred percent staring at you! Nuh uh, not me. Yes-huh, totally you…*

And when he fell back a few steps to get a break, he wound up next to Dava, Courtney's obligatory take along, who met his attempts at conversation with her signature nose blowing, and bewildered stare. Apart from the bookstore, Siddhi had no interest in the mall, and his burgeoning friendship with Travis gave Siddhi every motivation to skip it and stay home. "I'm gonna pass, but thanks anyway."

"Yeah. You'll probably have more fun finishing that math." She wasn't making fun. She was completely encouraging, a pain in the butt even, about his studies, but he'd already finished the math. "Whatever. Maybe you'll change your mind later. Jackson asleep?"

"Gone."

"Oh, right," she said and looked down for a second. Year after year, she managed to scrounge up fresh disappointment, like a bird dropping to the floor after the hundredth time it flies into a shut window. He wanted to beg her to stop torturing herself with gnarly fantasies about how it was all going to be great once they got a new mother or went to college or ran away to Africa, but if he was being real, he relied on her to do the hoping, for his were fewer and less. Maybe his own place. Maybe college. Maybe.

At some point over the next month or two, his dad would realize he missed his birthday and invite him out fishing, flip him some cash, which Siddhi would send down the mouth of the old tube sock under his bed where he'd stuffed most every dollar he'd ever obtained. His current net worth: two thousand and seventy-two dollars and sixty-five cents. He had to be the one to put some money together. If he left it to CeeCee, she'd be forced to try and barter using brownies and fringed leather boots.

She kissed him fourteen times on the cheek, which felt way more normal when he had turned seven. "Make a wish, Siddhi," she said gravely, for each silent yearning seemed to have both of their lives riding on it.

Siddhi closed his eyes and wished for some version of the same wish he wished on every birthday, to be heroic and to matter, to find himself with the power of flight and the balls to rocket hard and fast into the stratosphere, to find real girls to kiss instead of wanking to memories of Gloria's pointy tits overlaid on Elizabeth Shue's body, and to skate the hazy streets of L.A. with Lance Mountain...

"Siddhi, wax is dripping on your brownies!"

Siddhi huffed a big breath and blew out his candles with the force of another year's frustration, and CeeCee cut a big square and handed it to him with another kiss.

"Happy birthday!" she said, "Now, wait here!" She left his room for a minute and returned with a stack of boxes wrapped in splatter-painted newspaper and tied with a ribbon. "Now, open your presents!" She'd bought him many gifts since Christmas, she and Courtney trying to make him over, and thereby babying him, and hence excluding him, or maybe they just needed another focus for their shopping habit—moral CeeCee purposefully filching and then inadvertently laundering filthy coke money by exchanging it for size four Guess jeans—and he quietly fumed over it, furious as the hissing possum they once found in their trash can and failed to tame.

In the shallows of his thoughts, though, he was grateful for the recognition, and he thanked her and tore at the paper, and when it was over, he sat holding his gifts: a pair of black and white, checkered Vans; a beyond killer, Powell Peralta, Lance Mountain skateboard deck painted all white and covered in primitive cave paintings of hunters and animals with medium trucks and the illest, G-Bones street wheels; a pair of parachute pants covered in zippers; and a pack of white undershirts with cans of fluorescent pink and black spray paint; and a box of safety pins.

She'd gotten him perfect gifts, baked him perfect brownies, and still, he wanted to get away from her, because he felt so disgusted with himself for how badly he needed her to make him feel secure in the world, like he had any chance of making it to anywhere in the future, like he was a fucking baby.

Sienna grabbed the boombox, put on his Bad Brains tape, and announced, "Let's snarf these brownies and then go destroy those T-shirts."

*

Siddhi and his skateboard were not fast friends.

He started his practice before Travis woke up. Left foot on the front of the board, he kicked off hard, locked out his knee without meaning to, and took off too quickly on one leg. Lacking the awareness to tell the right leg what to do, it bent, dangled, and flailed, flamingo-like, then kicked out beside him, pulling his body backward, while the foot on the board continued to roll forward and away. Then he automatically leaned into the motion, jerking his arms and torso for balance, until both foot and board reversed direction and swept out from under him, leaving the flamingo leg and the whole rest of him to go splat, smashing down onto his right side, cheek, arm, and shoulder.

Wiping out onto asphalt was a remarkably contrasting experience to younger falls when he climbed too high in a tree and landed on a bed of pine needles and shock-absorbent soil. The force of impact with the driveway jolted back into his bones and muscles, tore open his skin, and drew blood. "Fuck! That hurts," he said, rubbing his shoulder. The sting did make him sit up straighter, manlier, but if Siddhi was going to learn how to do this shit without winding up in traction, he needed to dial back the speed and learn how to fall.

And he really couldn't stomach it when CeeCee came running out the front door with a wet washcloth filled with ice and, without even asking, placed it on his shoulder.

"Oh my God, Siddhi, that was like super bad. I don—"

"What the FUCK?"

He hadn't meant to scream it, and she drew back, startled. "I saw you fall and wante—"

"You were watching me from the window?"

She nodded.

"Because I'm six years old, right? Do you want to go get some fucking toilet paper and wipe my ass, too?"

"Siddhi, don't freak out on me. I meant to help."

Despite the pain and remorse on her face—he could see she knew exactly what she'd done and was already sorry—it didn't stop him from finishing her. "I don't need you to be my mother! Go get a fucking puppy or something." He kicked down hard on the tail of his board, and with a precision that can only happen by accident when you really need to look rad-as-possible, it popped up right into his hand, better than it had for Travis. And fuck if it didn't make him feel like a badass.

"Fine. Whatever." She shook the ice cubes out of her towel and went back inside.

He started again. This time walking the board around the driveway, bouncing his knees, searching for his center of gravity, waiting for Travis to wake up and Miyagi him through the basics.

He took several laps around the giant banyan tree at the center of the circular drive, past the remains of a dozen forts he and CeeCee had built and played in over the years, and then, almost diving, he fell hard again, rolling out fast, bending his knees, and pushing the board from beneath his feet, veering in the opposing direction, landing zombie-like on his other side.

Shoulder and ribs throbbing, Siddhi pushed and rolled through his apprehension, focusing his mind on dissecting the physics of his goal. Slower meant less balance and straight-down contusions. Faster meant more time to find level and a skimming fall, scrapes, and road rash. Either way, blood.

He closed his eyes and homed in on each synaptic flame. Then he opened them back up to examine his cuts. Thick blood rose through his abraded flesh, quivering up into a line of glistening, crimson beetles. He made no move to stop the flow but watched it move with his pulse and burble into a dark pool, fattening until heavy enough to streak down and drip over the edge of his forearm.

Something about the pain, accepting the pain, climbing into and inhabiting the pain gave him a peculiar awareness, awesome and terrible. The pain uncoiled his inner spring, that pissed off, furious feeling that, when he was a little kid, used to make him scream and cry, the angst, the restless worry, the sound and fury and futility of his life, and all that garbage...

He used to have to scream and punch and kick to empty his running thoughts, but falling, slamming, tearing skin proved sharper, faster, and way more effective at razing it to empty numbness. One solid shot of pain, and with no effort, he just disappeared.

CHAPTER 16

Sweet Sixteen, 1989 (Sienna)

When Jackson got back from Nassau with a boat full of product to move, he kicked off with a late-Fall free-for-all, different from the hippie orgy parties of Xanadu's past. Harder drugs and fatter price tags changed the crowd. Gone was the devoted, dancing bear set of tawny granola girls with scarves tied around their boobs and their lanky, meditative male counterparts.

Jackson's pep talks became far less *Vedic* and then disappeared altogether. He focused on matching up dealers with buyers, preying mainly on Yuppies in gray suits, college-boy hotshots who bought kilos and distributed to their college dorms and frat houses, and employees at office parks full of colleagues who loved their cocaine and quaaludes but wouldn't be caught dead at Xanadu. After these folks arrived and made their deals, most stayed to party.

The prep school kids, wealthy, wild, and barely older than Siddhi and me, were another party staple. They pulled through the front gate, five or six to a convertible Beemer, sometimes still in their crested uniforms or in linen Miami Vice suits or expensive jeans. They entered brashly and got wasted immediately, high fiving each other for being the coolest, before heading back to their parents' mansions.

Jackson made his rounds. He wore a chunky, gold Rolex that clunked into people as he patted them on their backs, did a line or two with those who offered, and made his way back out. "Hey there, munchie," he said, barely looking at me as he passed the couch and headed toward his room.

Siddhi skated obsessively with Travis in the driveway. Since moving to his own room, he'd become a stranger.

I ought to have sequestered myself as usual in my room, but the upstairs became a cathouse, and downstairs, drugs and drinks passed around on silver butler trays as "Fat Bottom Girls" blasted out of a new set of seven-foot-high speakers. A young hooker in a white dress danced on the coffee table, her right nipple peeking out each time she lifted her arm. A line of pinkish mucus dripped from her nostril. Another girl lay passed out on the bottom step, probably asleep from the Quaaludes.

I shimmied through people, trying to get out to the pool for some quiet, until I got waylaid by a vision...

The boy lay on one end of our couch, red-eye-baked, and splayed out, watching "Monday Night Football" on the new big-screen TV. I stared from a safe distance. He was tall, tan, and muscular, with long blond hair bunched in a messy ponytail and full, soft-looking lips. He looked close enough to my age to put me at some level of ease—a boy lay on my couch, a boy and not a man.

It had been over three years since I had any interest in romance. Over three years of replaying what happened at the ashram, having nightmares and conversations with myself before, finally, the fear sort of went dormant inside my soul. All of that along with the terrible loneliness gave me the courage to rediscover my interest. Only I didn't realize any of that until I laid eyes on this utterly gorgeous boy. I wanted his attention, and so I figured I could just pretend. I'd *act* bold and controlled, the way Jackson did when recruiting his Babies. Having this strategy and the fantasy of putting an end to my solitude gave me courage.

I hopped onto the couch and flipped my hair to expose my face, neck, and energy to his side. Then, I grabbed the remote, kicked my pink-painted toes up onto the coffee table, and changed the channel to "Newhart."

He groaned. I turned to face him, made a half-smile that I quickly retracted, and then looked back at the screen with a shrug, at once employing Jackson's bravado and adding in the dollop of *chutzpah* that Nana's friends assured me would lead to true love.

"What the fuck?" said the beautiful boy, and to my delight, he sat up, gave me the once over, and smiled back at me, "That was the game, kid."

"Seems like you have a problem, then," I said, still beaming. I laid my arm over the top of the couch, working every speck of my make-believe confidence. "See, this is my television," I said, adding Elsie's suggested wink, poorly conceived and a little pervy in a post-WWII milieu, but it was what it was. Blood rushed through my cells as the boy responded by sitting up and rolling out the rest of his smile. Major tingles, everywhere.

"But it's 'Monday Night Football,'" he said, turning toward me. "C'mon?"

Without overthinking, I moved one sofa segment closer to him. "Let me see if I can help you out with this," I said, placing my fingers on my temples like a mind reader, squeezing my eyes shut. "Wait, I see it…It's in the staaaaars…Yes, yes…San Francisco will destroy New Orleans," I said. I was, of course, full of shit, learning the team names right then from the screen. "I hope you didn't bet on 'em, kid."

As the boy's laugh rippled through the muscles in his shoulders, the muscles in my inner thighs shuddered in kind.

Since the ashram, I'd spent countless hours worrying, after-school-special-style, at how Mojave likely screwed me up for life, but the prospect of this beautiful boy, his touch, his company, and his interest in me, lit my body in a way that felt controlled and manageable. All I could think of was how best to act in order to convince him, entice his brain, to wonder about me, look at me, and want me.

"Why don't I bet you, and we'll watch together?" he said, smoothing a hand over the top of his hair, exposing his bicep, and staring straight at me. His eyes were gray-blue. He was unbearably gorgeous, pin-up hot. And when he said "together," something in me came back to life, and I moved the last sofa segment toward him.

"I'm Edsel."

"You're *what-sel?*" Again, he laughed, tan neck, Adam's apple, and I leaned in closer, maintaining my confidence, keeping total control. "Okay, Edsel," I put my hand down against the side of his leg. "What's the bet?"

∗

The 49ers whomped the Saints, 31–13, which I didn't find particularly affecting, but Edsel required a few minutes to pout and suggested I cheer him up by taking a walk. North Bay Road was peaceful in the night. Dim, amber streetlamps, palm fronds rattling in the breeze; I watched the sidewalk pass beneath our steps.

"So why are you at Xanadu?"

"The dude who used to hook everyone up left for Stanford."

I tried to keep looking at the ground, but I already missed his extra-long Snuffleupagus eyelashes, and I stole peeks at him as we walked. I asked questions, and he answered. He was taking a year off after high school graduation. Like Jackson always did when he first met a Baby, I let him tell me all about himself to make him feel comfortable. Most of his friends had scattered, but he wasn't ready to go to college yet. He was only nineteen. *What's the big rush for college anyway?* He had no siblings because his mom had bad endometriosis, and when he was little, they called him the Messiah, so, like, no pressure. His parents expected him to work miracles, and they were pissed off at him for deferring Emory.

He took my hand, laced his fingers through mine, and held it firmly, like a decision made. The feeling of being so chosen electrified my core. I imagined Edsel and me getting an apartment together, a condo on Collins Avenue with an ocean-view balcony and an extra room for Siddhi.

"You live in that house?"

"Since I was five."

"Jesus, that's kinda fucked up, but y'know, also pretty cool."

My heart pounded from my chest down to my knees as he stopped walking, turned me to face him, and backed me up against some other house's outer wall. "How old are you?"

"Eighteen," I lied quickly, "in January," because I'd already thought it through that he might be put off by my actual age of sixteen. What were a couple of fudged years between star-crossed lovers anyway?

He pressed our interlaced fingers to my hip, threaded his other hand into the hair at the back of my neck, and put his lips on mine. They felt as soft as they looked, and the kiss was slow, deep, and wet. I thought I would freak out, but he wasn't scary. I still felt the upper hand. And so, I kissed him harder and more hungrily.

Kissing and more kissing, the kind that sent live wires of ho-ly-shit-this-is-totally-happening vibrating to the farthest reaches of me, tendrils with tentacles and suction cups that spread out and stuck onto the insides of my skin. He never tried to hold my hands down by the wrists, cover my mouth, or talk nasty. He just whimpered and breathed and sighed. This kiss felt so...mutual.

Edsel embraced me, his arms trying at confidence, and pulled me up into his warmth, and the awkwardness, his pleading touches, and his neediness suddenly terrified me. I lost my breath, panicking at the thought of being known, of feeling that same neediness I used to feel for love, attention, and someone to come and help me. If sex was going to happen this time, I was going to be in control of everything. No needing.

And then the switch flipped again, and I was back to the pretending that had been so weirdly powerfully effective with Edsel anyway.

I premeditated every action. I skipped the wanton surrender and abandonment I'd witnessed with the Babies. The Xanadu sex scenes were dangerous. I stuck with the stuff I learned from movies, choreographed, purposeful sexy, romantic kinds of stuff I could control and dole out without ever ceding an inch of sovereignty. I kissed Edsel on his eyelids, belly, and toes, ran my fingernails over his thighs, and tickled him. I dragged my lips slowly over the fleshy lump of his earlobe and flicked the tip of my tongue lightly back into his ear, exhaling a little breath.

Encouraged, Edsel sought out my breasts. He fumbled with my bra clasp, quickly giving up on it, and instead clumsily worked them out from beneath the underwires so that my bra became a necklace. More kissing. He moved his hand down my belly to between my legs, inside my pants, but over my panties. I squeezed my thighs hard together against his hand before remembering to be cool, that I was running things, and taking hold and removing his hand, making sure to act like it was all too much, as if my passionate reaction to his manliness had stolen my equilibrium. I stumbled backward a couple of steps and looked down for a moment, innocently, coquettishly, and then back up timid and doe-eyed before rushing into his arms again for another passionate kiss.

I wrapped my legs around his waist and hooked them at the ankles. He held me up using his arm muscles and braced us against the wall so I could grind myself against the suffering hardness in the crotch of his jeans. I kept my arms wrapped around his neck and shoulders, squeezing him hard, and then, I got down and gently pushed away, acting embarrassed to have gone so far. I fixed my bra, knowing that forcing him to watch me compose myself would entice him to need me even more.

I made Edsel want me so badly that he begged for one more touch, and I began to really like the game. I was good at it. I felt protected. So, I hinted at giving one more touch, withheld it until just the right second, and then relented before again, pulling back with the shame of it, the all-too-much of it, and making him step away from the wall and see me in the light of the street lamp, have to grab me back, like, please, just a little more of you, until both of us, clouded in the perfume of night-blooming jasmine, braced ourselves against the wall and tangled into its vines.

My first real kiss wasn't the John Hughes experience I'd fantasized for myself, no Thompson Twins music rose in the background or feelings of deep love, but then, it wasn't technically my first anything. And all my movie sex scene acting left no room for me to feel my own experience anyway. This was Edsel's pleasure, provided by me, a small price to pay to try and get someone to really love me.

✱

We cruised around South Beach in his little red Corvette, listening to his tape of Prince singing, "Little Red Corvette."

"Ironic, right?" he said, and I nodded and ran my hand up the inside of his leg and touched him to make him feel manly again, even though he was completely unaware that he didn't understand irony.

The movie romance was going perfectly! Edsel taught me how to surf, throw, and catch a football, and tie my sweater around my shoulders rather than at my waist. With his wealthy upbringing and prep school tenure, it seemed to me that he knew a lot about class and sophistication and the right way to say and handle things, which made it easier for me to overlook it when he started a sentence with *"Supposably..."*

Siddhi, however, was not as deft at overlooking Edsel's imperfections. In fact, he sucked at it. When I tried to sell Siddhi on Edsel's virtues, he rolled his eyes.

"CeeCee, please," he sighed. "Money can't buy brains. That guy is an airhead," he said, "*and* a douchebag." He looked away from me before adding, "And you're becoming one of *those* girls now, the kind who drop everything for boys."

"One boy," I said, pretending he hadn't hurt me. "My *boyfriend.*"

"Yeah, well, I haven't heard much about Courtney in a couple months is all I'm saying."

Neither had I. For a back-to-school treat I'd stolen a bunch of cash and taken her on a shopping spree. She'd cried when she told me, but Mr. and Mrs. Laytner had taken one look at the thousand dollars' worth of clothes I'd bought her and banned me from their house. She rode by on her bike once or twice the week after it happened to give me back the stuff along with the requisite speech she was ordered to deliver, and then she snuck over again just for a hug, but she risked huge trouble with her parents for coming anywhere near Xanadu. And with all the drugs coming through the house, I didn't want her there either. I had to agree with Dr. and Mrs. Laytner: better to have her far away and safe.

Court was a true best friend, though, and refused to leave. So, after a failed bit of attempted cajoling, I had to do a trick I learned from John Lithgow in "Harry and the Hendersons." I made believe she was no big deal to me and that I didn't even want her over. I had an amazing boyfriend now, and he was all I needed anyway. She was a goody-two-shoes, and her parents were jerks who never let her do anything. I put on a cold, bitchy face when she cried. "You're such a baby," I told her. "Stop trying to slum it over here, and just get on with your life." It worked. She left.

"Whatever," I said to Siddhi. He'd been out on the boat, fishing with Jackson when it happened, and I was so mad at him for not being there for me that I simply never told him what went down.

Siddhi and I were no longer roommates. Nights in front of the TV grew quiet, except to ask one another, "How are you?" and to answer, "Fine," and to say, "Sleep tight." He spent his days with that scraggly punk Travis, a Xanadu dealer who looked like Shaggy-Doo with black hair and knobby knees. When the two hung out skating and laughing together in our driveway, Siddhi looked so much older than two months from fifteen, which, instead of concerning me for his well-being, bolstered my belief that I was pulling off eighteen. I let my brother ebb away because it was easier than figuring things out, because he wanted me to, and because I was distracted, allowing Edsel to flow in and fill my sagging life with his robust arms, upturned collar, privileged swagger, and car freedom.

*

Edsel liked to make bets. When I predicted sports wins (dumb luck), I won five-minute hugs and foot rubs. My best win—the Greek name of some minor deity I correctly sourced to Edith Hamilton's, *Mythology*—scored me driving lessons!

Since Edsel proposed most of the bets, silly things—"I bet you I make the next three lights," or "I bet you I can jump over your head," "I bet you I surf this wave all the way onto the beach"—he won often, and his preferred payment never varied. "And if I win, I'll take a *beejay*." I gave blowjobs the way I'd seen them given in orgy after orgy for as long as I had memories. Use the mouth on the top and the hand on the bottom, lick the lips and go slow; use the other hand on the balls, stop to lick the balls sometimes, and after a few minutes, just go fast until the end. Edsel couldn't get enough. I think he might have traded his inheritance for a beejay.

For Valentine's Day, Edsel gave me a gold charm bracelet. It had a ballet shoe and a horseshoe and a four-leaf clover on it, and I felt hard-pressed to interpret what those things had to do with a half-Jewish, hippie drug dealer's wayward blow-jobbing daughter, but it was a gift, a romantic symbol, and I wore it proudly. He also gave me a pale-yellow cardigan and his old tennis racquet "for, like, if we ever maybe play," he said. Edsel thought it was "cool" that I'd grown up in a psychedelic commune, "awesome" that my dad sold drugs, and "righteous" that I'd never attended school, while he'd grown up only three blocks down the street, eating beef *bourguignon* and doing his prep school homework while his mom piped the recording of him chanting his *haftorah* through the speakers in their house.

He sang badly to Tom Petty when we came up for air from fooling around in his car. And he was impulsively fun and even funny. When he made a big deal out of buying me my first Burger King Whopper, I looked up from eating to see a massive glop of ketchup on his left eyebrow, and Edsel, wiping his napkin at the right side of his mouth muttered, "What? Is there something on my face?"

And he did Monty Python bits to make me laugh:

Subway Employee: **What kind of cheese would you like on that, Sir?**
Edsel: (In an English accent) **Have you got any Red Leicester? Double Gloucester? Camembert? York Chester? Venezuelan Beaver Cheese?**

See, he *is* smart, I thought, and funny, and he knew how to break-dance, and he had these V-shaped muscles—Siddhi's anatomy book called The Adonis Belt—that ran like arrows toward his groin.

"People can be intelligent in different ways," I told Siddhi, who didn't even bother to answer, as he lay on his bed with no shirt on, reading. His own body was covered with cuts and bruises from falling off his skateboard. When I brought a potted aloe plant to his room, broke open a bit of it to salve his wounds, he scoffed at me and said, "Fuck off with that shit."

The skateboard helped him keep his knuckles out of the walls, and not a moment too soon, considering he had grown almost as tall as Jackson, his hair darkened to a ruddy, golden blond, and he wore it long and mussed, hanging over his eyes and shoulders. At least, I told myself, he had the skating now and a friend to help him blow off steam and keep him in the driveway and out of trouble.

It was a rainy Sunday afternoon in the 'vette with Edsel, and I'd been on the pill for over a month (Edsel took me to get the prescription), so it was safe to finally relent.

"Please, please, baby?"

"Okay," I said.

"Wait, *really*?"

"Um, yeah," I said between kisses. I hadn't held out because my body didn't want sex, but it was so much easier to run my game and sobering to stay focused on Edsel's pleasure. I might have wanted sex, but in my experience, it was not an act of love. Edsel already told me, immediately after every blowjob, "I love you so much, pretty girl."

So, with raindrops beating down on the hood of his Corvette, Edsel slid his penis inside of me, and it sort of burned down the sides, but was so different than before. Once he moved it back and forth a few times and I remembered I had all the power, it started to feel like love, and since I'd already promised myself that Mojave didn't count, with Edsel moaning and moving as fast as he could go, my real virginity became a distant blur in the rearview mirror.

The sex wasn't tender or candlelit; actually, the seatbelt stuck under me, stabbing at my ribs for the duration, but at least I chose to have this happen, and as a bonus, I got to put an end to the undies-to-undies dry humping that invariably concluded in a blowjob to relieve Edsel of the mysterious, chronic affliction he called, *Blue Balls*.

As a non-virgin and expert actress, I curated an extensive repertoire of moaning techniques and recreated all the worthwhile, romantic movie sex scenes. Edsel followed me around like a drooling puppy as I directed him in the shower, squatting hard and quickly on top of him. In the ocean, I wrapped my legs around him in the shallows, pulled my bikini to the side, grabbed him, and forced him up inside me. Then I pushed him down and got on top of him on the beach. Once, we did it standing up in the handicapped restroom at the Miami Seaquarium, and once—it was burning hot—I commanded him to "take me from behind" over the sunbaked hood of his car. I leaned over and lifted my miniskirt to expose that I wasn't wearing underwear, because I had that act pre-planned, as well.

Contrary to Edsel's belief about his own level of performance, real female orgasms didn't thunder into the light of day after twenty-three humps at a bad angle with one foot slipping off the soap dish. Adding in all my performing and staging of everything only made them more impossible. The movies were dead wrong;

orgasms don't proliferate on boiling hot car hoods or in salty, sandy waves. But I was a top faker. My pleasure cries rose and then crescendoed into explosive squealing when I knew Edsel was close to finishing, and he had no issue believing that my orgasms erupted exactly in time with his, same time every time, due to his evident sexual mastery. Miraculous. He usually held out for a couple of minutes (less than half the time that it took me with my own fingers) until he came, telling me over and over again, "I love you, CeeCee. Love you, sexy girl."

CHAPTER 17

Little Prince, 1989 (Siddhartha)

Siddhi learned over a few weeks how to control his board and how to have a guy friend. Sure, he'd made friends before, but not as a teenager, not as a real grown person, and not for long enough to ever feel like it was real friendship. He warmed up skating each morning while Travis slept in, and when Travis emerged around noon, the two skated out the front gate to Arthur Godfrey Road to buy bagels and sodas at the deli. While scarfing their food, they talked about famous skaters, the gnarliest tricks, who invented them, and who was sponsored. And after chasing the bagels with black and white cookies and more soda, it was back to the driveway for another session before Travis had to go to work.

Life was good like that for over two months until one afternoon, Travis said, "Your dad's totally over me, bro," which he punctuated with a heel flip, spinning his board around and popping it up on its side. He then balanced it on the upper edge for a good few seconds before he jumped and ollied back to neutral. "I'm probably hittin' the road soon."

Siddhi whistled his approval for the rad flip before what Travis said really landed. "Wait. Why?" He heard his own whiny voice sound too upset, way uncool. He took a second to chill out and collate reality, and then, "I mean, what's his fuckin' problem anyway?"

"Jackson doesn't like the way I run my shit."

"Like how?" Siddhi played it cool but lusted to hear someone (other than CeeCee) call out the weirdness of Xanadu. Siddhi never acknowledged that Travis was a drug dealer, like somehow, by not mentioning it, it could simply not exist, but if Travis vociferously admitted to selling weed and cocaine for Jackson, then Siddhi might have had a chance to ask questions to an actual friend about Jackson and why he did what he did. But there was no Sienna to be fucking found, because she had decided to lump her attentions onto Edsel, the Polo-clad Philistine, and his douchebag sportscar. There was only Travis and skating, and he couldn't take the risk, because no Travis and no skating meant all that was left was wanking it and reading and a sure descent to madness.

Siddhi aimed the side of his board for his ankle and scraped the rough edge of the deck down hard against his skin, banking on the resulting pain to white out the thought of Travis leaving for good.

Travis stood on his board, staring at Siddhi for a few seconds, nodded once and smiled a little, like he'd figured something out. Then he rolled into a rad 360 nollie. "I don't know. I don't work hard enough... make enough money... whatever," he said. "And I doubt he likes us being friends."

"Trust me," Siddhi said, "he doesn't give a shit about who I hang out with." Of this, he was sure: Jackson had no notion, let alone enough consideration to even form an opinion about Siddhi having a friend. When CeeCee used to go to Courtney's, or now with the dimwit boyfriend, Jackson rarely asked her whereabouts, and unless he needed to find the scissors, he was perfectly fine with Siddhi saying, "Out, I guess. Don't know," as an answer.

Rather than seethe, Siddhi let his mind hang on Travis's words, "us being friends." So awesome! Travis was a fountainhead of the skinny and dope on every notable skater and all things punk, and Travis regarded Siddhi as a friend. Siddhi hummed with the tenor of the word he'd been waiting so long to hear and believe.

With the ashram kids, he was a pup in a scrappy litter who unified their collective innovation for the majority vote, as boys will do when swings, rocks, sticks, and trees are paired with deep neglect. He remembered the ashram boys' first names, a few birthmarks, scabs, one appendix scar, one milk allergy, and the sound of their high-pitched voices shouting "mine" and "shut up" and "not it" and who liked peanut butter and who could pee the farthest and who hated girls. In short, they were "Litluns"—named for a post-ashram reading of *Lord of the Flies*—and "Litluns" don't know enough to exchange addresses and phone numbers, so there was never anything more to be heard from them. And the teenage girls who hung around Xanadu throughout the years treated Siddhi like the little kid he'd always been, petting his hair, talking down, calling him adorable, even carrying him kicking and screaming out of rooms when he refused to leave, and occasionally smuggling him a candy bar or bag of chips in from the outside world as if he never left the house. They all had been friends, sorta, but not like *friends* friends, not like he and Travis were friends.

CeeCee was not a friend. She had her own category. If Siddhi was like Antoine de Saint-Exupery's *The Little Prince*, the only boy on this tiny planet, then CeeCee was the planet itself, and in the past, she always made him feel secure by being the ground beneath his feet, the hook on which he knew to hang his hat. But that was fucking then.

Now, Siddhi was halfway to depending on Travis, and this dude planned to cut and run? He'd already told Siddhi how he ran away from his parents' house in Gainesville, hitching around, staying with friends until he'd turned eighteen. When Siddhi asked him how he got money, Travis told him about stealing, begging, soup kitchens, and even sex for cash with old married chicks who, "wanted it real bad."

Siddhi craved Travis's Zen with the board and his easy approach to life, treating the scariest things like they were no biggie. When they skated and talked, Siddhi swelled with community, but whenever Siddhi brought the conversation around to Jackson, Travis evaded, and when Siddhi dug in, Travis hocked up a lame excuse and split. Siddhi had to stand down rather than be left alone, and the frustration of giving up got lost inside him and needled him at random like the random stickpin they could never find in Nana's Afghan. Sometimes, they headed a few blocks down to Prairie Avenue to work kickflips on the basketball court, half-cabbing over the cracks and always talking.

Siddhi told Travis about the Ashram. "Bro, there was this old Indian dude, the guru, who made everyone go naked and meditate all day long and acted like he was God." He told Travis how Sienna's friend Wren told her she had a secret boyfriend, but Siddhi knew the whole time that her boyfriend was really the pervy old Indian guru. The guy could have been that girl's grandfather. He knew because he saw them doing it in the woods. Horrible. "But I was like so young, so I didn't have a clue what to do. I think I didn't tell anyone because I was afraid it would make my sister cry or something stupid like that."

Travis told Siddhi that Gainesville had the University of Florida, and their football team was called the Gators. He said his plan was to get his GED so he could go to college there and show his folks how he made it. "I'm gonna major in something rad, like psychology or some shit," he laughed, but because he was "true punk," he planned to take his degree once he received it and set it on fire on their front lawn.

"Why?"

"Because *fuck them*! That's why."

Travis said his dad used to ride him hard about grades, beat the shit out of him, and called him a loser when he failed a test or forgot to do his homework. This was how Siddhi and Travis talked to each other. Honestly. Openly. No shit.

Like it used to be with CeeCee.

He told Travis how Jackson used to be in a band back in the

Sixties and how he sometimes wondered what life would have been like if The Sandcastles had made the big time. And he told him that what he really wanted was to just pack up and move to Nana's condo, where life would be less shitty, more regular, and at least he could go to school. And he told Travis how he didn't even remember what his mom looked like until CeeCee showed him these crazy, naked pictures. "Like, how fucked up do you have to be to covet beaver shots of your own mom?"

"I don't know, bro. Depends. Was she hot?" Travis laughed, flipped his black, scraggly bangs out of his eyes. "Kidding. Kidding. I guess it's not so weird if that's all there is."

"I don't really love her, though," Siddhi said. "Not the way my sister does, and like not the way she wants to believe I do."

Travis Heli popped over a linear tuft of grass perforating the asphalt.

"Nice!" Siddhi shouted, adding, "Listen, don't mention anything about it to her, bro, because she gets all wacky when she's thinking about that shit."

Travis said skating was the thing that saved him. His goal was to save up for an NSA competition, rule it, get sponsored by Powell-Peralta, and travel around competing and selling his own signature decks one day.

Siddhi didn't have a goal to share. He just wanted to get away.

✳

The day he saw Travis come out to the driveway holding both of his boards, the crate of magazines, and his bag, Siddhi knew it was over.

The urge got hold of him, the rage, all of the unfair things coming to a head, and Siddhi left to sit with the throb of nothingness, his restlessness buzzing in him like a trapped swarm, vibrating in his chest, the punch that misses and swings you in a circle, that pricking needle in that fucking Afghan, stabbing the skin and then disappearing only to be almost found when it strikes again, not by your doing, not because you found it, no control, the needle in control, and Siddhi, left with no action, only reaction, found it unbearable.

And he had no other choice but to contain it. He was too old to scream, yell, kick, and punch the doors and walls of the bedroom Jackson always locked him in, a place containing no answers, no comfort, and no means by which to get the big bad thing out of his stupid little body. Too old for that, and so he had to; he had no choice this time. He had to go back to the rolled towel on the top shelf of the bathroom linen closet, he *had* to take out his Dopp kit, unwrap a fresh, clean razor blade, and he *had* to drag it three times across his thigh.

After he made his cuts, Siddhi sat back on the shower floor for a minute, breathing into the release, watching the blood bubble up, linear beads, like grass tearing up through asphalt and streak in several red streams down the cream of his flesh. Only the cutting recreated the numb feeling he used to get from the crying, screaming, kicking, and punching frenzy.

Siddhi could go a while without it, like when CeeCee went on her diet. Will power. He could endure the restlessness for a while, a week or even two, but then he felt hungry for it…The pain, the focus on the blood, made every terrible thing blur out and be replaced with, well, nothing. No need. No lust or want. Just a few minutes of being, something like high. What Jackson referred to as nirvana, except not with any clarity or enlightenment or any guru shit like that, just pleasant gray fuzz, that lasted long enough to keep him from going insane, and knowing he had access to the razor, that he could get numb when he needed, that helped, too.

He quickly cleaned up, bandaged the new wounds, re-hid his kit, threw his clothes back on, and headed out to say goodbye to his only friend.

"Ever thought about running away from here?" Travis asked. "It's scary at first, but then it's not that bad." He nodded his chin toward the house. "If the other choice is this place, you're probably better off. Just sayin', bro, you deserve better." Travis dropped his board and placed his foot on top, the skating equivalent to a key in the ignition. "You're like a genius, Siddhiman, y'know?

You gotta do something with that," he said, poking Siddhi in the head. "Like, go to college with me, or some shit."

Fresh off the razor, Siddhi felt good to go, to roll silently out the gate and never look back, but then he thought of CeeCee, and it all got complicated. He had to let Travis go, though. He wanted better for his friend than to be one of Jackson's do-boy crew.

Travis handed Siddhi the crate of magazines, one-third of his total possessions. "Here, hold on to these for me. You haven't really had time to read them all."

In fact, Siddhi had read each issue at least three times and fully memorized them. He'd never admit to the amount of time he spent by himself in his room reading, but in the past couple months, he likely added about a dozen trade paperbacks, the second half of *Halliday & Resnick's Fundamentals of Physics* (2nd edition from 1986, a college textbook he thought would help with the skating, and *it had*), couple of Hemingway's, couple of Vonnegut's, and a couple dozen trade Sci-Fi's. Book a day. Sometimes two. "No way, dude," Siddhi shook his head, shifting his weight; he pressed the heel of his hand on the new cuts, nonchalantly, not too hard. "That's your collection. I can't keep it."

"Hey, don't flatter yourself, fucker," Travis said, punching Siddhi in the leg. "I'm not giving them to you. I just can't carry them and all the rest of this shit and still skate." He laughed. Nice, Siddhi thought, to end with laughter.

Siddhi told himself a good ending: he would master skating, get sponsored, and go pro, run into Travis at all the competitions. He'd make enough money to get a house where he and CeeCee could move when they were old enough to leave. He would get free for real, maybe even be happy. Then he'd stop needing the Dopp kit and the shower drain.

Maybe Travis could move to the same town, maybe Los Angeles, where they might skate with Lance Mountain. Maybe start a skate shop together...

"Nothing stopping you, bro. Go throw some clothes in that faggot-ass backpack and carry the Thrashers for me? Come with?"

How pathetic did he look to Travis? The thought axed the numbness. "That'd be so rad." Siddhi wished like hell he could go. "But, like, I have Sienna…" He felt the rage return.

"Oh right, fuck. Yeah. I get that. Never see her here anymore. I near forgot about that chick…" He let it hang there, maybe to remind Siddhi it was he who had been his company for the better part of three months. "Your sister's a Betty, bro," he said. "I could work with that."

Siddhi winced.

"Oh shit! Sorry. That bothers you when I say that I'd like to make sweet love to your sister?" Travis was *taking the piss*—one of his awesome punk phrases—teasing Siddhi like a big brother or something. Smiling, Travis started rolling toward the gate. Siddhi put down the crate, walked alongside him.

"She has this jackass boyfriend now. Edsel. Some dumb shit from down the road."

Travis stopped at the fence, unzipped his fly, and *literally* took a piss on the bougainvillea.

"Guy acts like he's doing her a favor, and to hear her talk about him, she agrees. Fuckin' kills me 'cause she's a hundred times better than him and a thousand times smarter and there is no universe where he's anywhere near good enough for her."

"So? Let's go find him and kick his ass," Travis said with a smile, no irony.

"Yeah! Right? But y'know," Siddhi took a step back. "It's not like that. He's nice enough, just a total wanker. I can't fuckin' stand them together, but I think she thinks she's, like, sort of happy, so what can I do?"

"You can go get her and bring her to me!" Travis said, adding a Dracula laugh that gave Siddhi a real laugh.

Then Travis pulled a joint out of his pocket and lit it, and the tension whooshed back in. Travis had never smoked in front of Siddhi before. Siddhi felt the familiar disappointment. He had let himself believe that Travis was clean in the same way he and Cee-Cee were, as a mandatory fuck you to their dad, and he flushed with the embarrassment of his naiveté.

"Y'know how gnarly you get? Like fuckin sweaty intense…I get that way, too. It's total punk, yeah," Travis said. "But trust me," he said, passing Siddhi the joint, "for real, bro, this shit helps."

Siddhi had never gotten high on purpose before—not counting the contact highs from being a kid in the backseat of Jackson's car—but he was determined to stay level with Travis, to keep the friendship even, and he grabbed the joint and sucked his first ever direct hit. After which, he coughed out the smoke in his mouth and continued coughing, yawning, and choking to get the air back into his shocked lungs.

"Oh, shit. You ever smoked before?"

"I have now, bro," Siddhi said and took a second hit.

"Oi! Oi! Oi!" Travis yelped with a fist in the air while Siddhi coughed again. "Fuck all!"

"Fuck all!" Siddhi managed to shout back. He hugged Travis, holding his friend's wiry back a second past casual. Then Travis reached into his other pocket and pulled out a familiar orange fold of cardboard. *Zig-Zags,* Jackson's brand. "Here," Travis handed the packet over to Siddhi, who opened it to find an address scrawled on the inside. "That's the spot," Travis said, poking his own writing. "It's where me and my friends hang out." Travis had other friends! Of course, he did. Siddhi was heated with envy. Until then, he had pictured himself as Huck Finn to Travis's Jim Turner, the two of them stuck together, going somewhere, adventuring, but now it turned out, Travis had been free all along. "Sneak out," Travis said, "and come meet us."

Siddhi wondered how he'd get to the spot and then felt like an asshole when he realized his mode of transport was, at that very moment, parked under his left foot. He nodded and promised to try.

The high widened Siddhi's mind and left him mournful of the old days, sharing a life and a room with CeeCee, taking turns delivering the breakdowns of each of their days, different versions of things done together. Not like her current days, which all starred pretty-boy Edsel Chaiken, watching him do this or that, what he thought about that or this, and how his snotty parents treated her like trash the time they came home and found her over his house. Rich assholes.

Siddhi tried to psych himself up for a new destination, surely a better place than Xanadu, but he roiled with the shameful fear that made kids clutch the legs of the worst parents because "known" seems more survivable than "unknown," even when "known" sucks.

Everything was narrowing. Siddhi cursed himself for his ambivalence. If he went with Travis—a legal adult with undisclosed friends—then who'd be left for CeeCee but Edsel? Siddhi had for so long been the only one to file her sentences in his mind, to keep a record of everything that mattered to her, and to be honest with her no matter what.

But the honesty that once kept them safe had become alienating and risky, like when she described to him the gorgeousness of Edsel's house, all the floral patterns on the sofas and hand-painted Spanish tiles over the stove and blah, blah, blah, and Siddhi responded by reminding her that she wasn't even welcome there, that she didn't fit in with that kind of people, and she got quiet in a way that made her feel miles away. Maybe the address Siddhi held in his hand was meant to spur a new era: Siddhi's time to be good enough. Maybe he and CeeCee needed more time apart...

Travis turned to kick off. "See ya, bro."

"Hey, wait," Siddhi yelped. "Uh, where are you gonna live?"

CeeCee had called Siddhi naïve the last time they fought, when he demanded that she dump Edsel and help Siddhi save up so they could get out of Xanadu and get their own apartment. He wasn't thinking it through, she said, "You're too young to understand how the world really works," she said. "You're acting like a kid."

"I'll be cool," Travis breezed. "I'll crash on my grandma's couch. Most times she doesn't know what day it is. She won't even know I'm there!"

"She won't tell your parents where you are?"

"Bro, I'm legal," Travis shrugged his free shoulder. "Plus, the old bat talks to walls. I bet my folks don't even listen to her."

Siddhi was relieved that Travis had a place to land. He tasted the bitter sweetness of the marijuana on his cottony tongue.

"This Saturday night, bro." Again, Travis tapped the cardboard in Siddhi's hand. "Out front at like ten," he said. Siddhi managed the five-part handshake Travis taught him and threw in a nod. "Radical. Keep practicing, Siddhi-man," Travis said, hoisting his duffel on top of his shoulder, "See ya, wouldn't want to be ya!" he shot Siddhi the bird as he skated down the block.

Siddhi watched until Travis turned from North Bay Road, and then he sat for a long while watching a bee collect pollen from a pink hibiscus flower; it left and came back, left and came back, and no matter how long he watched for, it kept coming back and back and back.

CHAPTER 18

Leaving Them Where They Lay, 1989 (Sienna)

The Chaiken fortune was oldish and stealthy. Edsel's grandparents loved to endow things—The Marvin and Mildred Chaiken Tower at Mount Sinai Hospital, The Chaiken Fellowship to Yeshiva University, The Marvin Chaiken Memorial Library on the Emory Campus, and the never-to-be-discussed millions donated to The Simon Wiesenthal Center and Anti-Defamation League.

When I asked where all the money came from, Edsel explained that his grandparents, who got pogromed out of some shtetyl in Russia-Poland arrived in New York "with nothing," went to work at a box factory and then made their way over ten years to owning it. "And, well," he quoted his father and grandfather, "If you bought something in a bakery in the northern hemisphere in the past forty years, it probably came in a Chaiken paper box."

Paper boxes; such flimsy little things. I wondered about all the other seemingly insignificant items families manufactured that I took for granted, which over decades of toil and sacrifice made them rich: wire hangers, shoelaces, picture hooks, bed pans...cocaine?

Edsel was destined to report for work at Chaiken Paper Box upon his college graduation. Mr. Chaiken expected him to learn, manage, and inherit the business, as Mr. Chaiken had done from Edsel's grandfather. Any college would do, but Edsel had to be a college graduate for how it looked to the employees. Edsel preferred to get high and surf until the sun and salt bleached his shoulder-length hair to blond.

Mr. and Mrs. Chaiken had little patience for what they called his *prodigal phase*. So, if he and I were going to get married and be a real family someday, I had to make it my job to help Edsel appreciate how lucky he was to be handed the gift of a solid future. I checked out a business book from the library and used it to guide me as I edited and retyped his resume. And I denied him sex until he got a job interview, which led to a half-assed job hunt motivated by horniness that, maybe, because Edsel was so dumb-lucky, worked faster and better than predicted.

Edsel showed his parents his resume and promised, by my strenuous suggestion, that he was only deferring Emory (an acceptance he resented because it came about after Mr. Chaiken "made some calls") for a year of *real-world experience*. Once they had an appropriate story to tell people—"*Edsel is taking a year off to gain real-world experience*"—Edsel's parents cordially invited him to reclaim his seat at Sunday brunch. I begged him to bring me, but he insisted it was too soon. Xanadu was only five blocks away from their mansion.

At the brunch, though, he thoughtlessly asked them if they knew Jackson. "That man is the kind of garbage that shames the whole community," Mrs. Chaiken told Edsel in response.

It took a minute for me to register the meaning as Edsel relayed his mother's words. She thought Jackson was low-class, something I already understood about us. We weren't tennis people or Volvo people or people who "lettered" in lacrosse or people who had any *Gray Poupon*. And I hadn't had a vast experience of the upper classes, but I watched "Facts of Life," and I knew I was more of a Jo than a Tootie, Natalie, or Blair. How could I possibly have been surprised by being called "garbage?"

I was surprised, though, that she saw the truth so easily, and it made me feel naked in a bad way. Assuming I had been able to digest and accept that I was "garbage," Mrs. Chaiken had thrown in "shame;" not much chance of coming back from being a shame. Jackson said that shame was the power that fueled all fear, and even I could see how being ashamed had a way of shading all the good things by shining a bright light on all the bad ones.

Thing was, the Joneses lived in the shadows, and the Chaikens lived in the light, so who was I going to believe? I wished more than anything for them to be able to accept me. I'd even fantasized about them adoring me. Maybe, if I did everything right and impressed them enough, there might be a place in their family, a little notch they might sterilize, especially for the daughter of a shame?

"She called your dad a cocaine cowboy," Edsel added. "With his disgusting group in that tumble-down house." I shut my eyes for a minute as my innards sunk several inches, squashing themselves in my guts. I knew Edsel might stop telling it straight if I cried, but after "disgusting," the jig was up; no reason left to hold anything in. People knew. They knew all about us. It's one thing to be disgusting and a whole other to be called out for it, known for it. The Chaiken's acknowledgment that we were disgusting upped the shame a thousand percent. "Don't look mad, grouchy girl...I mean, like, I wasn't even gonna tell you, but then I thought, isn't it better, y'know, to hear the truth?"

The Chaikens had been extremely chilly the one time they got home early from the Miami Heart Institute's future Chaiken Telemetry Pavilion fundraiser ball and found their only son in their chef's kitchen with the likes of me, eating leftover *coq au vin* and watching "LA Law."

I thought it was because I was dating their coveted baby boy, like, of course, they'd loathe me, the way parents always did in the movies, rejecting on the grounds that I was "doing it" with their namesake.

"You told me to ask them," he said. "You started this," he said, rubbing my back when I cried. For once, I understood something about Jackson. Once you find yourself so far below the boundaries of what is good, so lost in the darkness that you no longer see any hint of light on the horizon, it almost seems insane not to just keep heading down.

Low-class. Shameful. Disgusting. Cocaine cowboy. Dreck… What in the hell was I supposed to do to surmount my station in the eyes of the Chaikens, my future in-laws, maybe grandparents to mine and Edsel's potential babies? Not a thing.

*

Edsel pulled into the municipal lot at Haulover, where we'd park in the shade and have sex before he planned to spend the afternoon surfing while I intended to sit on the beach and read *A Tree Grows in Brooklyn*. He put the car in park, popped in the tape marked SEX MIX.

"I got a job, kid," he said.

"Oh my God!" I yelled. "That's amazing. I am so proud of you!" I leaned over to him in the driver's seat, he put his hands up my shirt, and we kissed the best kind of kiss, the one for kissing's sake.

"Yeah, awesome, right? It's pretty sweet…G.O. at Club Med," he said, letting his hair down, running his fingers through it to smooth it out, and then carefully gathering it back up and retying it in a low ponytail. "It stands for *Gentil Organisateur*." He'd been forced to take French for all his years at Miami Country Day School, and after so many summers spent with the Chaiken cousins in Nice, he was more than fluent.

I listened to him describe the job while *"Let's Go All the Way"* played in the background. Then he gave me the look, and I yanked his shorts down to his knees and stroked his erection while he tipped his head back and closed his eyes. I took off my bikini bottoms, squatted over his lap on the seat, and lowered myself down onto him until he made a sound that told me I hit the bottom. And I stared out the tinted sunroof and thought of Club Med.

Jackson had taken Siddhi and me near there once when we were little. We flew on Chalks, a seaplane that landed in the ocean, and we stayed in another broken-down ashram on Paradise Island, where Jackson left us with one of his girlfriends for a few days while he did business in Nassau. We slept in camp cots, ate vegan porridge, and did yoga.

On the beach, we met Josh, a boy from Babylon, Long Island, whom I pictured as living in a biblical stone tower. Josh taught us how to tell his shirt was real Polo because the horse only had three visible legs, and he snuck us into where he was staying down the beach at Club Med and gave us ten plastic beads to trade to the bartender for virgin daiquiris. I couldn't remember the face of the girlfriend Jackson brought with us—I think her name was Wendy or Tracey—but I remembered Josh, his freshly cut, side-parted hair, the pink polo player on his mint green collar shirt, and how after his first sip of banana daiquiri, he said, in his wonderful accent, that the daiquiri only tasted, "mediocah."

"Wait, hang on a sec," I said and stopped humping but thought better of it and started again.

"Oh, God, yeah," said Edsel.

"Edsel, I can't move to Paradise Island. Jackson works with these bad guys who, I think, live right near there. I just…I mean, can't we just…"

He looked up from where he had his face wedged into my chest, "It's not in the Bahamas. There are a lot of Club Meds, kiddo. Shh."

Relief washed over. I readjusted my backside so that my lower back stopped hitting the steering wheel. "Oh, then where?"

"Shh. CeeCee, I'm gonna come!"

*

Goodbye calls? Beg me to stay calls? Nana was first. "Hello Sweethawt, what's doin' with you?"

"Nana, I'm thinking of going with my friend on a long trip. To Morocco, actually. I am not sure about leaving, but it seems

like a good chance for me to do something new and find a job
and a schoo—"

"I don't know what in the hell you think you're doing!" I got
excited about her reaction until I realized she was hollering at
someone in the background. "Oh, for Christ's sake!" And then
back to me, "Siennala, I'll have to call you back when this moron
electrician gets his act together." And she hung up before I could
say anything else, which was her way.

Next, I called the Laytners. "Oh, hello, Sienna. So nice to hear
from you," Dr. Laytner stated too formally. It had been over a
month since we'd spoken. Awkwardness abounded. I made small
talk and asked for Courtney, who was spending two months in a
summer program at Yale University. I hadn't even known about it.

The last call was to Aunt Paula. I was sure it would cost Jackson a fortune in long-distance charges, but I dialed the number
she left anyway, and after she filled me in on how happy she was
to be living in India and so much in love, and how her fifth husband Prakesh's sister taught her how to make *saffron pooran poli*,
I filled her in on my situation and asked her what she thought.

"I think nobody ever really regrets it when they finally gather
the courage to run away," she said.

*

Edsel held the cab in the driveway. I'd packed my purse, plane
ticket, passport, and the Franny and Zooey paperback Aunt Paula gave me before she left for Delhi. I included the jewelry box
filled with my life's spoils and my five pictures, all stuffed into my
Bee Gees backpack, which looked so much smaller than it used
to, back when I believed with all my heart that it had room to
hold everything I'd ever need. The cash I'd saved (meaning found
left around the house over a couple of months) came to twelve
hundred dollars.

A second bag was required, a small duffle for my clothes, me
flipping the bird at Jackson's one-bag rule. I decided to exhume
the treasure, and I almost went outside to the garden shed to fetch

a trowel, but then I passed Siddhi in the kitchen, and we shared a PB&J. When he chewed, his face looked so much like he did when he was five or six years old: feathery blond hair down his back, cartoon-puppy eyes, and pink cheeks from the exertion of skating.

I decided that, for Siddhi, the baby part that I could never leave, versus the current, grown teenager I needed to get away from, that the buried treasure had to remain in its place, just in case... If Siddhi had an emergency, I could direct him to the spot and solve his problem remotely, and knowing I had the power to do so helped me squash down the intense guilt I felt for convincing myself I had a right to leave for reasons that branched far beyond my one and only reason to stay.

I deserved to go do something purely for my own good for once in my whole life, and I'd dreamt of living in Africa since I could walk! Didn't I have a right to take care of myself and my future? Was I supposed to be my own mother and Siddhi's, too, at the tender age of sixteen and a half? Plus, with him on the other side of puberty, it felt ridiculous to ask him if he'd brushed his teeth, and moreover, it aggravated the hell out of him. He didn't need the kind of stuff for which I was capable anymore, and what he did need, whatever that was, I needed it, too!

We'd spent over a decade at Xanadu, plus or minus a few forays into shittier, less suitable locales, and I didn't stop rationalizing until I had convinced and persuaded and pretty much hypnotized myself into believing, full-on, that my leaving would be great for both of us, because in Morocco, I could grow up and find answers, and when I had, I would send for and rescue Siddhi. And I felt good about it, brilliant, for it was the best plan for everyone involved, even Jackson.

Not to mention that Siddhi—my one reason to stay—rarely felt the desire to spend his precious time with me anyway. He and I buzzed by each other, me coming and going from where Edsel and I were off to, and he on his way to skate, eat, or whatever gross teenage boy nonsense he did with all the hours he spent in the bathroom. The effect was that, at least on Siddhi, I didn't seem to have an effect at all. This was tough love. Not for too long. We'd blown entire years in the backyard. I was leading by example that we didn't have to blow another decade in that fucking house! And when Siddhi felt ready, I would know and then help him do the same.

The treasure would be left, unknown but to me, and saved for undeniable purpose.

Siddhi and I shared a long, tearful (me) goodbye earlier that morning with at least fifty hugs and promises to be good (him) and to write (both of us) before I walked him out, watching as he took off on his board and rolled out of sight.

The house was dead quiet. I left my bags near the shoe pile at the front door, and headed out back, through the sliding glass doors into the Xanadu yard. The avocados were ripe, and several had fallen off the trees and squashed on the weedy ground. The iguanas were too distracted by the food to scatter as I stepped past them toward the *Orgazmatron*, bobbing in its slip. As I walked the path to the dock, a sailboat idled by on the canal, and a little boy in a baseball cap, with zinc oxide war-painted on his nose and cheeks, waved from the deck.

I'd pre-planned how I wanted my Jackson-goodbye to go: me hugging him and saying, "Hey, I want you to know that I'm moving away with my boyfriend for a while. I have my plane ticket already. I'll be on my own now, so rather than try to stop me, just wish me luck, and tell me to take care." The expectation was for Jackson to look at me and see that despite his manifold failures, I'd grown into someone functional, good, maybe even beautiful, and at this realization, he'd choke up and say, "I am so proud of you, munchie. I know that I super sucked, and I'm sorry. I'll do better. It'll be different from now on. Please, please, don't go."

I boarded the boat and traversed the section of the cockpit where, years ago, I thought Smiley Guy was going to shoot Jackson in the head for the money I stole. The door was open as usual, and I peered inside to find the main salon deserted and humming with the white shush of the generator diluting "Zeppelin IV" playing on the stereo. Down the three carpeted steps, I walked back to the bedroom, and through the wide-opened cabin door, I saw Jackson and an unknown woman—too young to ever be a mother or even a friend to me—writhing in a big fleshy pretzel. Not surprising.

Jackson consistently obliterated my after-school-special delusions as fast as I could whip them up. I seethed with anger at my own self for being so stupid as to think anything would be different this time. Why would he, who possessed the power to fix it all with little more than a heartfelt *don't go,* be anything other than—for all his moments really— indisposed?

CHAPTER 19

Bye, Bye Buddha, 1989 (Siddhartha)

The whole thing got fucked up the week before, just after a late-night snack run. Bored and bummed out, Siddhi had smoked a joint solo, skated to Amoco for Devil Dogs, and lost track of time munching out and rereading *The Watchmen*. By the time he got back to his room, Sienna was sitting on his bed, arms folded, worry-faced, ready to act like his fucking mother.

"Where've you been all night?"

"What?" He had never been high in CeeCee's presence because he had always had the time to dodge her by faking sleep or hopping in the shower. Not that she even looked past her boyfriend…But this time, she had him cornered, wreaking with bloodshot eyes, mussed hair, and Little Debbie *schmutz* on his T-shirt. So busted!

"Siddhi, what…what happened to you?" She plucked a leaf from his hair, to which he flinched like she had the cooties, and then flopped onto his bed, trying to look casual.

"Nothing," he muttered. But his mind thrashed to prepare a better excuse.

"Wait. Are you…" She stood up and sniffed near his neck and shoulder. Siddhi had recently eavesdropped on the upstairs phone as CeeCee confided to Aunt Paula that she really wanted to go with Edsel, but she didn't know how to leave, *poor Siddhi*, home alone. "Wait! Are you *stoned*?" Siddhi was sick of being babied.

"That thing is so poseur," he said, wishing he could tear the gold charm bracelet from her wrist and chuck it into the bay.

"What?" She looked at her bracelet. "No. You're not doing that. Don't change the subject." But he knew she had heard him.

"I don't need you to worry about me, *Sienna*," he mocked her tone. "We wouldn't want to disturb Edsel's beauty sleep."

"Who ARE you right now?" she asked, and Siddhi wondered to himself about the same fucking question. He had no idea. Only that whoever he might become, he was never going to get there if she kept trying to handle him. She paced the center of the room, stopped, stared at him as if trying to make something out, shook her head, and resumed the pacing. "Hey, new guy, could you get in touch with my actual brother and tell him he's in big fucking trouble?"

"Oh yeah? Who cares? Last time I checked, my mom was dead, and my dad was a junkie drug lord!" The first tear spilled over the hurt in her eyes, leaving a wet comet tail down her cheek. Her apparent disappointment hung on her face like a mask she wore to separate her success from his failure, encouraging him to hate himself just a little more.

She stood staring, sniffling. "Don't go bad, Siddhi," she pleaded. "Please don't. I can't live with two…"

"No one's holding you hostage here, pretty, pretty princess." He nestled himself into his reading position and blocked his face with his book because it was easier to look away. "Why don't you just get out of here?" He felt awful about being nasty to her. He knew that she meant well and that he probably needed her as he always had, but he didn't *want* to, and something had to change. Honestly, he felt sorry, but rather than bring himself to say as much, he shrugged and went on with the fake reading until she stormed out and slammed his door.

As he sat on the floor of the shower, calming himself by bleeding down the drain, he fantasized about buying a cookbook and wondered why he had never thought of it before. He could follow a recipe and cook his own meatloaf. Maybe the point was to stop waiting for someone else, stop waiting for Jackson for sure, and for Aunt Paula. Stop waiting for Nana and her rancid refrigerator and her burnt pots and her kitchen bathroom that smelled like coffee shits and *Oil of Olay*...and he had to stop waiting for CeeCee!

When they were little, it had been fun to play her games: *Let's get her to be our mommy! Let's make this cozy hut into our new home! Let's play school!* Siddhi grafted himself to her notion that they had the power to drum up goodness simply because they wanted to... His dream had been an extension of *her* dream, that they would wake up one morning with a nice, new mommy, and their fixed family would move into a clean house like Courtney's, and they'd all eat that perfect meatloaf from the ketchup ad, with the baked-in eggs that showed up like protective eyes in every slice.

Siddhi had no more stomach for the disappointment that came from dreaming. The evening after she busted him high, after enough silent treatment that they both got tired of acting pissed off, CeeCee acknowledged reality.

"I get it," she said. "Things are different now." They were in her room. Siddhi sat on the blue velvet loveseat in the spot where his bed used to be. "But can I at least figure out how to get you into high school? Please?" She sat on her bed, rolling her favorite bits of jewelry into a few T-shirts, and stuffing one after the other down into her duffle bag. She still suffered from her delusion that if she had had a regular, normal family, nothing would have gone wrong.

"What's the point?" he said. "I'll be fine. Everyone gets fucked up somehow."

"Shit," she said. She dropped her backpack on her bed, sat next to it, and wept. "I can't..." She looked about to cry, her ambivalence seeming to pull her bilaterally outward, like taffy, thick on either side and the connecting bit stretched dangerously thin in the middle, threatening to break in two. Should she go, or should she stay with him in their crumbling limbo, waiting for what and for whom to rescue them? The occupation was so aggressively passive it made Siddhi sick. When she pinched her eyes shut like she always had when avoiding the truth, he threatened her.

"If you don't go, I'll run away," he said. "I'll disappear. You hear me? I won't come back. Travis'll teach me how to do it, so you'll never ever find me."

"Siddhi, c'mon," she sniffed.

"I swear. I'll do it." He hadn't been convincing, and his earnest fervor made her laugh. Not the pretty laugh that fluttered from her throat when he said something funny, but rather the involuntary, queer giggle she let slip, like the bursting humiliated *gah-hah* that slips out when someone walks in on you wiping your ass. They lived in the gray area now, no longer on the same page, not even in the same book! Siddhi understood that he didn't have all the answers, and he wasn't afraid to let the unknowns play out, whereas Sienna, clawed to hold on, out of what, sisterly love? Loyalty or good conscience?

"This is crazy," she said. "Look, I can be around here more," she offered. "Like before, and it'll be great."

But Siddhi just wanted her to stop bargaining, hovering, and coddling. He knew that to be brave enough to make a go of it for himself, he would need her gone. She taped the rips in his posters, folded his laundry, changed his sheets, and fluffed his motherfucking pillow. She didn't know how to back up and let him grow up. And he loved it, relied on it to a humiliating level that bordered on creepy. Telling CeeCee not to let the door hit her on the ass on her way out was his way to give them both what they really needed, less risky heuristics with the bonus of not witnessing each other's potential failures.

"Sienna," he said, rather than call her CeeCee, and her eyebrows noticed. "You already know you are fully out of here, so please, don't use your fear bullshit to try and give me a mindfuck, okay? I really don't have the patience to handle you all the time anymore, so please, just grow the fuck up!"

*

They said their goodbyes down in the driveway. CeeCee gave him the Club Med address and number, a promise to write, a pint of tears, and several rounds of hugs and kisses. Edsel was a moron and a priss, but he was her ticket to adventure, an opportunity to make her own new life and friends. Siddhi told himself these things because he wanted to stop gargling Scope to keep her from smelling the weed. He wanted to stop wearing long pants to hide his cuts and bruises. He wanted to stay out later than the curfew she had no right to impose.

"Have an awesome time," he said to her and meant it.

"Try not to bust yourself up too much while I'm gone, okay?" She teared up again and curled his hair behind his ear, which he wanted to like but hated. "I love you the most," she said.

And he told her he loved her, too. "Later, alligator," he said and then skated fast down the block, hating himself even more for how much he wanted to get away. When he got back home, she was gone, really gone, she and that Gatsby-little shit she'd weirdly and faithfully chosen to love.

*

The address looped Siddhi's brain like a stuck song. No way for him to guess what lay at that location, but the address itself, and the universe of possibility Siddhi assigned to it, gave 1445 Washington Avenue the promise of Oz... He had only to skate to Arthur Godfrey Road, over the bridge, and down Collins toward South Beach and 14th Street.

The hours slogged by as Siddhi paced the room, awaiting whatever gnarly sugarplums he sought to discover after dark. He read until two, worked *pop shove-its* for a few hours in the driveway, landed a fucking-brilliant *impossible* following something like fifty wipeouts, and then jetted to the shower on a nuclear blast of triumph, recalling something Travis once said, "Bro, every time I land an *impossible*, my dick grows half an inch."

Siddhi stepped out of the shower stall and stood naked, examining himself in the mirror. His biceps were nothing more than veiny little dinner rolls strapped to his upper arms, his pecs, skinny sand dollars. He had baby muscles, starter muscles, no mass to any of them, and a hairless chest apart from the contusions, ruddy patches of road rash, black-purple splotches of bruise, and on his thighs, fresh and fading lines in sets of three. What he saw was a little boy in an empty room with no mother or father or grandmother or aunt and, most vitally, no sister.

He unzipped his kit, turned the shower to a dribble, and sat on the tile floor of the stall. He unfolded the wax paper covering the new blade and found a clean expanse of skin on his right inner thigh. He breathed deeply in as he sliced the first line, and the searing burn delighted him as the blood leached out and the peace seeped in. He cut a second and then a third, paying close attention to the rubbery resistance given by his own body against this violation, this breach of his own innocence, and he sat for a few minutes, breathing, and resting his head on the wall, watching blood watercolor the tiles to pink, widen and spread, and narrow again to streak down the drain.

When he was about six, Siddhi once climbed the pine tree closest to the garden shed, so far up he was scared to get down. CeeCee didn't know what to do, but she couldn't just let him sit there, so she climbed up to rescue him until they were both too high, and she, too, was afraid to climb down. They spent what felt like hours shouting for a grown-up to come out and help, but no one heard or wandered outside. Siddhi remembered being committed to sleeping in the tree. CeeCee sighed and told him they had no choice but to do it themselves, and so they took turns watching each other, leading each other's feet, branch by branch, until they both got safely to the ground.

Siddhi cleaned and dressed his cuts, wrapped a towel around his hips, and took another look in the mirror. He crossed his arms to puff up his chest and tensed his abdominals, trying to make out Huck Finn through the filter of shower steam. Unimpressed, he headed downstairs to his joint in the kitchen, lit it, hit it, and left it smoking in an ashtray. He went to push his annoying, tickly hair out of his face and had another rad idea. He grabbed the sharpest knife from the block and raced back to the bathroom, where he flipped his head forward and used it to saw off his hair, a clump at a time, an inch or two away from his scalp at random spots until he had severed it all. He used CeeCee's blow dryer to defog the mirror, saturated what was left of his hair with a glop of her Dippity-Do, and for the hell of it, he backcombed the remaining inches into ratty, knotty spikes and then hung his head between his knees and blew the gel dry upside down so that when he flipped his head back up and checked his reflection again, he could barely see himself beyond the blaze of his smile.

*

Siddhi found 1445 Washington Avenue. He rolled down the street toward the haze of burning bulbs in the deco marquee. The Cameo Theater was once this elaborate 1930s nightclub, but by the time Siddhi skated up, the place had been ransacked by time and was billed almost exclusively for hardcore concerts. On the old-style marquee, hula-hooped in pink neon, Travis's invitation was spelled out in black letters: *TONIGHT: D.O.A.*

He knew the band. Travis had given him an old cassette of theirs. "Hardcore '81." D.O.A. was righteous punk.

Siddhi popped his board up, cuffed it under his arm, and walked over. With his enmity and the hacked-up hair to back it up, he blended in with the rest of the fans hanging around out front. A cloud of cigarette smoke hovered and stunk beneath the overhang created by the marquee. Jackson always banned cigarettes because they reminded him of his parents, which had the effect on Siddhi of making the whole rest of the world, when he was out in it, smell like cigarette smoke.

Siddhi backed himself up to the wall. No Travis...

He was still high and spent a few minutes busying his stoner brain. He stared at the sign.

TONIGHT: D.O.A.

TIGHT ON A DO.

NO AD GOT HIT.

O, NIGHT TOAD.

GITA, DON'T HO!

...when anagrams ran dry, he counted twenty-two punks loitering out front, adding himself made twenty-three. Prime.

A guy in a linen suit and pink T-shirt strolled past, hand-in-hand with a lady taller than him, her legs long and tanned, wobbling on stilettos. They chatted and smiled at each other and looked at the punk kids with curious suspicion as they passed by, and Siddhi was tempted to follow them down the street and throughout their lives to see if they'd have kids and fuck it all up. Then he lost interest in them and turned his attention to a skinhead dude making out with some pale chick up against a lamppost, and it struck him at that moment. The loneliness. So, he searched for a girl to imagine himself kissing, touching lips and tongues, breasts in his hands, sharp fingernails scratching down his stomach toward his...

A hard knuckle-punch landed sharply on his thigh, and he whipped around toward the pain. "What the fuck?"

"Relax, bro," laughed Travis. "I was like eighty percent sure it was you." He threw his arm roughly around Siddhi and pulled him into a friendly headlock. "C'mon," he said and dragged Siddhi toward the pizza place one door down. Travis had since shaved his head, leaving only a black curtain of bangs that stretched down below his chin. He had two safety pins jabbed through his left earlobe.

"You look different," Siddhi blurted, thinking himself a little boy and asshole for stating the obvious.

"You should talk, Sid Vicious!" Travis said and smacked Siddhi's cheek. And Siddhi felt their old rhythm, and he was at once relieved that their friendship, the ease, or whatever, was still alive.

The pizza place was packed with Cameo overflow. Punks

were standing and sitting everywhere, eating and wandering the crowded restaurant amid fumes of cigarettes, stale beer, and garlic. Travis bobbed his head to *"Holiday in Cambodia,"* playing on a hanging speaker on which someone had slapped a piece of pizza cheese-side-down. Siddhi watched a girl with bleached hair, a short skirt, and kohl-blackened eyes. He deconstructed her in his mind trying to figure out what she looked like without makeup to decide whether she was hot.

Travis grabbed his two slices from the counter, leaving the paper plates. He stacked the slices one on top of the other, folded them both in half, and took a huge bite.

"Whendyou go to the beauty parlor?" he asked Siddhi through his mouthful. Siddhi put a hand up to feel the hard spiked mess of his own hair and grinned. "Looks alright," Travis said warmly. "Hey, you bring cash?"

"Oh. Uh, yeah." Siddhi pulled out two twenties, half of what he'd brought. He hoped to spend as little as possible and return most of the cash back to his tube sock.

"Awesome," said Travis. He grabbed both bills, "Food and tickets," and ordered Siddhi two dollar-fifty slices of pizza and a fifty cent can of coke. The Cameo ticket would only cost fifteen. "Should we try and sit?" he asked, having mimicked Travis's pizza-stacking technique, which freed his other hand to carry his board.

"Yeah, it's covered. Follow me." Travis led him down the wood-paneled walls of the pizzeria, carved and graffitied top to bottom with dates, band stickers, and drawn logos, messages to enemies and pledges to friends, love-hate confessionals, poems, and curses.

Siddhi read a good one on a nearby wall: *I sat with the Queen at tea, and she asked of me, "Do you fart when you pee?" I replied with due wit, "Do you belch when you shit?"*

Scrawled above that one, in different handwriting, the wall said, *Jessica will suck you off for five bucks!*

Siddhi tried to stop himself from searching for Travis's old mop of black hair, forgetting, and losing, and then remembering and re-recognizing his stubbly head, as Travis pushed ahead of him and stopped at a back corner table. Two punks sat hunched over their food. They nodded coolly, acknowledging Travis.

"Oi! This here's my friend Siddhartha Jones." The big one smiled, the scary one sort of glared. And then to Siddhi, Travis said, "Yeah, so, this fat fucker is Christian." Travis punched the big one in the thigh, his violent calling card.

Definitively overweight, with caterpillar eyebrows and a demonic grin, Christian sported a spiked Mohawk with a Neapolitan dye-job; chocolate at the roots faded to vanilla in the middle and then it went strawberry at the tips. He wore a white T-shirt, plaid suspenders, and ripped jeans; under the table his feet rolled his board back and forth on the tile floor.

"What's up?" said Christian, holding up a clenched fist for Siddhi, who clued in and bumped his knuckles. "Nice hair." Siddhi liked the compliments and being the youngest in the room by at least a couple years, he'd take what he could get.

"You hungry?" Travis teased Christian.

"Up yours, asshole," Christian barked. Then he smiled huge, stood, and whaled Travis in the arm.

"Shit! You fat bastard! That fuckin' kills!" Travis rubbed his arm.

"Whatever, Grandma's boy," Christian answered. On the inside of his right forearm, he had a tattoo of a hand shooting the bird.

"And this," Travis said, with more finality and something like deference in his tone, "is Fox." The abrupt respect for the tall, skinny sneering kid with safety pins stuck through his ear, eyebrow, cheek, and nose indicated to Siddhi that Fox was the ringleader. "He's a phenomenal vert skater. Serious, bro."

Fox continued to stare, beady and relentless eyes searching Siddhi. His right leg thumped constantly, and then he seemed to decide about Siddhi, and he allowed one corner of his mouth to edge up into half a grin. He nodded in Siddhi's direction.

"Guys," Travis said, "Siddhi here's tough as fuck and good on a board. Yo! Be nice to this kid."

Fox sunk his grin, tipped his chin down. "I'm not fuckin' nice to anyone, T," he exacted in a chilly tone that revved Siddhi's pulse. "*Siddhartha*, huh? I read that book...Herman Hesse. You read it?" Siddhi flipped his chin up once, like he'd seen Fox do, presenting himself as tough. "Yeah, Travis said you're some kind of genius or something." Fox grabbed the ass of a beautiful punk girl walking past his chair. She turned and punched him, but she did it smiling, and Siddhi tried not to smile, too, because the whole move was the epitome of gnarly. This guy had something, at once keenly untrustworthy and totally badass. Then Fox was back on Siddhi's case. "You think you're so smart?" he challenged. The others went mute, waiting and watching. Fox stared.

Siddhi felt at a loss for what to do. He sensed enough to hang back, play it cool, but he also wanted to make a dent. "Two plus two is four," he said, in a sort of Lenny from *Of Mice and Men* voice. "I think."

Fox looked him up and down for an awkward minute. Siddhi stood firm, tensed his muscles, and kept his mouth shut, in a show of machismo, and stared back, took a big bite of his pizza, chewed, and swallowed, like it was all no big deal. Travis wouldn't let these guys do anything bad to him.

Fox stood up, popped a pepperoni into his mouth, and then, abruptly, quit leering and smiled wide, "*Siddhartha*," he hollered, clapping Siddhi on the back. "You're the fuckin' Buddha, bro!"

Next thing Siddhi knew, Fox grabbed him in a bear hug and bounced him up and down, and the other guys shouted, "Oi! Oi! Oi!" until Siddhi felt popcorn pop all through his spine and the fireworks of friendship, loud and bright, shot off in his head. Fox set him back down, gave him an approving smack in the face—that hurt like hell—and with Fox settled, everyone relaxed.

"You mosh, Buddha?"

"I what?" Siddhi stuttered, too drunk on ratification to be listening. They finished their food, taking frequent breaks to insult and assault one another, major laughs, no impetuses or apologies. Siddhi, both an outsider and a part of the scene, simultaneously being himself and watching himself interact with his new pals.

"Hey, motherfucker," Fox called to a younger punk kid two

tables over. "If you show your face in here with fake Docs again, I'll fuckin' brain you with my real ones!"

Siddhi waited to get a read.

Then Christian chimed in, "That you, Johnson? You freakin' *faggot*." And smiling to Siddhi, "Dude's a total homo."

And then Johnson, fattish, too clean, laughed and choked on his soda, to which Travis added, "If you fuckin' die, Johnson, I call your fake Docs," and everyone, even Siddhi, bent over pissing themselves with laughter.

He'd never bring it up to these guys, but the whole experience, the rebellion, tension, and resolution, made him think of a chapter from *The Stranger*, and he imagined himself at his own dead mother's funeral, sipping hot coffee with milk in front of the coffin containing her corpse, the corpse of his old life—his-not-good-enough, never-fucking-good-enough old life—and now, here he was pounding pizza and not giving a fuck, opening himself, like Camus put it so aptly, *to the benign indifference of the world.*

The Cameo was saturated with punks vibrating their cumulative aggression as they waited for the main act to go on. A couple of fights broke out, but people didn't seem to care much. Cigarette smoke swirled furiously in green columns of stage light, as hard-core music hammered through the sound system, and other than what Christian called, "poseur-pussies practicing dives," the stage was vacant.

Siddhi tried to hold the line, but he had no skill at weaving through a crowd. He looked up and around too much and soon lost his compatriots. It was useless to scan the quadrant for their clothes. There was no shortage of suspenders, Mohawks, or red plaid. The punks blended into a homogeneous, jumping mass as the opening band took the stage, and they howled together, thrashing about to release their rebellion into the atmosphere in the way Siddhi craved.

At some point, the din turned to a roar as the bartender handed Siddhi his Sprite—no cherries—with a twist of lime, to make it look like a real drink. He looked to the lights as the headliners were introduced and the band took the stage. The guys did some tuning and sound checking while the crowd chanted, "D-O-A! D-O-A! D-O-A!"

Another knuckle drove into the newish cuts on his thigh and caused him to spill half the soda up his nose and down his jeans.

"We been looking all over for you, asshole," Travis yelled over the barrage. Siddhi felt like the wound might have reopened, and he got a little high off the thought that his blood was shedding into his jeans. "C'mon, we got a killer spot over there." He followed Travis down the wall from the bar toward a place at the side of the stage where Christian and Fox waited.

Center stage, a lank man with drawn cheeks and black, mussed hair raked his guitar, and yelled into the microphone, "Hey everybody, how the fuck you all doing tonight?" The crowd was all screaming, cursing, thunderous stomping boots. "Same here," answered the man. Again, the crowd exchanged all the club's air for caterwauling. "No more fucking around," said the man. "We're D.O.A.!" And then, they played: fast guitar, crashing drums, a bassline that pounded Siddhi's chest, and harsh, fuck-laden lyrics that he could only decipher by distilling his consciousness and riveting his eyes to the skeletal lead singer as he hammered the microphone with intense, familiar anger.

Travis punched him again to get his attention—same bleeding, and now bruised spot on his thigh. "That's Joey Shithead, bro," he shouted over the noise. "He fuckin' rules."

Siddhi felt the rush, and dizzy with pain, he jumped with the music and nodded, more and faster, repeatedly bowing his head, bang, bang, bang, in unceasing agreement with the drumbeat.

"Now!" Fox commanded. He shoved and punched random others until he cleared a path for Travis, Christian, and Siddhi to the area just beneath the stage, where a hundred punks spun and flailed like whirling dervishes, body checking each other, veering, trouncing, swishing, smashing, like palm trees in a hurricane.

Fox caught Siddhi's eye and gave that wide, cold smile. "Bye-bye, Buddha!" he said and pushed Siddhi into the mosh pit.

PART IV

Time for Me to Fly

CHAPTER 20:

Little Deaths, 1989 (Siddhartha)

Nana always told him, "When you go to someone's house to visit, be a *mensch* and bring something." So, when Siddhi showed up to where the guys hung out at Travis's grandma's apartment in the Betsy Ross hotel, he went as a *mensch* with a fat quarter of Jackson's sticky, crystal-rich Kublai Kush, the fine weed that, until his dad got lost in the cocaine cash watershed, had provided the family Jones with what Siddhi considered to be a more respectable livelihood.

Jackson wouldn't have cared anyway. He left weed all over the house, fat roaches in the ashtray on the toilet tank lid, the glass bong bowl considerately packed for whomever might come next, close to an ounce spilling over the side of his rolling tray. Though marijuana was his comedown drug of choice, Jackson mainly kept count with the coke and pills. Siddhi thought of the current Jackson as the king in his counting house, counting out his grams and kilos…

None of it mattered to Siddhi because after CeeCee up and left, Jackson seemed to make the categorical decision that his kids were grown. He never really asked Siddhi anything more than, "Hey, man, how ya doin'?" and even then, he rarely hung around for the answer. They were men, and they each had their own lives.

Siddhi felt a far greater responsibility now to his friends than he did to his family. The math was simple: his friends knew and liked him as he was. They gave a shit and expected and included him. And though Siddhi was scrawny and barely fifteen, he quickly displaced Christian as Fox's second lieutenant, though really, it took no greater effort than having half a brain and funneling into Fox's thumb and forefinger a never-diminishing pipeline of gratis, pre-rolled joints, *mensch*-style.

*

Siddhi and the guys spent the brutally hot last Saturday of July getting high at Trav's and playing a couple of hours of Zelda before a day of skating, until the sun ran out and wound them up watching The Damned play at The Cameo that night. After the show, as they passed a joint in the alley behind the theater, Fox whipped out a full bottle of grain alcohol and passed it around, demanding they all take big sips.

"Don't you want some, bro?" Travis handed the bottle back to Fox.

"Stupid fucks," Fox said and laughed. "This shit isn't for drinking unless you're making garbage cans full of *Marielito* punch for *Calle Ocho*, or some shit like that."

Siddhi wanted to get the joke, but he sensed something more was coming, and, like the others, he waited for the explanation and possible further directions.

"Check this out!" Fox took a huge sip, but he held the 190-proof alcohol in his cheeks, swiped his Zippo back and forth on his jeans to light it, and spit hard through the flame, creating a massive raging fireball that shot right at Christian, who fell backward onto the sidewalk to protect his face.

"Whoa!" Travis laughed, clapped his hands, and then, gave Christian a hand getting up.

Christian had already taken hold of the bottle and opened his own lighter to aim and spit toward Siddhi, who was prepared to duck, and down he went, rolling out over the sidewalk to his friends' excited crowing. He stood up, dusted off, and shouted, "Stop! Drop! And?"

"Roll, *DICK*, roll!" they shouted together. Siddhi blew five fireballs of his own before Fox grabbed back the empty bottle, laid it on the street, and, wearing the brass knuckles he kept on his keychain, punched it into shards on the ground. Afterward, the guys went for pizza. While he waited for Christian to get the food, Fox summoned a pair of punk girls to the usual table in the back.

At first, Siddhi thought they were twins. Both wore short jean shorts with fishnets and combat boots. Both had impossibly red hair. Not ginger red, Magic marker red. But Siddhi could see that underneath, one was a blonde, and the other had darker roots. The blond girl, who had much smaller tits, introduced herself as Beth and hopped into Fox's lap as if she belonged to him, and they made out a little.

Fox kept his eyes open, half-paying attention to his tongue in her mouth like he was doing her a favor. Christian made a lewd noise, and Fox stopped kissing her long enough to slap him hard enough to leave a handprint on his cheek. Laughter all around, even from Christian. Fox nodded to the other girl. She winked back and then dropped into Siddhi's lap, and he stopped laughing.

"I'm Michelle," she whispered into his ear, and the tickle of her breath made his dick get hard so fast that it pressed sideways into his boxers. Michelle worked her ass into a better position to which Siddhi's boner found new length. When she turned around to face him, he saw that her green eyes were blacked all around with kohl, and she had a long nose with a cute little bump on top. He wasn't sure where to look, so he ran his eyes over her various earrings, all sizes of hoops and studs running the length of each of her ears, from lobes up to the cartilage.

"Hey," she said, her soft hands positioned his chin, and then she put her mouth on his—whooping from everyone at the table—and licked into his mouth. Siddhi scanned his mind for every kind of kissing he'd ever witnessed, and he delivered the deepest, sexiest one he could think of onto Michelle's welcoming lips. Lightning stole in through his tongue, banged round his entire body, and then—massive whoops—exited suddenly and crudely into his pants.

*

The first time the girls came over to hang out at Trav's, Michelle wore a white T-shirt beneath a plaid corset that forced her tits up like round tennis balls out the top.

"Oh shit! It's like a time warp to the Fifties in here," Beth said as Fox took her hand and led her toward the hall. "There's plastic on the couch. Oh my god!" she giggled.

Siddhi could tell by her behavior, her darting pupils, she was on something, uppers, maybe coke.

"Yeah, I know that," Fox said. "I've been here before." He let Beth walk ahead of him, and as he passed Siddhi, Fox stopped to shake his hand, transferring what felt like a plastic wrapped candy into his palm. "Raincoat, bro," he said with a wink.

Beth whined impatiently from the hall. "Fox!"

"Oh yeah, boys," Fox said. "She wants some of that hot beef injection." He slapped Travis on his bare back and trotted toward his grandma's bedroom. They all had claimed to have fucked in her bed, and though they all were in the apartment together all the time, none of them believed each other about the fucking.

Michelle sat on Siddhi's lap, which seemed to be her way of making the first move. Like before, her ass on his fly triggered an immediate hard on. Not that it took much to get him hard anyway, but he had to proceed with caution. The last time Michelle sat in his lap he let one go in his pants, and thankfully, no one noticed.

When the guys decided Siddhi had potential sex in his future, Christian sort of bragged to him that his foolproof secret to lasting for as long as he wanted was to picture Trav's grandma's varicose veiny legs. To which Travis told him to go fuck himself, as if he had ever shown her any respect, and Fox heaved Christian off the couch, wrestled him to the ground, and mashed his cheek into the peach-colored shag carpet, pulling his bent arm up behind his back, threatening to break it until Christian was forced to shout: "I have never been in any pussy, but my mom's when I was born!"

Still, the leg thing was good advice. The thought of all those subcutaneous blue spiders, squids, and caterpillars had the power to back things off. Michelle moved her ass in little circles over Siddhi's crotch. She spied the rubber in his palm, grabbed it, and giggled.

"C'mon," she said. She took his hand and pulled him from the plastic-covered swivel rocker that had become his assigned seat in the living room. He had no idea where she intended to take him, considering the bedroom was taken. Also, he wondered if he even liked her, but in the end, Siddhi followed Michelle across the living room because he was a fifteen-year-old boy with a pulse, and anything more could wait for later. The apartment was too small to give him time to get too nervous, and the guy-pressure made it impossible to bail.

"I'm next," Travis joked to Siddhi as he scooted past where they sat on the sofa playing Super Mario Brothers. Christian had bet him ten bucks he couldn't save the princess.

"Where are we going?" Siddhi asked, as he trailed Michelle down the hall. She exaggerated the shake of her hips when she walked, and she smelled like cigarette smoke and cinnamon.

"We gotta find some more fucking chicks, bro," he heard Christian tell Travis. The hallway walls hung with fifty years' worth of photos of Trav's grandma in her native Sweden and on her many travels. A whole life on one wall. One showed her in a sombrero, and another featured her in black and white, much younger, quite beautiful, with braids crossing each other over the top of her head, pointing to Niagara Falls. Siddhi thought of Sienna's pictures of their mother, just having fun with drugs and sex, and wondered about him and Michelle. What would their old pictures show, and to whom and when? And who would be around long enough or care enough to look at them?

Michelle led him into the bathroom, where she backed her body up against the door to close it and clicked the metal button in the knob to lock it. "Hi," she cooed, and since she had yet to say anything worth talking about, Siddhi went straight in to kiss her. She looked nothing like Elisabeth Shue with Gloria's tits, his spank-bank-go-to image. But that was probably a good thing because it meant that he'd succeeded in expanding his erotic life into the third dimension.

Siddhi pressed his body up against the length of hers, kissing and kissing, his hands locked on her hips because he'd learned from movies that if he touched the wrong spot, she might freak out and stop the whole thing cold. She pushed him backward a step, and he worried she might have changed her mind. His dick throbbed. *Trav's grandma's legs,* he thought.

"Hang on, slugger," she said, and he stepped back, pissed off that he'd ruined it. He tried to remember the stuff Jackson used to say when Babies thought of leaving that often worked to make them about-face and come back into the fold. But he was too distracted by Michelle's body and his own nerves to think of a single word to say. Beneath her over-thick makeup, Michelle's cheeks were young and round. She had downy brown hairs on the top half of her forehead, and her front teeth were a little oversized, more cute than beautiful. She was not a woman but a girl. She stuck her fingers into the space between the front of her corset and her T-shirt and fished out a little vial.

"It's always way better after a bump." She tapped a little mound of white powder onto the edge of the counter and used her finger to neaten it. Then she bent over the vanity and snorted hard until most of the powder disappeared. Siddhi wanted to get back to the kissing. Kissing her lips and pressing his body up against hers with his eyes closed opened some portal in him to a place without rage, a feeling of going somewhere, but with no resistance, floating. He put his hands in her armpits and tried to coax her back up to standing, but Michelle dropped down onto her knees.

Siddhi looked down at her as she lifted his T-shirt and made him hold it up with his own hand. Then she unbuttoned and then unzipped his jeans and, in one move, yanked pants and boxers down to his ankles, leaving him naked and releasing his boner so quickly that it flipped up and hit him in the stomach. She giggled. He felt like he knew where things were heading, and rather than worry too much about how it might go, he sighed and played with her hair, but the second he caught sight of himself in the mirror, the float was over, and all his pleasure ran scared. Everywhere, sets of three cuts all over him. He opened his hands over his thighs to try and shield them from Michelle's view.

"Guys say this feels awesome," she said. She took the remaining powder on the vanity and rubbed it inside her mouth, and then quickly grabbed his penis with her clammy hand and sucked the head into her mouth. Siddhi buckled with the sensation, so much more intense than the kissing and the rest of it, he had to lean a hand on the vanity to steady himself. Veiny legs. Veiny legs. Veiny legs... But it was no use. After ten seconds in her mouth, he came.

Michelle stood up and wiped her mouth. He awkwardly pulled up his pants and almost bumped heads with her. He reeled for the next move and grabbed and kissed her to buy time, but she pulled her mouth from his.

"Ew. There's still cum in my mouth. Guys don't usually kiss after head, you know."

Fucking perfect, he thought; *I'm the guy who doesn't know better than to eat his own cum...*

"Hey, don't look so mad! I'm just fucking with you." She turned and spat in the sink and then used a toothbrush—probably Grandma's?—to brush her teeth. Then she kissed him for another minute.

"So, what's up with the tribal shit on your legs, babe?" She *had* noticed his cuts, but also, she called him "babe." Every explanation sounded like bullshit or crazy shit, and he didn't even know this chick. She might become his girlfriend, or at least give him another round of "head," and either way, he had to say something not scary to make sure not to ruin his chances.

"Oh my god, you're like so shy and freaked out. Babe, I'm fucking with you again. I already saw your arm at the pizza place. That's why I picked you. Here, look…" She peeled up the side of her T-shirt, curling the corset upward just enough to expose a fresh bandage on her belly, to the left and right of it, Siddhi saw the pink and purple whispers of older wounds.

"But—" Siddhi's stomach turned, seeing Michelle's wounds.

"Since I was like ten," she confessed, like it was a turn-on that they had their deepest shame in common. She smoothed her clothes down, gargled some Scope, fixed her hair, and wiped a stray smudge of kohl from under her eye. As Siddhi watched her clean herself up to go back out into a room where everyone would know exactly what she had just done, he stared at her and wondered what he ought to do next. It would be a long day of not much else, and his dick was already half hard again, and he didn't want to be finished with her just yet.

He remembered a night at Xanadu; he had been young, seven or eight maybe, and had woken up in the dark, sick and shivering. Sienna told him he had a fever and took him to the bathroom for a bath in cold water. When they walked downstairs to see if there was any medicine in Jackson's room, Siddhi went in first and found Jackson naked, on his knees, using his hands between the legs of not one but two women at once. The sight had given him a funny sting in his groin, even then, and Sienna had led him away before he could see any more. Siddhi recognized that sensation now. Lust. Sex. And he wasn't ready for it to be over.

"Come here," he told her, taking Michelle by her hips but careful to be gentle when he touched her middle. "We're not done yet."

*

So that was how it went on…Beth and Michelle would rap at the metal screen door of the second-floor apartment, and after the girls and the guys all got crazy high on *Kublai*, Michelle would come and sit on Siddhi's lap in the swivel chair and wiggle her ass until Michelle—also fifteen and, "on the pill, so don't worry"—took his hand and paraded him past his catcalling friends, down the hall to the bathroom, and once they locked the door, she snorted her coke and rubbed some on the head of his dick.

Like him, she was cut to shreds, which didn't make him love her or even turn him on, but it made him feel even, level, okay to be whatever with her. She made no demands, never questioned or challenged anything, and he felt the sort of comfort he had when he was alone. And since he was comfortable, Siddhi fucked Michelle like she was the *Great Glass Wonkavator*. He took her upwards and downwards and sideways and slantways and wide ways and back ways and any different ways he could manage between the door and the tub.

Siddhi watched Michelle in the mirror sometimes, focusing on her scars and wondering about what drove her to cut herself to distract him and make it last. But he never asked her.

Michelle tipped her chin forward and kept very quiet. She didn't look into his eyes, and she always kept her T-shirt and corset on. He got used to not seeing her face and learned to do it the way she liked. He came either way. Like everything sleazy in life, sex had a short learning curve for a willing student. He hoped to feel love but never did.

CHAPTER 21

The Marrakech Express, 1989 (Sienna)

The blinding, blaring thrill of it all left no room for common sense. I shifted in my seat as the half-empty plane bobbed and jagged up, up, up, until I could look down at the clouds. I'd never flown without Siddhi sitting next to me, writing a story or listing NWA wrestlers and their weights and hometowns on his barf bag...but I promised myself I'd stop picturing Siddhi and what he'd do if he was there.

I hadn't been sure I'd even get out of the airport. I figured some stern and sturdy security guard would realize I was a runaway minor and whisk me into a holding cell while he attempted to call my parents.

The only reason I guessed it was worth a try was that I'd seen Jackson help Siddhi (whose hands were the only ones small enough) stuff packet after packet of wrapped marijuana down the narrow neck of a giraffe wood carving in Negril, which Jackson then had me lug through airport security and tell them the story he made me memorize about how it was my ninth birthday present and how I had to carry it all by myself because the giraffe was my favorite animal. Siddhi cried when we got home, and Jackson took a hammer and smashed the giraffe. I cried because I wanted a real birthday present.

When I showed my ticket to the agent, nothing happened. Nobody wanted to stop me. Nothing went awry. My ticket and I walked right onto the plane and sat in seat 25B, next to Edsel, who hogged the armrest, read an issue of *Surf*, and fell asleep on take-off while I took deep breaths, trying to acclimate to my reality.

I took out my five pictures of my mother, looked at them over and over using my Pan Am blanket to wipe the tears, and conjured daydream-montages of her, in clothes, on the stoop of a nice little house, watching me be brave and feeling proud of me, as the airplane ferried us over an ocean, across hours of time, a hemisphere away from home and Siddhartha.

*

I woke as the train whinnied to a halt. My throat crackled with dryness, and I had that half-dreamy, limbic weirdness that comes from too much sleep midday.

Edsel caught my arm with an elbow as he flipped his hair over his head and tied it back in a red bandana. He hoisted his baggage down from the overhead racks and pulled the travel guide I bought us from my loose, sleepy grip. "Someone I talked to while you were sleeping said we can find a really cheap hostel in this thing." He flipped the pages. "Cool as shit, right?" All around us, passengers stood, stretched, and gathered up their things.

"We're here already?" Marrakech *express* train meant one stop: here. "Edsel!"

"Yup! Psyched up, baby?"

"Why didn't you wake me after fifteen minutes like I asked? I missed the whole ride!"

Edsel shrugged. "Oh, yeah, no worries. You were tired, kid. You didn't miss anything; just like, farms and lakes and goats and stuff like that, nothing worth seeing. Wait till you see the resort! It's like a nod to the history and stuff, but all modern and gorgeous in the amenities."

Siddhi would have *needed* to wake me whether I asked him to or not, knowing it'd be better, funnier, and prettier if we saw it together. He'd point out a goat chewing like Nana or a peasant with a Jew-fro or feed me the highlights of a book he read on Moroccan history, maybe pose one of his famous questions like, "What if Morocco's gravity held down the people and buildings and stuff but not the sand?" and make me argue the hypothetical...*Stop it,* I told myself. *If you keep thinking of him, you won't really be here. You haven't really left.*

As we waited for the herd of passengers to push their way out of the train car, Edsel broke into his sexy, fluent French with a group of backpackers ahead of us in the aisle. He gestured to me once or twice, sounding more sophisticated than he ever had in English, while I waited for some sort of introduction that never came. I cleared the sleep from my eyes, fluffed the heat out of my T-shirt, and fixed my hair. Casablanca and the train ride were behind me, but the vast cinnamon landscape of Marrakech lay just outside.

*

The lobby of Hostel Taziz, the hallways, and our small room all reeked of the same chemical floral. I'd smelled it before at Nana's when I used to unzip the garment bag in the way back of her closet and hug myself into her furs. Mothballs.

Room 4's powdery blue walls were bordered by painted garlands of kaleidoscopic flowers that also framed the doors and the one five-pointed window, unglazed—it was more a star-shaped hole in the wall that doubled as easy access for an unceasing, dotted line of black ants. The bed had clean blue sheets to match the walls. A low table in one corner held an old, rabbit-eared television like our first set at Xanadu when Siddhi and I took turns holding the ends of the antennas for better "Hee-Haw" and "Lawrence Welk" reception.

Immediately after the room-christening sex, Edsel flipped on the TV and leaned back against the pillows. I locked the bathroom door, peed, and then stared at my face in the small mirror, trying to call out some fresh enthusiasm. I'd made it to Africa! And yet my face, like my new life, seemed underwhelming and burnt, like a movie line Siddhi and I overquoted until it lost all its funny. I kicked off my flip-flops, bent to scratch an itch on my leg, and felt it covered in a crust, like dried blood.

In fact, my right leg was covered with crumbling brown vines, tiny polka dots, petals, and paisleys that sprouted at my big toe and then grew all around my ankle and up almost to my knee.

"Something's wrong with my leg!" I yelled from the bathroom as I unlocked and opened the door and came out. "What did you do to me?"

Edsel burst into laughter. "I was wondering when you might notice that, jet lag girl. I paid some Arab chick on the train five bucks for *mehundi*."

"Meh-what-zee?"

"It's *henna*. All that stuff falls off and stains your skin, like a tattoo. I actually told her to write 'drunken whore,' but she only knew how to do that flowery pattern."

"You *tattooed* me?" I shouted while marching toward the bed. "What in the fuck were you thinking?" Nana lectured us about tattoos and banishment from Jewish cemeteries, grabbing Elsie's arm and holding it up to show us her six, blue-black numbers from Auschwitz.

"Whoa, whoa, whoa. *Chill...*" he said, taking my hand and tickling the inside of my forearm. "I said it's *like* a tattoo. No worries. It fades away over time."

"How much time?"

"Fast, okay. It'll be gone in a week or two. I was being nice. It was a fucking gift. It's sexy, you know, pretty."

"Wait, you wanted 'drunken whore.' Was that pretty?" But I'd already fizzled down, the henna design was actually very pretty, and I was too tired to care. Plus, I didn't want Edsel to think I was uptight. I was a cool, flexible, laidback traveler. I climbed back on the bed and straddled my legs over him in the way he liked best.

"No, not pretty," he said. "But it'd have been funny, which, last time I checked, you loved about me." He pulled my face forward over his and kissed my ear and neck. Kissing back was effortless. The flowers on my foot and ankle were exotic, and it seemed easier, more fun, and adventurous, to sink into the bed with Edsel.

I nuzzled his neck and conceded, "You *are* funny."

"Funny enough for a beejay?"

As Edsel pushed my head toward his pelvis, my thoughts flooded my brain. *I really should give him head, because why not? He takes me places and buys me things and wants me and loves me. And it would really smooth things over to just go with the flow, and it's better than fighting, and as soon as he comes, he'll pass out, and I can look at him while he sleeps, which is how I like him best, but we already had sex today, plus the beejay in the train station bathroom, and how did I not feel something being done to my body while I was sleeping? Did they do anything else to me, Edsel, and those backpackers? Did they laugh at me? Drunken whore? How did he think that was funny? But I need to be cool about little things, so I don't sound like a kid, and I'm still so tired...*

"Hmm?" he asked again, poking me with his erection.

"You'll never be that funny," I said, kissing him once more, to show how cool and fine I was, before rolling over into my pillow.

"Aw, c'mon..." But I ignored him, closed my eyes, and let myself drift. "Okay," he said and wedged his face between the back of my neck and the bed. "Goodnight, crazy-sleepy-girl."

We spooned. "Goodnight, discontinued Ford."

✻

For the first few days, we woke up hours before dawn. We filled the time with morning sex, followed by Edsel watching French game shows while I read beaten-up copies of *Winnie the Pooh* and *Naked Lunch* I found in the closet.

Pooh was sweet-as-could-be, and I read it greedily and too quickly and went on to the Burroughs book. The incomprehensible rambling, odd stuttering, brutal scenes, petulant orgies, and especially the sickly "black meat" took me back to Xanadu, where we had many a naked lunch, and where sex and drugs meshed with snakes and trumpet vines in a sinewy marijuana-smoked dream that, with Siddhi and me tangled in its growth, sprung mythically whole from the head of Jackson Jones.

I wished I was Christopher Robin, in a life of warm familiarity, in my own little abode in the peace of the Hundred Acre Wood. I couldn't shake the idea that I had something to be ashamed of, like how I quit when the going got tough, like how I drained Siddhi out with the bathwater. I reminded myself that Siddhi wanted the space and that I deserved this adventure. My adult life had begun, and I owed it to myself and even to Siddhi to dedicate to Edsel and the present. I owed myself Africa.

And when the sun finally rose, Marrakech more than delivered.

Hostel Taziz was a short walk from the *Jemaa el Fna*, the market square, packed with tourists and hawkers and sellers of spices, sandals, and leathers, roasted meats served on beds of steaming grain, and teahouses full of Arab men with nowhere else to be at ten a.m. on a Thursday but sipping hot mint tea from delicate little glasses.

We walked for miles, holding pinkies and sharing tastes of a bag full of unrecognizable chips and dried fruits, feeding them to each other with our eyes closed, and playing name that food. Edsel was good at the game. By noon, I owed him two beejays.

We wandered in and around the old city, meandering down small streets that wound, Seuss-like, up and into the hills, some leading into the *medina*, paths that led past mosques and homes, and beneath the dusty, striped awnings of the never-ending *souk*. Edsel taught me a little French and bought me a bangle bracelet, and he slid it on my wrist, kissed my hand, and mouthed, *love you*.

The ancient walls were thick and solid and the same clay-orange as the ground below them, making the entire old city appear as if it rose from the earth at one time and in one piece. Siddhi would have compared it to The Fortress of Solitude. I tried and failed not to think of what he would say or do if he were with me and why I hadn't just brought him in the first place. When I first had the thought, its simplicity knocked the wind out of me, and I had to sit down and catch my breath, wait for my stomach to untwist before I was able to convince myself once again that things were as they should be. I had to stop worrying about home and Siddhi and let my mind and heart fill with sand and saffron and possibility. Instead of missing my family, I imagined myself on a farm outside the city, a Mother Theresa type, doing vital public work, building a hospital, or teaching English to poor children. And I pictured myself as Indiana Jones, mentally prepared, if the need arose, to escape being shanghaied to a Sultan's harem. I really was in Africa, and anything was possible.

I wrote Siddhi a letter a day, saying in each that everything was awesome, and then spending a couple of pages describing one Moroccan thing I'd done.

Dear Siddhi,

Have I told you how awesome it is in Marrakech? Tomorrow, Edsel reports to Club Med for his training week, but today, we rode a donkey cart through the leather tannery.

The guys working there were impossibly skinny, and they pulled us around so we wouldn't fall into any of the pits and gave us bouquets of fresh mint to hold under our noses to block the death smell of offal and rotting flesh. We saw them dehair, stretch, and buck the animal hides. And their hands were all peeling and red from the wood ash and lye because they didn't even wear gloves! They soaked the skins in deep pits, and then they pulled them out and dried them in the sun, massaged them with oil, and I invited all the wretched poverty and filth to feel elegant to me like I was a princess on an exotic holiday. (Aren't I? Hee hee.)

In short, Marrakesh is totally awesome! How are you, Nana, and Jackson?

Love and miss you,

CeeCee

P.S. I bought you a belt in the gift shop. It's beautiful, hand-tooled leather, and it's going to look so crazy great on you, but warning: even after all that sun and washing and special treatment, it still smells like shit.

*

Come Monday, Edsel left off his usual over-washed Van Halen T-shirt and jeans for a crisp, white golf shirt and a belted pair of chinos, no more than a change of clothes transformed him from a mussed traveler back to a boilerplate trust fund brat, but he did take extra time to brush and style his hair. I guessed I was nervous about him starting work, too, because my stomach kept cramping up.

A week later, Edsel moved to *Club Med*. For the first week, exploring without him was fun. I got so familiar with the old city and the square. In week two, I met some American tourists, a mom and dad, and their little kids, and I did my thing, like Siddhi and I used to at HoJo's, and joined the family for the day. Then, there were Canadians, Swedes, French, and Germans who had good English. I found people, got some company, filled the days, free lunches in exchange for being a nanny and tour guide, and all that. When he made the agreed-upon Wednesday night call to the hostel phone, Edsel said he missed me and assured me I'd love the Club Med staff quarters once I got a job there, too.

He returned from the village on his first day off, after two weeks away, with a deeper tan and a bouncier step. We had sex twice before he broke the news. "So, like, they can't really hire you if you're under eighteen." When, on the plane, I'd finally told him the truth of my age, he'd roared with laughter and couldn't have cared less, though I'd been premature in my relief that my age lie was no longer a problem.

"Oh, right," I said, wondering how madly rushed and blindly stupid I'd been not to research such a vital fact before moving to another continent; my faith and foolishness left a gaping hole in my plan. Like that picture of my mother, standing with the two of us as babies, young and alone, with no end in sight. "No worries," I borrowed Edsel's standby when there was nothing good to say.

*

"How long are you here for?" I asked Edsel's new friend Paolo at dinner. We sat at one of the tables in the eating area of the *Jemaa el Fna*, the central square and the best place to be at night.

Spice vendors, snake charmers, *Chleuh* dancers, and acrobats put on shows for tips. Arab boys in blousy pants walked the perimeters with Barbary apes on leashes. Flashing orange cook fires sent smoke pluming up into the black sky above the food stalls, and strings of lights, looped post to never-ending post illuminated heaps of vegetables, grains, and rows of disembodied goat heads, set jowls up, eyeballs bulging, watching the sky even as they roasted. Walking the *Jemaa* at night was like watching poetry.

I thought of Oscar Wilde, whom Jackson quoted often: *We are all in the gutter, but some of us are looking at the stars.* I didn't share the thought with Edsel. I didn't know why, but I needed to keep it for myself.

We were a little group. There was me and Edsel, a couple of girls also from Club Med, and Paolo, who exuded what a Brazilian national should: athleticism, sensuality, and the *espirito de Carnaval*. He danced in his seat and bought us a round of watery Moroccan beers, which I drank to feel less outside of things. He said he'd transferred from Club Med in Cancún, because they needed a Portuguese speaker in Marrakech.

"Two years contract, everywhere een Club Med," he explained. After Portuguese, Spanish was his second language, then French and Italian, with English coming in at a distant and broken fifth.

"Two-years? Is that what you said?" I looked at Edsel, who sipped his beer, avoiding my eyes. "Does *everyone* sign a two-year contract?" I asked.

"No, ehhh, some peoples can just one year."

"Babe, what about you?" I asked Edsel. "Did you sign for one or two?"

If Edsel had paused before answering, to consider my position, if he'd stopped talking to Becca Lynn, the ethereal Australian red head (who was taking a break after medical school to work the Club Med infirmary, and whom *all of us* found hotter and more fascinating than me), if he'd known that I spent my days trying to make three-hour friendships with fluent English speakers by getting their babies to laugh at my funny faces from the next table at the café, wandering the medina, and reading sandy paperbacks from the hostel shelves, or if he'd known I was so homesick I counted and recounted my twelve hundred dollars (that he didn't really know about) to be sure it was enough for a return ticket... If he'd made eye contact so that he could share the hurt from the blow that he was staying, regardless of me being an unemployed, runaway minor who was not even allowed to enter the Club Med village, only a ten-minute walk away from the hostel, while he ate chocolate croissants for breakfast and played *le football* with French tourists... If Edsel had done literally anything before shouting, "Two years, baby!" and high-fiving Paolo (the one he was actually calling baby), I might have been able to settle in, calm down, and stop feeling so nauseated.

I forced myself to eat half a plate of plain couscous, taking comfort in its starchy softness but also in its name: *couscous*, like kiss-kiss, the sound of warm, enduring love. Siddhi would have suggested it as a pet name for a homeless kitten or a sad amusement park fish alone in a baggie.

Edsel reprised his Monty Python cheese shop bit (I pictured Siddhi rolling his eyes), to which Becca Lynn threw her head back in laughter—silky ginger waves bouncing everywhere. I shifted in my seat, pulled my knees up to ease my tummy. I reminded myself that by the time I turned eighteen, Edsel planned to be the Village Chief, and he promised to have some sort of interior decorating job waiting for me on my birthday! We were in love, and not the Jackson kind, where the minute someone acts a little differently than before or needs a little more of the focus on them for a while, you cut and run. It was Edsel's turn, and I supported him.

To me, love meant being there at the table with Edsel and getting to know *our* new friends.

But even with my head in line, my stomach refused to cooperate. A few more swigs of beer, and I got so queasy I had to head back to the room.

"Sure you don't need me? Cause, like, it's our only night off this week?" Edsel looked at me and then back over his shoulder at the table.

"Stay. Have fun," I said, wishing he hadn't given me the choice. "I'll be fine."

"Cool. Meet you there later," Edsel said, kissing my lips and returning to his conversation with Nava, the petite Israeli tennis pro. The last time I looked back at them, Edsel was laughing and fixing his ponytail.

I barely made it into the room before shoving my head into the toilet bowl to wretch an undigested tummy full of couscous and beer. Then I let the shower run over me until it turned cold before getting into bed to sleep it off.

Edsel clamored into the room in the middle of the night, soused. He knocked the books off the nightstand. "You won't believe this. You know that tiny guy near the sandal place? The one who stands on the glass? Total hook-up! Guy sells hash. Hashish? Ever smoked it? Pretty good." I knew the man to whom he referred, a ninety-pound street performer I walked past each evening on the way to the stalls for dinner, whose schtick was to stand barefoot on a pile of broken Coke bottles while holding a little money cup at his waist, a meager income that he'd clearly figured out how to supplement. "Anyway," Edsel stripped naked and slipped into the bed. "After the hash, there was this cake shop. You know the one? And the girls got these pastries with almonds and honey and orange oil and cloves and all this aromatic shit in them. Horrible munchies. I guess I'm spoiled now from Club Med. The desserts are *Français et délicieux, du vrai chocolat et crème, Napoléons et éclairs...*"

"Baby, you're speaking French," I whispered, adding a little burp that smelled unquestionably like vomit. "I don't understand what yo—"

"Whoa," Edsel sat up. "Pukey-girl! Drank too much? Yikes. How you feeling?" Edsel asked, tickling my back as he edged away. "Sorry, babe. Your breath sucks."

I kept my eyes shut, wishing he would shut up. He got out of his side of the bed and moved around, pushing me to move forward so he could scoot in behind me. He kissed me on my back and neck, which felt nice for a minute or two before I felt myself drifting off. I dreamt of goats, feathery white hair billowing over cashmere bellies. One stood facing me, and in my dream, I knew it was Siddhi. I wanted to go pet him, pick him up, and cuddle him, but there was a crackling sound under my feet and sharp pricking pains. I was standing on broken glass.

*

The next day, after Edsel returned to Club Med, I caught a break. Farid, the Taziz manager, who, if he had a few more teeth, might have made a nice living impersonating Edward James Olmos, found me sweeping the halls out of sheer boredom and offered me cash to clean the hostel. He spoke little English. He grunted and handed me a mop.

When I nodded with a big, grateful smile, he nodded back, no smiling, and took me to the linen closet where there was a worn, mimeographed list of instructions in terrible but understandable English. And my nod gained new vigor. I had a job!

"Yeah. Yes," I told him. *"Iyyeh! Iyyeh! Oui!"*

"Mezyan," he said, which I guessed meant something like, okay, because he handed me a ring of keys, scratched his belly through his *djellaba,* and shuffled off. Of course, there was no paperwork, but I knew he'd pay me something. Sienna Shiva Karma Jones: hotel maid. Not a nice hotel like Boardwalk or Park Place, Hostel Taziz was more like one of the cheap, dark purples that came right after *GO.* Hostel Taziz was mainly patronized by loud and rowdy backpackers, insects, rodents, and a tentative black cat with no left eye, who followed me around at a distance.

My duties included sweeping, dusting, wiping, laundering linens and towels, folding, hauling trash, bed-stripping and making; unclogging toilets stuffed with used tampons, saturated rolls of toilet paper, and splattered traveler's diarrhea; mopping away booze-scented puke; and sweeping up piles of tracked sand and bushels of fallen hair.

Once I started working, I made a chart to organize and accomplish it all as efficiently as possible. I changed the sheets twice a week or when a room was turned over. Maybe only five rooms per day needed anything more than a wipe down, sweep, and fresh towels. The bathrooms were the worst, often grossing me out to the point of getting sick myself (though I'd never been so squeamish before). I did them over the morning hours so I could be through with puking by lunch. Then I took an hour nap to gain back strength for the dusting, sweeping, and linens. With the extra time, I organized closets, cleaned out, and rearranged the furniture in the lobby. Moved things in a way that worked better. I took pride in the job, but also it filled the time.

Farid liked to deliver directions in Arabic. With his meaty hands clamped on my shoulders, he blew spittle onto my face and neck when he spoke, though he'd never notice with his eyes permanently glued to my breasts. He always ended with, *Wah?* To which I agreed, "*Wah.* Okay," and referred to the mimeograph. The job was physically hard, especially with my stomach being so testy, but Farid paid me five hundred *dirhams* per week, basically fifty bucks, plus no more paying for my room. That made about a hundred and twenty-seven bucks a week, and for how little I ate, it was enough so that I never had to dip into my cash from home.

My efficiency and organization built on itself so that I often finished early and lay in bed reading the copies of *Shogun* and *Enderby Outside* I found in Room 8 and chalking the loneliness, sickness, and exhaustion up to being a traveler, gathering tales to tell our kids someday. By the fourth Wednesday, Edsel forgot to call.

On Thursday, Farid burst into my room, shouting incomprehensibly, saliva whitening the rabid corners of his mouth.

He yanked me up to standing and thrust the broom handle into my hand. He wanted me working, even though the job was long done. So, for the remaining daylight, I wandered the halls and swept. I was too queasy to wear any more than my *djellaba* and sandals, and with my own deep tan and wild black hair, I really looked like a local. Most guests didn't even make eye contact, let alone speak to me, except to command me in French or Arabic, to which I nodded, offered more towels, and returned to sweeping.

In bed for the night, with One-Eyed Willie curled around my head and purring steadily, I lay awake missing my family. Was Aunt Paula still in Delhi? Still married to Prakesh? And if so, which Muppet would Siddhi say he resembled? Was Nana sitting at her gray-blue card table sucking the candy coating off a Jordan almond and calling out *Mah-jongg*? Was Jackson giving a new girlfriend a tour of Xanadu and reciting the Coleridge poem from rote? And, best for last was Siddhi, whom I took the time to remember and miss at all his ages, doing anything and everything I could remember. I might have cried for a bit, but I was half asleep and couldn't be sure.

*

After the first month of work, Edsel got a whole weekend off, and he returned with a big smile and a bigger posse. Paolo, Nava, and Becca Lynn were back, along with Rasheena from Christchurch, Sadie from Greece, and Ishtvan from Budapest, each one more attractive, robust, and upbeat than the next. When I wrote to Siddhi, I joked that Club Med must have recruited and fostered all the happy, dancing, robot-kids from the "It's a Small World" ride. Everyone was on their way to the beach in Agadir.

Edsel was the self-proclaimed "Ferris Bueller of the G.O.s." When he found out he no longer had to pay for my room, he used the money his mom wired him "for fun" to buy several rounds of beers for his friends, who laughed as he told his stories and chimed in with satellite anecdotes of their own, all roads leading back to Edsel for a "Fuck yeah!" or a "That's what she said!" or a closing joke or a segue or spiral into another of his own stories. He ran his fingers through my hair, kept his hand on the small of my back, and claimed me in a way I needed.

"So, you work at the hostel?" Becca Lynn said in her accent. Her skin was as luminous as mine was dull.

"As a maid," I said too eagerly, happy to be talking.

She pressed her lips together to staunch a giggle, "Oh. Eh, sorry, then."

"It's not that bad," I answered, noticing just then her exchanging a glance with Edsel and him looking quickly away. I wasn't sure what she was up to, but it didn't seem friendly, and I wanted to let her know she'd better get used to me. "It won't be long before I'm working with you guys."

Then, she really laughed, and Edsel shot her another look. "Sorry. Of course, because you're only sixteen, yeh?" She must have had some confidence with Edsel to have this information.

"*Yeh*." I mocked her accent, but she'd missed it, turning quickly to Nava for a bite of her lamb.

The pang was a familiar one: I was on the outside, and the normal, pretty people, who dwelled so easily in the regular lovely places, were in. I mouthed to Edsel, *What's up with her?* He shrugged. But then, he made out with me at the table, which felt perfect in all the important ways. And when they begged him again to join them, he refused. They left for the train, and Edsel stayed with me. He loved me. This was where I was supposed to be. This was growing up.

So, when we got back to the room, I ignored my stomach, and when he pushed gently on my head, I went down and gave Edsel his favorite prize.

CHAPTER 22

The High Seas, 1989 (Siddhartha)

Siddhi heard them mention the bust on the fucking ten o'clock news, Happy and Smiley taken into custody, lots of charges, ongoing investigation. The D.E.A. raided the Guy brothers, and though Jackson's reaction was familiar—contracting *the flu*, kicking every dealer and scrub out of Xanadu, and disappearing into his room—something massive had gone down, and now Siddhi had to brace for the recoil.

After a couple of days, Jackson emerged looking sick and like he hadn't slept, and when he told Siddhi he was headed for some fresh air and asked if Siddhi wanted to go fishing, Siddhi surprised himself by deciding to skip Travis's and accept the invitation.

Jackson agreed to prep the boat while Siddhi skated to *LaGorce Market* for a couple of sandwiches, a six-pack of Cel-Ray, and some chips and cookies, and when he returned, the two set off into the bay.

Siddhi was psyched at first about the raid on the Guys. Jackson was awful around those two, and their goons, and their guns. All his mojo vanished. He tripped over himself and became embarrassingly deferential as they verbally abused him like a fraternity pledge. And Siddhi felt embarrassed for him when he saw them off and then covered it up by saying something pathetic like, "It's always great to meet up with friends, huh?"

Siddhi certainly would not miss seeing Jackson with Happy and Smiley, and their motley crew of freaky yeoman, tied up behind Xanadu at night for a boat-to-boat exchange of laundry bags of cash for coolers of fish on ice, layered over plastic-wrapped pounds of weed and kilos of cocaine.

But now that they were in custody, was Jackson in danger? He and his dad were sitting on the Guy brothers' old boat, though Siddhi had no idea who currently owned it. Had it been Jackson who turned them in, he wondered, and if he weren't the snitch, then who was to say he wasn't next? He was curious, sure, but Siddhi wasn't dumb enough to ask the risky questions. And with enough weed, Jackson, at heart a storyteller, could monologue for hours.

Once they got out of the channel, Siddhi brought out a bag of joints, lit one, and passed it to Jackson. He was nervous to do it, but the punk voice in his head told him to ignore his nerves. *Who fucking cares, bro?* They had only been high together once before, right after CeeCee left, and Siddhi got home a little early from Trav's to find Jackson watching "Saturday Night Live." Siddhi had said, "Pass that," all casual-like and his dad paused for a second, laughed a little, and then *did.*

And since they never really talked anymore, not like they used to when Siddhi was a kid, passing the joint felt to Siddhi like the Jones version of having a catch.

CeeCee had been gone for weeks before Siddhi got a letter from her. "We made it to Marrakech!" He couldn't imagine how she might hear about the raid, but just in case, he sent a reply in which he described Jackson and Xanadu as "pretty much the usual." He shouldn't have lied, but what good was there to gain by telling the truth? Keeping Jackson's world secret from the outside world was a comfy old habit, and CeeCee now lived in the outside world. Siddhi added a postscript lie—*Jackson said he hopes you're having an awesome time adventuring.* But Jackson hadn't even mentioned her. And with CeeCee gone and Jackson a basket case, Siddhi had exactly zero reasons not to go get high.

They killed the motor in the good fishing spot and let the boat drift. As they set up the rods, Siddhi broke the silence, "So, when did *you* first smoke pot?"

Jackson laughed. "Heh. Well, it wasn't with my father," he said, the implication clearly being that Pop Pop wasn't as cool as he was.

Jackson seemed more relaxed, so Siddhi let himself chill, too. "Was it with Mom?" Jackson didn't answer. The pause made him nervous, but he could see Jackson thinking about the question. He took another hit, allowing Jackson the freedom to continue.

"My father was a real son-of-a-bitch," Jackson said. "Not cool like I am with you, munchie." He gave Siddhi a firm pat on the back of his shoulder. "He rode me hard. Wanted me in sports, working, in college, and up all the girls' skirts."

Siddhi laughed. It was hilarious, considering Jackson's abilities regarding getting laid.

"Listen, it wasn't so easy to get a piece of ass in the Sixties!" But he also chuckled. "This was before the Summer of Love, man. You were lucky if some girl in your school let you hold her hand. Anyhow, Pop was always calculating and coveting other men's successes." Jackson cast his line out into the bay, "He hated that he worked so hard for a home life that really was middle class and shit boring. The dinners, the holidays, and Bridge nights, everything repeated. Monday was Ma's no-flavor roast and pinochle in the Goldstein's den, and Tuesday was overcooked spaghetti, Hitchcock, and maybe some Dick Powell. Wednesday, I remember, tuna casserole—Jesus, every Wednesday—and then what was it on Thursdays? Maybe Veal Chop, and more TV. Forget his bookkeeping! Whisky was his real full-time job. He even spiked his coffee at the breakfast table. Real nasty drunk." Jackson cuffed his rod to secure it, and then he lay back on the cockpit settee, folded his hands over his abdomen, and closed his eyes.

"He took me to Pinochle once. I was younger than you, maybe

twelve, and I heard him tell Goldstein and his friends that Ma was a cold fish, that she'd hung up her saddle. That's what all those guys said about their wives. Most of 'em had girlfriends, but Pop liked whores. He had a few I think, but I only knew about Maggie. Fridays, between work and Shabbat, Pop saw Maggie."

Something nibbled at the line, but Siddhi ignored it, not daring to stop the story. If he didn't stay focused and quiet, his dad might spook or veer away from the subject, maybe never to return. So, Siddhi held his breath, buttoned up and expectant, letting Jackson drift with the joint and his memories.

"What are you, about fourteen now?" Jackson took another big hit. Exhaled. "Have you ever been laid?"

Siddhi's fifteenth birthday was four months past, but to both questions, he gave an indiscriminate "Mm." He knew Jackson would keep talking.

"When *I* turned sixteen, Pop had some kind of epiphany. 'You've had hair on your *schmeckle* for years now,' he said to me, 'and you can't get one little girl in the whole neighborhood to take hold of the damned thing!'" Jackson gave a chuckle that turned into a cough, and Siddhi noticed the cherry on the joint burning closer to his fingertips. He hoped it would hold out until the end of the story. "So, the next Friday, when I walked out of school with my friends, there he was, leaning against his Bel Air. 'Hey Pop.' I asked him, 'Uh, what's wrong? Something happen?' He ordered me into the car. I told him, 'I don't understand.' See, I was afraid of my father."

Siddhi remembered Aunt Paula telling them how Pop Pop beat Jackson with his belt when he failed to make the football team.

"He got in the car and patted me on the leg, all friendly and happy-like, and scared the shit out of me. With Pop, I was always waiting for the other shoe to drop, y'know?"

"Totally, yeah," Siddhi encouraged.

"Right, yeah. So, I asked him. 'Where we going?' And he said, 'Put on the damned radio!' I thought I did something wrong, and he was taking me home to kick my ass, but then he turned north. Told me, 'If Paula wants to iron her hair and dress like a communist hobo, that is your mother's problem, but YOU have to carry on the family name, and the job of making a boy into a man lies with the father.'

"Maggie's house looked like the rest of Surfside, *little boxes made of ticky-tacky* and all that. Pop told me his time was three o'clock because Maggie took care of her grandmother. He got all puffed up about how this beautiful blond girl seemed to think Pop was the end-all. He was so fuckin full of himself." Jackson toked again, sharply inhaled, crossed his ankles the opposite way, and opened one eye long enough to pass what was left of the joint to Siddhi.

"Anyway," Jackson said and exhaled a smoke ring. "Pop opened the front door to Maggie's like it was his own house and walked us right in."

A boat sped by, too close, and they rocked in its wake. "EASY!" Siddhi and Jackson shouted in sync. Siddhi took the opportunity to recast his line and to take a last hit. He lay back down and was quiet for a moment, but Jackson didn't resume.

"The door was unlocked?" Siddhi prompted. Stupid question, but it did the job.

"Well, no one locked their doors back then, but at least we knocked. Not Pop. I remember the foyer smelled like mothballs, and then this fuckin' beautiful girl, maybe sixteen, seventeen, clacked out wearing high heels with white feathers on the toes, and Pop kissed her on the cheek and handed her a five-dollar bill and a twisted little grin.

"Understand, I had no idea Pop meant to get me laid, y'know, not a clue what the fuck was going on. So, then this girl takes me down the hall to her bedroom. I'll never forget she had pink and green, seahorse wallpaper. And she had an Elvis poster and a record player.

"When she came onto me, munchie, I was so surprised, I kinda jumped back and fell off her bed!" Jackson burst out laughing. "Knocked over a lit candle and damn near caused a fire!"

Siddhi laughed, too, and flicked the spent roach overboard.

"'Just tell him we did it,' she said. And since Pop paid her, she told me to come back Monday, by myself, for the real thing. Before we left her room, she put my hands on her tits, like a little sample, and I gotta tell you, man, to this day, that was the most erotic moment of my life." He paused, cracked a soda, and handed one to Siddhi.

With Jackson's face soft in the brightness of the sun, Siddhi could make out the boy from Nana's photos, when Jackson looked fresh and new. "After that, she led me to her living room where Pop sat with his shoes off and his feet kicked up on her coffee table. 'So?' he said, and I thought I was gonna puke right there. I think I shrugged, and then he threw me his keys and told me to wait for him in the car."

"Ew, shit! He went right after you?" Siddhi hadn't meant to say this out loud.

"Well, at that point," Jackson defended, "I hadn't been with her yet." Siddhi felt himself rooting hard for his dad, the marijuana in his brain looping him through the very real truth that the hero in this story would grow up to be his own oppressor. His Pop insisted on school, whereas Jackson locked him in a room and forbade it. Really, truly, there was no fucking difference, but weaving a double helix of father-son irony wasn't going to get him the end of Jackson's story.

"So, you went back on Monday, right?"

"Hell, yeah, I went back on Monday! I skipped geometry and took the bus up to Surfside. I picked a little bouquet of flowers from the hedges I passed walking from the bus, and when I went in the house, Maggie was happy to see me and kissed me at the door. She took the little bouquet and went to the bathroom, and when she came back, she was in this sheer nighty… Man, I could see everything, and she had all the flowers woven into her hairdo. I made a bunch of amateur moves on her, and she told me I needed to relax, and asked me if I'd ever smoked grass."

This reminded Siddhi of his original question. "And that, munchie, was the first time I ever smoked pot!"

"So, Maggie was, like, a wasteoid?"

"No. Siddhi, c'mon? You're old enough to understand this,

man. Maggie wasn't a junkie like your mother. She just did what she had to do to take care of her family." Siddhi never thought about his mother the way CeeCee had, but he didn't like to hear her described as so broken. CeeCee would spontaneously combust from this story, but Siddhi wanted the rest.

"So, for Maggie, it probably just took the edge off of, like... being a whore?"

Jackson shrugged. "Heh, probably. It takes the edge off a lot of things...things you never let yourself believe would ever come to pass." He trailed off, distracted, looked out over the water, and scratched his head. Siddhi knew there was more to his thought; there had to be some reason he had all this shit on tap today, but he didn't want the metaphysical lecture. He wanted the rest of the story.

"What happened after you two got high?"

"She avowed me to her mysteries, man. And it was redolent... symphonic...tantric... Maggie hypnotized me."

Jackson told Siddhi how he traded afternoons hanging out with his friends to work as a part-time bellhop at the Eden Roc Hotel, so he could afford his Mondays with Maggie. He said Murray teased him for thinking he was a "big working man" and once gave him the belt out of pure spite because he said, "You think everything comes so Goddamned easy, dontcha?"

Maggie asked for five dollars, and Jackson paid her ten, for which she promised to stop the Fridays with his Pop. She listened to him as he lay in her arms and told her of Murray's evils and about how Jackson always felt outside of things, a bad fit, and then she spread her legs on top of him and told him, "You're a good fit with me." Sometimes, they had a few minutes left for a third time. Sometimes, they said, "I love you."

"I told her, 'When I'm eighteen, we'll get married, pack up, and drive away,' and I meant it, man. I even saved up for a ring." Jackson rubbed his eyes, and Siddhi saw they were more bloodshot than usual, sadder.

Siddhi *got* the teen version of his dad yearning to flee home and never look back, and in this way, he realized he understood

CeeCee, too.

"So, then?"

"So then, the first Friday of summer vacation, I was in Flamingo Park about to leave for work, and Pop pulled into our house for lunch, but when he left, he headed in the wrong direction, and I got this tragic pang in my gut. I stashed my guitar in the bushes and ran to the bus, telling myself all the way there that she loved me, she promised, she'd never. But I had that sick feeling right in here," he circled his fist over his gut. "I sprinted to the bus and then to Maggie's, and wouldn't you know it, there was Pop's laurel green Bel Air, parked along the grass.

"I wanted to peek through a window, but I feared what I might see inside. Like, how could she spend Friday humping the guy who gave me the same welts on my back that she just kissed on Monday? I thought, no way, man, never. I was madly in love with this girl!"

"What the fuck did you do?" Siddhi asked, ever more invested.

"I hid!" Jackson laughed. "In the bushes! Like a nutball, crouched there in the rain—it was pouring, did I mention that? Until my clothes were soaked through, and then the rain stopped just in time for Pop to stroll out to his car and drive off like the cat who ate the fuckin canary.

"I got up the nerve to try the door, but it was locked. I knocked and waited. Knocked harder. And then I knocked on the window and peeked in to see her right there. Her lipstick smeared a little on her chin. She looked right out at me. And then I saw, it wasn't her, well, it was the same person, but her face wasn't my sweet Maggie. This girl was someone else. Her eyes were dead. She looked bitter, sick of it. Her energy was so different, man. Like a hundred years old in a bad way." He cleared the emotion out of his throat.

"I smiled at her anyway. Made a signal like, 'let me in.' She didn't smile back."

"Think by going there on Pop Pop's day," Siddhi asked, "you, like, broke the hooker laws?"

Jackson laughed again. "I think exactly that. Anyway, Maggie shut the drapes on me, and that was that."

Siddhi took his own deep breath. Even though they were on the other side of years, Siddhi now understood that not only did his dad *not* get the girl, but also that THE girl, Jackson's one-that-got-away, was not Siddhi's poor, dead mom. Still, it moved him that Jackson once fought for love. He wondered what happened to the hard-working idealist. Could it be that with one heartbreak, Jackson up and quit? And why did he choose today for father-son bonding? Today, suddenly, Siddhi deserved to hear the whole story? Siddhi tensed up and felt the usual rising rage, the kind that, when it boiled over, had to be cut and bled out. He felt so conscious of his skin, wanting to slice it. He lit a fresh joint and took a big hit.

Siddhi couldn't help doing the math, putting Pop Pop Murray's age in 1963 super close to his dad's age now, and was amazed at how his dad seemed completely oblivious to the parallel between Murray's whoring and his own M.O. of fucking girl after girl after girl, none of them far north of twenty. "So, then what?"

"Whaddaya mean, what? I left and went home in tears. That's what. By the time I grabbed my guitar from the park bushes, I was dead set on running away. I stayed in the park long enough to let Pop get home first, and when I finally showed up, it crushed me to find Ma in the kitchen peeling carrots and Paula braiding the challah dough like it was any other Friday. And Pop at the head of the table waiting like the fuckin king of the manor."

In his bedroom, he lit the joint Maggie gave him on his last real visit and smoked it out his open window. That was the moment, he told Siddhi, that he distinctly remembered thinking, *Who fucking cares?* And he packed away his love for Maggie, *his* Maggie, and the scent of her bouncing ponytail, her voice, and the faint pop of her lips opening for a kiss.

"I picked up my guitar and put it all in the song, three verses, a chorus, and a bridge. I'd guess most love songs happen something like that."

Siddhi stared at the open ocean, feeling in awe of the series of unlikely almosts and thuds that brought him and his dad to this day on this boat where they lay, high off their asses and with no happy ending anywhere on the horizon. No wonder he felt so depressed. The condition was genetic. The rest of the story, Siddhi knew by heart. He'd heard it told to many rounds of Babies over the years.

One Sunday in the summer of '63, a man in a shiny suit heard his dad playing "Tiny Flowers" in the park.

"That's a hit, kid!" he said and set Jackson up with a shiny blue suit, a drummer, and another boy on rhythm guitar and dubbed them *The Sandcastles.* "You'll be the Beach Boys of the East Coast!" He signed the recording contract—ten thousand dollars—and changed his name from Johnathan Schmuel Litzkin to Jackson Jones. "Better to be less...*ethnic*," the man said, handing over the check.

"Jackson Jones, the big shot from the Sandcastles, is my *son!*" Murray told the pinochle fellas, the rabbi, the waitress at Wolfie's, and most likely, he told it to Maggie. To his son, Murray cautioned, "How 'bout you don't screw this one up?"

The Sandcastles toured around to county fairs, convention halls, dance halls, and variety shows. The drummer taught Jackson how to drive a car and come onto women. The other boy, on bass, introduced him to the Bhagavad Gita, fasting, and meditation. Each time he sang "Tiny Flowers," he thought of Maggie, a year of nights, singing her song to a sea of new ponytails—a different one after every show, quick, in dressing rooms and cars, after they'd smoked enough grass with him to forget they were nice girls. But, soon after, Ed Sullivan bumped *The Sandcastles* for Topo Gigio, radio play dried up when Bob Dylan and The Beatles put out new albums, and the man told Jackson, "Sorry, kid. That's show business."

Siddhi's mom came around right after the music went kaput, like one of the new girls at Xanadu. The only thing that made his mom more than just a chaser for Maggie was her timing and demonstrative fertility; she managed to produce Sienna and Siddhartha, two anchors she chained to Jackson just before she did what she had to do to cut her own self free.

"You've got one!"

"What?" Jackson got up to grab Siddhi's rod just before it flew out toward the water. Something had bitten and was taking the line down deep and away. It was a big one, and the weight of the fish bent the rod and pulled Jackson way forward. He leaned out and in and out and in, each time pulling back to reel in another two or three feet of line. Siddhi stood behind him to try and lend a hand, but he couldn't get a good angle, and then there was a big yank and a snap, causing all the pressure to vanish. Siddhi reeled to the end of the line, but with nothing to weigh it down, what was left of the lure practically leaped out of the water.

*

The morning after their fishing trip, an hour earlier than the earliest Siddhi had ever seen his father rise, Jackson came out in a new suit, pale gray, with a crisp white shirt and a pink tie. He'd cut his hair bizarrely short and shaved his face clean.

Siddhi thought he was someone else at first, never having seen, for the length of his life, the bare skin of Jackson's cheeks and chin, nor had he ever seen Jackson be stone cold, sweaty sober, like an anxious boy headed off to his bar mitzvah. Siddhi wolf-whistled to acknowledge the makeover.

"You planning a big day with Nana at Temple Beth Shalom?"

"Hey, munchie, seen my keys?" he asked, popping a pill that he chased with a whole glass of water. He patted his pockets and exhaled a sigh. Siddhi thought it looked like the suit was wearing the man, and he understood something had gone badly for Jackson. CeeCee remained AWOL, and Siddhi finally realized he was scared. He found the keys where they always were in the bowl on Jackson's dresser, returned to the foyer, and handed them over with a weak smile.

"Hey, you alright?" His dad wasn't really listening, but he took the keys, gave Siddhi a grateful pat on the arm, and headed for the door. "Jackson!" Siddhi hadn't meant to shout. His dad was startled, stopped, and looked back, took off his suit jacket, folded it shoulder to shoulder, and laid it over his left arm. All of it seemed so alien like it was happening with two other people in some other house. "Where are you going?"

"Court," said Jackson. "I've been indicted." And he walked out, leaving Siddhi standing in the open doorway.

CHAPTER 23:

No Flow,
1989 (Sienna)

The first week, I was sure it was menstrual. My period was imminent, and I always had a queasy PMS day. The second week I figured traveler's diarrhea, then food poisoning, then stomach flu, and now, after a third week of sickness, I was too taken up with staggering to the bathroom to experience some form of vile deluge from either one of my ends to worry about what to call it.

Of course, I thought of going to the doctor, but I still had to change the sheets in at least three rooms per day, sweep the sand from the whole building, do the laundry, and clean the bathrooms. I had no additional energy or clarity to even plan anything and used all remaining time to sleep and sleep and sleep. I fell into my bed every night with a weak prayer that I might get better soon.

On Tuesday, I called *Club Med* and left Edsel a message asking for help. He never got back, but on Friday afternoon, at the start of his August weekend off, Edsel showed up alone. He said the crew was headed to the beach in Essaouira this time.

"Everyone's staying in this place where Janis Joplin and Jimi

Hendrix used to hang out," he said. "And the surf's up!" He was so chipper, I decided not to mention my deeply unsexy issues of late period and diarrhea.

"Want to see my new space?" I asked from the lobby chaise where he found me napping.

"New space?" he asked, and I let him pull me up. He went to kiss me, but my breath was puke, so I gave him a medium-long hug.

"You changed rooms?"

"Had to." A summer rush at the hostel the week before inspired Farid to kick me out of Room 4 and show me to a former exit vestibule with a filthy bedspread and a window-sized hole where it was clear someone bricked up half the back door. I'd spent weeks passing bits of time with strangers and hedging the lonely nights (two weeks since the last time he slept over) with the promise of Edsel figuring out a way to rescue me from what seemed to be a bad plan.

When I came in from my last day out with short term "friends", Farid said, "You here!" And when he pointed to the grimy little corner, I was too nauseated to protest. Instead, I used my remaining strength to scrub the filthy walls with a bleach solution and nail a spare bedspread tightly all the way around the "window." I wore myself out, but each day since, I added something: a lamp, a fan, a candle, a vase of feathers, the white and gold leather pouf I bought at the tannery, to make it feel less like a cell. I made my space look the opposite of how I felt, and I had to say, it was quite pretty.

Once I shut my door, Edsel came up behind me and kissed my neck, walking me toward the bed. Usual me would have welcomed him by slinking slowly out across the covers, but the new me concentrated on getting back to sleep as quickly as possible, preferably with Edsel reassuring me he intended to take over my care.

"Looks really nice," he said with a smile and no further questions.

I tried to use some idiotic love-telepathy to get it to be his idea to pick me up and lay me gently on the bed, tell me everything was going to be okay, and then call the Club Med doctor to come give me medicine and while we waited, maybe even hum Cat Stevens songs to me like I used to do when Siddhi had the croup cough, but Edsel hadn't even looked at me yet.

"They moved me, too! I got this awesome room with Paolo and Ishtvan. It's a corner unit, so we have cross-ventilation, and all the G.O.s hang out there. Everyone loves it. Awesome, right?" He pulled my hips toward his groin. "Mm. Take these clothes off, sexy girl," he cooed into my ear, "I brought you something." He rubbed my fingers over the crotch of his pants.

When I pulled back my hand, he chuckled, "Oh! Heh. Got it. Aunt Flow visiting?" I was supposed to be done with my period. I was already through a week and a half of the new pill pack. I wasn't sure if I'd been sick long enough to have puked up too many pills last month and gotten myself pregnant. No. But then, wasn't a missed period the universal indicator of a pregnancy?

I remember Wren Raintree's mom used to tease her that she was a diaphragm and foam baby, like that was something special about Wren, like she'd think that was hilarious. We didn't want you so much that we used two kinds of birth control! I supposed parents just stumbled through all this shit by accident, like Edsel and I were right then. A couple of horny dummies playing a bizarre version of house, and now, because we were both so irresponsible, we might be adding on.

"Be right back," I told him as I left for the bathroom, barely making the stall before heaving until the little bit of food and water I'd managed to swallow was out, and nothing came up but foamy bile. The dark circles under my eyes and my caved-in cheeks, made me look a little like Siddhi had the time he got food poisoning at Lum's, and Nana took us to the clinic that had a slide in the waiting room. I didn't use it because Siddhi was too sick to use it, and I didn't want to make him feel worse. I missed him, Aunt Paula, and Nana, even Jackson, in a way that made me weak, and my guts squeezed into a cramp that brought me to my knees on the cool tiles. If this was morning sickness, I had trouble believing we hadn't just let humanity die out.

To be sure, Edsel would be shocked at first if I told him I might be pregnant, maybe even pissed. He might go off on me and say a few things he didn't mean, and I'd hang in there until the end of whatever and forgive him. And he was also adventurous and impulsive, so there was an equal chance he'd drop to his knees and spontaneously propose. We'd get married, have the baby, and deal with everything together as a family. I wouldn't be a bumbling, accidental mother. I'd attend, adapt, and abide. Another round of dry heaves, and I cleaned up and brushed my teeth.

On my way back from the bathrooms, I ran into Nava in the lobby. "Hey, you," she called in her Israeli accent. One-Eyed Willie spied me, ran over, and made furry figure eights through my ankles.

"Nava! What are you doing here?" I didn't want a visitor, and Edsel had a way of making me feel invisible whenever the Club girls came around. She bent to pet the cat, who bolted for safety.

"Eh, I don't know best to say this, so please you deedn't know this from me..." She shifted around, anxiously, like she wanted to leave as much as I wanted her to leave.

"What? I don't understand you. I didn't know what from you?"

"Eh, Edsel, when you called heem, he deed not want to come to the phone. He said to tell you to cheell out. But CeeCee..."

"What, Nava? What is it?" *IT* was that even though he was in my room for the moment, the truth was that I was all alone, that Edsel lived over there, and that he was laughing about me and telling his friends to hang up the phone when I called for help!

"Please. You didn't know from me," Nava repeated. "He is with Becca. In the village, he goes with Becca Lynn."

"What?"

"Becca Lynn. He is with her. Please, CeeCee, because I feel so badly for you. You deedn't know this from me. I must go now," she said and almost ran from the entryway out toward the square.

I hid in the phone closet in the Taziz lobby with my new pile of unwelcome, semi-reliable information. Edsel was with someone else? For a year, I made him the person I believed kept me safe, the one who loved me the most. I let Courtney go, and Siddhi, my family, and I'd been positive that Edsel and I had created a life that led us to Africa. But in the end, Edsel Chaiken was in Morocco, and I was in Morocco, of course, but we—that is Edsel and I as a family—were not together. He had no hand in anything I'd done to date, from buying the ticket to packing and coming to getting my job to filling my lonely, painful days.

Back in the room, I found he'd dozed off on the bed. I slammed the door accidentally on purpose, and he opened his eyes to slits. I'd stripped off my sweaty *djellaba* and stood by the bed in my bra and undies stilled by futility. He sat up, and I let his eyes roam over my body, and the three seconds of *being seen* sent surges of energy, joy, and humiliation to my crampy muscles. For the moment, I was so weak and lonely, it felt better to ignore Nava's revelation.

"Wow," he said, rubbing his eyes, hair mussed from sleep. He looked sweet and handsome, all cuddled up in my pillows, and I grinned against my will. "What've you been up to over here?" he asked, smiling back.

"Yeah," I said weakly. "It's sorta been a rough couple of weeks..."

"You look so *skinny*," he interrupted. "Jesus, kid. You must've lost like ten pounds or something." I sat on the edge of the bed.

"Okay, so, yeah," I began. "It's been kinda bad for me here, like really bad, and, um, I know I should've told you everything, but I didn't have the—"

"You look *hot*!" he interrupted. "Holy shit! Come 'ere..." He scooted over and reached for me, came around for a kiss. Self-conscious about my breath, I avoided his face. Looking down, I saw him work his erection out through the slot in his underwear.

"Are you serious?" A rush of stingy acid shot up my esophagus and ended in a burning, bubble-pop belch.

"I don't know, *am I?*" He reached back to unclasp my bra, and too weak to react, I made no move to stop him, though I winced against his touch. I curled forward to lie down, which Edsel took as an invitation to roll on top of me, smooshing me beneath his weight. "I mean," he pressed his boner between my limp legs, "have you seen yourself?"

He kissed my neck, trying, fumbling to find his way inside of me, and I pulled at the mattress corner to get leverage to roll out from under him. The effort caused a sharp stomach pang and I rolled off the bed with a cry of pain. On my knees on the floor, I heaved up a bit of saliva onto the tile. "Mostly," I said, wiping my mouth with my forearm, "I only see my reflection in the toilet bowl."

"What'd you say?" He laughed, missing it. "What are you mumbling about now, skinny girl?"

Help me! Please, help me! I begged in my thoughts. "I'm *SICK, okay?*" I finally shouted to him. "Can't you see that I'm sick? I've been sick for weeks, almost the whole time we've been here. Do you know I can't even pee? I don't think I've peed in like two days. And I cry all the time, but I can't even make tears come out anymore. I am *dying* in this dump while you fuck around in your *cross-ventilation* with Cubby and Annette, and the rest of the Mouseketeers!"

"Who's *Cubby?*"

"Never mind. Just move over." I got back on the bed and pulled the sheets to my chin. "I need to sleep."

"I don't know what you're imagining in that crazy little head of yours, CeeCee, but I've been *working*. And you never said anything about being sick. How was I supposed to know?"

"Maybe if you looked past the beautiful continent of *Australia.*"

"What? Oh, I see. Now you're jealous of Becca Lynn?" He got my drift too quickly on that one. He wasn't quick enough to make that sort of connection unless he was guilty. "Oh sure, now I am *cheating* on you with everyone! I guess that's why I came here to bring you to the beach on my only weekend off."

"I'm not jealous," I said, and it was true, I really wasn't. "I'm just sick," scary sick, dehydrated, and wasted with a near constant headache and partial consciousness, like sick-sick, like drop dead in Morocco at sixteen for being an ignorant, pregnant, cheated on moron sick. I'd only written lies to Siddhi, stories all about what I *wanted* Edsel and this place to be.

"Yeah, well," he said. "You don't need to jump down my throat. I didn't make you sick."

Farid gave me the afternoons to rest rather than have me quit, but even afterward, I had trouble carrying the sheets or lifting the broom, let alone cleaning the whole building. I rolled toward Edsel, put my head down, and ran my fingers through his hair the way he liked. "I know you've been working hard. I'm proud of you."

"*Thank you,*" he said, relaxing into my fingertips. He put his arms around my waist.

"I just, I *really, really* need you to take me to the doctor." I had canker sores on my gums, and my lips cracked at the corners, my heart pounded into the top of my head. Let the doctor announce the pregnancy. Then, they might give me the right medicine to help me regain the strength to figure it all out with him afterward.

"I really want to help," he said. "I just, I have a lot of errands to do today, and I need to work out..."

"Right now, Edsel!" I got up, picked up my *djellaba,* and motioned for him to help me on with it. He looked confused. I tossed it to his hands and put mine above my head.

"Okay. Like how long d'you think?" He pulled the garment over my head as I threaded my hands through the sleeves. "You probably have like a bad stomach bug. It happens all the time in the village. I mean, I don't think there is any real medicine for it. You probably just need a shitload of Gatorade."

"It's right across the square. Please, let's go." Without waiting for his answer, I put my arm around his shoulders, and the exertion of standing again so soon caused me to lose control of my bowel for a second, not enough for Edsel to notice, but enough to restart the trembling and frighten me into thinking about dying, being painless and peaceful. At my little funeral, Jackson would speak about immortality and quote from the *Bhagavad Gita: Never the spirit was born; the spirit shall cease to be never; Never was time it was not; End and Beginning are dreams.* If Edsel showed up, I pictured furious Siddhi telling him how his relationship with me was symbolized by the skid mark they found in my underpants when I died. The thought made me laugh, which confused Edsel.

"Let's just go!" I said.

"You really do look beautiful," he said again, as he dispatched me from the hostel and led me out into the square. "I'm not an asshole, CeeCee. When you're all better in a day or two, you'll see." He looked at his watch and then picked me up to carry me more quickly toward the green crescent moon sign for the pharmacy. Inside, he lowered me into a chair in the chilly waiting area and signed me in. I patted the empty seat beside me, but he stayed on his feet.

"You're sick, babe. They said a few minutes." I felt keenly aware of my disappointment in his every gesture, every choice, but what did I want him to do? The ultimate fantasy involved him running erratic, Shirley MacLaine in *Terms-of-Endearment-esque* laps around the waiting room howling, "Sienna is in pain. She's in pain! Help her! Someone, help her! Give my girlfriend the god-damned shot!"

Edsel checked his watch again. "Look, I-I'm going with them to the beach this time. I know this sounds bad, but I haven't gone once yet, and you know how much this means to me. I only get one weekend off, and I can't just, like, lay in bed the whole time. You stay here where there is help, and I'll go pack and nap and stay with you tonight. I'm going to do that even though it takes a night off my trip since you probably can't come. I'll leave in the morning. Okay, pukey-girl?" He popped his eyebrows suggestive-ly. "Rest up. No school today," he joked, offering a pathetic grin.

I wanted so much to be angry, to yell and scream about what I deserved to get from love, but my experiment had failed. Barrel-bottom least, though, I thought he'd wait with me, but he kissed the top of my head, stroked my hair, and pulled what Siddhi called a Huckleberry Hound. "Exit...stage left!"

✳

"Parles tu anglais?" I asked the handsome, Moroccan doctor, in my pitiful smidgeon of French. "Speak English?"

He shook his head. "*Uniquement en français et en arabe.*"

"Um, okay. French. Uh, I mean, *français.*" I pointed to my stomach and wrung my hands, "Ahhhhh...*Estomac...comme ça?*" Then I threw in some dramatic pointing and groaning. "Uhhh oooh...*Vous comprenez?*" He nodded that he understood. And then I heaved to illustrate vomiting, which aggravated my gag reflex, though nothing much came up. The doctor watched patiently. I waved my hands in spastic waterfalls from both my mouth and backside. "Um, uh, *très malade. Malade estomac.*" And finally, I threw in the encore. "No, um, no period, *vous comprenez?*" I folded my arms in front of my belly and rocked the air, "No menstruation." I pointed to my crotch. And then I scooped up the air and laid it over my shoulder to burp it. "*J'ai bébé?*" I broke and began to cry (no tears though). "*Est-ce clair?*"

"*Oui, ma chère,*" he nodded kindly. "*Je comprends.*"

Thank goodness, I thought, hopefully, he really does understand because the only French words I had left in my vocabulary were *croissant, soufflé,* and *voulez-vous coucher avec moi ce soir?*

The doctor pinched the skin on my cheek and then released it, staring as it held in place for far too long. He sighed and then repeated the pinch on my arm, belly, and thigh, sighed again, and even tsk-tsked through his considerable mustache.

The nurse took four stabs before finding a cooperative vein, and they kept me laid out and shivering on an I.V. for a few hours. They spoke to one another in Arabic. After piping two whole bags of clear fluid into my veins, they were able to take some blood.

"Shh," said the nurse, "*Repos.*" But I couldn't rest. The blood would be for the pregnancy test, to be sure. They'd confirm what I already knew, that I was no better than my mother or Jackson or all those Babies who followed their selfish whims away from their responsibilities and the people who needed them and loved them the most. I fell asleep wondering if my mother and Jackson, like Edsel and me, were just living their lives and trying their best.

"*Oui, ça va?*" The doctor was back. I wasn't ready to be a mother. And Edsel—a guy who needed to take a nap more than he needed to take care of me—was sure as hell not ready to be a dad. Nana would likely disown me as my mother's parents had, and it wouldn't change a thing. No one would have me like this. Not Edsel's parents. God! Not even Edsel, who suddenly seemed of little importance to me now. The doctor clapped his hands together.

"*Ce est bon, mon cher, vous avez un parasite,*" he said. "*Giardia. Est-ce que tu comprends?* Okay. Gi-ar-di-a."

"What about the baby? Uh...*le bébé?*"

"Ah! *Non. Non. Non. Tu es très déshydraté. Pas de bébé. Non!*"

Dehydrated from a parasite, not pregnant. No baby. No. No. No. The gentle and kind Moroccan doctor wrote me a prescription. And just like that, I was not a mother.

As the nurse helped me from the exam room back into the waiting area, a cute backpacker stood at the pharmacy counter buying Band-Aids and speaking pretty fluent French. The nurse sat me in a chair to rest for the walk back across the square, and I looked up when I heard him count his money to himself in English.

"Excuse me," I said. "Sorry to bother you, but I am not sure if I got the right medicine. Can I borrow your French?"

The guy was tall and awkwardly attractive in that way a guy could be who was no longer a teenager but not yet thickened into a full man. He had eyes the same rainbow hazel as Siddhi's and an oversized Adam's apple that rolled up his neck when he said, "Oh, you're American?"

I smiled. "Yeah. I am. I'm Sienna."

"Jeez, no offense, Sienna, but you don't look so good." I chuckled, and he assumed I was insulted. "I mean, you *do* look good, attractive I mean, er, but you know, not so *healthy*...oh jeez, you know what I mean?" He put his forehead in his hand.

I was pretty sure he was flirting. "No. It's fine," I said. "But can you check this and tell me what it is and how to take it? It'd be super awesome if maybe I didn't die."

Kevin, from Michigan, laughed. He was twenty-two and traveling with friends after graduating from Haverford, "a pretty good college in New England," he said. I'd never heard of it, but the name summoned boys with side parts in argyle sweater vests who spoke Latin and snuck cigarettes behind the school chapel. Kevin had a chat with the doctor, and after five minutes, I learned that I had been dangerously dehydrated, that I needed to drink a lot of fluids, and that the four pills I took would kill the Giardia parasites before they killed me.

"It says that even though it works, you're still gonna be sick and have symptoms for up to two weeks. Uh, no raw food, and don't drink the water here. Drink Coca-Cola and juice and stay in bed. It says *a lot of rest*." Without me even asking him to, he helped me walk all the way back to the hostel.

"Thank you so much," I gushed. "Really, this is so nice of you." And with my arms wrapped around cute Kevin and his backpack, my hand hit up against something in the side pocket, and I couldn't help palming it as a memory of this selfless person who wanted nothing in return for his help.

"No problem," he said in a slightly different voice. "Hey, uh, what's your deal?" he asked with a different smile. Whoa! Kevin *had been* flirting.

I thought, *you just finished telling me how sick I am, and now you want a date?* "I think my deal is to get in bed and try not to barf myself to death."

"Heh, yeah, no," he laughed. "I know. I just mean, like, are you with someone?"

"Let a man lift himself by his own self alone, let him not lower himself; for this self alone is the friend of oneself and this self alone is the enemy of oneself."

Kevin blinked.

I'd fallen asleep a little, and in my daze, I mumbled a quote from the *Bhagavad Gita*. "Oh man, did I say that out loud? That's embarrassing." I tripped and almost fell.

Kevin put both of his arms around me to strengthen his hold and keep me upright and moving. "Um, I meant, do you have a boyfriend?"

"Honestly," I said. "I don't really know."

Back in my room, I shoved the plastic lens cap from Kevin's Nikon into my Bee Gees pack, and definitively unpregnant but far too ill to work, I fell into bed. Edsel had left me a note saying he caught the earlier train to the beach, hoped I felt better, and he'd be back early on Sunday night to see me before returning to Club Med. That was it.

*

By the end of the weekend, the Taziz was such a god-awful mess I stopped leaving my room. Farid came in spitting fury, but I didn't even lift my head to acknowledge him. He said something that I took to mean I was fired and stormed out.

After another ugly round in the bathroom, I checked the mirror on my way out to find that I'd broken a bunch of blood vessels in my cheeks and in the whites of my eyes. The medicine had done nothing yet to heal me. More than anything, I wished to call Siddhi to hear his voice, but making a phone call or mailing a letter might as well have been climbing Everest.

It was dark out when Edsel clamored in drunk. As usual, he got naked and into bed, spooned up behind me, and wrapped me in his warmth. He smelled horribly of beer, and when I "slept" through him poking me with his hard-on, he jerked off and passed out.

Around four, I crawled from the room because, thanks to the I.V. at the clinic, I had to pee! Then I changed into my clean, blue *djellaba* and had to rest again after all that movement. I lay down and watched Edsel breathe for a while, kissed his cheek, and said, "I really wanted to love you." And I cried (with tears) because I knew it hadn't ever been true, not once in all the thousand times I'd said it to him.

Walking slowly through the lobby, carrying my Bee Gees backpack and my twelve hundred dollars, I had an idea. I grabbed the big scissors from the drawer in the front desk, and feeling an intense desire, desperate to be remembered, I crept back into my room, and, with great care, swiftly separated Edsel from his beloved ponytail—which had been inexplicably crimped.

"I'm breaking up with you," I whispered and then headed for the train.

CHAPTER 24:

STOP!
1989 (Siddhartha)

Fox tore into the Betsy Ross Hotel with a gnarly shiner on his left eye and ordered everyone to follow him. Siddhi and the rest grabbed their boards and followed in formation. They skated all the way west and over MacArthur causeway until Fox made a right onto the bridge to Star Island, a private, man-made circle of killer-rich mansions in the middle of Biscayne Bay.

Siddhi couldn't be sure whether Fox was giving them a work-out, messing around, or if they were headed toward more mayhem, as they had the week before, when, after Siddhi convinced him not to *remove* stop signs, Fox bought a can of Krylon and defaced every stop sign around Fienberg-Fisher Elementary:

STOP *pissing me off!*

STOP *being a SHEEP!*

STOP *sucking cock!*

At least the stop signs stayed in place and the *sheep*, as Fox called all non-punk civilians, would still know when to stop, Siddhi thought. His friends could get their jollies without hurting people. Two days after he vanished, Jackson had called to say something about his lawyer making a plea deal and, "Tell your sister." Siddhi was baked off his ass when he'd answered, the connection was all static and crunch, and he hung up before asking any follow-up questions, like, *What in the fuck do I do now?*

Siddhi thought to call Nana, but he couldn't be sure if Jackson had told her anything, and he didn't want to make the situation worse. He considered staying with Trav for a while, to stop spending his nights at home spooked, cutting, and too high to cry. He felt like a fucking idiot for doing nothing, but this was no after-school special; it was his life, and he wasn't going to throw his dad under the bus or chance missing CeeCee's next letter by leaving.

The guard at the security gate made no move except to wave Fox on as he ollied his board over the speed bump and hung a right.

"What is this place?" Siddhi asked when Trav caught up. "What's he up to?"

"Don't know," Travis shrugged, *"but we're movin' on up. C'mon, bro!"*

Fox skated a lap around the whole island. Most of the properties were elaborate mansions, like Xanadu, only meticulously maintained. Fox stopped at a coded keypad, typed, and then led them through the automatic gates toward a three-story gleaming white mansion with a tiled roof and a manicured front garden.

"Yo, Frandy!" Fox said, high-fiving a Black dude in khaki coveralls who worked a sudsy rag over the lacquered hood of a Rolls-Royce Corniche out front of the opened bay of a five-car garage.

"Yo, Mista Fox," Frandy called over his shoulder in a Haitian accent and turned back in time to nod and wave at the rest of the group before returning to his duties. Siddhi waved back as he passed close enough to see the sweat beads on Frandy's forehead and upper lip, the deep wrinkles around his tired face, and the wiry infestation of grays in his hair and eyebrows.

"Hi," he said to the old man, who had looked much younger

and stronger from farther away.

"Hello, mista, sir," Frandy said in his servant's timbre, punctuated with a noticeable head bow that made Siddhi wonder how old was too old to be sweating your ass off sponge-bathing some rich fucker's Rolls-Royce. Siddhi's guess: about Frandy's age.

To the far left of the façade, Fox turned behind a perfect stand of arborvitaes that shielded the side porch. He hooked his board by one wheel on a line of rope, strung for this purpose outside the *Service Entrance*, which was embossed on a brass plate on the door. The boys followed him in and down a hallway into a huge kitchen of white marble and dark wood that seemed eerily familiar.

"I've seen this place before," Siddhi blurted. "I-I can't figure out how I know it…"

"Oh shit, then I'm not crazy, right?" Travis said, "I've seen it, too."

"Yeah, me, too, douchebags," Fox snarked. "It was on the last episode of "Miami Vice." My father is best-faggot-golf-buddies with one of the producers." He plucked a grape from the fruit bowl and lobbed it to Travis, who caught it in his mouth.

"Nice!" Fox laughed. "You're like Salty the fuckin' sea lion, bro."

"So, like, you're rich, dude," Christian said, helping himself to some grapes.

"My *father* is rich," Fox said as he wrenched a jug of apple cider and half a fancy cake from a carved wooden cabinet that turned out to hide the fridge. "I'm the little prick he wishes was never born," he added. "Take some of this. The maid soaks it with booze." They tore off pieces of cake and ate with their hands. Fox opened the juice bottle. His Mohawk hung soft over the brown stubble on his scalp. He was seventeen, two years older than Siddhi, but swigging from the bottle in his fancy kitchen made him look like a little boy.

Fox led them back outside, and they followed him, each grabbing back his board. Behind the house, they walked a brick path that cut through the long, velvety back lawn to the seawall. Fox flew past on his board, stopping just at the edge of the open bay.

"Siddhi-man," said Trav. "This is like is the mega-version of Xanadu, bro."

"What?" said Christian, but he clearly wasn't interested. Siddhi dragged his finger across his throat, and Trav nodded, being exactly smart enough to *grok* that Xanadu was not up for discussion.

Even at Siddhi's last lunch with Nana, where they munched knishes and mustard at the deli, Siddhi avoided the subject of Xanadu. Nana may or may not have known about Jackson, but when she asked Siddhi about home, he said something like, *Fine. Usual.* And she moved on to Siddhi's appearance. "Well, you look like a derelict," she had said. "What is this *meshuggah* haircut, sweethawt? *Feh*!" She filled her mouth with knish and chewed, and then, she surprised him by adding, "You're a good boy, Sid. Don't use your father as an excuse to be a moron."

"Fox!" An unfamiliar and, for sure, female voice called out from behind them. Siddhi turned to see a girl about his age limping down the brick path. Slight and pale, but pretty, like a feather, the girl held a leash in one hand, and in the other she used a kind of metal ski pole for balance. Her back was crooked and S-curved beneath her sundress, pulling her right hip up a couple inches above the left one; the sole of her right shoe had a thick pad attached to even the lengths of her legs. She ferried along with a gondolier's grace, stirring in Siddhi some novel feeling, nothing like those he had for Michelle.

"Dad wants you to walk Edward and feed him," she said. "I did the food for you, but you know I can't do the walk." Her fragile body did little to hide her power, which was so great that in her presence, Fox lost his. Siddhi watched the girl's soft brown eyes scan over him and understood the source of her interest, being himself an expert in all things lonely.

"Uh, hi. I'm Fox's little sister," she said, parting petal lips to expose a trussed metal smile.

"You have braces," Siddhi blurted. He liked them. He had a little gap that never closed between his own front teeth. Braces meant someone cared about you.

"I'm Dove," she said, smiling wider, so that he had to smile back.

"Fox and Dove?" Siddhi puzzled.

"Where's Squirrel and Rabbit?" Christian joked.

"Our dad's a big hunter," she giggled adorably and tucked a lock of hair behind her pearl-studded earlobe. "He loves animals, so he gave us dumb names."

"If he loves 'em so much, why's he hunt 'em?" asked Christian.

Siddhi ignored him. "Dove's a nice name," Siddhi said, aware he was flirting.

"But the fucking dog he names Edward," Fox mumbled, eyes trained on the bay. He spat into the water, turned, and wailed Christian in the upper arm for his bit of sass.

"Ow! Shiiit, that was hard!"

"Whatever." Fox shrugged and kicked at the stone balustrade running the length of the waterfront. Fox bragged about getting expelled from four different private schools. Siddhi wondered if Dove also went to a fancy school, or if she was home-schooled because of her crooked back.

"Fox!" Her tone was fearless.

"I heard you!" He barked. "Got it!"

Dove nodded and tossed the leather leash on the pavers near his feet. "Thanks a lot for introducing your friends," she said, "and for being such a sweetie." Mightier by far than she appeared, she pivoted to return to the house.

"Thanks for being a little bitch about it," Fox mumbled, making Siddhi want to pin him to the ground until he took it back.

Siddhi remembered this little baby barn swallow he had found years before at the ashram. He had dropped mushed bits of earthworm into its mouth, and for two days Siddhi stayed in his bunk, keeping the baby fed, nestling it in a washcloth in his lap. When he brought the baby with him to the dining hall, Jackson delivered a spiritual sermon to the whole kids' table about how the baby was not meant to survive. Its mother had thrown it from the nest because it was defective, deformed, he said. "Mother Earth seeks balance, and death can be beautiful." He ordered Siddhi to put the bird out of its misery, and when Siddhi cried and refused, Jackson lost patience, took the washcloth, wrapped it over itself, and squished the bird.

Siddhi watched Dove moving forward, poling her way steadily toward a future of straight teeth and, maybe, some happiness. He imagined himself taking her out to dinner and a movie, a real date, at the end of which he longed to bring her home to meet Jackson and let him know that Mother Nature could go fuck herself.

"Was that your sister?" Christian asked. Stupid question. "What's with the crutch?" Stupid.

"Severe scoliosis," he grumbled. "She was born with it."

"Like Quasimodo?" Christian asked. Trav shook his head at Siddhi. Fox turned back around and slapped Christian hard across the face. Dove went in the French doors and out galloped a donkey-sized bloodhound, madly wagging his tail as he took the time to check out each of the three new people; he jumped his huge paws up onto Siddhi's chest and licked at his chin while Siddhi scratched his flanks. Christian and Travis pet him a bit and then grabbed their boards and skated back up the path to look around. Siddhi stayed back with Fox and the dog.

"Edward, I presume?" Siddhi put on an English accent. "He's bloody brilliant, mate." Edward finished tongue-bathing Siddhi, but stopped shy of Fox, and when he spied the leash in Fox's hand, he crouched low, his tail fell limp and tucked between his legs, and oddly, he dragged his belly along the ground as he crawled toward Fox looking terrified.

"What's up, fucker?" Fox spat, and Edward flinched then rolled on his back to submit. Fox clipped the leash on the etched, leather collar, yanked Edward up, and walked him a few steps, then gave the dog a swift kick, causing Edward to yelp in pain.

"Whoa! What the fuck?" Siddhi shouted, instinctively grabbing for the leash. Edward returned to his cower, tail tucked, crying. Siddhi bent down to pet and hug him.

"Back off, Buddha," Fox warned, yanking on the leash to pull

Edward from Siddhi's protection.

Siddhi's stomach lurched, and rage spread up and heated his chest, the kind of fury that sought release in his Dopp kit. "Why'd you fucking kick your dog, man?" Siddhi yelled.

"You think you know me, bro, but you don't know me. You don't know what it's like here. How he fucking treats me and then goes and spoils this little bitch." Fox yanked Edward's collar once more, dragging the trembling dog over the grass on its back before shouting, "Get up!" Edward obeyed.

"Still," Siddhi dared. "It's not the dog's fault your dad's a dick."

"Yeah? Well, it's not my fault either," Fox said, calming down. "Look, I'm sorry, alright? I won't do it again."

Siddhi nodded but kept Edward in his periphery because Fox almost never kept his word. His code of morality was as curvy as Dove's spine. "Hey, why don't you check on the douchebags, and I'll walk him for you?" Siddhi offered, scratching Edward's neck while holding out his other hand for the leash.

"Just…mind your own business, Buddha." Fox deadpanned. He circled the yard until Edward managed to piss and shit, and then he yanked him back toward the house. Siddhi said nothing but hung near enough to intervene in any further abuse.

"Yo! Check this out!" Christian shouted as Fox put Edward in the house. Siddhi tried to look over, but the sun whitewashed his view.

"They found it," Fox said, sounding more like himself. He led Siddhi to the other end of the house, past more gardens to the edge of the pool, drained and dry with scuff marks war-painted over its steep aqua walls. Some were black, and some dark brown, but Siddhi knew right away which came from the board and which were blood.

"He let me drain it like a year ago," Fox said, absently touching his bruised eye, "but I still hate his ass."

He kicked off from the shallow end and looped the pool on his board. His performance was radical and taking his own turn at pool skating gave Siddhi an adrenaline rush that felt way less lonely. Fox had skated these curves and stained them with his blood. Siddhi knew the power and permanence of shedding blood for betterment, for liberation. Fox had kicked the dog, but his own father beat the living shit out of him whenever the mood struck. Fox had said it started after his mom got diagnosed, but "when she died two years ago, he started using closed fists."

Fox's body, like Siddhi's, was thatched with wounds both given and made. They were skaters, Spartans, with no one to depend on and nothing to return to.

*

Fox and Siddhi met up early, around ten, and got a bunch of take-out Cubano from Puerto Sagua. They skated up Ocean Drive, past the nursing homes and efficiency hotels and all the residents, lining the porches in rows of chairs. Siddhi thought of visiting Nana there on a warm future morning, and maybe eventually Jackson, if in time each of them wound up in some nice place and Siddhi stuck around long enough that it even mattered at all.

"Promise to put a pillow over my face and OFF me if I ever get that old," Fox said. "Look at 'em, all debilitated and shit." Fox didn't mind pointing.

"What? You'd have them all report to the Ethical Suicide Parlor in Hyannis?" Siddhi countered. When it was just Fox, Siddhi could be himself and make his literary references. Fox was rebellious but also educated. He read a lot of books and had attended and been expelled from four different prep schools.

"I don't get the reference, but it sounds gnarly."

"*Welcome to the Monkey House.*" Siddhi considered Kurt Vonnegut a close friend. "Read it?"

"Nah, bro. I read *Slaughterhouse-Five* for school, though. It was badass. Maybe all these fuckers are only old for now? Like Billy Pilgrim, right? 'Unstuck in time.'" They rolled past another porch full of senior citizens.

Siddhi focused on their faces, weathered and overgrown, veiny, spud noses, dark crescents beneath their eyes that saw their way through decades, read whole libraries, survived concentration camps, and fought in wars.

"This doesn't make you sick, bro?" asked Fox.

"Nope. Fine with me," he said, and Fox gave a creeped-out shiver. Siddhi might never have gone in for all that hippie shit Jackson peddled over the years, and yet, Fox's energy was missing something. Reverence. Fox revered nothing. Siddhi liked seeing the people safe and content, and he respected that they had conquered the pain of existence long enough to be able to just sit down in a chair all day and let the sun warm their faces. He exchanged a few waves and smiled.

"Fuckin' Buddha," Fox chuckled as if Siddhi was kidding. "Don't depress me."

"Serious, bro. My mom OD'd on heroin when she wasn't much older than you. If I'm lucky enough to get old, I must admit, I'd be hard-pressed to say no to a nice pudding cup and a front-row seat to the sunrise." Fox gave him a questioning glance. "Heroin," Siddhi repeated.

"Christ. That sorta sucks worse than cancer, right, because it's like she asked for it or whatever." He stopped near a man in a parked wheelchair and patted him on the shoulder. "But if I ever get like this guy right here, please, show up at my house and nuke my ass to death."

Embarrassed, Siddhi smiled at the man, who had clearly heard and moved himself quickly away. "Now you hate old people, too?" he asked Fox.

"Don't be a smartass, bro. They're sheep. Look at 'em, sitting and waiting for the grim reaper to call their bingo number. So passive, it pisses me off."

"Okay, so when I show up to kill you, what will your smelly old ass be doing?"

"Don't know. Hanging out with my wife or some shit."

"And what do I tell your wife I'm there to do?"

"Fuck my wife!"

"Yes, of course. But *after* I fuck your wife..." They had to stop skating to cackle.

"Seriously though, I'll live dangerously. Nietzsche, bro," said Fox. "I'll be in my La-Z-Boy building up the energy for another go at my twenty-year-old, fine-assed, gold digger wife who married me for my daddy's millions."

Siddhi jived with Nietzsche more than with Fox, who kinda didn't seem to get Nietzsche. Nietzsche had lost his father when he was five and was partially raised by his aunts, grandmother, and older sister. A lot of the crazy-sounding shit he wrote was quite sensible in the context of his experience. Used as a defense for Fox's punk bitching, though, it came out sounding defeatist and whiny.

"Fuck all," said Fox, needlessly pushing over a corner trashcan. "God is dead, bro." Fox used Nietzsche as lighter fluid, while Siddhi found his words exegetically comforting like others felt about the Bible. He answered Fox with the same quotation Jackson used years back when he introduced Siddhi to Nietzsche, "*You have your way, I have my way. As for the right way, the correct way, and the only way, it does not exist.*"

When they arrived at Trav's grandma's apartment, Siddhi considered his friends as they sat on the plastic-covered sofa, getting high and eating Cuban sandwiches. Fox was a medium-sized monkey who dealt with being beaten by the big monkey by finding and pummeling smaller monkeys. Christian had dyed his hair green because he said, "Fuck it." He had no content, Siddhi realized, other than aimless negativity. Whatever IT was, Christian was against IT, for no good reason, a solid "NO" without any respect for the question. Christian was a stock character. A redshirt. Siddhi felt guilty for thinking this, but only because it was so comically true.

Travis was a tenacious and talented skater and a truly nice guy. His tragic flaw was that he had no purpose of his own other than to be a good soldier and to follow orders. He would have been equally dedicated to Martin Luther King or Adolf Hitler, whoever hired him first.

All these observations made Siddhi feel ashamed. His need for camaraderie and skating, his daily choice between rage, fear, and loneliness, had made him blind, deaf, and dumbass, a follower, a sheep. And his shame suddenly gave birth to a new, intense feeling that his *real* time had come, for once, to do something—no more mayhem—something good, the right thing, on purpose.

*

After deciding to rent movies, get high, and chow down for the afternoon, the crew wandered Video Vida, searching the rows of tall shelves for the right videotapes to complement the joints and junk food that awaited them at Fox's house. Siddhi had no desire to hang out there now that it was mid-August and Dove had returned to her boarding school, plus being at his house put Fox on edge. But it was a good skate to get there and way more comfortable than Trav's grandma's.

"Here's one for Christian!" Trav announced, holding up the box for "The Jerk."

"It's right here, bro," Christian said, laughing, grabbing at his nuts and shaking them in Trav's direction. They all laughed, and Siddhi gave Christian a friendly slap on the back.

"Here's one for Fox," Christian said. He read the title aloud, "'Private School.'"

Fox's father had called in a favor. In two weeks, Fox was packing off to an expensive liberal arts academy on pain of being "cut loose" if he refused. The guys all knew about it, but they'd been smart enough to keep their mouths shut. Siddhi had no explanation for why Christian would poke the beast, except what Nana would say: *That one is not playing with a full deck!*

"Motherfucker," Fox said, in a harrowing whisper. He chucked movie boxes, rapid-fire, at Christian.

"How about 'Porky's?'" Fox grabbed another, "Oh, wait, here, 'Octo-PUSSY,'" he said, hurling another. "No, no, here you go fucker!" he shouted and ran over and whacked Christian in the face with "Tootsie," destroying the box and sending chunks of Styrofoam flying.

"You leave now," yelled the store clerk, a bantam Hispanic

man with glasses and a graying comb-over. "Or I going to call the *policia*!"

"Oh yeah, big man? You gonna call the *policia*, you fuckin' spic? Why don't you tell them I did THIS!" Fox screamed.

The clerk cowered toward the back wall as Fox kicked down a ten-foot-high set of shelves, laying waste to three more rows of shelving units with the easy physics of dominos, leaving half the shop reduced to a leveled mound of scrap metal, busted particle board, and exploded Styrofoam snow.

Blood dripped from Christian's right eyelid, and after the crash, he did the smartest thing Siddhi had ever seen him do. He grabbed his board and high-tailed it from the shop, an act so brilliant that it changed Siddhi's whole opinion of him. Travis stood firm by Fox, his commanding officer.

Siddhi picked up his board, and nodded to Fox and Travis, expecting that the next move was to bail. But Fox was on a tear, and Siddhi had to scramble into the clear as Fox let out a yell and kicked down the other four rows of shelves in the same manner as he had the first. The entire store was now on the ground, leveled.

Siddhi looked right into Travis's eyes and, as authoritatively as possible, commanded him, "Get the fuck out of here now!" And Travis tipped his chin, grabbed his board, and obeyed. Siddhi felt sorry for the clerk, but in the rush of the moment, since no one was hurt, his instinct was to grab Fox and hightail it to the relative safety of the Betsy Ross. *Exit, stage right!*

He grabbed his own board and began to climb the crushed mess of the shelves to get to the door, but when he pivoted back to call for Fox, he saw the clerk grab the phone and dial.

"C'mon, bro," Siddhi yelled to Fox, purposefully not saying his name, catching Fox's eyes and widening his to ask, *What's up?* And nodding toward the door, *Let's get the fuck out of here.* Siddhi must have let his guard down because he started and stumbled backward, almost falling when he saw Fox sock the little man in the jaw, dropping him to the floor behind the counter with an anguished cry.

"What the fuck?" Siddhi heard himself shout, and he scrambled over the ruins of the displays, away from the exit, toward the counter at the back, watching as Fox hauled himself over the Formica and disappeared down over where the clerk lay out of view.

"No," Siddhi heard the clerk wail. "Please, please." He'd almost climbed to the front of the store when he caught his thigh on a stray shard of metal, a wound deeper and more severe than the ones he'd sliced into his own skin, and when he glanced down to check the damage through his pants, he heard Fox cursing and landing punches. The puncture to his leg felt real and frightening and dangerous and not at all good. More punching, and there was no time to do anything other than throw his own body over the counter, past the cash register, where he found Fox straddled over the clerk who was curled like a shrimp, moaning and bleeding.

Siddhi flushed and shivered with terror at the sight of so much blood splattered over the pink wall, innocent blood, blood from someone who hadn't chosen to bleed. Siddhi grabbed for Fox's elbows, but he moved too quickly and, amidst the chaos, had no choice but to bear hug Fox from behind his back, using all his leverage to smash Fox down onto the clerk, effectively suppressing his ability to punch. The man's eyes and cheeks looked like pizza, and he appeared to be knocked out. Siddhi couldn't tell if he was breathing. Fox cursed and elbowed Siddhi's ribs in his struggle against the hold.

"Fucking STOP IT!" Siddhi yelled. "He's not your dad!"

Fox stopped. "Okay," he said and took a deep breath, convincing Siddhi to release him.

"You gonna psychoanalyze me now, Little Buddha?" Fox rounded to face him and spat on the floor. "I know he's not my dad, you fuckin' Mary." His eyes were all hatred, and his face was flecked crimson with the poor clerk's blood. No truth or release to it, this man's blood was wasted.

Fox gave Siddhi a hard shove, and surprised, Siddhi fell back on his ass in time to see Fox go back and punch the clerk again and again and again. Knowing he had to stop him—how was there so much blood—all he came up with was to grab the clerk's umbrella and wail Fox across his back.

"STOP! You're fucking killing him!"

"FUUUCK YOU!" Fox screamed, and then the clerk was somewhere in the background. And Siddhi was on his back, looking up at Fox and the glint of brass knuckles on his friend's right fist as it sped toward his face, hitting hard enough to make Siddhi hear a very wrong sort of snap, crackle, and pop inside his cheek. Another glint, and he heard the cartilage in his nose break and splinter, sending a tidal wave of agony down his spine. Fox sat with his knees, pinning Siddhi to the ground by his shoulders, wailing him above and below with the hard, shiny knuckles, his frothing mouth making words Siddhi could no longer hear.

There was so much pain, white-hot pain, and then there was blurriness, eyes veiled in red, and then darkness that squeezed in from the sides, and then nothing.

PART V:

The Family Jones

CHAPTER 25:

Seized,
1989 (Sienna)

The airplane was so cold that visible condensation clouded out of the vents. The stewardess who helped me back and forth to the bathroom spoke gorgeous, stunning, perfect English and gave me extra blankets and chilled cans of ginger ale with cups of ice. I napped and woke up sweating. I puked the soda back up into a barf bag but still had the wherewithal to wish Siddhi had scrawled on it first. I grew sicker rather than better, but knowing that sometime in the next day, maybe, I'd set eyes on my family, on Siddhi, made that seven-hour flight worth ten times the seven hundred and fifty dollars I had paid for it.

My personal finances were in shambles. The transportation from Marrakech to the airport in Casablanca had cost all the money I had left from work. I had a grand total of thirty-one dollars and thirty-seven cents left, and other than to hug Siddhi, apologize to him for leaving, and tell him what really happened on my trip, I had no substantive life plan.

But wasn't my one-way destitution the poetry of Xanadu? I expected after I spent my last dollars on a ride home, that there it would all still sit, a tad better for the fixing or a little worse for the wear, chock full of freshly tapped hippies, hookers, homeboys, and homeless, rolling in and out with the late summer tides. Jackson would either have the flu or not, be home or not, have coke or pot, be naked with a woman or not, or maybe be away on the boat to make a drop. Siddhi would be reading or skating, and Nana might show up unannounced bearing tepid chow mein.

No one answered my call to the home number, more than expected, because no one ever answered the phone, but strangely, neither Nana nor the Laytners had picked up either.

Outside of the airport, Miami was hotter than it had been in Africa. The smokers smoked, and people waited with their suitcases full of bullshit. I tried to work out a shuttle bus fare, but everything looked blurry, and the nausea grew big and bad. When I saw no one in line for a taxi, I gave up trying to save money and surrendered to the cushioned backseat. The driver lowered the windows, and I stuck my head out into the humid whoosh of home, which still smelled like Miami: salty, floral, and tinged with notes of rotten mango and fishy garbage.

Only once did I force the worried driver to pull over into the emergency lane of the Julia Tuttle Causeway, a move that irritated an old lady who could barely see over her steering wheel and who honked and gave us a reproachful shake of the head as she cruised by in a Buick the same silvery blue as her hairdo. The driver at first refused until I promised him that if he didn't pull to the side, I'd be sick in his car.

Trembling, sallow, and greenish, I sank back into the seat. The driver looked me over, sweating his concern, not the sort of person to kick a skinny, sick girl out on the side of the highway, but also not cool with that girl retching or plotzing on his watch. The breeze blowing past the speeding window ruffled my cheeks, and I closed my eyes, smiled a little, let my head relax into the white noise of the rushing air, and let my enervated mind blank out.

*

"Excuse me. Wake up, Miss." The cab stopped. I heard the hazards blinking as I opened my eyes to the cab driver standing outside of the open back door with his hands on the hips of his trousers. "I must go now. Please, miss."

Sitting up from where I'd passed out on the seat, I left a smear of drool, horrid, but a galaxy less humiliating than other possible fluids. I considered us both lucky but refrained from pointing it out as I paid him the twenty-five dollars, plus tip, and reoriented myself, me and my Bee Gees backpack, same as always give or take a dollar and thirty-seven cents, on my feet outside the familiar gates of Xanadu.

The rusty, wrought-iron latch hung open, and I entered and limped the circle of the driveway, all the way around the colossal old Banyan tree, glancing up into her million tendril roots to see if Siddhi, conspicuously absent from the driveway, might be perched on a bough, rereading *Atlas Shrugged* and waiting for me in some new structure he built based on the ideology of Ayn Rand...He wasn't up there.

My eyes drew down from tree to ground too quickly, I had to sit down to stop the spinning. I pulled the blue *djellaba* over my folded knees to brace myself for sitting up. The garbage truck sailed by without stopping, though it squealed to a stop at the house next door. Typical Xanadu. Jackson and whatever burnouts he had over that night had forgotten to put out the cans. Garbage collection meant it had to be Wednesday, around 6:45 a.m.

Once upon a time, Siddhi and I would've been the ones to drag the cans out to the street before wandering back inside and out to the canal to look for seahorses in Biscayne Bay, or take a swim, or get on each other's shoulders to pick mangoes off the low boughs for breakfast. The thought of surprise-waking him, how his dirty room would stink like feet and be littered with tear-outs from skating magazines and Skinny Puppy posters after I hadn't gone in to clean it in almost three months, filled me with joy and gave me the zip I needed to get up and head inside.

Fallen palm fronds and Poinciana seed pods littered the driveway. I put my focus on not tripping until I got safely up the front steps. The door was locked, and the welcome mat missing. The hollow key rock where Jackson kept the spare key no one ever needed was upturned and empty. There was a sign posted on the front door in warning-colored, fluorescent orange paper:

SEIZED! THIS PROPERTY HAS BEEN SEIZED FOR NON-PAYMENT OF TAXES AND IS NOW IN POSSESSION OF THE STATE OF FLORIDA. ANY PERSON WHO ATTEMPTS TO TAMPER WITH OR INTERFERE WITH THIS PROPERTY WILL BE PROSECUTED TO THE FULL EXTENT OF THE LAW.

Panic surfed the bile to the top of my throat. Where had they taken Siddhi? Wading into the stucco planters on each side of the front stoop gave me a leveraged view into the foyer windows.

The place was a mess, but no more than any other morning after a party. All the furnishings were still in place. The pile of shoes by the door. Dishes on the table, and a pizza box left open on the foyer table where we always scuttled pizza boxes when we didn't feel like taking them out till morning. Same old house. A couple of palmetto bugs skittered across the white of the pizza box, but even roaches were status quo for a Miami Beach morning. The sign said to stay out, but I wasn't going anywhere with less than two dollars, no Siddhi, and no clue.

I sat on the deep windowsill to rest until I realized I had no way to find my brother, and my heart began to beat so anxiously that I had to wretch into the planter. Ginger ale, and then acid, and then nothing, before finding my way out of the bushes back onto the stoop for a rest. When I could manage to get up, I limped around the back, checking all the windows as I passed them.

I had to press myself up on the other windowsills to see inside, and the strain squeezed my stomach into cramping. Kneeling on the rotted wood, I cupped my hands around my eyes against the glass. The dining room table was littered with dishes and glasses, but no usual cutting board of weed, no ashtray of abandoned joints.

In the living room, the trusty couch sat in its spot by the big screen. The hole in the sun porch had been boarded up, as had every window where a tree branch grew into the house. I lowered myself down and rested for as long as my worried brain would allow. Around back, the Chattahoochee stones had come loose and crumbled up the surface of the side porch. The waterfall to the pool was shut off, the pool water half-evaporated, the surface slimed over with algae and floating dead fish. The air reeked of decomposition. The sliding glass and sun porch doors each had their own boards and seizure signs to remind me once again that I was breaking the law. At the dock, rope lines dangled from the pilings into the empty boat slip, and I imagined Siddhi and Jackson somewhere on the *Orgazmatron*, hopefully fishing, possibly fleeing.

I sat down on the dock and looked out at the bay, already knowing it had zero answers for me. I thought this was the all-is-lost part of the movie. I was broke, had no ride, was too sick to get anywhere, and had no one who'd help. But this was not a movie, this was my actual life.

Limping toward the sunporch, where I planned to sit and breathe, maybe take a nap, and dream of what in the holy fuck to do next, I tottered past the pine tree, the tallest, prettiest pine tree, and I remembered.

The shed brandished yet another seizure sign, but it wasn't boarded up. No need. The door was rusted shut at the hinges, but that was only if you were a Fed. Any real Xanadu Baby knew that a little upward thrust released the stuck hinges, and the door swung open without so much as a squeak. I had to sit down on the grass to untangle a shovel from the weedy tangle of gardening tools that hadn't been in regular use since the summer after we lost Ximena.

Standing in the yard with the shovel about to dig up untold thousands of dollars in drug money I stole and buried as a very young child didn't imbue me with the confidence to believe I was any more capable of a normal life than poor Ximena—whom I could still picture exactly as she looked, far too skinny, playing

Monopoly, loaning me some lip gloss, tripping on the Chinese jump rope, convulsing, and blacking out on the cold terrazzo floor. It had been over ten years since I'd interred my treasure, but I remembered perfectly my six-year-old intention from the moment I had dropped the duct-taped package into the hole. *For just in case we ever need it.*

I dragged the shovel over the lawn toward the base of the tree, dry heaved from the exertion, rested, and then dug some more. The excavation was slow going. My rubbery and tired arms did little to get the shovel submerged, lifted, and replaced. I lost my breath a couple of times, and halfway through digging, no way to hold it in against the pain in my guts, I had to lie on my side and rest. The summer-dry earth was hard-packed and covered in a ten-year-thick blanket of rotted pine needles. I got down about eight inches before I reached the sandy soil of memory. Every part of the scene looked smaller to me than it had when I was little, the roots closer together, the tree shorter and less protective.

I had to stop again to let the lightheadedness and spinning subside, catch my breath, and slow my heartbeat. A few shovels full after getting back on task, I hit the root that told me I could dig no further, but I'd found no treasure. Pivoting on my knees, I tried to triangulate the yard. Counting the trees to confirm I was in the right spot. My hollowed-out stomach and intestines flooded with fear, vibrating with anxious desperation. I had nothing, no chance of anything, without this money!

Letting the shovel drop away, I leaned into the hole and scratched at the soil with my fingers, and after a minute or two, hysterical, furiously hand-digging with my fingernails like a frightened raccoon, I got hold of something that was not a root, and not pine needles or soil. Tape. I retrieved a torn, twisted clump of silver-tape, wadded up and wound into itself, filthy and ruined, left to rot, and stuck to nothing.

*

It took forty minutes, with ample stopping and resting and one inadvertent catnap on the sidewalk, for me to walk around the block to Alton Road and down the few blocks to Courtney's house. I didn't want to do anything but make it to her front stoop and cry until I fell asleep for a week, but that all disappeared when measured against my desperation to find Siddhi.

Cars sped down the busier road as people left home for carpools and work. A couple slowed to eye with obvious suspicion the disheveled girl in the dirty, blue robe, not how I'd intended to bring Africa back home. Each blade of grass on the Laytners' bright, happy lawn still glistened with droplets from the early morning sprinkler bath. The front walk puddles had already receded, leaving their dark prints shrinking on the pavers.

I rang the bell. No answer. I rang it again and again and again. After several minutes of ringing and knocking, I leaned back into the front door and slid down to sitting. Of course, I realized, I knew just where they were, and it wasn't home! I remembered counting down each boiling day of one of my Laytner-free Augusts by striking big Sharpie X's on a 1986 Playboy Playmate calendar I had found somewhere in our house. Court and Dava would be in North Carolina, tucked away at Camp Blue Star, while Dr. and Mrs. Laytner would have rented a car and driven around a new country in Europe. I even knew this year's location was Ireland because they bought the tickets right before we stopped talking to each other. Mrs. Laytner couldn't wait to kiss the Blarney Stone.

I understood they were gone, but I couldn't handle it being true, so I shouted at the door. "Please! Court! Mrs. Laytner? Please! Help me. Someone, please help me. I need HELP!" It wasn't insanity, I just wanted the truth to be different for once, for one time, to change my mother from dead to alive, to change Jackson into a functional, legitimate person, to change Siddhi from lost to found.

Two doors down, a woman came out of her house, an older neighbor lady whom I didn't recognize. Housecoat and slippers deployed, she waddled down the sidewalk, slowly approaching the questionable character wreaking early morning havoc on her otherwise peaceful, upper-middle-class street. "What are you banging?" she called to me from down the block, repeating it a few times, coupling each with its own exasperated hand gesture.

Nana used to say, "Throw a rock in Florida, and you'll hit a *yenta*!"

I wanted to jump up and shout at the lady, "It's okay! I'm not a *meshugganah*! I'm a *shana maidel! Schmaltz! Schmuck! Schmear! Shmageggy!* Don't look at me like I don't belong anywhere, lady, because I'm from your people!"

She'd hear my considerable Yiddish and realize that I was no infiltrating bag lady, but one of her own, partly, at least, Jew-*ish*, and returned a teensy bit late from wandering in the desert. But all that good sense was too tiring, so with abridged awareness, I continued shouting for the Laytners to help me—with brief intervals of rest, which no doubt made me appear even more insane.

"Hey!" she shouted. She'd come closer, just on the sidewalk in front of the Laytner's walk. "What's the mattah with you? You don't come ovah heah to bang on doors and holler in this neigh-bah-hood, like some kind of lunatic!" When I ignored her and cried out again, she took a few emboldened steps up Court's front walk. But she hesitated, staring at me like I might sear her with laser beam eyes, breathe fire, take flight, set her home ablaze with mental telepathy… The notion that this little *yenta* probably thought me crazy, someone dangerous to be approached with great caution—*Cujo, you're rabid!*—was frankly hilarious, and at a loss for anything else to think of, feel, or do, I burst into laughter, bizarre and hammering and then soundless laughter. And the two being so very closely linked, I went ahead and shifted into sobbing.

Distracted by the agony and the ecstasy, I forgot about my hand that, without my conscious command, continued to rhythmically rap at the door like a metronome. And looking as I did at that point in my illness, drawn face, foreign clothing, hair wildly curling down to my waist, filthy from digging, and laugh-cry-knock-loitering for my friend, who wouldn't proceed with caution? I'd fully intended to explain myself and ask to use the telephone, but first, I leaned forward up onto my hands and knees and gagged up some more bile over the striped welcome mat that Mrs. Laytner bought the year before, when I joined her, Court, and Dava for back-to-school shopping at Zayre.

And there on the stoop, came a terrifying line of crimson blood from deep inside my body, and when I tried to stand up, both of my calf muscles knotted up in unbearable cramps. No shocker that my subsequent collapse, combined with my bloody face and wails of calf agony, startled the *yenta*, who jumped up and down and shouted, "*Oy yoy yoy*," before turning around and trotting off toward her house.

CHAPTER 26

The Place to Be, 1989 (Sienna)

The Mount Sinai Emergency Room bore a shroud of mystery I'd only ever associated with the shameful death of a sick girl I'd been too young to help. Through the automatic doors was a vanilla room with pink chairs; it was thick, calm, and empty but for the piped-in symphony. I must've puked myself crazy, because as I stared up from the gurney, I heard the paramedic tell the triage nurse something about me being disruptive and disoriented.

"Possible homeless," he said. "Local homeowner phoned Emergency." Then everything softened, spread out, and blew away. I lay there for the moment unable to place myself in time, but present and accounted for. And still listening to the Muzak, I thought about how cool it would be if I had that skill, like sophisticated people in movies, to name the composer of any random piece of classical music as it played.

"Shh!" I'd demand. "This is Mozart's Concerto Number Seventeen!" I promised myself I would learn all of that and more if I didn't die, and then I could no longer keep my eyes and ears open, and the quiet dark whooshed me away.

*

I woke up in a hospital room, the patient in the bed. It was meat locker cold, and my blanket felt more like a big paper towel. Striped wallpaper, beige and pink, covered the walls, and the drop ceiling had four squares that were a different shade of white from all the others. There was one mirror, a bank of windows, and over the empty bed on the other side of the room, a framed print of the *Saturday Evening Post* cover where the little boy is pulling down his pants while the doctor readies his syringe. Norman Rockwell. Nana had a coffee table book of all his covers, most depicting the childhood of my dreams.

When I got out of the hospital and found Siddhi, I thought, tears welling, stomach starting up again with my wakefulness, he and I would laugh our brains out for a whole afternoon coming up with the Norman Rockwell covers of the *Xanadu Evening Post*: a smiling little boy and girl hide in their tree fort above a cloud of pot smoke coming from below them where four naked women dance in a circle around two more naked women on the ground erotically massaging their father...

And then I wanted to cry because if Siddhi were there, it really would be okay to laugh, but without him, it just sounded sad. The piano and sax from the elevator were gone and had been replaced by the whirring, humming, and bleeping of hospital machines interspersed with random hallway tumult. And with the bit of medical knowledge I'd picked up from my clinic visit in Marrakech, along with a little boost from innumerable reruns of "Quincy" and "Trapper John, M.D.," I concluded I was getting more I.V. fluids and maybe some other type of medicine from the yellowish bag, and they were monitoring my pulse and blood pressure.

Every so often, the cuff inflated and woke me, squeezing the crap out of my left arm before stopping and then exhaling slowly, growing looser and looser, until it released and changed all the numbers on the screen. The bag must have contained some good medicine, I decided, because nothing hurt and I felt no need to move, and though I knew I should be upset, worried, looking for

Siddhi and freaking out, my body and brain refused to muster any discomfort.

To take advantage of the numbness and escape the chill, I decided to try for a record-breaking sleep. When the blood pressure cuff startled me awake, a pretty nurse stood next to my bed checking and adjusting machines. She wore too much blush, and her hair was pinned in a stiff, French twist. I lay shivering in a head-to-toe puddle of wetness that cooled to freezing in the air conditioning.

"Did I pee in the bed?" I asked. My voice came out all groggy and scratchy.

She chuckled. "Welcome back to the world, sweetie!" She was maybe thirty, a slightly chubby woman with fair, freckled skin and purposeful but gentle hands, nurturing mother's hands. "You are far too dehydrated to wet a bed. The wetness is from you breaking that nasty fever." A man came into the room, an orderly if the medical shows served, and he and the nurse exchanged glances.

"If you let me and Andy here help you move onto the other bed for a bit, we can get you some dry linens. How's that sound?" Her sunshiny, upbeat offer inspired me to play along.

"Sounds like a plan," I said, my throat still raw, but my spirit climbed the charts and carried with it my sanity. "But only if you bring me a few more of these sheets you are trying to pass off as blankets." Hospital banter was fun; I felt like a witty guest star on "St. Elsewhere."

"You bet, sweetie," she said. She elbowed the orderly. "I think we've got a live one here, Andy. Let's get her up!" Surrounded by strangers, it seemed less painful to pretend everything was coming up rainbows and lollipops, and even though I almost puked myself into an early grave at sixteen, I could pretend I was past all that now, off in the clear blue yonder. And I was happy to get on the denial train because what else was I supposed to do, ask the nurse to adopt me or buy myself a whole new life with two dollars?

They moved me, changed the bed, moved me back, and added

blankets, and they fed me—salty broth, apple juice, red Jell-O—and once I was warm and changed and fed, the doctor showed up to have a look at me. "Hello, young lady," he said in a decently thick Cuban accent. "I am Doctor Jesus Beraja." His glasses were almost as thick as his black, side-parted hair, and he was, well, the opposite of tall.

"Hi, Doctor Beraja. Am I going to die?" Even tongue-in-cheek, it was a fair and primary question. He looked at me like I was nuts, furrowed his brow, and tipped his head to the side, and I understood the game was over.

"Probably not today, I think," he answered. He pushed his thick glasses farther up on his nose, took out a pen, and marked my chart, all business. "You came into urgent care severely dehydrated, with an elevated pulse, low blood pressure, fever of 104.2. If you hadn't gotten here when you did, *mija*, it might have been a different story."

"I threw up blood," I suddenly remembered. "Am I bleeding internally?" He popped his eyebrows and made an amused, chuffing sound.

"You had some inflammation of the gastrointestinal tract from so much vomiting," he said, noting the chart. He wore a fancy gold wristwatch. "Not too bad, I think. But you also came in with a rotten little case of pneumonia. This over here," he pointed to the yellowish bag, "seems to be taking good care of tha—"

"I was right!" I was on some kind of medicine. I couldn't help myself, punch-drunk and molded to the bed and pneumoniaed up as I was, I had this very turned-on feeling about the hospital. The order, the precision, the cleanliness, and routine...

Dr. Beraja smiled and scanned my chart. "Eh, Marnie?" he said to the nurse, "she has *Jane Doe* still here. We need a history right away, please. Before she goes back to sleep." Dr. Beraja enticed me with his firm calm. I could accept him without second-guessing. "Okay, *mija*," he turned back to me. "Nurse Marnie is going to get your information so we can get you processed. You need to rest now, understand? No getting up without calling the nurses, yes?"

"Yes," I agreed. He nodded and went to leave. "Dr. Beraja?"

"Eh?"

"Muchos, muchos gracias."

"De nada, mija," he said and patted my shoulder before leaving the room. Marnie poured me some water and stood right up against the side of the bed.

"Okay, sweetie. Get comfy. Name?" I answered her question, and she followed with fifty more. I did my best to interpret whatever knowledge I possessed about myself and the history of my family. I couldn't help her with anything from my mother's side other than to say deceased, drug overdose, Minnesotan, and never met them. Jackson's side was more colorful, and I did the best I could, even throwing in Pop Pop Murray's alleged angina and diverticulitis and Nana's alleged gout, which she only complained about when she ate too much-chopped liver. I told the story that began in Marrakech and wound me up retching blood onto Court's doormat. I told the truth about almost everything. When she finished, Marnie clicked her pen.

"Okay, Ximena," she said, calling me the name I'd decided to give instead of my real one. I lied and said my name was Ximena Pajinas, the poor, starving girl who almost died in front of my eyes years before. "Not too bad, right? Time to get some more sleep, okay?"

Siddhi and I had a rule. I used to test him on it when we were little. "If you ever get lost," I'd look into his eyes and quiz him, "and you can't find me or Jackson," I'd ask slowly, "what is the rule?" The rule was to call Nana. She hadn't answered my call from the airport, but it had been the middle of the night in Miami. There in the hospital, though, it was late afternoon, and when all the medical distractions died down, I gave them a dead girl's name as a proclamation that I seemed to have no past and no future, thin and sick and alone and afraid, I admitted to myself that I was lost.

Shifting my body toward the bedside table, I used whatever energy the yellow medicine and red Jell-O yielded to pick up the phone, follow my own rule, and once more, not knowing where to begin or end or even what I wanted her to do for me, I called Nana. I listened to it ring at least fifty times before I hung up.

*

The blood pressure cuff struck again, and I woke, dazed but still in daylight, with Nurse Marnie again at my bed, pursing her lips. She had too many freckles to ever look mean.

"So. Ximena Pajinas, huh? Well, you're either a liar or a time-traveler," she sat on the edge of the bed, "because the only Ximena Pajinas who ever visited this hospital left with her mom and dad back in 1985."

"She's alive?" The news rushed me with adrenaline and shot me up to sitting, squealing, and thrilled that my hare-brained "I Love Lucy" scheme had worked! Nurse Marnie nodded. "She lived!" I practically shouted, and then the corners of my vision turned to black shadows, and I fell backward into the pillows.

"Easy. Listen, sweetie, you can't move around like that yet." She fixed my pillows and resettled my head. "Now that you've tricked me into I-don't-even-know-what—"

"Sorry."

"It's quite alright...once. I'm glad it worked out for your... friend?"

"Yeah. I guess so. She was once."

"So, how about you reward me with your actual name?"

"Oh, yeah. Of course, sorry. Sienna Shiva Karma Jones."

"Great. Pleasure to meet you. I'm Shirley, Shirley, Bo Birley Banana Fana Fo Furley," she said, visibly annoyed.

I assured her, "No, that is really my name. I swear it."

*

When she next returned, Nurse Marnie looked less mystified. "We found your passport, Sienna," she smiled. It was in the ambulance with this," she held up my Bee Gees backpack, and I felt relieved and then embarrassed, someone had dug inside for my ID, seen my naked photos and old stolen junk.

"We are going to move you shortly, okay, sugar?" But it wasn't okay! I liked my room. It was safe, orderly, and sensible, and only nice people who took good care of me walked into and out of it. I'd grown accustomed to Marnie and Andy and the unrelenting chill, bleachy-crisp sheets… By trial and error, I'd almost achieved the ideal level of warmth by layering two booties on each foot beneath five blankets, all burrito-wrapped and tucked under my legs. I even bonded with the gawky Rockwellian kid in the picture. I'd named him Farnsworth.

"Why can't I stay in here?"

"We have a better place for you," Marnie said, her tone resolute.

"What about Farnsworth?" I tried to entice her with the banter that had worked for me so far. "Marnie, meet Farnsworth." I gestured toward the picture. "He can't be left alone to take that shot without holding my hand. He totally needs me here, or he'll cry."

"Andy will be in shortly to take you downstairs."

"Please, Marnie. Why?"

"We had a request from your grandmother that you be moved into the same room as your brother."

"One, two, three," Andy counted off with the other orderly as they hoisted me and my blanket chrysalis off the gurney and into the empty bed in the new room.

Siddhi's room!

I struggled to see past them until Andy pressed me gently back against the mattress.

"Hey, not so fast. You can't get up yet, okay? Here," he said, using the bed controls to elevate my head to a raised angle. There. *Right there!* In the bed to my left lay Siddhi. His face was half-bandaged, and the other half was bruised and stitched. His one, visible eye had swollen into a bruised and lacerated, bluish-green popover.

Nurse Marnie wouldn't give me any details other than that he'd been found three days ago, badly beaten. "But he's stable, sugar. He's stable." He had his own set of machines fluid-filled bags and blood pressure cuff.

I was about to try and sit up, to get closer to Siddhi, shake him awake, and beg him to forgive me for what I let happen to him. I was about to formulate some plan for how to make it up to him, when I heard, "Let me see her! Move away already, will you, and let me see her!" She burst through the door in her emerald-green Sergio Tacchini tracksuit zipped down to expose her Star of David, and she shoved Andy aside to get close enough to lean over my bed.

She took my cheeks in her chilly hands and stared into my eyes for a few seconds. I kept myself from crying because I knew she had no patience for it. She looked like she might cry herself, and I had to question at that moment whether she didn't love us more than anything in the world. Then, she dropped her eyebrows, and all the softness left her face.

"Well, you're a godforsaken mess!" She smacked a kiss onto my forehead. "I'll tell you something, you are done with this moron boyfriend business, Siennala, you hear me, goddammit?" Behind her sneer, there was deep concern. The intensity of Nana's nastiness had a strong correlation with her level of concern.

"Yes, Nana, I understand, but I just need to…" When I tried to get up and go to Siddhi, Nana began shouting for Andy to do something, and when I tried to push poor, well-meaning Andy out of my way and get out of bed, he shouted to the hall and a new nurse ran in and injected something into my I.V.

"This'll help her calm down," Andy said to Nana, using one of his forearms to secure my chest and his other to keep Nana away from me. After that, the more I pushed against Andy's restraint, the more I shoved at him to try for a better look at how to get to Siddhi, calling his name at my greatest possible volume to try and wake him, stretching to see if his chest was breathing, the harder it became to fight the fast-growing weight of my own body. After the injection, every single one of my cells began to pull hard toward the bed. My eyes dropped closed without my doing. "Nana, where's Jackson? Where's Jackson?"

"*Aiysh*! I am not gonna talk about this," she said more to Andy than to me.

"Siddhi? Siddhi, wake up. I'm gonna get us out of here now! Siddhi?"

"This is my nightmare!" Nana shouted. "For Christ's sake, will you stop fooling around and put her out already!"

That was the last I heard.

CHAPTER 27

The Water and the Whale, 1989 (Sienna)

"CeeCee." It was his voice, Siddhi's voice, calling me. "Cees?" My head felt like it weighed fifty pounds. My eyes strained from the dryness. Each swallow was a knife dragging down my throat. I tried to sit up, but someone had turned up the gravity. I felt heavy, like a beached whale. Siddhi and I once watched this documentary where a bunch of good Samaritan volunteers stood in line to pour buckets of water over a whale that had stranded itself on their shore. They tried over and over to get it back out to sea, but the poor thing kept turning around, swimming back, and getting stuck again on the beach.

"CeeCee, your breathing sounds different. Like you're awake," Siddhi whispered. "You up?"

It took me a minute to bring my clothes and the covers with me as I forced my body to tip left. Siddhartha. He lay right there in the other bed, flat on his back, with only his head turned to face me, eyes closed. His sheets were a twisted mess. His whole right leg bent up and out of the gown and covers, and the usual whiteness of his thigh was taken up with cuts and bruises.

"Siddhi," I whispered back. In the smallest, most important way, I began to feel more than motivated to make it all okay; now that we were back in the same room together, I was compelled to fix things. He cracked open his eyes. "Siddhi, what happened to you?"

"It'd probably be stupid, right now," he whispered back, "to say, 'you should see the other guy.'" He laughed weakly and followed up with a pained moan. He adjusted his chest, laying his hands down by his sides, exposing more bruises and a mess of little cuts, lines all over, regular lines, new ones and scabbed ones, pink ones, and white scars, oddly, three-at-a time.

"I think *I'm* the other guy," I told him.

My brother said he had four broken ribs, fractured bones in his cheek, a mild concussion, and that Fox's beating had collapsed a lung. They did something in the ambulance to reinflate it.

"Oh, Siddhi," was all I could say because I could not let myself imagine his pain and still summon the energy to tell him how I planned to make things right. I even felt tired from the little bit of talking and from memorizing the stitches tracking over and around the sunset-colored swells of his damaged face. Really, I just wanted to sleep, but it was my job to get us out of this mess and into a better situation, and likely more quickly than I had time for dredging up the needed resources. I took the deepest breath I could. "Okay," I said. "This looks pretty bad."

"Mazel tov on that astute observation," he said. "You're some kind of genius."

"You're pretty funny for a dead guy," I said back. He was still Siddhi, so I just resumed being me. "We're the Joneses, right? We're going to be fine, Siddhi. We can get ourselves out of anything," I said, feeling my heart pound and my head cloud with the excitement of the moment. "Always have and always will." I thought I heard him answering me, but it was all gibberish. The room spun once around and nosedived into my periphery, and I must have followed it because I was for a little while down in the quiet blackness.

For the minutes and maybe hours in between being awake

and talking to Siddhi, I dreamed the dreams you feel but can't remember. I knew I was dreaming, making my way through big landscapes and bigger feelings, but when I woke in between them, in our dark and humming room, the doors to whatever I'd been trying to figure out in each dream had shut gently behind me, locked from the inside. For a little while, I lay semi-awake, still climbing the steps up from the fuzzy to the clear part of wakefulness. When I looked over, Siddhi's eyes were closed, and in the sameness of the hospital room, there was no way for me to be sure if another day had passed. I cleared my throat, and Siddhi stirred but kept his eyes closed.

"I think you might have narcolepsy on top of the pneumonia," he said.

"Mm. How long was I out?"

"What does it matter?"

"Siddhi, that's not the spirit we need right now. What I was gonna say was…ah…what was I going to say? Something about, like, my plan…I…ugh, I seriously don't remember."

"Don't worry about it, CeeCee, I have no intention of biting this time anyway," he spoke to me, but kept his eyes closed, and it seemed a brilliant conservation of effort. I closed mine, too. "Don't get me wrong, I am glad you're back, and all that. But believe me when I tell you that you don't know me like you think."

"I know you had something bad happen here, and I'm so sorry I let that happen to you. But don't tell me I don't know you. I think I know you better than you think I do. So…"

"You fucking don't," he said it deadpan. He didn't sound like himself.

"You're scaring me even more than I already am. Cut it out, Sidd—"

"You DON'T!" he yelled, and the shouting took it out of him. Rather than risk riling him again, I waited for him to breathe and hopefully explain. Slowly, with a lot of effort, like a hundred-year-old man, he maneuvered his arm out of the covers, led it away from his body, and pointed to his ruined leg. "These here," he said, "all these and those, and the ones here on my thighs…

none of those are from the fight. You get that? Right?" I focused more closely on his leg as he ran his fingers over the multicolored sets of cuts and scars, sort of counting and pointing them out to me. "You understand that Fox didn't hold me down over months and like, carve little sets of lines all over me with a razor blade. I saw you notice my cuts. You shouldn't skip over shit like that, CeeCee. The inexplicable shit, the secrets and shame, that's the most important shit," he whispered. "And if you look in the mirror, you'll see that you're running a decent goddamn shitshow of your own, and you fucking know it."

He took a few breaths. And in the space of his silence, I knew he was right. I hadn't asked about the cuts because I didn't want to know.

"I've been doing it for over a year," he said. "I learned it from Gloria. She was hanging around the house one time, after that Christmas, you were at Courtney's, and I was so humiliated after that thing with her underpants on my face. She was all coked up and half-naked like usual and razoring her next line, and she told me before she found cocaine, she used to cut herself with the razor to get brave."

I opened my eyes and looked over to see a stream of tears drawing steadily down from the corner of his good, closed eye and running over the bridge of his nose and down past the sunset eye until it landed in dark spots on the pale blue of his pillowcase. "It's the only way I have to really calm down."

"Don't cry, Siddhi," I pleaded. I would have done anything to stop him crying, give him a whole plan for how we would heal his bad habit, get him happy and whole, save or steal money for therapy or rehab or just stay in the hospital until he was all the way better, but it was so unlikely, and so damned exhausting, I said this instead: "I think I ran away with Edsel because I thought he was the only one other than you who'd ever love me. Like I was going to eventually lose you, you know, to growing up and stuff, and I needed to find a replacement or something."

"I'm no expert, but I'm pretty sure love doesn't work that way," he said. "You're my family, and I can still love you even though I'm broken." Siddhi's tears had doubled the size of the dark spot on his pillow. I had no idea what to do, other than to know that for the length of his life when Siddhi hurt, I wanted to be the one who knew what to do for him.

"But it doesn't have to be that way. It's just temporary, all this craziness, Siddhi. You're not going to stay broken. We are totally going to fix you. We'll do all the stuff they tell us to do, and once you're fixed up, we'll get out of here. I am already thinking up the beginnings of an awesome plan for us to ge—"

"SHUT UP!" he barked at me, and the force made me jump.

"What? What's wrong?" I asked.

"I'm telling you I'm fucked up. I'm not asking you to fix me. Try to hear the difference!"

"What I hear, Siddhi is that you take razors and purposefully cut your skin. That is more than fucked up. It's dangerous, and you're all ready to decide for us that it's over and done with and broken forever without at least trying to fix things? Without even trying..."

"Whoa! Hold on. You know how Nana said that thing about how people in glass houses shouldn't throw stones?"

"What? Now I'm a hypocrite? No way, Siddhi! I don't cut myself, and I sure as hell don't visit Kublai Kush La La Land to avoid my problems."

"Oh? How was your big adventure in Morocco? Did you get that job at Club Med? No? Did you see all the cultural sites? Did you visit lots of museums like you described in your letters? Did you hike up mountains and camp in the desert? Did you ride the ferry to Gibraltar? Did you meet lots of new and interesting people to keep in touch with?"

"Some of those things."

"Ha! Your letters were the most inconsistent bullshit I ever read. Sometimes you put yourself in two different cities in the same afternoon. You're full of it! A liar. I bet you spent the whole time decorating your hotel room with throw pillows and shit to make it all organized and 'comfy' and waiting for Edsel to get home from work so you could feed him the Moroccan version of tuna casserole and bring him his pipe and slippers and then do whatever he wants in exchange for like a pat on your head?"

"Siddhi! That is not wha—"

"Oh, right sorry, I forgot to add in the part where you shop-lifted and stole a bunch of worthless crap and shoved it in your 'Saturday Night Fever' bag of stolen dreams!"

When he mentioned my stealing, my stomach and chest collapsed in fluttering, humiliated fright. I'd been one hundred percent positive; no other soul had even a whiff of my little idio-syncrasy. "I just...I—" I was at a loss.

"And how about the part where you stare over and over at those fucking pictures? How many times have you flipped those pictures, like Hades is going to release Mom and then the crazy shit you fantasize about with this family is ever gonna happen? Newsflash, CeeCee: it never is. It's NEVER going to happen!

"We're fucked up, okay? We're all fucked up and you can't fix it! You can't. Not today, not tomorrow. So, how about you shut up, and we just lay here a while without one of your cute little plans? I'm sorry we're not under the blanket fort in our living room and probably never will be again, but at least we're together, so, like, just... fucking... for once, just... let it be."

I always thought that if presented with the chance, I'd surely have been one of those good Samaritan volunteers, standing on the beach filling and passing the buckets of water down the line, hopefully, and altruistically working hard to help shimmy a fif-ty-thousand-pound animal off the shore so it could swim away and survive. Siddhi pointed out how I caused my problems, then noticed, turned around, and tried to solve them. I steered myself repeatedly out to sea, and then, each time, made a one-eighty and drove myself back up onto the beach. I lived by turning in futile circles, at once the water and the whale.

*

When next I woke, a ray of sun seared through the window,

illuminating the swirling dust. Siddhi and I used to swish our hands through the lit particles when they shone through the back windows at Xanadu. Jackson once told us that the dancing specs were just dead skin, dust mites, and lint, but Siddhi and I called them disco dirt. If I weren't so pasted to my bed, achy, dry, and out of breath, I could have gotten up and disappeared them with one pull of the pink curtain. "I can't help thinking," I said, "that if she lived, if she showed up today…"

"She didn't live," Siddhi said, half into his pillow. He turned his head, and his voice got louder. "She's dead. She quit the gig before she even got to know us." He shifted in his bed and covered his poor legs with the lousy blankets.

We breathed for a while, and I thought about what made me keep circling back to my mother, knowing full well there was nothing and no one there for me to find. "I miss her. All the time. I really miss her."

"Who? Nana?" he laughed. "Me, too. I am dying for some hot cereal…"

I had to giggle. "Seriously, though, I do."

"No. You don't. You don't miss our mother because you never had her. And I don't miss her because I didn't either."

"So then, why do I feel like this?" He was quiet for a while, but I didn't talk, because I knew he was thinking.

"Phantom leg syndrome," he finally said. "That's what you've got."

"You mean like Tomatoes?" I remembered him scratching an itch on his prosthetic shin.

"That guy thought if he read enough philosophy and ate enough fucking tomatoes, or got enough girls, or smoked enough weed, he could stop feeling his lost leg, but all that stuff was just what he was doing to avoid admitting something was lost. That dreamy denial shit'll kill you, CeeCee. You keep flipping those pictures and you're going to waste the rest of your life. She's not real. Wave your hand around in the space, it's empty. Just accept it and then fill it up with something-fucking-else!"

One of his machines began to bleep. Blood pressure. "Okay,

okay, Siddhi. Please, calm down," I urged. "You're gonna pop something."

"*I* am your family. *You're* my family. You and me. That's fuckin it!" He coughed hard, heaved a sigh of resulting pain, and rolled toward me on his bed. His hair looked like an electrical accident, greasy and spikey, his face was splatter-painted with bruises and scabs, swelling and stitches, but the hazel of his good eye glowed through the slit. "It might not feel like two legs to either of us, but it doesn't matter, because it's all we have." He coughed again. The bleeping stopped. "Man, CeeCee, I'm insanely tired."

"Let's just sleep," I said. "For now, let's sleep."

"Yeah, okay."

I rolled onto my back, re-tucked the holes where cold air breached my blanket shell, and let myself sink almost to sleep before mumbling, "Siddhi?"

"Huh?" He breathed.

"Let's never do this again, okay?"

"Good plan, CeeCee. Tell Nana that when she gets back."

"She's still here?" Of course, Nana showed up in a pinch; that was her big move. She wouldn't do much more, but she always showed up with a strong opinion and a bag of not-very-good-food, not such a bad little something to count on.

"What'd she bring?"

"It was grayish-green with little orange spots floating in it that may or may not have been carrots, and I think it was trying very hard to be soup." We laughed together until I felt the wetness of tears on my own pillowcase. Siddhi winced from the pain in his ribs.

"Knock, knock?"

"Maybe no more jokes for like another week?" he laughed and moaned again. Then his eyes rolled back to closing. "I love you, Cees," he said before nodding off. And even with tissues for blankets, I finally felt warm.

"Wait, Siddhi, one more thing…"

"Mm-huh?" he mumbled.

"Where in the hell is Jackson?"

"Oh. Yeah," he answered. "Jackson's in jail."

CHAPTER 28

A Major Find, 1989 (Sienna)

MIAMI HERALD
FEDERAL
Agents Seize Fourth Largest Cocaine
Haul in US History
FRIDAY, DECEMBER 1, 1989

Tuesday afternoon brought a new development in the saga of the "Cocaine Catacombs." At three o'clock, twenty-four federal agents raided a ramshackle storage warehouse off Biscayne Boulevard and Thirty-fourth Street in downtown Miami, where they seized more than five thousand pounds of cocaine.

No one was present in the warehouse when the agents raided the site, but much like they found in Los Angeles on Monday, the building was loaded from floor to ceiling with massive concrete blocks. Plastic-wrapped, kilo bricks of cocaine were stuffed into hollow chambers inside the blocks, prefabricated for road and building construction projects. The hollows of these 'cocaine catacombs' were then sealed with more concrete.

The lease on the building is currently held by a company called T.S.I., an acronym for Trabajando Sol Incorporated, registered in Delaware, that has been linked with other leases held in California, Texas, and Venezuela. Tuesday's find adds much-needed new information into the case against Venezuelan brothers, Happy and Smiley Guy, A.K.A. Herman, and Solomon Gutierrez, under investigation for alleged ties to several cartels.

The twin brothers along with multiple known underlings, have been indicted for narcotics trafficking and are being held without bail as they await trial.

Edward H. Frances, U.S. Customs Special Agent in Charge for Dade and Broward Counties and lead investigator in the Catacombs case, elected not to comment on alleged ties between Happy and Smiley Guy and the Rodriguez Orejuela brothers of the notorious Cali cartel.

"This was a major find," said Frances, "a huge boon for our case."

*

As Siddhi and I continued to convalesce, first in the hospital and then at Nana's condo, I rehearsed Jackson's eventual prison release in my mind with cinematic flair: In Mellow Yellow, waxed-up and spit-shiny, Siddhi and I would drive up with some emotional road song streaming from the tape player, something Bob Seger, maybe Neil Young, tires crunching over the gravel, kicking up dust behind the car to symbolize that we were leaving our murky past behind us to make a new start.

We'd park in an old lot of potholed shale and weedy puddles before a formidable, cinder block wall topped with razor wire and gun turrets, but all on a sunny day. A stray dog would trot over, lift a leg, pee on something, and wander back out of frame. Siddhi and I would get out and lean up against the side of the car, sunbaked and ruddy but cool, arms folded across our chests, knowing eyes trained on the gate.

At the agreed-upon hour, the tower guard would blast an air horn to signal the gate, and the door would open to expose Jackson, ageless and alone, with his top button undone, looking well, and carrying a manila envelope containing his personal effects. He'd step out and pause, turn back to shake hands with the gate guard, whom he'd grown close with while serving his time. The guard would deliver some gift for the future, a slip of paper.

"Call that number. My Uncle Tony will hook you up with a job…"

Then they'd embrace, exchanging manly back pats, and Jackson would tell the guard, "Thank you, brother," in his way.

He'd walk over to us, his teeth brilliant white in his familiar smile, but with a new, repentant lining, his rehabilitation apparent, embroidered over every part of him. He'd walk up close, pause, and we'd nod our forgiveness, making a silent agreement that he'd do it better from then on.

Siddhi and I would sit up like always, on top of the seats in back, and he would tell us, *no way, drop down and put those seat belts on*. And once we buckled up, he'd hop behind the wheel and drive us into the setting sun…

I didn't have to get it right just yet. There'd be ample time for me to play with details of the scene because, in exchange for his testimony against the Guy brothers, Jackson's plea bargain included five years in a minimum-security prison.

CHAPTER 29:

Now What?
1990 (Sienna)

The front of the bus reeked of armpits, smoke, and some kind of cooking spices. I walked the aisle toward the back, getting the once over from everyone I passed, and to be fair, I couldn't help staring back. The other passengers' eyes were fat with questions and judgments, nothing like the staring contests I used to have with Siddhi, where my only goal was to try not to blink while also attempting to pick my nose with my tongue to make him laugh. To my left, two old ladies sat next to each other with coupon circulars spread out over their laps, clipping away. Sisters, I thought, and by their relaxed teamwork, I figured they'd been riding this bus for years.

A couple of rows farther back was a Haitian mother with a white scarf tied over her hair, her children spread across the aisle. She shouted in Creole laced with the "F" word, spanked her crying toddler, and shoved him into the seats with his brother and sisters. All the kids were well groomed and clothed in vested suits and ironed pastel dresses. The girls had heads full of colorful plastic barrettes peppering their hair which was sectioned into straight, clean, mother-made parts. Behind them sat an obese mother arguing in Spanish with her bony teenager. I could tell he was her son by the look in his eyes, hate framed in love. Kids get good at recognizing the pain that comes with wanting to be with someone but wishing for a better translation, a new and improved version in a far safer place.

Each empty headrest on the bus sported a wide vertical rainbow, put there to seem comfortable and inviting I guessed, but as I made my way down the stink and groove of the center aisle, looking for an empty seat, I found a child sitting at each rainbow's end. But this was nothing like the school bus rides I once craved, the kind that started at home, ended at school, and ran that loop, round and round, in a way children could trust.

Jackson used to tell the Babies that everything circles. Did it count—I wondered but never asked—if you ran away or died or went to jail before things curved around?

I thought about bailing, but I'd already put off visiting for close to eight months. Jackson never tolerated such trepidation. He told Siddhi and I that fear-bullshit was the seed of war and every monster that ever lurked under a bed. I managed to agree completely, yet still found myself scared stiff, sweating, and sick with fear.

"You want some a dis, *mami*?" said a hulking man exiting the bathroom. Taking a step toward me, he grabbed his crotch and gave it a little shake. Jackson used to preach that we were all infinite energy shifting and changing over eons into microscopic bits of flashing consciousness that lasted for a quark, and then changed forever into something else, equally necessary in infinite space, time, and existence. If that were true— and for much of my life, I believed it was—then this dick-shaking *putz* was as significant to the complete and living universal field as anything and anyone, vital as air, great as Gandhi, Galileo, God…it didn't seem fair to those guys. The guy had a tattoo of a teardrop under his left eye and another of a bird flying on the side of his shaved-bald head. I told myself he was nothing for me to fear. How tough could someone be when he'd just finished using the bus potty?

Siddhi always found it hilarious to imagine important people peeing and pooping. "I bet," he said once, back in the day, "that President Reagan would be at least ten times more likely to start a nuclear war if he had a dingleberry!" I wished Siddhi could have come with me, but it was better that he prioritized work. In only two months, he'd already gotten a promotion.

I held my hands at my chest to skinny myself and squeezed past the pervert. "Where you think you goin', *mami?*" I needed to get to my seat and rehearse what father-daughter talk Jackson and I might have during my first visit. It was no surprise he didn't write. He wasn't the type to funnel his big thoughts through a ballpoint to be trapped and diminished by the bordered, white insignificance of a sheet of paper. And I wasn't the type to write to someone who wouldn't write back, not that I had any idea what to say either.

I wrote with Courtney, though. Once she moved to the dorms, she sent me long letters, her tiny, perfect script on monogrammed stationery. She had a boyfriend at Swarthmore. She decided to major in Economics. "So weird, right?" She wrote to me, "But I want to go to law school, I think. Hurry up and ace your SATs so you can come replace my heinous roommate. She has like eight cat posters over her bed, loves mayo, practices violin three hours a day, doesn't watch TV, and chews egg salad with her mouth open." Nana was a pain about the long-distance bill, and even though we occasionally snuck lengthy calls, the writing was a better way to stay close.

I could write to Courtney for hours, but I couldn't think of anything to write to Jackson. I'd spent my entire life by his side. Siddhi and I were his lap dogs, his houseplants, his droids, the crown prince and princess of his alternate universe. And even though I felt long passed up for it, the world had placed me near him again, raw and clueless.

"Yo, I'm jus' playing witchoo," said the dick shaker, sticking out his tongue and laughing.

The only vacant seat was the middle of the bench on the rear wall, next to the stinky bathroom. Two Indian ladies in shimmering sequined saris—bright purple and hot pink—had claimed it to lay out their buffet, a fuss of plastic containers and bowls with peeled-back foil, forks, and plates balanced on their laps as they served themselves rice.

I smiled and nodded my intention to sit, to which they kindly cleaned up, and the purple one slid over to the pink, leaving me the seat by the window. Right as I sat down, the side door squealed shut, the bus hydraulically hissed up to level, and off we rolled, the traveling innocent. We cruised beneath overpass after overpass, through exchanges, and past weedy, graffitied cinder block warehouses. Not one of Miami's virtues was visible from these roads. No palm trees or trailing streaks of neon light. No ocean. We passed Waterbed City, where Jackson used to sell to a few of his regulars. Let loose in the giant store, Siddhi and I would run amok, wandering its wide aisles, trying out each configuration of wood and lacquer furnishings, narrowing our choices until we were ready to call dibs on the bedroom set we felt sure would make for the coziest home.

When the bus turned on an unfamiliar stretch of highway, I took a few deep breaths, willing my stomach to cooperate. In the many months since the hospital, Siddhi and I had both returned steadily to health. We looked mostly back to normal, at least, but neither of us had reached a full recovery.

After a while, the pink lady pointed toward the window, jingling her bangle bracelets to signal her purple counterpart to brighten up with powder and freshen her lipstick. In that moment, I realized how most people—regular, run-of-the-mill people—were lucky enough to live their entire lives without ever having to learn where they keep the prisons.

*

The facility looked more like a junior college than a jail. A necklace of parking lots surrounded a clump of pale orange buildings, ringed with trimmed hedges, and everything was tidy and in order. Of course, a wire fence ran around the perimeter, barbed loops at the top, but no walls, no turrets, no dystopian monochrome gray, nothing like the Victorian dustbowl in the unfettered wilds of my mind's eye. The flag on the pole in the grassy median out front hung limp in the heat.

Despite a valiant effort by the little A/C dart on the console above my head, my armpits, knee backs, crotch, neck, and the spot where my lumbar spine met the itchy rainbow bus seat were all damp with sweat. My seatmates had brought along handkerchiefs for brow mopping, and they passed a powder compact and patted their bodies and faces. I scooted forward, fluffing my T-shirt to fan myself, as the bus pulled in and parked in its long parallel space. Stacking my steps, one in front of the other, I zeroed in on the swish-swish-swish of everyone's legs as the lot of us inched off the bus. The woman and her four children stayed in their seats as we all filed past. Her baby lay asleep in her arms, and across the aisle, the two toddlers slept on each other, curled like kittens. I looked down at her, thinking I might offer to help, perhaps to carry someone, but she shot me an angry, suspicious glare.

I shuffled my thoughts, trying to make the right face back at her, but she turned her head toward the window and made that tongue-suck noise that, if you lived in Miami long enough, you came to know meant any version of fuck off. She hadn't asked for my pity. She could handle her own children.

I shouldered my bag, just a brown leather purse now, and walked on. After almost a week in the hospital (Siddhi had needed a month), the Feds had escorted me back to Xanadu to retrieve any of the stuff I wanted to keep. I took Siddhi's stories and my old letters and greeting cards from my bedroom, but I left the rest.

So, all I owned in the world were those papers and my Bee Gees backpack. The next day, I mailed the jewelry box to Aunt Paula along with a note apologizing for stealing it from her bedroom and did the same with Courtney's Easy Bake pan. I kept the pictures of my mother and threw the rest away. I'd been tempted to leave it all, and start fresh, but keeping the five pictures was the right move. My social worker explained to me that it is forgiving, not forgetting; that really does the trick.

Forgetting didn't work. I'd already almost died trying. Paused in the vestibule between the two sets of automatic doors, I let the bug fan blast me with cool air and enough decibels of clean, white noise to blanket over the riot in my head.

"Miss, please step all the way in," said a plus-sized, wooly guard in a dull, white button down, the gold epaulets at his shoulders looking mangled and worn, likely having joined the rest of the shirt in the washing machine.

"Sorry," I said and moved through into the sterile lobby. At the metal detectors, I showed my passport, signed in, and handed over my purse in exchange for a numbered claim ticket.

"Name?" another guard barked in my direction. He had a chin mole with two long hairs coming out of it. My legs began to tremble at the idea that my turn had come up for anything—pat down, cavity search, Silkwood shower—before they sent me in.

"Sienna Jones," I said. He sucked his tongue and looked at his colleague, who laughed, leaving me another step further into my debasement.

"No, baby girl. Prisoner name. Who you coming to see?"

Everything in the waiting area had that horizontal, angular Sixties feel, all pointy wood veneer desks and tables, sticky vinyl chairs, muddy green linoleum, nothing soft, so as to tell you: *Don't get comfortable here!*

"Oh," I managed, and then, if I didn't feel conspicuous enough, I inhaled a bit of my spit and began to sputter and choke. Unmoved by my coughing fit, the guard waved me through the next set of doors.

"You'n go on through. Next desk, sign for yah inmate." The next room contained bars, glazed over and part of a modern locking system, but, to my sensibilities at least, it seemed more overtly penal. I found the clipboard and signed in. When they said it would only be five minutes, wait here, something turned over in my stomach and I ran to the bathrooms, where, despite the noxious combo of pink hand soap and institutional bleach, I looked in the mirror, calmed myself and breathed. The waiting area contained only pamphlets for halfway houses, rehabs, and

job programs along with a discarded issue of *El Nuevo Herald*.
The second I sat down, a new guard came through the bars.

"Jones!"

"That's me."

"Who?"

"Sienna."

"Who's your prisoner, miss?"

"Oh. Jackson Jones. My father."

There was another rush of cool air as I followed him through
the bars.

*

Jackson smiled when he saw me come in, bright white teeth, like
always. The guard warned me I could give him a hug and a kiss
in the beginning and again when we said goodbye, and then no
more touching. Jackson seemed to know this already and stood
up to grab me in a tight hug, adding an extra squeeze at the end,
planting a wet kiss on my cheek, and then, right on the guard's
time schedule, he released me and sat down. He wore the same
denim blue shirt and pants as the other twenty or so inmates in
the "Visiting Parlor," as they referred to the room when they read
us the rules. Visiting Parlor. It sounded like a place for men in
bespoke suits and top hats to come smoke their pipes and pontif-
icate about Tammany Hall.

But this room was windowless and bare, a blond wood table
with two plastic chairs for each inmate and his corresponding
guest. Everyone got right into a cloud of chatting, and the structure calmed me, much like it had in the hospital. In the Visiting
Parlor, even Jackson Jones had to follow the rules.

"Hey there, munchie! It is so great to see your face." He
knocked his knuckles on the table like a drum roll, as if to punc-
tuate his delight. He smelled like ivory soap and peppermint gum.

"Sorry, Siddhi couldn't come. He had to work."

"Oh yeah? Good to know he's all healed up. Ma told me he
took a little beating." I wondered if he knew the extent of his

son's injuries. Nana was a master of denial. I thought of telling Jackson the whole story, shocking the shit out of him by recounting the mess he'd made for us.

I had a whole speech prepared and was loaded and ready with all the details. The plan was to spend the whole hour unloading on him, level him with the truth of how extensively he had done us wrong and leave him with five years' worth of something to think about, but as he sat across from me, thumping his leg and saying hello to the couple of inmates he knew in the room, I felt relaxed, almost tired. And seeing Jackson in his numbered clothing made my big plan to let him have it seem redundant and not at all worth the bother. "Siddhi is all healed up," I echoed.

"So, what are you two munchies up to these days?"

"We're both taking a couple of classes at Miami Dade Community College. Prerequisites. For the spring semester, we are taking Anatomy, Biology, and Statistics, and we both get straight A's so far," I said. If I wasn't going to deliver my big speech, I was at least going to fill the time catching him up on how much had happened since he'd been incarcerated, with a sure focus on how far we'd come without him there to oppress us.

"When I don't get something, Siddhi is the one who tutors me! Oh, and he got a job at the Hebrew Home for the Aged, on Collins. He is like *amazing* with the elderly. He loves all the residents, and they totally love him, too! The little old ladies all fight over him, and for a while, they thought his name was 'City,' like a metropolitan city, when they all realized they had the wrong name, he corrected them, and then, since they all have New York accents, they called him 'Sid-Arthur,' and he let that go for another while, and when he tried to correct them again, they were so confused and embarrassed they just decided to call him 'Handsome.' So," I giggled, "now all the residents and even the administrators just call him Handsome. Isn't that hilarious?"

I skipped telling Jackson about the rehab, plastic surgeries, and therapy, or that Siddhi could get depressed and needed help not to fall back to cutting himself, that I had an odd habit of shoplifting little things, waiting for a bit with my heart beating in anticipation, feeling my little high, before bringing them back to the store clerks and apologizing for my, "mistake."

Keeping it to myself was the right move because Jackson wouldn't have even heard me. He was distracted, mouthing something to the guard across the room, who pointed at me and mouthed back, "That your daughter?" To which Jackson puffed up a bit and nodded. And the guard nodded back. And I got a shiver because I could tell he was proud of me. I wondered if I ought to repeat the "Handsome" story, not sure he'd been listening then either, but when Jackson looked back at me and smiled, I figured I'd just move on. "Anyway, after only four months, he got a raise."

"Who got a raise? You got a raise?"

"No. Siddhi did."

"Oh, greeeaaaat. That's great," he said. He ran his finger through his hair in the way he always had and as he pulled it backward, I saw it had grown wildly peppered with gray.

"Yeah. He got a raise, and then it didn't take them long to figure out how crazy smart he is, so, they got him into these training classes to earn some kind of certification, so he'll qualify for a promotion soon, too." When had his hair changed? Did the first gray hair sprout up in prison? Maybe it happened years before, and I just never noticed. "Best part is that he actually loves working there."

I couldn't be sure Jackson was listening to anything I was saying, but that was nothing new with Jackson. And whether he was, or he wasn't, made little difference to me because nothing I chose to say took any risk or made any sacrifice. "I got a job at *Häagen-Dazs*, which is great for me because working there has made me so sick of ice cream, I think my whole ice cream craving is forever cured." I took up at least five minutes with telling him how I was psyched when people ordered vanilla, because it was so much easier to make a nice perfect scoop with the vanilla, and that when there were chunks in a flavor, pralines or chocolate-covered almonds or whatnot, the scooping was unpredictable, tougher, and the scoops came out uneven. People even complained. "About ice cream! They are always asking for extra. Everyone wants more."

"So, that's cool," he said, just to say something, I thought. He observed a nubby bit of cuticle on his pointer and for the moment, gave his awareness over to his finger. I might have asked what he was thinking, but if I were being honest, I really didn't care to know.

"You know the funny thing about *Häagen-Dazs*?" I asked.

"What's that?"

"It's not real. It's all invented. They made up a European-sounding name to fool people into believing they were getting something exotic and fancy and unique."

"Oh, yeah?"

"Yeah, but at the end of the day, it's just plain old ice cream." He might not have been thinking of anything except the annoyance of a hangnail, or what it would have been like if he hadn't been arrested, or what it would have been like if he'd never been left with us, or whether there would be any good TV on later in the rec room, but deep or mundane, it stayed inside his head. He didn't share it with me, and for the time being, I felt no pressing need to draw him out.

Right before my eyes, Jackson was doing his level best, like all the other prisoners, like anyone, and his best just didn't happen to be good enough for me. Such a tiny thought I had, and it came so easily to me sitting there in the Visiting Parlor, blabbering on and on about whatever nonsense I could muster—Nana won seventeen dollars in mah-jongg on Tuesday—any and every sundry detail of our steady climb from the bottom of the hole where he'd left us.

I'd arrived that afternoon ready to battle Kublai Khan, to hold my ground to the bloody death, throw down the pain of my existence at the foot of my oppressor, and demand, if not a solution, then truth, repentance, groveling, drooling, sniveling, tearful apologies. The only thing I hadn't anticipated was being where I sat, staring into the face of my father and already feeling like I'd won, like anything I said or did would be overkill, and the win was a distinction, a power shift, but a joyless one, like I'd been shipwrecked and washed up in a safe harbor, and it seemed like a waste of energy, and quite frankly silly as hell, to stand there on the shore and tell off the sea.

"Siddhi and I both took the SATs. We get the scores back in ten weeks." Jackson nodded along, sometimes interjecting, sometimes looking around the room where other inmates sat visiting with their loved ones. "I had a first date with Courtney's cousin Alex when he was home from Dartmouth for President's weekend. We ate steak and held hands. It was nice. He calls a lot." He bit his cuticles some more and smiled at my pauses.

"Aunt Paula came to stay for two weeks and taught us how to cook a full Indian dinner, and we are saving up to go and visit her and Uncle Keshie next year."

He said she visited him when she came.

"Nana falls asleep while reading the Sunday paper on the poufy white couch in her condo and farts herself awake and then blames it on the coffee." To that one, Jackson and I finally shared a laugh. When my mouth was tired and I had no next story, I thought I'd give him a turn. "So, how are you?"

"Oh, well, not too bad. Not too bad," he said like we'd bumped shopping carts in the produce section. "My cellmate is quite a guy," he began.

I had been prepared to engage and answer some follow-up questions about Nana's legal guardianship of me and Siddhi. The papers had been sent to
him months before.

"Carl Greenstein. Ha! He got two years for tax evasion. He took all the money he would have had to pay in taxes and buried it in his yard. And you know what I told him? I told him how my daughter tried to do that with *my* money when she was a baby. Remember that, munch? You probably don't even remember, but it was so cute. So smart of you when you grabbed a bunch of cash and toddled out into the backyard and put it in the ground? You had so many clever little games, even then." He said it so casually.

I was stunned silent. He'd known the whole time, probably

went behind me, and dug up the money the next day, the next minute. It had never been there to protect me. I protected myself by believing in it.

"All the guys in here, when you ask them, they're in for tax evasion, no matter what they really did, they all say they got nabbed for tax evasion. Carl's cool. He showed me the ropes. He's an older guy, sixty-four, funny, funny cat. He gets the *Reader's Digest,* and then he tells everyone the jokes.

"When he told me his age, I broke into that Beatles tune, you know?" He interrupted himself to sing it, "'*Will you still need me, will you still feed me?*'" He thumped his foot to the beat. He had the top three buttons open on his shirt, whereas everyone else in the room left only one button undone. He laughed after he sang, having amused himself, and I added a little laugh of my own, just to keep it all nice as it was, and keep him talking.

"So, uh, yeah, we have some deep chats sometimes about his life and how to meditate on those weaknesses. I think he really gets it, but, you know, people know how to let those fears creep in and take root. Oh, and uh, he's a terrible fuckin' snorer. Wakes me all night with the snoring."

He went on to tell me how he and Carl passed the time playing chess. Carl taught him tennis, and he was getting pretty good. He taught Carl to play the bass and the two of them, along with another guy—a "real cool drummer named Sally"—started a band.

"We call ourselves *Joe's Garage*, like the Zappa song," he said. "We play gigs in the mess hall once a month, and everyone has a ball." His leg stopped thumping and crossed over his other one. He shifted and scratched his stubbled cheek, his tan faded to tawny olive. "Joe's Garage!" he announced in a lightly raised voice.

"The guards are huge fans," he said so that the guard standing nearest our table could hear him. "Isn't that right, Mr. Davis? You love the band?" Mr. Davis stood tall and still, made a sour face, and shook his head, but ended with a grin that sent Jackson into stitches of laughter, and again, I joined in. "Mr. Davis loves the meatloaf here, don't you, sir?" This time the guard nodded.

"Mushy as hell," he said, mostly to Mr. Davis. "Terrible meatloaf here. Zero stars!" And back to me, "Some of these guards have chips on their shoulders, bullies, you know, vendettas, but not Davis. He came here from Ghana when he was around your age, he and his brother, and then they got hard at work at any job they could until they saved up to bring their mother over…"

As Jackson kept talking, I let him, and I listened, positive I could have gone home and taken a shower and come back to find him still as he was, shifting every so often in his red plastic chair, and somewhere in the telling of another story about another cool cat he'd gotten to know, and another deep guard, and another, and another, and another.

I wiggled my toes in my Converse and let the visiting time tick away until it came to an end with one more sanctioned hug and kiss, and I followed the crowd back to the bus.

Maybe on another visit, me and Jackson would curve our way back around to talking about all the things that we decided to leave buried. Maybe he would resolve all my mysteries and make me whole. Maybe he would even repent, come around, and see me as a young woman he could be proud of and learn from and respect. Maybe he would share in the rest of mine and Siddhi's lives, clean up and reengage, respect us both, and watch us graduate from colleges, have careers, marry people, and have our own families.

Maybe someday…

And then again, maybe not.

THE END

Acknowledgments

I offer my deepest gratitude and love for the support of my husband Joshua Kowan, and my children Brandon and Roseanna Smith (and my granddaughter Anya), Claire Cohen, Miles Cohen, Max Kowan, and Shepherd Cohen.

Thank you to my parents David Wallack and Judi and David Lazan.

Posthumous love and gratitude to my grandparents, Amy and Ben Snetiker, and Florence and Irving Wallack.

To Tracey and Andy Neuberger, Wendy, and Dan Schmerr, Joshua and Toops Wallack, Kevin and Rachel Lazan, and Joe and Julie Kowan, thank you for the brother and sister love and encouragement.

Special thanks to my writing teachers and mentors: Dani Shapiro, Hannah Tinti, Karen Russell, Tom Jenks, Nan Gatewood Satter, Susannah Applebaum, and Marie Helene Bertino, and to my agent and friend Victoria Sanders.

I cannot trip over myself fast enough to thank my dear, ideal readers and editors Rasheena Taub and Benee Knauer.

And I am so grateful to my generous, early readers: Rebecca Merritt, Trudy Wallack, Barbara Buck, Jacinta Bunnell, Susie Warren, Liza Darnton, Alysa Wishingrad, Tova Mirvis, Robin McLean, Jacqueline Dooley, Julie Fogliano, Adam Cohen, Elizabeth Indianos, Elise Title, Aileen Weintraub, Leah Glennon-Gleason,

Lauren Grabowski Lauterhahn, Sonia Resika, and Bernadette Baker-Baughman.

Thank you, dearest friends, who inspire me to love and know myself: Nava Sabag, Saydi Keefe, Rebecca Merritt, Jessica Applestone, Jana Sperry, Jacqueline Dooley, Rasheena Taub, Justine Gray, Annaleise Maynard-Cooke, Karin Lipke, Allison Berman, Nicole Jurain, Nikki Davis, Dana Silver, Zsofi Postyn, Debbie Dor, Doni Zasloff, Jennifer Borerro, Wally Nichols, Andrew Singer, David Keefe and Josh Paynter, Michelle Mavorah, Blaze Buck, and Jill Olster.

And a unique thanks to Mr. Gary Glick, my 12th-grade Advanced Placement English teacher at Miami Beach Senior High School, and his evil, purple grading pen for figuratively kicking my ass about passive voice and giving me an "A" on my satire.